RATTLESNAKE

A Novel by

STEVEN I. DAHL, M.D.

Rattlesnake Published March, 2015

Editorial and Proofreading Services: Eden Rivers Editorial Services

Interior Layout and Cover Design: Howard Johnson, Howard Communigrafix, Inc:

Photo Credits:

Kotangens, *Active Lifestyle Concept*, February 14, 2013. Depositphotos.

Monk, Stuart, *The Landmark Charging Bull in Lower Manhattan Represents Aggressive Financial Optimism and Prosperity*, August 3, 2012. Shutterstock.

Reichner, Tom, *Western Rattlesnake Coiled with Rattle Erect and Forked Tongue Extended*. Shutterstock.

Downtown Manhattan Wide Angle - Stock Image, December 12, 2013. iStock.

Author photo courtesy of Steven I. Dahl.

 **SDP Publishing**

Published by SDP Publishing, an imprint of SDP Publishing Solutions, LLC.

SDP Publishing
Permissions Department
PO Box 26, East Bridgewater, MA 02333
or email your request to info@SDPPublishing.com.

ISBN-13 (print): 978-0-9862896-2-0

ISBN-13 (ebook): 978-0-9862896-3-7

Library of Congress Control Number: 2015932787

Printed in the United States of America

To my beautiful and long-suffering wife,
Paula, for nursing me through the past year
in medical hell.

Acknowledgments

Many thanks go out to my patient publisher, Lisa Akoury-Ross, and my even more patient editor, Lisa Schleipfer. Special thanks to my designer, Howard Johnson, for his expertise. Many friends and family have given me good ideas. Thanks to all of you. The Colorado setting was the home of my uncle and aunt, Carl and Helen Seely, who rescued me from city life each summer to enjoy the freedom to live in the majestic mountains near Meeker.

Good health is a marvelous gift from God that we too often take for granted.

When it's springtime in the Rockies, there is not a more beautiful time or place on earth than in the deep valleys and mountain peaks of Colorado. The valleys are covered with a green, velvet coat of new growth, and the mountain peaks are radiant with their still-heavy blankets of the whitest snow, contrasting against the bluest sky in the entire universe.

Bricklyn Wahl Junior—known as Brick to everyone on earth, except his mother and his wife—would be the most adamant to defend the Rocky Mountains' beauty, but also to explain its dangers, especially in the spring.

Sitting on a narrow rocky mountain trail, astride his $5,000 Trek mountain bike with the early morning sun heating his hands and cheeks, he took in the panoramic view below. He was waiting for the rest of his four-man group to catch up. If there was anything wrong in his whole world, it was the heaviness he felt in his belly from the 24-ounce T-bone steak he had inhaled the night before at the rustic Meeker Hotel. He had never eaten a more tender or flavorful piece of red meat, but at the moment, it felt like it was still sitting on top of his heart— the entire pound and a half of it.

"What's the holdup? Are you guys riding with your

brakes on?" Brick hollered down the trail as the others caught up with him while he caught his breath.

"Sorry fellows, I'm sure I'm the holdup. Ever since I earned that yellow jersey in the Tour de France, I haven't been able to muster the same level of stamina. Of course that was forty-some-odd years ago," said Edward Foster III. His voice had a slight foreign ring to it—British or maybe Australian or maybe just New England—Brick couldn't be sure, but he was already forming other opinions about the stranger who wore a big smile as he spoke.

The Tour de France comment brought a winded laugh from the others, echoing off the face of the rock canyon below. A joke? Perhaps, and yet Brick couldn't help but wonder if the stranger—"just call me Ned"—wasn't for real. Derek and Dave both gave a sideways glance—with a synchronized rolling of their eyes—to their buddy Brick. Before they caught up with Brick the two friends had been at least a quarter mile behind Foster.

The three close friends and the grey-haired stranger had first met in front of the Meeker Hotel the previous evening. Both parties were getting ready to check in when they had begun to visit. A single, high-end, carbon-fiber mountain bike was in the bike rack atop a powder-black Porsche Cayenne-Turbo. The limited-edition, crossover SUV had blacked-out custom wheels, darkly tinted windows, and a fine layer of road dust. Wearing New York State license plates, it was parked immediately next to the three friends' five-year-old Chevy Suburban. The presence of mountain bikes on both vehicles had precipitated a conversation among the four men that in turn, led to an invitation for the older, but very fit-looking, Mr. Foster to join the three friends on the next day's mountain trail ride.

From the passenger side of the Porsche appeared a tall, stunningly beautiful woman. She wore her silky, long, black hair pulled back in a single braid. No wedding ring was visible on her left hand, but lots of glittering bling hung from her ears, neck, and wrists. Her voice was soft, and yet confident in a wifely way.

"I would like you men to meet Willow," Ned announced as the woman opened the back door and removed a leather briefcase. She apparently was not a mountain bike rider, as there was only the one bike on the Porsche. She appeared to be in her late thirties with a figure more like a runway model than that of an athlete. She moved about with a grace and agility that attracted the men's attention more than they should have let it. While the men chatted, she moved deftly around the running boards of the Porsche, unfastening the latches on the bike rack, and then passing the bike off to Ned. The woman stayed busy unpacking the car, and out of the conversation until it's end when she paused beside Foster to ask a question, and was introduced individually to the three young men.

"Willow," as he called her, seemed cheerful about the news of being abandoned during the next day's ride, commenting that she was looking forward to spending the day painting spring flowers and old barns. Having their car at her disposal would be a real plus. She seemed very pleased that Ned had found someone with whom to ride and gave a friendly wave to the group as she headed up the wide staircase toward the Foster's third-floor room.

The men didn't see the woman again that night,

but had lingered, visiting for some time with Ned at the check-in desk. He had dropped a few names of people he knew in Arizona, but the three friends didn't know any of them. For the three of them, New York City was on a different planet. None of them could come up with a single person that they knew personally whom Ned could possibly know. After a good thirty minutes of visiting, Ned said good-bye and went up the carved staircase.

They ate their carnivorous dinner in the old, historic hotel's rustic dining room where they were observed by dozens of glass-eyed trophy animals mounted on the dining room walls. The buffalo, elk, mule deer, and antelope were most likely many years older than the men. After the 700-mile drive, and the huge dinner, all three men had gone straight to their rooms where they slept through the night as though anesthetized.

Breakfast for the men had consisted of a couple of hard-boiled eggs and some power bars from the gas station out on the highway. They washed the food down with Gatorade. They left sleepy Meeker and drove partway up the twisting mountain road, and parked the Suburban at the base of their intended trail. By daybreak the four bikes were assembled and rolling. There were no other cars in the gravel parking area—a bit of a surprise to Brick. On his previous trips the place had been packed with hikers and bikers. The plan for the day was to ride all the way up to Trapper's Lake, arriving before noon. It was about twenty miles of rough, uphill terrain, but the trail itself was usually in good shape. They would eat lunch at the lodge, and then ride back down using the smoother, forest service roads and a couple of steep, shortcut trails. It was to be the best ride of the year for the three Arizona guys. The only question in their minds was if the older man could handle it.

"Is this your first time riding in the White River area?" Brick asked Foster as they both gulped their water.

"It's my first time riding anywhere out in the West," Foster said, his accent more pronounced with his strained breathing.

"One thing I can't help but mention is that we all should keep an eye out for bears and snakes," said Wahl, as the four men readjusted their helmets. "The locals here in Colorado claim that unlike rodeos, if you've seen one, you haven't seen them all." His joke produced a nervous laugh that didn't stop him from continuing. "The bears are a family-oriented species, and the sows are the most protective mothers known. As for the snakes, the eggs are hatching out these last two months. The adults have been in hibernation, and their venom is the most concentrated it gets all year. If you do see a rattler on the trail and can stop well back of it, do so; otherwise just keep moving. If you're going to run over it and have choice, pick its head or upper body."

"I think I'll let you go first, Brick," Dave said. "You kill them and I'll cut off the rattles."

"Whatever you do … do not crash your bike trying to stop for the critters," Brick said, still in a business tone, as he clipped into his pedals and headed out. He rode less than twenty yards when he stopped again, bringing the parade to a halt. "Did I mention the bears? A big, black bear killed two dozen of my uncle's lambs just up the mountain from here."

He received a big "boo" from the cluster of sweaty

guys, which continued until he was around a bend and out of sight.

In spite of the warnings and trying to concentrate on the trail, Derek Morris couldn't stop thinking about the possibility of coming upon a mama bear with little Teddy or Honey close by. He had watched enough Discovery Channel and Animal Planet to know that the threat was real, especially in the springtime. He looked over his shoulder at his cousin, Dr. David Felshaw, peddling effortlessly behind. He was the closest thing Derek had to a brother. Brick, up ahead, was his best friend and had been since eighth grade when they shared a math class with a male teacher who liked to give shoulder massages. It was Brick who had suggested taping thumb tacks—upside down—on their shoulders. The teacher tried his massage therapy during a pop quiz, but had to dismiss the class early because his hands wouldn't stop bleeding. Two weeks later the teacher was reassigned. It was the men's lifelong secret joke.

The bleeding from a potential bear attack crossed his mind, but not for long. He heard crunching to his side and glanced over to see the old man, Ned, closing on his left. "Go for it, grandpa," thought Derek, pulling close to the edge of the trail to let the man pass.

"I hope to be that strong when I'm your age," Brick yelled as Ned passed him and their shoulders brushed. Matter of fact, he wished he was that fit right now. Sitting on his butt twelve hours a day, trading commodities and stock portfolios of foreign corporations whose names he could barely pronounce—let alone explain to his friends or wife—wasn't the best way to stay in shape. Thanks to Derek and Dave, he had made the decision to close out his accounts for a week-long breather, and introduce them to the wilds of the Colorado Rockies.

"Sorry to pass you gents this early," Ned yelled back. "Dust gives me a bit of wheezing and that starts a cough. I'll try to get far enough ahead so you don't have to eat mine."

"No problem," Brick said. "You can scare off the bears for me."

He changed his thoughts from pondering the past week's puts and calls, to wondering about Edward Foster III. *Who's he kidding with that name, and what's with the trophy wife? She has to be at least twenty-five years younger than him. Maybe I've seen her before—maybe in a movie, or on the cover of a magazine?*

If the men had been observed by a camera from the sky above, the observer would have seen nearly perfect spacing between the four riders—about two hundred yards. It was enough space for the dust to settle between them, and for each to enjoy the exhilaration of the high-mountain solitude. The vistas were fantastic, and when valleys popped up below the tree tops, they were truly majestic—almost enough to make them stop, but not quite. Every once in a while the riders would cross the dirt road maintained by the U.S. Forest Service. That too might have seemed like a good place to stop and rest, take in the view and enjoy the milieu, but their endorphins were flowing and the clock was ticking.

Brick's goal of reaching the lodge and the lake by noon had both planning and wisdom behind it. He had ridden the trail before, and though it had been a few years, he knew how fast the sun disappeared in the late afternoons and how very cold spring nights could be. A flat tire, a broken wheel, a snapped chain, or a stripped sprocket could end a climb early, but a late start down the mountain from the top of the climb could be the beginning of something very bad.

There were no bears on the trail and no snakes had been spotted as they approached the old, hand-hewn timber lodge at Trapper's Lake. The building was the epitome of the rustic West, and yet appeared in excellent repair. There was even a triangular dinner bell hanging from the covered porch, and a rusty, hand-pumped well complete with a wooden bucket dangling from a stout, nylon rope. Hot food was foremost on their minds as the four riders pedaled up to the lodge's front door only to find it bolted and padlocked. Disappointment struck hard.

"Crap," Derek said to Brick. "Didn't you say that you checked it on the Internet and it was supposed to open a week ago?"

"I did just that, and I even spoke to one of the Forest Service managers last fall about it. He said it opened every spring once the snow was gone," Dave said. "Like clockwork … he promised."

"Hey fellows, not to worry," Ned interjected. "I brought extra jerky and a package of Oreos. It should be plenty to get us all down the mountain."

It didn't take long to devour the sparse picnic. After lunch, a skinny dip had been planned in the crystal clear mountain lake, but when Dave—stripped to his briefs—wadded into water near a sandy beach area, he bellowed with pain.

"It's far too cold for any human," he said, teeth

chattering as he headed back for his clothes. He picked his cargo shorts up from a grassy patch and gave them a good shake just to be safe. One could never tell what might wander into anything warm and soft lying on the ground. To his surprise his efforts were rewarded when a tiny chipmunk chattered it disapproval and ran off into the bushes.

The men had each found a soft, comfortable place to relax, and Derek had even dropped off to sleep. It was Foster who broke the peaceful mood suggesting that they start back toward the bikes.

The ride down the mountain was fast and furious for the first part of the twenty-plus miles. Some parts were steep, and several slippery, mossy spots were crossed, demanding caution. Then they encountered the obstruction.

Their stories didn't vary too much from man to man— as was seldom the case after such an event. Although each man told his version from his varied angle of view and distance as each had seen and experienced it, they all pretty much agreed on the basics.

Leading the pack downhill, Edward Foster III, beaded in sweat, coated with dust, and with endorphins flowing, squinted against the afternoon sun when he spotted the problem. Sure of the reality of his sighting, he thought momentarily about laying the bike down on the rocky trail. He need not have bothered. There wasn't just one rattlesnake in his path, there were two long, fat, momma rattlers lying stretched out across the narrow trail about thirty feet apart. They were apparently very content to remain right there in the warm afternoon sunshine, storing up body heat for the night's hunt. His scream could be heard echoing up and down the trail when Foster bellowed the word "Snakes!" as a warning to the three riders behind him.

The three following close behind hit their brakes, skidding and sliding on the shale-like rocks and mountain dirt. Foster would have braked and slowed down, but instead he made an instantaneous decision to roll straight across the reptiles' extended bodies and to do it as quickly as possible. It worked on momma number one—causing her, no doubt, a mortal injury. The second rattler, however, reacted instantly, coiling like a steel spring and then uncoiling with the force of the end of a bullwhip. Foster stopped peddling, giving the viper a relatively static target. The dual fangs might have penetrated his leg deeper had he been standing still, but not by much. The momentum of his bike and the momentarily attached snake carried all three—man, bike, and snake—down the steep trail, twisting, rolling, and scraping for fifty feet before the snake pulled free, having delivered its load of clear, yellow venom. Apparently unscathed, it slithered off into the sagebrush never to be seen again.

Derek, Dave, and Brick each heard the scream, and then watched helplessly as the cloud of dust erupted, the twisting bike skidded, and the body of their new friend lurched, tumbled, and finally came to an agonizing halt sixty feet beyond the lifeless body of the first snake. All six bike tires rolled across that first snake before coming to a safe stop alongside Foster's still body. At their first glance, all three friends thought with certainty that the man was dead. Laying their bikes against some bushes, they surrounded him and carefully began extracting his limbs from the mangled bike.

"Don't move his neck," commanded Dave, the physician of the group. Although he hadn't moonlighted in the emergency room for a couple of years—since finishing his orthopedic residency—he hadn't forgotten the first rule of head and neck trauma: Stabilize the neck before you move the patient. With Derek's muscular arms and hands holding Foster's neck in a fixed position, the other two straightened Foster's scraped and abraded arms and legs. That's when Dave and Brick saw the double puncture marks. Unlike the other skin injuries, which were oozing blood, the evenly-placed puncture cavities were filled with blood, but neither was actively draining.

"Is he breathing?" Dave asked his cousin.

"I can't see his chest heaving, but I feel his neck pulse in my fingers," Derek said.

"That's good! Just keep his neck fixed while I check him over," said Dave.

Brick was silent, his worst fears building in his gut as he watched Dave pull up the shirt and examine the abdomen and chest of the muscular, 200-pound man. Foster had the chest and pectoral muscles of a thirty-year-old body builder, and his belly showed six-pack abs any college athlete would be envious of. The hair on his chest was grey, consistent with the salt and pepper rim of hair around his balding pate. When Dave re-examined the arms and then the legs he paused, staring at the two puncture wounds. He shook his head and looked up at Bricklyn and Derek.

"Damn it, do you think he got bit?" Brick asked, already knowing the answer.

Derek, losing his concentration and grip, leaned forward to get a glimpse of the leg. He started to feel light-headed, realizing that they were dealing with a lot more than a serious bike wreck. Having had a weak stomach most of his life, in spite of causing his share of physical injuries to others on the football field, he took a couple deep breaths then twisted his head away from the others and threw up his small lunch.

"You okay?" Dave asked his cousin.

"I'm feeling better already. His head and neck are fine right where they are for now," he said. "I'm going to grab some water from his backpack."

Foster's pack had been ripped off his shoulders and was another ten feet down the trail. Derek retrieved it and poured bottled water onto an extra shirt, and began dabbing at the blood around the wounded man's face and mouth. There was still no sign of consciousness. Dave completed his bone-by-bone exam, finding no sign of obvious fractures, knowing that only a series of x-rays and CAT scans would tell the final tale.

"He is pretty much intact, bone- and joint-wise. He probably has a concussion, but the threat to his life right now is the snakebite. The longer it takes us to get him to a medical center and get on antivenom, the less chance there is to save his leg or even his life."

Brick had his cell phone out, and began walking to higher ground to get a functioning signal.

The voice came back through the phone, "Nine-one-one operator, what is your emergency?"

"I have an injured bicycle rider who is unconscious, and who has sustained a probable rattlesnake bite."

"If you could tell us your location we will send help as soon as—" static replaced the voice.

Brick repeated the message two or three times, but

could never make the operator understand because of the poor reception. Finally, the phone signal was lost; only a single bar was showing on his phone. Frustrated, he returned to the cluster of men to find that Foster was starting to move his hand and feet and blink his eyes.

"Derek, I'll keep an eye on his neck. I need you to ride up the trail to that higher peak and see if you can get a message through to the 911 operator. Tell them we need a helicopter," said Brick. "My phone battery is low. Maybe your new Droid will get better reception."

Foster's movements increased and suddenly he opened his eyes and looked Dave straight in the face. "Who the hell are you?" he asked, in a voice full of self-assurance. "When will the town car be ready to leave for the downtown office?"

The reaction to the concussion might have been funny if it weren't for the snakebite and the remote location. Foster continued asking the same questions over and over. "Where are we? Why am I lying on the ground? Why don't you have Willow bring me a drink?" Over and over he asked the questions. He shook free of Brick's grasp and tried to stand up, which was reassuring to Dave and Brick, ruling out any serious neck injury. With some effort they forced him to lie still, waiting for Derek to return with some kind of news.

"Yes, I can hear you," the emergency operator said. "We will send an ambulance to the forest service road, and can probably get within a mile or two of your location. That's as close as we can get."

"What about a helicopter?" Derek pleaded.

"The nearest one is in Steamboat Springs, and that would take two hours to get there. Then, since you are in the forest, there is no guarantee that it could land anywhere close to you. It would be better if you carry the patient to the forest service road. We will have an ambulance meet you there."

Derek pulled the topographical map from his backpack and studied it until he found their exact location, and then punched a hole in the spot with a twig. He determined the closest place which they could intersect the forest service road, but that was an uphill climb. He found another spot downhill, then called the operator back and gave her the coordinates where they would meet the ambulance. Now all they had to do was carry Foster to the road, and be sure it was the right location. It would be up and down unmarked trails for miles. How they were going to manage that, he hadn't the slightest clue.

The world's availability of snakebite antivenom is a hit-and-miss thing. Some large American hospitals in "snakebite" areas stock supplies of rattlesnake antivenom, and so do major hospitals in India and Indonesia for bites from cobra and asp vipers, but these hospitals are also the first to run out of the serum on busy "bite days," usually weekends and holidays. The first thing Meeker Hospital's emergency room doctor did when he got a call from the 911 supervisor was to place a call to Denver as one of the nurses called the University of Utah in Salt Lake City. Within half an hour the two regional poison control centers had coordinated their supply inventories, and it was decided that a courier airplane at Salt Lake City

International Airport would be loaded with ten vials of the newest generation of antivenom. A flight plan direct to Meeker was being filed. Without even confirming that the patient in Colorado had, in fact, been bitten, or how deep the bite actually was, the emergency air transport was already in the process of saving the life of Edward Foster III.

Up on the mountain trail, nine thousand feet above sea level, the three Arizona buddies had abandoned their bikes, and were beginning their tag-team-like piggybacking of Mr. Foster down the mountain. They had brainstormed to try to figure out some type of gurney or stretcher, but with the clock running on his snakebite they gave up and hefted the semiconscious man onto Derek's strong back. The plan was to trade off every couple hundred yards. The thousands of dollars' worth of bikes and gear left behind would have to be dealt with later. At the last second, Brick snatched up a CamelBak he had filled with water from the mountain spring that fed Trapper's Lake.

What had looked like a mile of downhill trails on the topographical map turned out to be closer to two miles with hundreds of up-hill climbs and slippery downhill skids and slides. The worst was a 200-yard trail around a slate hill where all three men had to hang on to Foster to keep the piggybacker upright.

The men could hear the siren of the ambulance long before they got to the intersecting mountain road—the welcome sound giving them a boost of energy. Foster was unconscious and unresponsive when Dave and the paramedic transferred him onto a stretcher and then into the ambulance. His leg had continued to swell and his forehead was burning up with fever. The only glitch with the ambulance was that only one of the three men could ride along in the vehicle.

"This guy will go," Derek and Brick said in unison, both pointing to Doctor Dave.

Derek and Brick would return to the site of the accident for the bikes and then go to the trailhead parking area where they had left the Tahoe.

Meeker Community Hospital was far from modern but technically quite good for a small ranching community. Quality x-ray, MRI, and CT equipment was on-site and used with regularity, although reading of the images was done by doctors in Denver. The on-call emergency room doctor had been notified of the estimated arrival time and the status of the patient by the ambulance driver. The staff was anxious for the arrival of the mystery snakebite patient. The airplane delivering the antivenom from Salt Lake City was in the air and the on-call ICU nurse was en route from her second job: cooking for a ranch crew ten miles up the White River.

The ambulance driver made Grand Prix-like time to the hospital at the expense of the equilibrium of the paramedic and Doctor David Felshaw. Both admitted to car sickness when they finally hit the straight, paved highway into town. An IV of D-5-lactated Ringer's solution was running into Foster's left arm as they descended the mountain. He was seldom alert, although he was moaning and groaning with every twist in the gravel road and every cattle grate and pothole. His left calf was swelling at a rate Dave had never witnessed, not even with a compound fracture.

Once at the hospital, the ambulance doors were ripped open from outside, and a team of urgent health workers rushed the patient into the small emergency room. The fight to save Edward Foster III's life was already three hours old. The deadly venom from the recently hibernating rattlesnake was doing its intended work on Ned's vital organs.

Although exhausted and nauseated, Dave hadn't forgotten about his friends back up on the mountain. Once out of the ambulance and having given as much of a report to the new team of health workers as was possible, he reached in his pocket for his cell phone. He found it right next to the keys to the Tahoe—the Tahoe that was still up on the mountain.

"Nice going, Einstein!" Derek said to his cousin over the static riddled airwaves. "We're not even halfway down the mountain trail ... carrying your bike I might add ... and now you tell us that the SUV is locked up and you have the keys?"

It wasn't as if the day had been hard enough. Brick and Derek had made good time getting back up the two-mile trail to retrieve the bikes and backpacks, but they were exhausted and choked with thirst when they arrived. Skittishly, they rounded up the broken pieces of Foster's bike and scattered debris from his personal gear. They were very aware that more snakes had to be nearby. The body of the first one—Foster's bike tire kill—still lay stretched across the trail fifty yards away. It wasn't going anywhere until dark, when some lucky coyote or bobcat would drag it away for dinner. Derek started to leave it but then pulled out his pocket knife and cut off the rattles—they would be a lasting souvenir of the horrible experience.

The next decision was whether to try to ride their bikes and carry the two extra bikes, or leave them there on the mountain and come back another day. Not wanting to ever think about that particular trail again, they elected to ride. Helping each other, they discarded Foster's twisted wheels and handlebars and strapped the frame onto Derek's back. Dave's good bike—brand-new three days ago—was strapped onto Brick's back, and the two friends set off down the trail. By the time they reached the first crossing of the forest service road they were both exhausted: the heat of the day, the altitude above 8,000 feet, the lack of water, and the gradual decline of their adrenalin blood levels made gear shifting and peddling difficult. In addition, each man had pain where the sharp bike parts were digging into their skin. They had stopped to rest when Dave called them with the bad news about the locked Tahoe.

"Thanks for the good news," Brick said.

"The good news is that a plane is going to land in a couple of hours with a load of antivenom to treat Foster's snakebite," Dave told his friends. "As soon as things are squared away here I'll borrow or rent a car and bring you guys the keys."

"How about the guy's hot girlfriend? Just call her and borrow Ned's car to come get us. She'll need to stay at the hospital with him anyway," Derek said.

The suggestion was a good one, except Willow was nowhere to be found. The hotel clerk tried to be helpful, but there was a shift change and none of the new people had a clue where she might be. Dave put a call into the sheriff's office and explained the situation to the dispatcher who agreed to put a call out to all the cars (both of them) to be on the lookout for the Porsche SUV. In the meantime, Dave paced the halls waiting for the sound of the airplane entering the little valley. He checked on Foster a time or two, but the staff was still cleaning up the abrasions, suturing lacerations, and getting x-rays.

The three Arizona guys still had four more days of biking and a river raft trip planned. Dave's concern was that if they were to call their wives and relate the disaster—along with the news that the mountain was alive with vicious rattlesnakes—he doubted that the planned activities ever would happen. He began to worry that wives would insist on them coming home early, and probably make them take the family to the beach or Disneyland, or even worse, his wife, Debra's, favorite resort hotel in Sedona.

It was nearly four o'clock when Dave finally walked the few blocks to the hotel. No one at the hotel had seen or heard from Foster's lady friend, Willow. Foster had been given Demerol for the increasing pain in his leg, and he was unable to even remember his car's license plate number. Dave offered the night clerk twenty dollars to borrow her car, and then headed up the highway to take the Tahoe's keys and several bottles of cold Gatorade to his friends.

Brick and Derek were thirsty, sweaty, and dusty; they lay down on a patch of wild grass waiting for Dave to arrive. Any positive memory of the morning's exhilarating ride up the mountain was long since erased by the reality of the bicycle crash, the rattlesnake encounter, and then the painfully urgent transport of Foster's heavy, limp body up and down the mountain trails to the ambulance rendezvous point. From there on the men's thoughts had become a blur of pain and deprivation. They were both city boys, not eighteenth century mountain men. Brick was especially soft and out of shape for the task they had been forced to perform. Years of early rising, long hours of sitting in front of computer monitors, and his habit to constantly snack while he traded commodities had transformed his young, athletic body. Derek, on the other hand, had been into twice-weekly workouts at a local fitness center. Spin classes and swimming were his favorites, leaving his upper body and legs strong, but his endurance—especially at high altitude—lacking.

The steep mountains already were shadowing the rays of the afternoon sun, thus dropping the ambient temperature to a crisp fifty degrees. When Dave finally arrived, both men were shivering from the combination of the cool air on their sweaty clothes and bodies. Mild dehydration didn't help their state of exhaustion.

The bikes were haphazardly thrown into the back of the SUV, and the heater was turned up to high for the drive back into town. Derek wasn't sure he was up to the driving, but the car was his, and he doubted if Brick felt much better. They followed close behind Dave in the borrowed Toyota so they wouldn't miss the unmarked turn toward town.

The two vehicles were just pulling into guest parking spots in front of the hotel when the black Porsche SUV pulled in beside them. Willow rolled down her window and craned her neck looking for Ned. When she saw the crumpled bike being unloaded, she jumped out of the Porsche, yelling at the men; asking what they had done with Edward, as though they had abducted him.

"Settle down ma'am," Dave said in a calm voice.

"I won't settle down until you tell me what happened to Edward's bicycle. And where is he?" she demanded.

"We were in a bit of an accident up on the mountain trail. Mr. Foster is down at the hospital getting cleaned up. Why don't you do the same and then I'll drive you there and you can get the whole story from him."

Willow looked like she needed to go through a car wash, not just get cleaned up. Apparently, she had been collecting riverbank red clay for her turning wheel. Foster had mentioned something about it on their drive up the mountain that morning. The woman had streaks of red mud on her face and in her silky, black hair, which she had pulled through the back of a New York Yankee's baseball cap. She had on no makeup compared to the evening before, and had dusty, red hand prints streaked up and down her powder blue slacks and navy shirt. The mountain sun had given her face and arms a bright, pink glow. She apparently had forgotten her sunscreen.

Willow slowly calmed down and agreed to meet Dave back at her car in ten minutes, which turned into twenty by the time she reappeared: scrubbed, dressed, and dripping water from her wet hair. Her scowl had been replaced by a nervous smile as he opened the door for her and accepted the keys to the four-door, German hot rod. Brick and Derek were showering and promised to come pick him up in half an hour. By now, they all had another round of juicy, rare Colorado beef on their minds.

Foster lifted his head from the pillow and attempted a smile as Willow and Dave pulled back the curtain in the ICU cubicle. His leg was suspended in a sling, with what looked like ice packs on the upper thigh and a sterile dressing covering the site of the snakebite. Dave had explained the basic medical facts and problems to the woman, as they drove the few blocks to the hospital, in order to ameliorate her shock when she saw her battered man. Scrapes, scratches, and bruises covered his face, arms, legs, and especially his hands, where he had attempted to break his fall on the downhill rocky path. Dave had guessed that Foster was traveling about eighteen miles per hour when he crashed.

Willow gushed empathy and concern for the injured man as tears the size of gumdrops fell on the sheet covering Ned's battered torso. She hovered over him like a humming bird looking for nectar, but Dave noted some very odd things during his observation of the woman. She never actually touched Ned. At first he wondered if she was afraid to hurt him, but then he wondered if it was the venom circulating in his blood. Lay people had strange ideas about contagious diseases and poisons. Perhaps she thought the snake's venom would rub off on her, or maybe she just wasn't into touching.

"Have you had a good day, honey?" Foster managed to get out in a whisper. "This man is a real human being," thought Dave as Foster, in spite of all the drugs, showed concern for the woman. "Would you mind getting my wife a chair?" he asked Dave.

Before that could happen, the attending doctor entered the curtained-off area and began a lengthy explanation to Willow about the antivenom and the prognosis. Brick and Derek showed up just in time to hear the man explain that Foster had received ten vials of the latest form of the antivenom.

"We were so lucky that I called Salt Lake when I did and could pull some strings to get the airplane in the air so soon. Had there been any delay we would be in the operating room right now amputating your whole leg," he informed Foster in a tone that implied his sense of great worth.

"As far as I'm concerned, it was an unnecessarily dramatic explanation," Brick told the other two men when they finally got back to the hotel and sat down to dinner. The hotel's chef had agreed to stay late to accommodate the Good Samaritans. Word had spread fast through the little town about the daring rescue: "Imagine piggy-backing a full-size stranger down the mountain trails to save his life!"

"You've got to give these ER docs their due," Dave said in defense of the man. "They wait around for weeks treating colds, flu, and sprained ankles, before something exciting like Foster's snakebite comes through the door."

"I agree," said Derek. "Besides, there is plenty of glory to go around for everyone. The newspaper reporter caught me on the staircase when we got back from the hospital. She made me promise her an interview at breakfast. Who knows? Maybe we'll get our picture on the cover of the *Rolling Stone*."

"More like the cover of the local grocery store advertisements," Brick joked.

The men had a hearty meal, then sat back and discussed the plan for the next day. In the middle of their raspberry bread pudding, Willow came through the lobby's entrance into the restaurant and gave them a wave. Dave pulled a chair up to the table for her and got the waitress from the kitchen to fix her some tea and toast—she declined anything more substantial.

"So was he able to get to sleep?" Brick asked.

"He is in lots of pain, but the doctors gave him a long-acting narcotic and told me to leave. I guess the next forty-eight hours will tell whether he keeps his leg or not." Her tone of voice was somewhat flat, leaving the three men to wonder how much she even cared about Ned.

There was a pall of quiet around the table, interrupted only when the waitress came with the tea and the check for the men. Everyone was exhausted but remained at the table until Willow finished eating, and then Brick offered to accompany her upstairs.

"If there is anything we can do for Ned, just let us know," Brick said as they stood in front of her room while she found her key and opened the door. "I'm just down the hall in number twelve. Don't worry about disturbing me. If they call from the hospital during the night one of us will run you up there."

She thanked him and closed her door. There was no offer of a hug or even a handshake.

The walls of the old hotel were constructed of sturdy, hand-hewn timbers, but were not so thick as to conceal all the sounds of the guests occupying the individual rooms. Soon after the lights in the lobby were turned down, the soft rhythm of men's snoring could be heard in adjacent rooms. Running water and a rattling pipe added to the cacophony of muted sounds, as did the lonesome sobbing of a female guest somewhere on the third floor. There were no televisions in the hotel, however, a one-sided conversation also could be heard;

though the precise words could not be understood by other hotel guests as Bricklyn Wahl spoke with his wife about the day's activities and disasters.

It was difficult for him to keep his voice down as she relayed information about her stressful day from her end of the satellite's relayed connection.

Debra Wahl was exhausted. She had just turned out the light and settled into the soft, goose down pillows on her king-size bed. It was still cool enough in Phoenix to keep the windows open at night, but with her husband gone, she had experienced a shiver of angst while she was putting on her nightgown, so she had locked up the house and set the alarm, something Brick never did when he was home. With him gone and the baby asleep, the house seemed bigger and just a bit spooky.

The musical ring of her cell phone, which was in its charger in the hall niche, startled her. She had a fleeting moment of anger, assuming the call to be from Brick, and that he had called her cell rather than the house phone sitting on her nightstand. She got back out of bed and walked into the hall where she kept the charger.

"Hi, sweetheart," he said. "How was your day?"

"It was fantastic," she said, letting just a bit of her frustration bleed through into her tone. "The baby was fussy all day cutting her top front tooth, and she pulled a table lamp over and broke the shade. Mom had another breathing attack which the doctors say is par for the course with her emphysema and it should only get worse. It took sixty dollars to fill your truck with gas and on the way home from Costco a cement truck threw a rock into the windshield. How about you guys, did you have a great bike ride?"

"I'm sorry to call so late," he said, sensing that she wasn't bubbling with joy at the sound of his voice. "I called your cell so the phone wouldn't wake the baby. You are never going to believe what happened."

He was correct with that deduction. She didn't believe him at first, thinking it was another of his fabrications, which he liked to create at parties and family get-togethers, only to say at the end that he was joking.

He gave her a ten-minute, shortened version of the last twenty-four hours, enjoying the telling of the story as much as the sounds of her surprised responses. When he took a breath at the end, she took the stage.

"Well," she said. "My day was nowhere close to the excitement of yours, but there was a rather tense moment when I was checking out at Safeway and our MasterCard wouldn't work."

She let this news settle for a second before continuing. "The bank said we had maxed out our card and that you had already been notified. Thank goodness I had my emergency hundred dollar bill tucked under my driver's license, otherwise I would have had to take back all of the food. Do you know anything about this?"

"I took care of that last week. The guy at the bank said it wasn't a problem and that the credit limit would be increased."

"But I thought we were paying off the balance each month. Haven't you always done that?"

"Our cash flow has just been down a little the last couple of months. It's nothing to worry about. But I've had some awesome trades the last few days. I'm sorry you had to be embarrassed by the experience. I'll make another call in the morning and get it all taken care of."

They said good night and Debra tried to settle back into the pillows. What she soon realized was that she would never get to sleep until she did a little more checking into their finances. She got up and tiptoed past the baby's room and went down the steps to the room Brick called the "Star Chamber." It was intended to be a guest bedroom, but he had taken it over to do his commodity trading. The walls were lined with open file cabinets, and three folding tables were set up in the middle of the room in an open triangle with a high-back, leather "judge's" chair in the middle. On the tables were five large computer monitors, two on each side, and one in the middle behind a sophisticated keyboard. Off the backs of the tables ran enough wires, electrical cords, and cables to wire the average house. The ceiling lights had red bulbs to make staring at the computers all day easier on the eyes. Off to one side was a real desk, an old oak roll top where the family finance records were kept.

Debbie hated the red lights. They made it hard to read anything but the computer screens. From well before the start of the trading day in Chicago until hours after the close of the Chicago Board of Trade, Brick would hole up in the room, making the computers' screens dance with numbers. He traded four main commodities: wheat, soybeans, pork bellies, and eggs, but occasionally ventured into exotic metals such as platinum and rhodium. Why those particular items, she only could guess. Maybe it stemmed from his summers spent on his uncle's ranch. His explanation to friends was that there always would be a need for food, but not necessarily rare metals or oil.

She went through the files until she found the folder marked "credit cards," then picked out the last few months of the MasterCard statements. Sure enough, just as the service center's operator had explained, the credit card limit was at a maximum. She was astonished. They had two other credit cards, but had agreed to use them only in situations where it was a must. Just like the MasterCard, those cards had big balances as well.

She replaced the files and returned to her room—her head full of questions about her husband and his lack of discipline with the plastic. She had glanced at the charges and none were blatantly foolish—except maybe for the new bike, which she had agreed would be his first-ever Father's Day gift. There were none that could have been for gambling or support of another woman or any outrageous expenditure like that. When she went back to bed and tried to get to sleep her mind wouldn't stop rerunning the figures and the questions. *How in the world did we accumulate so much debt?*

Edward Foster III awakened from a drug-enhanced nightmare—the details of which were immediately erased from his mind—to a real nightmare as he looked around the hospital room trying to remember where he was and why he was there. His body was screaming with pain, especially his leg, which was suspended with a traction-pulley, making it impossible to turn to his side. Somewhere in the back of his mind was a memory of an unknown doctor telling him about antivenom, and how they were going to give him all ten vials and how it was very expensive, and that sometimes it had side effects like allergic reactions and kidney damage. He shuffled through the sheets and blankets for the nurse call-button, but soon gave up and started hollering for assistance.

"Mr. Foster, you finally woke up," the short, grey-headed nurse said with a forced smile. She pulled back the blue cloth curtain surrounding his bed, allowing sunshine to flood the cubicle from a window on the other side of the room. She took his blood pressure and handed him a glass of fresh, cold water. "Let's have a look at that leg," she said turning back the sheet and blanket.

He couldn't get a good look at it from his angle, but could see that his toes were closer to the color of plums than strawberries and were just as fat. "What do you think?" he asked, as his memory of the reality refocused in his mind.

"I'm just the nurse. The doctor will look at it when he gets here. He usually comes in about eight on his way to his office. I can tell you that the swelling has stopped increasing. See this pen mark on your thigh?" she asked, hiking the sheet up nearly to his naked groin and pointing to a thin, black marker line.

"Is that a good sign?" he asked, tugging the sheet back downward.

"That and the fact that your vital signs are good both are indicators that the antivenom is doing its job—which it dang sure ought to for as much as the stuff costs," she said.

His mind was full of questions, but he felt a wave of nausea from the lukewarm water he had downed too quickly, so he laid his head back in the pillow and closed his eyes.

The morning passed by slowly for Ned. There wasn't a TV in the ICU, and after a breakfast of pasty oatmeal and overdone bacon he lost his appetite. A visit from the doctor didn't tell him much more than what the nurse had said. The man did agree to move Ned to a regular room twenty-four hours after the administration of the antiserum.

Edward kept glancing at the door, expecting Willow to appear at any moment, and by the time the aide brought his lunch tray, he was getting worried and a bit angry. He had been living with the woman for several years, and though she definitely had an independent streak, she had been very agreeable as a companion. It wasn't like she was a kept woman either. She was widowed after just a few years of marriage; her college sweetheart was rear-ended by a city bus, leaving her broken-hearted and financially secure. She had grieved for nearly three years before she took a job as a secretary to a VP at Goldman Sachs, and started meeting Wall Street's movers and shakers as well as Manhattan's beautiful people. Meeting Edward Foster III had been the best day of her new life—or so she told him.

When she did finally breeze into the ICU cubicle around two in the afternoon, he was back in a deep, drug-induced sleep and in the depths of another tortuous dream.

"Wake up, Mr. Foster," Willow said, whispering into his ear. She slipped her hand around the curve of his cheek and began a gentle messaging of his neck muscles. When he finally opened his eyes she bent down and gave him a soft kiss.

Ned lifted his head off the pillow to look at the wall clock. "Where have you been?"

"I called here this morning and they told me you were not to be disturbed until two o'clock visiting hours," she replied. "This hospital sure has strict rules for a hole-in-the-wall town."

His memory of the morning already was fuzzy, so he relaxed his head back into her hands and felt his tension melt away. He sensed the aroma of her perfume and shampoo. Closing his eyes, he pictured them back on his yacht in Newport, listening to the ocean's waves crash against the rocks and the seagulls filling the air with their cries. Willow was the best. Willow had saved his life. He liked to think that each day they spent together, day by day, luxury by luxury; he was paying back the debt he owed her. But he always remembered that he could never repay the permanent loan of her kidney.

He was working on his third or fourth million when she had shown up at the front desk of his fledgling investment company's office with a resume in hand. Her looks alone would have been enough to get her the job. Her aristocratic stance and the way she flipped her bangs out of her eyes were breathtaking. In addition to her tall, well-configured frame and cover girl face, she had brains. From their first handshake, she made it plain to him that she was there for the executive assistant's job and *nothing* else. Out of curiosity he had called on her references at Goldman's. He thought the guy on the other end of the phone was going to start crying when he realized that Willow was really leaving the firm, and all because one of the jerks in mergers and acquisitions had made an inappropriate comment about her low-cut dress. She had slapped the guy and demanded his termination. When that didn't happen immediately, she gave her notice, as well as hired an attorney to sue the idiot.

Now, ten years and two Edward Foster wives later, she was still with Foster's company and with the man himself. His kidney failure had come on after an attack of dengue fever that he picked up on a honeymoon skin-diving trip to the island of Palau in the Eastern Pacific. Not knowing what was wrong with him when he returned to New York, he had self-treated the "break-bone" pain with large doses of naproxen and gin. When he started bleeding from every possible orifice, his new wife, Wanda, took him to the ER at Columbia University where they were able to reverse his disseminated intravascular coagulation (DIC), stopping his bleeding, but the medical team was unable to cure the kidney failure the disease had precipitated. By the third month after the infection had begun, Foster had wasted to 70 percent of his ideal weight and visibly aged fifteen years. Wanda had asked for an annulment, having spent less than two weeks of normal married life with him. He didn't blame her or resent the $500 thousand it took to satisfy the woman.

When dialysis began to fail and the question of a kidney transplant came up, Foster found that none of his relatives were compatible or agreeable to a painful and somewhat risky kidney donation. The national organ banks were scanned, but to no avail. Money wouldn't buy him a place at the front of the two-year-long waiting line. Travel to a foreign country was considered briefly—Kiev was the surgical tourism hot spot at the time. Obtaining an illegal organ purchase was even suggested, but quickly rejected. The risk of anything but a first-class transplant from a fully-compatible donor was out of the question for Ned. However, he was rapidly running out of time.

Willow, by then his executive assistant—just like she promised him she would become—had managed to hold his business together through the several crucial months during which he was present in body only. On a whim she went to the Red Cross one morning to donate blood, and for the first time in her life she discovered her blood type. After long nights of lying awake worrying, she gave Foster's nephrologists a sample of her blood, and found out that she was a fully-matching kidney donor.

Edward Foster III was dying. His multimillion-dollar business was going over a cliff when Willow approached him one evening, knocking on the door of his upper Manhattan town house with a plate of homemade cookies in her hand, and an offer to put on the table.

"Everyone in the company needs you to get better," she pleaded. "I need you to get better. You are the catalyst that makes the business work. If you don't get better, we are all going to eventually be out on the street; and Edward, your clients are going to lose out as well. Now, listen closely to what I have to say then think before you answer. I want to give you one of my kidneys. I want you to get better."

"There is no way I can let you risk your health that way; besides, you have to be a compatible match," he protested

"I've already done the testing and we match, Ned. We match perfectly! But Ned, I won't do it for nothing. I want a significant ownership in the company. I checked with lawyers. It can be done quite easily and quickly. We can get married on Monday."

Foster blinked a couple of times, took another bite of his cookie, and then started crying. Willow would never be sure whether this rare expression of emotion was because he was grateful for a new lease on life, or because it was going to cost him more money than both of his previous wives and all of his bad trades put together.

When the final legal documents were drawn up, Willow accepted 40 percent of the Foster Company's assets, and a $5 million "signing bonus" to be electronically credited to her Grand Cayman bank account the moment her kidney's blood supply was clamped off and the ureter transected during the surgery. There would be no backing out for either of them.

To avoid the question of her selling her kidney, the wedding took place in the chapel of the Massachusetts General Hospital a mere sixty minutes before the anesthesiologists gave them both their pre-op anesthesia. The head transplant surgeon, Dr. Douglas Rose, stood in as the witness to the wedding. Seventy-five minutes later he made the skin incision.

There was never any guarantee that the donor kidney would work or that Foster's body wouldn't reject it. There was likewise no guarantee that Willow's single kidney would pick up the slack to do the task it and its partner had been doing since her birth. If one would have asked either of them on their first wedding anniversary if they had any regrets, both just would have smiled and changed the subject.

The three young vacationing cyclists met for breakfast in the historic hotel's coffee shop. Brick wanted to sit on stools at the bar so he could watch the *Opening Bell* financial show on TV while they ate, but by the time they ordered, all three agreed that they needed to sit in a padded booth since the day ahead would include lots of sitting on a hard bicycle seat. Their original plan was to be back up on the mountain trails by seven sharp, but plan B, to ride along the winding White River trails, was easily agreed on since they were all feeling the aches and pains of the previous day. Dave made a call to the hospital to check on Ned Foster, but the charge nurse didn't know him and would say little except that Ned still didn't have a room number. Thus, Dave concluded that the poor guy was still in the intensive care unit.

With breakfast under their belts, they sorted through the jumbled mess in the back of the Tahoe where everything had been tossed during the emergency. They straightened things up, went over their bikes and equipment, and proceeded to load their bikes onto the roof rack. Brick looked over Foster's $8,000, mangled bike and decided to leave it inside the hotel. When he asked the desk clerk what to do with it, she handed him a room key.

"Just put it inside the Foster's door. Someone might steal it out here. I'm the only one here right now so I can't leave the desk," the grey-haired woman said.

Brick was a little winded when he finished the three flights of stairs. Room thirty-two was at the end of the hallway. He was somewhat uncomfortable opening the Foster's door; he really didn't know the woman and for sure wished he had never met the man. He shifted the broken bicycle into his left hand and knocked on the thick, pine door. He waited, but there was no answer. Knowing the boys were waiting downstairs for him, he inserted the key and turned the door handle.

The room was enormous compared to his. There were two large, leather couches in the main room and what appeared to be two bedrooms. Finding this unusual he closed the door behind him and laid the bike parts against the wall. He knew he should leave, but couldn't keep himself from poking around. In the first bedroom the dresser and large bed were strewn with men's toiletries and clothing. The second bedroom was definitely occupied by the woman. The open closet held a row of feminine clothes, and the bathroom had her cosmetics scattered out on the counter. He had just picked up a cut crystal perfume decanter when he heard the door open.

"Can I help you?" asked the woman's voice.

Only dumb luck saved him from dropping and breaking the bottle. He set it down then turned to face Willow. She had her huge, leather purse on her arm and a paper coffee cup in her hand. To his surprise she said nothing further, but did glance at the twisted bicycle and then proceeded to the couch where she sat down and crossed her long, tan legs. She was wearing loose-fitting shorts and a simple, snug, red T-shirt. Staring at him over the top of the cup she took a sip, and then raised her eyebrows as though posing a question.

"The light in my bathroom is terrible. I've been trying to get something out of my eye ever since last night," he said turning back toward the mirror and lifting his eye lid.

Willow didn't budge from the couch, but listened to his lame excuse as though she had heard better ones. "There is a doctor at the hospital who could take a look at it. Maybe there is nothing there and you scratched your cornea. That can be dangerous. You could lose your vision. Of course, searching through other people's rooms might cause you to lose more than your vision."

"I was bringing your husband's bike up to the room. The desk clerk gave me the key," he said defensively.

"Well, in any case, I hope you found what you were looking for," she said. "Incidentally, your friends are waiting for you at your car. They asked me, if I should see you, to tell you to hurry up. Unless, of course, you would like to continue your search ... for the object in your eye?"

"And why were you poking around in her bathroom?" Derek asked Brick as they headed onto the main highway.

"It wasn't like I intended to snoop around. It was just too tempting. Either of you would have done the same thing. I mean, the rooms were enormous compared to ours. They obviously sleep in separate beds."

"Not me," said Dave. "I don't mean sleeping in separate beds. I mean I would not have cased out the room. I value my life way too much."

"But think about it. Isn't it pretty weird the way she acted at the hotel when she found out about the snakebite? And who is she really? Her name is just Willow? Not Mrs. Foster or even Willow Foster. How many women do you know who have just one name?"

"How about Cher?" Derek said. "Or Rhianna, or Madonna?"

"Well, what about the wedding ring?"

"What ring?" asked Dave.

"Just my point … she doesn't wear one. Every married woman wears a ring. So when I saw two bedrooms and two bathrooms it made me curious about just what's up with these two?"

"Get real, Brick, older people like their space. Nobody goes poking around their bedroom. Their life is none of our business. So he has a mysterious girlfriend or a wife who hates rings, who cares? By the way, had both beds been slept in?" Derek joked.

It was nearly noon by the time the men had filled up the Tahoe with gas, bought snacks, and readied their bikes for the ride. The White River was rushing, and was nearly overflowing the tops of some of the bridges as they pedaled their way along the county roads. The bike ride was far from the stressful ride and piggyback trip of the previous day. Likewise, the adrenaline rush was nowhere as close, but it was beautiful just the same. By the time they returned to the hotel four hours later, they were in a quiet funk, grumbling about how they practically wasted the entire day on an easy ride that they could have done in their neighborhood desert trails back home.

"I saw a marked-up trail map in Ned's room," said Brick. "He had a trail outlined in yellow marker that went up toward Flag Creek. Remember the sign we saw on the outskirts of town? Maybe we could try that tomorrow."

"Why not," said Dave. "Since you and Willow are like old friends now, you should ask her to borrow the map. 'Pardon me, Willow sweetie, you know when I was checking out your bathroom and going through all of your dresser drawers this morning, I noticed a map—' Ouch!"

Derek settled the two friends down and suggested they shower, and then stop by the hospital to check on Foster before dinner. They were still full of gas station junk food snacks, so they agreed on the plan.

Foster's Porsche SUV wasn't in front of the hotel or in the hospital parking lot. Ned was still flat in his bed in the ICU with his leg elevated in a sling. Dave was the first to notice that the black marker line demarcating the highest point of swelling was slightly above the redness in the skin. A small TV mounted to the wall was on, but the patient's eyes were closed.

"Mr. Foster? Ned, are you awake?" Brick asked.

A nurse appeared at the door and asked if the men had signed in at the desk, then recognizing Dave, changed the subject. "He's pretty stable right now, Doctor. He may have had a slight allergic reaction to the antivenom, but the swelling almost has stopped increasing. His intake is adequate, but his urine output has decreased, just when we thought he would start getting rid of some of the swelling fluid," she said to Dave, ignoring the non-medical visitors.

"Is he mentally alert when he is awake?" Dave asked.

"He is pretty good until just before his next dose of Demerol is due, and then the pain makes him disagreeable.

He keeps asking about his kidney. Did you know that he has a kidney transplant?"

Surprised, they all shook their heads to the negative. Dave actually lifted Foster's sheet to look for the scar, but was on the wrong side of the bed. The over-informative nurse nodded to the patient's other side. When Dave followed through and looked on the other side he saw a nine inch scar curving around beneath Ned's ribcage. The commotion stirred Foster, who opened his eyes and blinked, studying the faces of his visitors.

"Ah, my life savers," he said with a weak smile, then turning to the nurse, explained to her how the three men had carried him down the mountain to the hospital. He made it sound as though there wasn't even an ambulance involved. By the end of the story his voice was getting weaker.

"It looks like the medication is working, Ned," said Brick, leaning over the bed, talking louder than was necessary.

"Have any of you seen his Willow?" the nurse asked and then blushed thinking that may have come out wrong. "You know his lady friend, Willow? We need to get copies of the records about his kidney operation, and she was going to bring them from the hotel."

They all shook their heads and decided that was a good time to leave. They offered to do anything they could to help him, but Foster waved them off telling them to go have fun and to do a steep trail ride for him.

"Knock on Willow's door when you get back to the hotel and let her know that I'm fine, she doesn't need to come by tonight. She has to get up early every morning to take business calls from New York and Europe."

"Sure, Ned," Derek said, starting to shake the man's hand, but then realizing it was still attached to an IV line. "Brick here has visited with Willow this morning. He'll be happy to take care of it. We'll check on you tomorrow."

"Thanks a lot," Brick said, giving Derek a friendly shove as they walked to the car.

"Don't you guys think it's pretty weird that she isn't sitting at his bedside? If it was one of us in the hospital, our wives would insist on being there 24/7," said Dave.

His question went unanswered as the three heard the sound of the Porsche's turbo engine whine as it came around the corner. Willow was driving, but in the diminished light of dusk, must not have seen the men. She did slow as she drove by the small ICU wing of the building, and then accelerated, heading down the street toward the highway, away from the hospital and the hotel.

The Lazy Z was a steakhouse about ten miles up the White River from Meeker. The Michelin travel-guide recommended the place for a "great local steak," giving it two out of three stars. The last thing Willow wanted to do was to share dinner conversation with the folks at the hotel, hashing over Ned's snakebite again—especially with the three Arizona bikers. She was tired and hungry and needed a change of scenery. She had been on the phone to their East Coast contacts most of the day, during which time she had reiterated the snakebite story more times than she could count.

The Lazy Z was a rustic place with a gravel parking lot that was illuminated courtesy of half a dozen neon beer signs. After one look, she hesitated even getting out of the car, but then saw two couples going in with teenage kids in tow, so she guessed that the guide might be right. At least the place would be safe. The guide book promised the "best buffalo burger on the planet and Black Angus steaks that are aged till they can be cut with a fork." The concrete floor inside was covered with sawdust and peanut shells. The music was loud and twangy—some melody she vaguely remembered from her childhood. She was shown to a table against the far wall, and was quickly visited by a waitress who took her drink order and gave her a menu. Two minutes later her drink was on the table, and she had ordered the half-pound buffalo burger with mushrooms and a small dinner salad. She settled in, her back against the wall, and observed the people in the busy place, making comparisons to her favorite night spot in The Village in Manhattan. "Like a different planet," she thought, "not just a different state." She actually was beginning to relax and enjoy herself, tapping her foot to the music's beat. Then trouble started.

"Hi there, Missy," a rumpled, cowboy-looking guy said in a tone she recognized immediately as a come-on. "My name is Rowdy, and just what might yours be, little lady?" he asked, offering her his weathered and scabbed hand. He was short, wiry, and looked like he had forgotten to shave for a few days. His pearl-button shirt had a brown stain on one pocket, and his boots were scuffed and caked with brown mud, or whatever else he had slogged through.

If Willow was anything, she was tough on men. She had been mugged once in Central Park and had made it her mission to never let it happen again. Self-defense classes had been her obsession for the next year, and she made that knowledge part of her daily fitness routine. Since the man was just an innocent local she didn't want to make a scene, so she took his hand and told him her name was Brenda Lee.

"I think I heard your name somewhere. You must be famous. Mind if I join you?"

"That would be a problem," she said, shaking her head slowly and avoiding eye contact. "My husband is just cleaning his handguns out in the pickup and will be in any minute now."

Rowdy wandered off toward an old Wurlitzer jukebox. Moments later Willow's enormous buffalo burger was served; it was steaming hot with what must have been three or four whole potatoes worth of golden brown, curly fries, making her salad look like a garnish. She was working her way through the delicious meal, enjoying the music and watching a few of the couples dance on the weathered hardwood floor, when Rowdy showed up again, this time with a beer bottle in his left hand.

"If I didn't know better I'd be thinking your husband must have a lot of guns to clean, or maybe he just shot himself by accident. Why don't you give that burger a rest and take a little spin around the dance floor with me?"

"No thank you," she said, not making eye contact with the guy who now appeared to be a little tipsy.

"Now, little lady, I must insist on a dance with the sexiest woman in the room," he said, reaching down and grasping her left hand. Had he grasped her right arm or hand he might have been okay, but she held the long-tine dinner fork in her right hand in a firm grip. The second his calloused hand tightened on her wrist, she drove the fork deep into the stringy muscle of his forearm. He jumped away from her, knocking over the table behind him, sending the dishes and glasses crashing to the floor.

"You're crazy lady!" he screamed, shaking his arm, unsuccessfully trying to dislodge the imbedded fork. Blood was weeping from the wound by the time he mustered the courage to pull it out. His second scream was laced with profanities, which brought absolute silence to the room. The jukebox kept playing but the dancers were frozen in place. Attention was focused on his wounded forearm, which by now was dripping blood between his fingers onto the floor. No one seemed to notice that the chair beside the table was empty, nor did they hear the guttural roar of the German V-8 engine as Willow's Porsche exited the parking lot.

CHAPTER

The men were sitting in a booth eating breakfast when Willow approached the table. Dave already had been on the phone with the hospital, and had reported Foster's stable condition to his friends. Willow was dressed in crisply-pressed, tan cargo shorts and a snug-fitting, red sleeveless top. She had on a thin, gold necklace with a teardrop diamond. The studs in her ears matched the size and shape of the teardrop. She was carrying an alligator-finish laptop case and a folded *Wall Street Journal*.

"Good morning gentlemen," she said, nodding at the empty place next to Brick. "Is someone sitting there or may I join you?"

"Please do," said Derek, starting to stand up, but trapped by the snug table.

Brick scooted over against the wall to give her more room, but still found his bare knee accidently brushing against hers.

"Are you sure you have enough room?" she said, making no attempt to move nearer to the outside edge of the booth or to move her smooth shaven leg away from his hairy one. "Aren't you guys starting a little late in the morning? It's already seven."

"We were almost ready to leave, but couldn't resist

53

the smell of the bacon and pancakes. Would you like to order something?"

"No," she said, "but I'm glad that I caught you before you head out. Is that how you say it out here in the West, 'head out'?"

This brought a round of chuckles and a significant decrease in the tension because of her presence. She waved over the waitress and ordered a cup of coffee, and then accepted an extra slice of bacon from Dave's side order plate. This she ate politely with a fork and knife. She asked about their upcoming ride for the day, and seemed to know something about the trails, especially how the trail guides rated the grade and difficulty of the terrain.

"You sound like you must do some riding yourself," said Brick, again bumping his knee with hers. "You sure you don't want to join us? There is a bike rental shop out on the main highway."

"Heavens no," she said. "I haven't ridden a bicycle since I was in middle school. I only know about the trails here because Edward has me do all of his planning. I do everything but pedal the bike for him." This brought on a laugh from the men. "He became spoiled when he rode professionally, you know, everyone bowing and scraping to the famous riders, especially the yellow-and-polka-dotted champions."

"When was that? And where did he ride?" asked Derek.

"He was on an Italian cycling team in the seventies. That is how he got his start in business. You mean he hasn't already told you all the details of his Tour de France yellow jersey?"

The conversation was interrupted by the waitress delivering the check, which the men insisted putting her coffee on, then her iPhone rang and she abruptly excused herself, nodding her thanks for the coffee and bacon. The men lingered for a minute in the lobby, but she didn't return.

"How weird was that?" Dave said as they started up the mountain road.

"Weird what?" said Brick.

"The woman hasn't been the least bit friendly to any of us. Then she pops in and practically sits on your lap. And what's with the Edward business, and how about the confirmation of his comment about winning the yellow jersey? And she didn't mention anything about Ned being in the ICU. That is not a normal husband/wife relationship."

"You're just jealous that your wife won't call you by your proper name and plan all of your daily schedule for you," Brick said. "My wife calls me Bricklyn all the time."

"Yeah, when she's pissed at you, or when you're snuggled up close to a foxy woman and your face is turning beet red," Dave said. "What I still don't get is the no wedding ring."

As they drove to the trailhead, they all became quiet, lost in their own thoughts and perceptions of their new friends and the mystery surrounding their relationship. All three had done some traveling and met people from different walks of life, but none quite as mysterious as Willow.

They were halfway up the twisty, dirt road to the top of Flag Creek. Derek stopped and checked his phone signal, and called his secretary about an ongoing commercial building project. The static was starting to overwhelm their conversation when Dave's phone rang.

The nurse on the phone was calling from Meeker Community Hospital. "Is this Doctor Felshaw?" she asked.

"Yes, this is Dr. Felshaw. Could you possibly speak a little louder?"

"Sure. The patient from New York, the man with the snakebite, Mr. Foster, is asking to speak with you."

At that moment the phone cut out and both Dave and Derek's calls were dropped.

For a brief moment the three discussed the possibility that they should turn around and return to town, but then just as quickly dismissed the idea. Derek's call was almost finished and they already told Foster they would visit him after their ride.

While the boys were gleefully trudging up the slippery dirt trail to a natural spring in the middle of a mountain meadow, their three wives were discussing their absence and adventures while sitting around a glass-top table near Dave and Melody's pool. The toddlers were playing in the shallow end of the pool, and the Wahl baby had just finished nursing and was ready for a nap. The women had become friends because of the men's long-lasting friendship that went back years before wives entered the picture. Fortunately, the couples had progressed through college, grad-school, and businesses at the same pace. Although the Wahl's had been late-comers in the baby business, their interests and concerns and general incomes had run parallel with their close friends.

All three families had started with little or nothing and all carried debt, which up till now, had been manageable. The problem was that those salaries and commissions that sounded so good coming out of school were now being chased with extra obligations previously unanticipated.

"It's the darn insurance salesmen!" said Natasha. "Just when we think everything is going along great one of those guys shows up on the door-step and gives Derek a guilt-trip about what would happen if he died or had a stroke or whatever. Health insurance is one thing but life insurance, disability insurance, liability insurance. Did you know that my homeowner's insurance won't cover me for accidents with that old golf cart I got from my dad?"

"I'm glad the boys got away," said Debra. "Bricklyn hasn't taken a day off since the baby was born. He thinks that if he misses one day of market trading, it will be the day the lid blows off the pot and the market doubles or triples. He sold out every position he held in the market before he left just in case there is Armageddon while he is gone." She got up from the table and went to the pool edge to dangle her feet. Her long brown hair glistened in the morning sun. She always had been slender and shapely, but had struggled to lose the twenty-plus pounds she had put on during the pregnancy. She looked great in her new two piece swimsuit, which she could finally wear. Her usual summer tan was still a few weeks off.

"She seems pretty stressed out today. Money or the baby? What's your guess?" Natasha whispered. She was sitting in the shade of the large umbrella. Her skin was bright pink already and the day was young. Her naturally blond hair came with skin that never tanned, but just turned various shades of red. Her deep blue eyes gave an aristocratic air to her high cheekbones and fantastic smile. Nothing in her appearance hinted of her brilliance or of her tenacity.

"I think it's the changes of the new baby. And the two-is-company-three-is-a-crowd thing with Brick, her, and the baby. He's used to being the center of her world and can't quite get used to the new world order," Melody said. To call Melody analytical was an understatement. No less beautiful than the other two women, her master's degree in clinical psychology allowed her insight into relationships most others missed. Her personality however, was strictly that of a redhead. She was kind and fun but not someone to get on the wrong side of.

"Well, one thing is for sure," Natasha said. "When it comes to our husbands, there will never be a day in their lives when there is too much money or too many fun things on their to-do list. We're in the same boat as Brick and Deb. The last day of the month used to be the best because it was payday. Now that the paydays are at odd times, the thirtieth is always bill-paying day, and it's the worst day of the month. No matter how much money is in the account on the twenty-ninth, it will be down to almost nothing by the first."

The phone rang inside the house four times before Melody made it to the patio extension. She listened for a couple of minutes then made a comment and hung up.

"Have either of you heard of Edward Foster?" Debra asked, loud enough for both ladies to hear.

Both shook their heads, dismissing the question until Melody went on. "That was Dave's office. They wanted to know if it was all right to give someone named Edward Foster Dave's cell phone number. They said the call was forwarded from a hospital in Meeker Colorado. They said that it was urgent that this Foster guy get in touch with Dave as soon as possible. You think I should have said no?"

The hotel manager met the three bikers before Dave could turn off the SUV's engine. She was waving a note and trying to explain it before they even opened the door.

"The hospital called and needs you to go down there as soon as possible," the woman said as they got out of the car.

"You two go," Brick said. "I doubt they are calling for me. I'm feeling a little carsick and also need to make some phone calls. I'll meet you downstairs for dinner in about an hour or whenever you get back."

Derek was wishing he had come up with the excuse first, but now felt obliged to go with Dave, thinking that it must be a medical matter, and all Derek would do is sit in a waiting room watching the black-and-white TV and smelling the hospital's sickening aromas. Brick was inside the hotel before Derek conceded with a shrug.

Both men were sweaty and feeling grimy from their ride when they entered the immaculately clean ICU, expecting to see an improved Ned Foster. What they saw instead was the curtain pulled, and half a dozen feet below the green, dividing curtain's hem.

"You go in and see what they want," said Derek. "I'll just get in the way."

What Dave found was astonishing. The heart monitor showed a rapid but regular cardiac pattern, but Foster's breathing rate was triggering an alarm bell. There were the remains of an attempted cardiac resuscitation scattered around the bed—sterile white wrapping papers, plastic needle caps, and a Silastic intubation catheter still coated with K-Y Jelly. Even the defibrillation machine stood beside the bed with one of its paddles dangling from its cord. Three young nurses, dressed in jeans and pink scrub shirts, were trying to put a different airway tube down his throat to enable Foster to breathe. From Dave's perspective, none of them had a clue what they were doing. Meanwhile Foster's face and arms and hands were getting bluer by the second.

"We got his heart rate back with chest pounding, but when I tried to intubate him his vocal cords were swollen shut. I think he had an anaphylactic reaction to the last dose of antivenom," said one of the nurses.

It took Dave less than a minute to verify what was happening and to take command of the code. He barked like a boot camp sergeant, ordering a cut-down tray and a tracheotomy tube. While one of them ran to find the supplies he took a look down Foster's airway and then clamped an oxygen mask on his face and reached across the bed to turn up the flow rate.

"Get in here and help me," Derek heard Dave command.

"Who? Me?" Derek asked, sticking his head through the curtain.

"Hold this mask while I get this ready," Dave said, turning toward a bedside table to open the surgical tray. The other nurses were starting a second IV and trying to stay out of the Arizona doctor's way.

With the speed of the striking snake that had precipitated Foster's problems, Dave swabbed the dying man's neck and not taking the time to glove himself, picked up the scalpel and made a one-inch-wide incision into the trachea, just below the cricoid bone. Reaching out for a Kelly clamp—which to Derek looked like a skinny pair of pliers—he inserted it into the incision and spread the teeth. A second deeper incision produced a bubbling of blood and air, which was followed by the immediate insertion of a curved plastic tube with a floppy rubber flange in the middle. Dave would later sew the tube in place using the flange and neck skin.

"Oxygen," he ordered, reaching out for the connecting hose that Derek already had unhooked from the mask and was attaching to the tube. Derek then began slowly squeezing the black Ambu bag about every two seconds.

Still holding the tube in place as blood welled up around his bare fingers, Dave looked up at Foster's pink face and then at Derek.

"How did you know how to do that?" Dave asked his friend.

"I saw them do it on *Grey's Anatomy*," Derek answered. "Can I leave now? I think I'm going to faint."

When the nurse finally attached the ventilator to the tracheostomy tube, Foster started to twist and grab for the tube as his body began to regain a pink color, and he regained consciousness. Derek held the older man's wrists and talked to him, reassuring him that everything would be all right, not knowing if he was lying to Foster or not.

"Give him some morphine and get me some 2-0 Prolene suture," Dave ordered the nurses, who by now were standing and staring in shock. "And while we're waiting, would someone like to tell me where the on-call doctor is—who should be doing this stuff in the first place?"

The explanation was complicated, but Dave and Derek finally learned that the in-house doctor on call had jumped in an ambulance to go out to a ranch house a few miles out of town to deliver a baby.

Foster—with his hands now in soft restraints to prevent him from pulling out the tube—was becoming more alert, and began responding to yes and no questions. By the time the town's doctor returned from the home delivery, the room had been tidied up, masking any appearance of the catastrophe.

Dave and Derek were sitting at the small ICU desk after having scrubbed their hands and downed bottles of drinking water. Dave was writing up a procedure note and some orders for follow up medications.

The town doctor apologized for his absence and explained, "Foster's leg started swelling more this morning. Ten more vials of antivenom came in with the UPS delivery, so I called the university and the snake guru there told me to give him all ten. The patient insisted I put a call in for you this morning. I even had them call your home in Arizona. When you hadn't called back by noon I went ahead and had the nurse start the infusion. I was already out at the ranch, up to my elbows with a stubborn baby when the nurse called to say he was having a reaction."

"Don't you have a backup doctor to call?"

"That's a laugh. We are lucky to have the two of us. I go through a new contract doctor every year. The one you met yesterday is fishing today. He's single—thank goodness—or he would have been gone by April. None of the married guys last more than a year. Their wives don't want to spend the winter belly deep in snow with the shopping malls three hours away. Even the bright, local-born doctors and nurses, those that grew up around here, they get a taste of the big city while they are away at school. Then if they do return they soon find that this hick-town is too small for their britches. Not to mention the fact that they can earn three times as much in the cities."

"The lifestyle looks pretty good to me," said Derek. "Fishing, hunting, mountain biking, and not having to put up with traffic and the noise of a big city. They should be grateful for the small town life. I'd move my family here in a heartbeat if I thought I could earn a living. I guess the grass always looks taller and greener on the other side of the fence."

"Well," said the doctor. "My brother-in-law owns an office building just up the street that has plenty of vacancies. You could try your hand at real estate development here in Meeker. We could use a nice little shopping mall."

The three men laughed, in spite of their grim surroundings.

Brick was starving—so he finally called the hospital to check on his buddies. He got a way too vivid description of the event at the hospital from Derek, who was still in shock from having played scrub nurse. Foster was now stable, though mentally out of it from the morphine. Unable to be of any more assistance at the hospital, the three friends agreed to meet back at the hotel dining room. Through all the confusion and drama of the previous hours, no one had seen or heard from Willow. As they drove back to the hotel, Derek was the first to notice the $100 thousand

SUV sitting in front of the hardware store, half a block away from the hotel.

"There's her car. I wonder where she's been all day," he said. "Everything about that lady is weird."

"I don't know about everything Derek. She is pretty darn good-looking and she has a certain elegance about her. I think she's kind of classy and yet mysterious. But yes, you are partly right. She's a little weird too."

"That's just great, Dave. Her husband or sugar daddy or whatever he is, owes us his life. Especially you. And now you have the hots for his woman."

Dave laughed at the absurd inference. Of the three friends, his marriage was the most solid, but that didn't mean he didn't appreciate beauty and elegance when he saw it.

The men parked, locked up the car, and headed into the hotel dining room. Both were famished. As they walked past the mounted elk and mule deer heads lining the wall, they heard Brick's familiar voice and then another. The dining room had six or eight tables occupied with early evening customers. Sitting at the only round table, laughing at Brick's joke, was the mystery woman, Willow.

The two men pulled up chairs nodding, but not saying much. Dave waved for a menu from the waiter, but didn't interrupt the heavy conversation at the table. Willow and Brick were discussing some intricacy of the international monetary trading market.

"The Euro took a substantial drop today, and we were right on top of it," she said, looking at both of the newly arrived. "I spent the whole day online and on the phone."

It was hardly an explanation for why she hadn't responded to the calls from the hospital.

"Did they tell you that Ned had what could have been a fatal reaction to the second round of antivenom?" Dave asked, interrupting.

"Bricklyn here filled me in," she said, patting his arm. "He assured me that you had the situation well in hand. Trust me; I've spent more than my share of time over the years sitting at Edwards's hospital bedside. He is a very private man, and doesn't like his friends and employees groveling when he is in poor health."

All three men darted their eyes at one another as they pretended to study the menu.

"I felt uncomfortable being the one to make decisions about his care when a family member should have been there to help," Dave said.

A bucket of ice water dumped onto the table could not have chilled the conversation any more. Luckily, the waiter appeared—as if heaven sent—and took their orders.

When the waiter turned back to the kitchen, Willow leaned over to Dave and with a smile said, "Doctor, just like you don't expect me—or any of your patients—to understand all of your medical decisions, I don't expect you to understand or agree with decisions regarding my personal matters. That includes my use of my time, my marriage, and my businesses. I apologize if you were offended that I wasn't at Edward's bedside. He and I have a unique relationship, one which doesn't necessarily involve all of the usual husband-wife synergy. Thinking of me more like his business partner than his wife might help you reconcile yourself to the facts. I truly appreciate your expert medical care of him, and what you were probably thinking then—at the hospital—and now. Just give it a little time and you will catch on to what I mean."

Willow had eaten dinner with them, listened to their biking talk, and then promptly left the table without saying good night, jump in the lake, or boo. The men watched her leave in disbelief.

"Catch on? What the heck did she mean by 'catch on?' The woman is a literal nutcase," Derek said. "I couldn't believe my ears when she was giving you that lame explanation."

The men stuck around for dessert and refills on their drinks. When Brick asked for the check the waitress said that it had already been paid.

"She may be a nutcase, but she is a good-looking nutcase, and as long as she foots the bill for our steaks, I'll sit at her table anytime," said Brick.

"Yeah Derek, at least we got paid for our two hours of slave labor in the ICU, but barely above minimum wage," Dave said.

"And here I thought you were the president of the Willow Admiration Society," joked Derek.

Dave made an under-breath comment about where Derek should spend eternity and then finished his bread pudding. As the men got up to leave, Dave leaned over and whispered to Brick, "If you're starting to think that Willow is good-looking, you better go Skype with Debbie before you go to bed. Your wife is a thousand times more beautiful than that New York nutcase. Plus, Brick, Debbie isn't crazy."

"Where did that come from? It sounds to me as though you are the one who needs a Skype session," said Brick.

Thirty minutes later and eight hundred miles southwest of Meeker, Debra Wahl looked at the screen of her laptop and quizzed her husband's grizzly face about his day. "Are you really not going to shave for a week? You already look like something that escaped from the rehab center," she teased.

He gave her his second-hand version of the melodrama up the street at the hospital and how Dave had saved the New Yorker's life for the second time.

"His name is Foster, right? Some kind of stuffy first name and the third or fourth stuck on the end?"

"How did you know that?" he asked, staring into her blue eyes. She really was just as beautiful as Dave had said.

"I was with the girls and Melody got a call from Dave's office asking for permission to give out his private cell number. But that's not all. There was a second call an hour later; from his office again, but this time it was a woman with a New York area code. She wanted yours and Derek's phone numbers as well. We told her to call back in a week. Who was she, and what was that all about?"

Though the endotracheal tube had been in place in Ned's trachea for only thirty-six hours, to him it felt like it had been there a year. During the drawn-out hours of increasing mental clarity, he was able to understand most everything that was happening to him. As his brain cleared, his throbbing leg pain increased, and he experienced continuous waves of scalding fever and then teeth-chattering chills. Though nearly all of the faces he saw were strangers to him at first, they gradually became like his best friends. Even the lovely, older woman, who straightened and cleaned his room every few hours, would smile at him and called him "Lucky Señor Foster. We are all praying for you."

Visits from the three Arizona men blended in with all the other faces and events. He had frequent visits from the local doctor, and of course, the nurses. An attorney from Steamboat Springs showed up after apparently reading an article in the local newspaper about the accident. One of the friendlier local nurses whispered to Dave and Brick that the sleazy attorney figured he could build a liability case against the bike manufacturer and possibly the out-of-towners.

Foster had spent enough time in hospitals over the

past years to recognize that he was probably getting good care, but he still told Willow that he wanted to be transported back to Massachusetts General Hospital, in Boston, where he had once been a patient. He wanted to go as soon as was possible. His private jet was on standby in New York, but the Meeker doctor was hesitant to release him to fly on a conventional airplane while he was still intubated.

Since he couldn't really talk with the tube in place, he did a lot of listening and some note writing on Willow's iPad. It took a while to get things sorted out, but Willow finally made arrangements for an SOS air-evacuation jet out of Denver to fly into Meeker. The local doctor finally consented to the transfer and to removing Foster from the ventilator. Dr. Dave agreed that it would be safe for Foster to make the flight as long as there were trained personnel on board. The swelling in his leg was slightly reduced and his skin color was improving. There was, however, one more major problem. His kidney functions tests were getting worse. When Willow heard that news, she went off on a tirade about how she should have insisted on his being air evacuated the first day, and then went on about how the second round of antivenom wasn't necessary and how he had been getting along just fine until then. The one thing she didn't find fault with was the life-saving care Foster had received from Doctor David Felshaw.

Once an accepting internal medicine doctor at the Boston hospital was arranged, she put in a call to Doctor Rose, Foster's previous transplant doctor, who insisted on her faxing him all of the pertinent lab work. The last rounds of dialysis previous to his kidney transplant had been hard on the Wall Street tycoon. Dr. Rose always was quite frank with his patients, and stated his concern that the newest complications from the snakebite and the antivenom could very well lead to Ned's demise.

The Bombardier air-evacuation jet landed in Meeker just before dusk. The tiny airport's runway was barely long enough for it to stop. Its two-man team of no-nonsense paramedics rode to the hospital in Meeker's ten-year-old ambulance with lights flashing, and then spent (what seemed to the hospital staff) an excessive amount of time checking paperwork and re-examining the patient. Foster was then carefully loaded into the ambulance for the short trip to the airfield.

Brick, Dave, and Derek stood by the chain-link fence waiting for the ambulance to arrive and pass through the gate leading onto the runway. They had cut their last day of mountain bike riding short in order to bid farewell to Ned and to Willow as well. They had stopped by the hotel to shower and change clothes and afterwards were told that she already had checked out.

The entourage arrived at the gate, led by a police cruiser with lights flashing. Then came Willow in the Porsche SUV, and finally, the ambulance. Willow parked her car right next to the three men and as per the pre-discussed plan, the ambulance also stopped at the open gate. The ambulance side door opened and there lay Edward Foster III. He waved the men toward him, trying to elicit a smile. With a weak voice, harsh from the recent endotracheal tube, he again thanked each of them for their help and promised, "I'll be in touch with you three once I'm settled at Mass General." The door then closed and the vehicle drove the final hundred yards to the side of the jet.

Willow waited for the ambulance to pull onto the tarmac and then got out of the SUV, tugging a huge, baggy purse onto her shoulder. She was dressed in a plain, black jogging suit and running shoes. She walked up to the three men and dropping her purse on the pavement offered her hand, first to Derek, then Dave and then, to everyone's surprise, gave Bricklyn a brief embrace.

"Thank you, each one of you. You saved Edward's life, at least up until now, and believe it or not, you have been a great source of strength to me. None of you will be forgotten," she said, then turned toward the plane. After a couple of steps she stopped and turned back. Digging into her purse, she pulled out a large key ring and pitched it underhand to Brick.

"I almost forgot. Would you please drop the car off in Grand Junction at the Porsche dealer? It's on your way to Phoenix. The directions are on the seat. They will ship it to New York. Edward suggested giving it to the three of you, but no one in town had a big enough metal saw to cut it in thirds." She laughed at her own joke then turned toward the plane. It was the first time any of them had heard her laugh.

By the time Willow walked the distance, the patient was on board and the engines were spiraling up to power. Seconds later, the door was pulled up, latched and the $30 million airplane was rolling toward the far end of the runway where it turned, and without hesitation, came back toward them gaining speed and volume. Seconds later it was aloft and disappearing into the waning dusk with just its navigation lights visible—blinking farewell.

The three men stood shoulder-to-shoulder watching the airplane disappear over the mountain top, each lost in their own thoughts: the steep mountain trail ride with the jovial and talented Ned, the accident, the snakebite, the piggybacking of Ned down the mountain, the antivenom reaction, the tracheotomy, and the many strange encounters with that beautiful mysterious woman, Willow. Would they ever see those two again?

When a guard arrived in an old pickup and chained the gate closed, they finally turned toward the vehicles.

"I'm riding with him," Derek said, nodding toward Brick and the Porsche. You can bring the clunker."

Dave started to protest, but then just laughed at his friends instead.

They returned to the hotel and ate a hearty dinner—including the biggest steak on the menu. After the gluttonous meal, topped off with homemade ice cream sundaes, they stopped at the desk to check out. They had given up the idea of a last early morning ride, thus planned an early morning departure. When their three hotel bills were itemized for meals, room, and laundry, they each owed around $900. At the bottom of the bill, where the amount due was listed, there were zeros. When they questioned the figures, the desk clerk just smiled at them. "Lucky you," she said.

The next morning was beautiful, but went unappreciated because the drive to Grand Junction was fast and furious. None of the three men ever had driven such a magnificent machine as the Turbo-Porsche. Each of them took a turn at the wheel, leaving the Tahoe far behind to catch up with each changeover. The dealer in Grand Junction was expecting the car and didn't even need instruction on the shipping. Willow apparently had it covered.

The long drive back to Scottsdale was a real drag, with nearly twelve hours of High Plains driving cutting across southern Utah, the Navajo reservation, and then the desert heading into Phoenix. They did have a chance to get caught up on their sleep while each one took their turn driving. By the time they arrived home they were looking forward to being with their wives, kids, and catching up with their work.

For the next several weeks, each of the men went about their daily agendas of work and family: Dave had a backlog of surgeries and a double-booked office schedule; Derek needed to argue the benefits of a new shopping center in front of the city council; Brick's hopes of a turnaround in the pork bellies' market came about just as his options were about to expire, giving him a near heart attack followed by a handsome profit. Other than the basis of a terrific story to share with friends, Edward Foster III and the mysterious Willow were fading memories.

And then their UPS packages arrived.

Massachusetts General Hospital is a sprawling collection of buildings that dominate entire city blocks of Northeast Boston. There are never-ending expansion and renovation projects going on, giving an impression of unsettled chaos surrounding the around-the-clock lifesaving medical miracles. On the top floor of the surgical tower are a group of hospital rooms, which appear more like they could be VIP rooms at the Bellagio or Wynn hotels in Las Vegas. Tucked away in regal splendor, Edward Foster III lay in a hospital bed with his leg elevated, his mind sedated, and a high-definition, big screen TV reviewing the Wall Street activities of the day. Willow was seated beside him in a leather recliner with her laptop resting on her indigo-colored, silk slacks.

"Are you okay with the Boca Raton purchase?" she asked.

He lifted his head off of the pillow to look at her then let it sink back into the fine cotton threads. "Tell me again what the project is," he said.

"It's a cluster of three-story houses that line the sixteenth fairway. Remember, there are ten of them all on that dogleg right. The street approach ends in a cul-de-sac. They are all finished, but haven't been lived in. We can pick them up for $2 million apiece. The listed price is four point two each. I can find a buyer in Qatar for the package for thirty-two to thirty-four. That's a $12 to $14 million profit. We can keep the money in Dubai so you don't need to worry about your buddies at the IRS."

Willow didn't wait for an answer from her boss and legal husband. She already had committed to the deal while they were in Colorado. Today was the first time she considered him lucid enough to remember anything she had previously said. The first three days back in Massachusetts his kidney was completely shut down. Only after massive doses of steroids and anti-rejection medicines had the transplanted organ shown any sign of coming back to a function good enough that there was hope of saving it. Foster still needed dialysis twice a week and bed rest—lots of bed rest.

Willow had split her time between Boston and Manhattan, carrying the full load of responsibilities they normally shared. In the past Foster's company had full access to over $100 million in cash, plus the responsibility of $2.5 billion in real estate scattered around the world. The slumping financial markets had affected their bottom line on paper only, since Edward never dealt with banks, using only his money or that of private investors. None of them had been forced to liquidate any major assets, but Foster liked to pump up the cash reserves from time to time. No telling when a "fire sale" would pop up and that's when cash was king. His company's staff of employees ran the day-to-day operation and management of the properties, but the decisions always had been made by the boss. Nowadays it wasn't certain who really was the boss.

The TV sound went off, interrupting her Internet search of the commercial real estate market in Athens.

"Have you come up with any ideas on how to reward those Arizona boys for saving my life?" Ned said to Willow, shifting his diminished weight in the bed so he could see her face.

If he'd asked once, he'd asked her a thousand times. She had given it some thought, but still hadn't come up with anything except the repugnant idea of dishing out cash to them, which to her was like rubbing her cheek against a cat's wet nose. She did have one brainstorm, and decided to give it a spin.

"How about we bring them into the multilevel investment plan we talked about last winter? Remember, the one you dreamed up of buying Florida and Las Vegas condo buildings one at a time and letting the investors sell them off to their friends. And those friends sell them to theirs. Remember the gig?" she asked.

The idea was a takeoff of some of the liquid vitamin drinks and skincare multilevel marketing companies. She had built a computer model of the project, which made it appear both feasible and profitable. All that was needed was a pool of people who had a little discretionary money, a lot of friends just like themselves with a desire to get filthy rich on real estate, and a personality that hated to see their friends make more money than they did. With the stock market in the tank, there wasn't a better time to dangle a real estate worm on a tempting hook.

"We could bring them into the new project. We can probably add them to the base-level group without any upfront cost ... instead of the usual big-dollar buy in," she hinted, knowing that he would jump at the chance.

"They might just bring in a lot of their friends giving us a new client base in the Scottsdale area. Did you realize Phoenix is the fifth or sixth largest population area in the country?"

"That would be great!" said Foster, relaxing his head back into the pillow. "Then, I can quit worrying about rewarding them."

"They aren't your little toddlers," she said. "You don't have to give them anything."

"No, but there was a time on that mountain when I was like their toddler. Have legal draw up the paperwork and let's go forward with that business plan. If we get them in on the ground floor, they'll be millionaires in six months."

"Have you decided on a name for the project?" she asked, not expecting an answer.

"How about The Giza Relay," he said with a smile. "You know, like the pyramids in Egypt?"

"Edward, the last thing you want the world press to know is that you are building a financial pyramid. If you're thinking of it as a sort of relay race, how about calling it Baton? You know, like the runners pass to one another in a relay race."

"Or would they think about the Baton Death March in the Philippines during the war with Japan? What about Strike, as in 'strike it rich'?" he asked. "Ouch, that made me think about that damn snake."

"Why not call it like it really is. Call it 'TAG' like the game of tag? If you are lucky enough to get touched, then you're it," she said. "To make your investment pay off, you need to find others with money to invest and tag them."

"So is that your impression of the project? If you're dumb enough to let somebody talk you into investing in it then *you're it* and have to save your assets or ass by tagging someone else? We might just as well really be up front and call it Rattlesnake. If you get bitten, then you have to bite several others to save your own life."

"I thought you believed in the project?" she said. "You're just depressed since your accident. Give it a week or two and you'll be the biggest cheerleader for the investment project. I need to give the attorneys and the printers a name so they can write up the prospectus and all the legal documents. I think 'TAG' is perfect. It has a simple power to it but doesn't strongly hint of a multilevel marketing scheme or a Ponzi rip-off."

"Fine, call it TAG," Foster said, losing interest in the conversation. "Just make sure you include the three Good Samaritans in on the deal. Who knows, maybe they would be interested in helping run it? I'm certain that the team downtown doesn't want anything to do with it since I resigned as chairman last month. You and I can take the new company and run it independently."

Foster's head was pounding and his nose was running—he was trying to withdraw himself from the narcotic pain medications and was having significant withdrawal symptoms already. His kidney was his major concern—not making another $100 million for himself or anyone else. He did have a sense of satisfaction from the conversation with Willow, knowing that his Good Samaritan Arizonian friends would be rewarded, especially if they could sign up a big group of their friends and acquaintances, and then have the good sense to get out of the project before it got too big and collapsed or got shut down by the Feds.

His thoughts were interrupted by the nephrologist, Doctor R.P. Damon, the kidney specialist assigned to him. The man was six feet, six inches tall and rail-thin, with glasses hanging off the end of his nose and coffee stains on his white lab coat. He may have looked the role of a generic research technician, but the name embroidered on his left coat pocket caused medical students, residents, and fellow staff members to clear a path for the man. His reputation as a world expert in kidney disease, and a personality some would compare to *The Godfather's* Don Corleone, preceded him through the corridors of Mass General, like the calm before the tempest. He didn't have to open doors when he entered rooms—they seemed to spontaneously open ahead of him.

Damon plucked the chart out of the hand of the senior resident and flipped through the pages. He looked down at Edward Foster III with a look of disdain. "I just returned from a conference in Vienna. I would like to hear the story firsthand of your injury and the antivenom you received in Colorado," he said, then leaned against a nearby wall and listened, impatiently tapping his finger on the bedside stand. Foster had told the story one too many times to friends, family, and anyone else who asked, so he gave the doctor an abstract-length version that lasted less than a minute.

He looked at Ned's swollen leg and then palpated his abdomen. Turning his attention toward Willow, he said, "It seems that I recall a previous conversation with both of you about risky activities. In my book, downhill bicycle racing and close encounters with rattlesnakes would fit into that description. And then to let you be treated by a bunch of bumbling country idiots is beyond my comprehension. Just how stupid could one be … really, Mr. Foster?"

Willow arose from the recliner and closed in on Damon's personal space—something no other mortal seemed willing to do. She faced him, just inches from his nose-perched glasses and raised her index finger between their faces.

"My husband has been through a difficult week. He nearly lost his life on two occasions, but was saved by the intelligence and fortitude of the doctors present at the time. While you were stuffing your face with Sacher Torte and listening to violins, they were living life like real men and did an excellent job of it—"

"Who do you—?"

"Don't you dare interrupt me, you shriveled-up wimp. We will be transferring to a hospital in Manhattan. Now leave the room before I call for security. You are fired from my husband's care," Willow concluded.

The next hour brought a chain of visits from hospital administration, hospital legal, and from the transplant doctor, Dr. Rose—a man they had both loved when he cared for them previously. Excuses, apologies, and promises finally settled Willow down enough to agree to stay in Boston until Foster's kidney function stabilized, but only if the arrogant Damon stayed away. When all was said and done, she vowed to include Doctor Damon in her financial plan for the future—the last man into the Ponzi.

During the entire encounter and follow up visits, Ned had remained absolutely quiet. Not that he was fully alert in the first place, but he did remember enough of the exchange between the doctor and Willow to realize that today, more than ever, she was sliding the reins of his business out through his fingers and into her tight grasp, an inch at a time.

Regardless of the many protocols the doctors in Boston attempted, Ned's transplanted kidney continued to decrease its ability to filter his blood. After two weeks in Boston, Willow arranged for a limousine to transport them back to their penthouse in upper Manhattan. His name was once more added to the national renal transplant list. His private secretary was installed in the dining room, and dialysis was arranged at a private clinic nearby.

Willow began spending most of her day at the corporate headquarters where, unknown to Ned, she moved her personal things into his private office, seriously doubting that he would ever return to work there. She guessed that without another donor kidney Ned was going to die within the year. She had no intention of letting the financial empire he had built die with him. The basic structure of their new venture, TAG, was about up and running. The prospectus was printed and the phonebook-size ream of documents each client needed to receive and sign was already in the hands of their top fifty clients. For many of them, the minimum $500 thousand buy-in was a small formality. With a promised upside of one to 200 percent per year, compounding each year, combined with Foster's track record of turning real estate dirt into gold, none were worried that the return wouldn't be there. More importantly, none could resist the gamble.

Willow had a staff of ten working exclusively on the deal. This required her to be there every day to ride herd over them. She wasn't trying to hide anything from Foster, he was simply too sick to get dressed and go through the hassle of traveling the few miles to the office each day. They had been back in New York a couple of weeks when he reminded her about his self-promised reward for the Arizona boys.

"Are you sure you want to give them each a $500,000 position?" she asked. "That's a stupendous reward for you to just hand out."

"They saved my life, for goodness sake! If I didn't have the other investors already signed up I'd give them more. Matter-of-fact, I want you to give them a full $1 million position. It isn't going to cost you or me anything."

"If you say so, Edward. I'll go ahead and prepare the packages. I liked the boys too. I suppose you want to invite them to the kickoff meeting as well," she said, resigned to keep the dying man happy, and actually feeling a slight rush thinking of seeing the three young, handsome men again.

"That's an excellent idea. And have them bring their wives ... no kids ... just the wives. Perhaps you could arrange for a catered dinner here at the town house the night before the investor's meeting. It'll give me a chance to thank them personally."

Willow turned toward the door, her mind already planning an event that she suddenly found way more interesting than Foster's next trip to dialysis.

Dr. Dave Felshaw was in his backyard on a very hot Saturday morning, trying to repair the drip lines to his cactus and sun-drenched row of native desert shrubs, when he saw the UPS truck pull up to the front of the house. The friendly driver waved, and then made a beeline straight to the front door, where he rang the doorbell and promptly dropped a thick envelope on the door mat. Within thirty minutes, Brick Wahl and Derek Morris had received a visit from the same truck and driver. Each was delivered an identical overnight express package.

Except for an occasional generic, "He's slowly getting better," e-mail, sent to hundreds of addresses and signed simply, "W," it had been three weeks since the three young Arizona men had heard from the Fosters. Brick had e-mailed the address on Foster's personal business card, but hadn't received a response.

"I just received a package from New York. Do you have any idea what the heck this thing is?" Dave asked Derek over the phone. "I started to read it, but can't make heads or tails out of it. You're the business wizard. How about coming over for a minute and helping me out? I'll have Melody fix us a sandwich. I think I'll give Brick a call and ask if he received anything."

Just as Derek walked to his front door and confirmed that he had received a similar package as Dave, his call waiting beeped and he saw Brick's name come up on his smart phone. "That's Brick calling me now, why don't you bring your information over here and I'll have Brick do the same. My sister took our kids to the park so we'll have some peace and quiet. Give us half an hour to pick up the house. Bring your wife if you can. Natasha says she's tired of getting all the stories about our New York friend secondhand. She wants to meet the guy."

Dave and Melody's kids were sent to the neighbors to play, and the Wahl's baby was given a bottle of juice and left in the stroller. The three couples sat around the Morris' dining room table and began to dissect the contents of their packages, page by page. Each of the packages was individually addressed and yet visibly identical. The face letter started with a profuse "thank you" to each of the men for their time and effort to save the life of the then stranger, Edward Foster III. Next, there was a short medical update on Foster. A new paragraph included an invitation to come to New York in a little over two weeks, to learn about a financial venture called "TAG," which in its short summary, sounded like it had an incredible upside. Foster was offering—as an expression of gratitude—each of the men a share in the venture. There was no downside for them since the described buy-in was being covered by Foster himself—again it stated, "... in appreciation for their heroic efforts to save my life." Enclosed was a thick prospectus explaining the venture with page after page of legal verbiage and disclaimers. The last page was an engraved piece of stationary with fancy calligraphy initials at the top. It was an invitation for the six of them to come to dinner at the Foster's Park Avenue townhome the evening before the business meeting.

"So, what's the catch?" Debra asked, staring her husband in the eyes.

"Your guess is as good as mine," Brick said.

"I don't think there is a catch," Dave said. "We saved the man's life and now he wants to reward us and has the means to make the reward something special."

Natasha, being the most skeptical in the group, stood up and leaned over her husband's shoulder to get a better look at the letter. "Why not just give each of you a check for some money? And why the fancy dinner? We don't know these people, and why would they want to get to know us? Besides, what will I wear to a fancy dinner in Manhattan?"

This brought a laugh from the group followed by some individual chatter. The men would all have to adjust their work plans and meetings, and Dave would have to arrange for his practice to be covered and postpone a few surgeries.

"The invitation doesn't say anything about kids," Melody said. "We'll all have to get babysitters."

"Sounds good to me," Natasha said.

The excitement in the room built up as they readjusted their mindset to plan for the unexpected trip to New York. When they dug a little deeper into the thick stack of papers, each found first-class tickets for the flight, and a reservation confirmation for deluxe rooms at the Helmsley Palace Hotel. Nowhere in the information package was the actual value of the investment stated, leaving them to wonder just how this could or would change things for them in any substantial way.

Brick immediately pulled out his iPhone and tried to find information about the financial entity, TAG, but only got the watchmaker's information—nothing about any financial or real estate enterprises. Even under Foster Ltd., the holding company of Ned's apparently vast holdings, there was nothing that indicated anything called TAG.

When he reported his lack of findings to the others, who had started making sandwiches from leftover roast beef, Dave lifted his head from the food assembly line and said, "So what? My guess is that we'll have a great time in New York. It'll be an adventure! I'm already tired of being back at work, let alone the summer heat. I say we go for it. Send them an e-mail saying that all six of us will be there."

Everyone made comments and excuses, but eventually everyone seemed to agree—though for their own different reasons. When a vote was taken, there appeared to be no dissenters. Brick tapped in an e-mail message of acceptance for the group.

Just like most Arizona families, the Morris's, Wahl's, and Felshaw's summer days flew by. During the next few weeks the everyday activities of the kids: soccer, T-ball, dance, swimming, tumbling, camp, the men's work, and the excitement of the upcoming—first-class—trip to New York added a zest to the lives of the three young families. The summer heat wasn't as hot, the daily work wasn't as difficult, and the family relationships were definitely sweeter.

Each of the women found time to go shopping for clothes, both smart daytime casuals and stylish evening glitz for the planned dinner with the Fosters. Dressing for a Broadway show or two was also anticipated since the return date on their airline tickets was open. Little thought was given to the men's clothes. Debra was nervous about leaving her nine-month-old until her mom stepped up and agreed to come and stay in the house with the baby. Neither Melody nor Natasha had any trouble finding babysitters from their list of college girls who were out of school for the summer.

On the day before the New York trip, Brick closed out a contract on September wheat, netting him a whopping $18,000 profit, thus getting his family's finances out of the red for the first time in months. To celebrate he ordered a limo to take the six of them to the airport the next day.

"We can take the Tahoe and leave it in long-term parking. All six of us will fit with our luggage," suggested Debra when she heard the men discussing the plan. "Spending $200 on a limo is ridiculous."

"Why not?" Brick asked. "Foster is going to give us something that will more than make up for it."

"I'll tell you what. You give me the $200 and I'll make you feel like you've been to the airport in more than a limo."

The smirk on her face broke the tension between them. He stood up from his home office desk and started toward her.

"Later, Romeo," she said, closing his office door before he could reach her.

She had a hair appointment and needed to get her nails done, not to mention the pedicure she had looked forward to all week. Two-hundred dollars should just about cover it.

"All three lab tests are elevated, the blood urea nitrates more than the others," the nurse's voice on the phone repeated.

Willow looked at the phone in her hand and tried to decide whether or not to pass the bad news on to Edward. The call from the doctor's office had come at the worst possible time. Both her cook and the evening maid had shown up late. The planned dinner was at least half an hour behind schedule.

She thanked the nurse and confirmed Foster's appointment with the doctor for the following evening. The business meeting was planned to start at nine in the morning, which should give them time to come home and for him to rest before the doctor showed up. They had resorted to one of the concierge medical practices in mid-Manhattan to save Edward having to get dressed and travel back and forth for his office visits. It was an extra $300 a visit, but under the circumstances seemed like a reasonable expense.

Edward Foster III's name had been on the national transplant registry for three weeks, but he had yet to even be given a waiting number. Again, he and Willow had discussed the pros and cons of going to an international market for a transplant. The $200 or $300 thousand cost wasn't of concern, but the reliability of a foreign doctor's technical skill required to do a successful second transplant, and the increased risk of a contaminated kidney or a bad crossmatch worried them far too much to consider it yet. Unfortunately, time was running out. The dialysis treatments were slowly failing to do their job, as proven by the poor lab results.

"Margo, make sure you have the dessert forks and spoons at the top of the plate; some people prefer spoons instead of forks for their baked Alaska," ordered Willow. "And go ahead and start heating the crab and artichoke dip now. I still don't understand why you started from your mother's home so late. You should have anticipated problems with the subway. It seems that the least you could do is to be on time for something important like this."

The veteran employee rolled her eyes and sighed, probably wondering why she bothered putting up with the woman. She had worked for Mr. Foster for twenty years and never had anything but compliments and joy in her work. Ever since the new Mrs. Foster arrived there seemed to be nothing but turmoil. Even before his kidney transplant the woman would show up unannounced and begin barking orders to her and to Benjamin, the boss's butler. Every day that Mr. Foster's health worsened, "Willow the Witch" became more difficult to please, even though she spent less and less time at home.

"Margo, I can't believe you ordered red roses for the table. You know that I don't like roses, and red? It looks like we're celebrating the Fourth of July."

"But Ma'am, Mr. Foster said he wanted to have red roses to give the lady guests," Margo tried to continue, but was cut off and scolded even more. She turned away, vowing to begin searching for another job. She could see death lurking in Edward Foster's eyes, and wasn't about to continue working just for Willow. If he didn't survive planned treatment, she was gone.

The massive, hand-carved wooden door opened slowly, allowing a cool burst of air out to greet the six dinner guests. Unused to the humidity, all six members of the party had tiny beads of sweat forming on their upper lips and foreheads as they stood under the portico of the elegant town house. Even the women's lightweight evening dresses didn't save them from the oppressive humidity of the July evening in the Big Apple. Each however, looked fantastic, and each of their husbands beamed with the bliss of being married to such a beautiful and desirable woman.

"Good evening ladies ... gentlemen. My name is Benjamin. Welcome to Edward Foster III's home.

Now, please come in," the butler said in a tight-clipped New England accent, holding the door as they entered. Taking his time to close and lock the door, he then led the group down the hallway to a large drawing room lined with new but very fine furniture. There were no antiques anywhere in the house. Foster's first wife had been an antique fanatic. When she left him after twenty years of fruitless marriage he had gladly emptied the house of everything older than six months of age.

The room was lined with paintings, mirrors, and arched window casings. The beveled glass window panes looked out onto a lighted swimming pool, which was enclosed in glass and surrounded with tropical vegetation including fruit-bearing banana and papaya trees. Orchids grew from hanging baskets, and three large bird cages held cockatiels and macaw parrots.

They were left in the room for several minutes before Willow appeared in a slinky black dress cut above her knees, and scooped low enough that all eyes in the room went directly to her cleavage, the valley of which held a sparkling teardrop ruby the size of a Brazil nut. It was suspended by a thin gold chain that looked like it would break under the weight of the stone.

"Bricklyn, David, Derek, ladies ... how nice of you to join us."

She swept across the room and embraced the three men then offered her hand to each of the ladies calling them by their names and asking about their children; she had obviously done her homework. After a couple minutes of greetings, attention turned toward the clatter of an aluminum walker in the hall doorway. Edward Foster III inched his way into the room, smiling at the guests, who approached him with friendly greetings. All of the men were shocked at the morbid appearance of this man, who just weeks prior had led the three of them up a difficult mountain bike trail.

"Look at these three beautiful ladies," Ned exclaimed to his wife and the three men. "How did three ruffians like you attract these Greek goddesses?" he said with a lusty chuckle. He gave each of the women a soft cheek embrace and balancing his weight on his left hand gave a firm-gripped shake to each of the men.

"I see you have met my dear wife, Willow," he said to the three wives. "Without these four people," he said with a sweep of his hand, I would be dead and buried now instead of just gimping around like a ninety-year-old war casualty."

Faux compliments were extended to the man, in spite of his appearance, and jokes were made about the Colorado trip and his stay in the tiny Meeker hospital. Willow was a congenial hostess, and joined in the conversation, chatting with the ladies and flirting with the men. Margo and Benjamin appeared with silver trays of appetizers and the drinks each had ordered. There was a background of soft music mixed with the tinkling of glasses. After drinks were finished, the double doors were opened into a spacious dining room by Benjamin who said in a rather formal voice, "Dinner is served."

All of the westerners had seen rooms like this in the movies, but none had ever been entertained in such lavish splendor. From the Murano glass chandelier, to the inlaid Italian serving table with its Irish linen tablecloth, and napkins embroidered with the initials EFIII in the corners, the setting was regal. Even a small, engraved menu with a tiny, blue bow was lying beside their place cards.

The food came in a series of slowly served and consumed dishes, each prepared and cooked to perfection. The guests later would learn that the entire meal was catered by the Four Seasons. Taking silent clues from Willow, the guests managed to use the correct forks, spoons, and knives at the appropriate times. As Benjamin lit the baked Alaska, sending a blue flame into the air and leaving the lingering aroma of toasted marshmallows behind, Brick leaned over to Willow and expressed what a wonderful chef she was.

"Oh darling, I didn't cook a crumb of this meal. I can barely make coffee. I can do a lot of things well, but not in the kitchen."

This brought levity to the party, which up to that point had been heavy on formality. Foster made an attempt at leading the conversations, but was easily discovered to be not just under the influence of medication, but severely weakened by his medical condition.

"I'll bet you're about ready to throw that walker under a city bus," Dave said.

Foster and Willow glanced at each other then with a slight nod from Ned she said, "Actually, Edward had an unsuspected complication arise as a result of his rattlesnake bite. He had a reaction to the second round of antivenom as you are aware. This, unfortunately, has had a negative effect on his kidney function. Sorry to bring the subject to the dinner table," she apologized.

Dave turned to Ned, put his arm on the back of his carved chair, leaned toward him, and gently said how sorry he was to hear about the kidney ailment.

"You needn't extend sympathy to an old man who has lived a great life," Foster said. "Besides, even though the dialysis isn't working that well anymore, I'm still on the transplant list. Matter-of-fact, I think I hear the phone ringing right now." He cupped his hand to his ear as though listening, then laughed. "I guess it was just a neighbor's cat."

The guests were stunned, not knowing whether to laugh at his joke or extend comments of sympathy. Thankfully, Willow stood and suggested they walk out by the pool. It was an obvious prelude to ending the evening, and a welcome relief. As they filed toward the glass French doors, Foster excused himself explaining that he would see them at the meeting in the morning. The visit to the pool was brief and the departure from the town house again quite formal. Willow didn't seem able to leave her role as the hostess and the business woman. However, her last words to the six visitors as they said their good-byes were not, "Come again soon."

Settled back into the plush leather seats of the limo, Debbie was the first to speak. "Can't something be done about his condition? I mean ... you hear all the time about them transplanting everything in the body. Surely it can't be that hard to find a kidney."

"The problem is getting a perfect match, and performing a second transplant isn't easy, let alone being approved by the transplant committee. The wait list is very long," Dave explained. "It might seem that he could buy his way to the front of the list, but the government watchdogs are keeping a real close eye on anyone or any organization that tries."

"Well, if he is in such poor health, I'm not sure that

we want any part of a business that he is running. What if we just get started then put time and money into it, and he dies?" Melody asked.

"Why don't we just wait until tomorrow and see what this whole thing is all about? It could be something that is already up and running and doesn't need anything from us. It was Willow's name on the paperwork. She must have an important role in the thing so that if something did happen to Ned, it would still keep on going."

Although everyone was looking at Brick as he spoke, they were tired and their minds already were drifting into their own imaginations about what this wonderful reward for life-saving valor was all about. They had talked at the airport about going to see a late night show Off Broadway when the dinner was finished, but were now showing signs of their early morning departure, and the stress of getting ready for the days away from home. When Natasha mentioned the play to the others, she drew a blank look that generated the enthusiasm of getting one's teeth cleaned. They took a quick vote and decided to make it an early night to bed and to have the concierge at the hotel reserve them tickets for a real Broadway show the following night.

When the wake-up call came at seven the next morning, their brains were still on Arizona's Mountain Standard Time—4:00 a.m. Everyone but Brick thought there must be a mistake. He was used to rising early to glean as much as possible before the Chicago commodity markets opened. By the time everyone was up, dressed, and had met for a quick breakfast, the limo was waiting to take them to the Foster building. Limo riding was getting to be old hat, but entering a thirty-story building on Wall Street with their friend's name on the entrance wasn't. The express elevator whisked them to the penthouse where they were greeted at the elevator door by a perky young administrative assistant named Jaden Allen.

The woman, dressed in a tailored, grey pinstripe suit with matching skirt and a frilly, royal-blue blouse, greeted them each by name—obviously she too had done her homework—and led them into a very large conference room which held theater-type seating for at least a hundred people. About half of the seats already were occupied. The plush reclining chairs faced a podium and a fifteen-by-twenty-foot flatscreen. A buffet of coffee, tea, and fruit juices was against one of the walls and was being enjoyed by a handful of serious-appearing men and women who had not yet taken their seats. The three couples barely had time to help themselves to the refreshments when the lights dimmed and a video production lit up the screen.

The twenty-minute color promotion, accompanied by catchy music and the strong, deep voice of Edward Foster III, outlined the history of the last twenty years of real estate in the country. It criticized the government for sticking its nose into the private sector's business and even touched on the foreign markets' ripple effect. Foster explained that the time was now ripe for a harvest of the mistakes of others through aggressive buying of both residential and commercial real estate. "The market is 30 percent overbuilt, but occupancy is starting to steamroll back to full, and the construction industry won't be able to retool, rehire, and re-plan fast enough to meet the demand. Now is the time to get off of the sidelines and buy, buy, buy!" he said as the Hollywood-quality production came to a symphonic end and the lights slowly returned back to normal.

"I have selected you, my longtime associates in wealth development, to go for another ride on a shooting star—a Foster shooting star." The young couples' new-found friend Ned exclaimed, standing at the podium looking ten years younger than the night before. "I believe in this project and hope you will too. I'll now turn the time over to my Willow, my best friend, my partner, and now the executive director of TAG, to explain the details and to answer any of your questions."

Debra was the first to admit she had a splitting headache as they rode back to the hotel in the Mercedes limo. The midmorning traffic was plodding. Sitting backwards with the start and stop motion of the car was making her ill. "I need to go back to the room, take four Advil and lie down. Then, maybe I can figure this whole scheme of Ned's out," she said.

"It sounds simple to me," said Melody. "All I have to do is find ten friends who are willing to invest over $100,000 each and then they each find ten friends of their own to do the same and I'll make $1 million. The only problem is that I don't know a soul who could afford to invest $10,000 let alone a hundred thousand."

"Don't get in too big a hurry to dismiss the idea, let's just give it some time to sink in," Derek said. "But for the rest of the day let's just have a good time on Ned's tab. I want a ride through the park in a horse-drawn buggy and to eat a Pastrami sandwich at a real New York deli.

Tonight I want Italian food at Mama Luigi's, and then I'd like to see a good Broadway musical."

It spite of their lingering concerns, they laughed, and then the ladies started planning the rest of the day in chattering voices. A busy afternoon beginning with the deli was agreed on—just as soon as they could get into some comfortable clothes.

The six adults spent the rest of the day having the time of their lives. They ate until they couldn't have taken another bite, they walked until their feet throbbed, and they laughed like ten-year-olds. Melody had never ridden a subway, so they took the train out to the north and got off at the new Yankee Stadium. Though they had no idea of the team's schedule, they arrived during the eighth inning of a Red Sox game with the score tied. No one was guarding the entry gate so they just walked in and found some scattered empty seats right behind home plate. The game went to eleven innings giving them a taste of East Coast baseball at its best. They had to rush to make the eight o'clock curtain call for the remake of *The Sound of Music*, which was fantastic. By the time they limped back into the hotel lobby they had completely forgotten about Foster, Willow, and that morning's meeting and their supposed new wealth.

CHAPTER

Armon Dupree sat two rows behind the Arizona threesome in the Broadway theater as they watched and listened to the dialogue and music of the sixties hit musical. He had seen them that morning at the Foster meeting and couldn't help wondering what in the world these six small fish were doing in such a big pond. It wasn't that the couples were particularly odd in their dress, nor ill-mannered, nor did they have unfamiliar accents. Perhaps, he thought, it was that they looked so pure and innocent. What surprised him the most was how familiar they seemed with Edward Foster III, and that snake of a partner or lover or wife—whatever she was—Willow.

Dupree had known Ned since they were classmates in prep school, and they had crossed paths in the financial world a dozen times. He even had allowed Foster to manage a portion of his family estate when his mother finally gave up the ghost, leaving him and his two sisters with more money than they could ever possibly squander. The only reason he had come to the meeting that day was to satisfy a curiosity that was pricked when he bumped into the Fosters' doctor at a cocktail party, and overheard the man talking about a rattlesnake bite and how it had put the Wall Street Midas into kidney failure. Although the doctor was doing his best to conceal the patient's identity, it was well known around The Street that Foster had been bitten while vacationing out West. When Dupree saw the invitation to attend the launch meeting of Foster's new investment company, TAG, he had rearranged his tennis schedule.

Never having worked an honest day in his life, the Manhattan socialite had what many would consider the ideal life. Standing six foot four, Dupree had wide, athletic shoulders and hands which could palm a basketball; he was a readily recognized face and figure around Midtown and among the power brokers of the city. He had always been an athlete, having played basketball against Powell High and Lew Alcindor—later known as Kareem Abdul-Jabbar. He played college ball at Davidson and then gave it up for yacht racing. His family always had played a discreet role in the city's political scene. He especially liked funding the political campaigns of the new faces. Those who knew him well recognized that he always had an open door into the Mayor's office.

At the end of the performance, Dupree sat in his Bentley observing the couples as they exited the theater. He toyed with the idea of having his driver pay a quick visit to their limo driver—a crisp hundred dollar bill often gleaned a lot of information—but he changed his mind and decided on the direct approach and quickly got out of his car.

"Pardon me madam, I believe you might have dropped this," Dupree said, holding a rumpled twenty dollar bill out to Debra Wahl.

She was standing in front of an announcement board waiting for the rest of the group to return from visiting the powder rooms. They had decided on a late night piece of real New York cheesecake before retiring.

"Thank you, but it's not mine," she said.

"My mistake," he apologized, stepping closer to ostensibly view the announcement board with its list of planned activities and conferences for the following day. "Are you here attending a meeting or just for fun?" he inquired.

It wasn't the first time the attractive Debra had been approached—hit on—by a stranger. Though she could put up a huffy front at being offended, she, like any red-blooded women the world over, liked to believe that in spite of her age and recent pregnancy she was able to attract handsome men. This was definitely a handsome, though quite a bit older, man. She was, after all dressed in her evening best, the most reveling dress that she owned: a sky-blue silk number with narrow straps and a scalloped hem. Even her hair, pulled into an up-do for the evening, had a sultry look.

"It's a mixed visit to the city," she said, keeping her eyes on the board. "Half-pleasure and the other half is for fun."

This brought a chuckle from Dupree who now turned to face her. "I don't suppose that I am so lucky as to find you unaccompanied and willing to share a bottle of wine?" he asked, knowing full well that her husband and friends were due to show up any second.

"Thank you," she said, now facing him with a smile. "Actually, my husband and two other couples are with me. Matter-of-fact, here they are now."

Debra introduced her new acquaintance to the others and after a few interchanges he turned aside to her.

"My apologies," he said with a bit of a faux blush. "You must think me a cad."

"Would you like to join us for a light bedtime snack?" Debra asked, causing a subtle start in her companions. "Perhaps you could give us some insider tips on what to see and what to avoid while we're here in New York."

"Oh, I wouldn't want to crash your party," he said, again turning to leave.

"Not at all, come join us," Brick said after he had received a quick jab in the kidney.

And so he did. The group found a table in the hotel's coffee shop and for the next hour visited and laughed at Dupree's wit and at their own naivety. New York really was a different world. It was well into the conversation when the Foster meeting came up. Dupree listened to the six of them openly discuss TAG, not revealing that he had been at the meeting or that he was well acquainted with Edward Foster III.

As the group said good night Dupree gave each of the men one of his business cards and invited them to spend a day with him on his yacht, should they return soon to the Big Apple. He shook the men's hands and gave each of the women a cheek-embrace, lingering an extra second with Debra.

"What a charming man," Debra said, dropping her dress into a heap on the floor and collapsing into the king-size, down duvet. "It's too bad we don't live closer and we could take him up on his offer of a ride on his yacht. That would be the life!"

Brick didn't answer, but his mind was definitely

working over a variation of the same idea. "You know, I can work from just about anywhere. Maybe living close by, you know, here in the area, Connecticut or New Jersey or even upstate New York, could be fun."

"You've got to be kidding. You hate the snow and the cold and the humidity and the crowds. One guy who says he has a yacht and talks a smooth line isn't going to make all of the negatives go away," Debra said, rolling off the bed and heading to the bathroom to wash off her makeup.

Brick took off his shoes and hung up his slacks. He looked around the small but luxurious room wondering just what it was that he found so intriguing about the big city. He parted the curtains on the window looking out at the city lights. He almost felt dizzy looking down the fifty stories to the street. He sensed that he was being seduced by a force beyond his control, but couldn't isolate any one thing that would make him change his present lifestyle, unless it was the possibility of vast wealth. For the first time in his life, at the meeting today, hearing all the huge numbers being thrown around, he wondered if real wealth was more than a fantasy—a realistic possibility. The people he had met at Foster's meeting weren't just talking about millions; for many of them billions was a realistic goal.

He felt Debra's arms slide around his waist and her head resting on the back of his shoulder. He started to turn to face her, but she increased her hold, not allowing him to turn.

"Just look at all of those people out there," she said, gazing past him out the window. "I would bet that 99 percent of them would trade you their claustrophobic apartments and their lifestyles in a heartbeat for our home and pool and four-car garage, not to mention the way we live our lives each day."

"You are probably right, but I don't want to be part of the ninety-nine. I want us to be in the filthy-rich, one percent."

"I don't really like that modifier," she said.

"What do you mean?"

"I mean that even you, an honest, hardworking family man, say that you are desirous of wealth. The problem, as I see it, is that you can't just be rich without in some way, shape, or form becoming filthy."

Breakfast together at a deli on Third Avenue, and some last minute shopping, was followed by the limo ride to JFK airport. Brick, Dave, and Derek had expected some sort of farewell from the Fosters, but received nothing. Dave even had tried to call to check on Ned, but was only able to leave a message. Even at the airport the men looked around expecting a last minute note or greeting, or at least an e-mail or text message, but again there was nothing. It was as though they had been checked off of some mental payback list and forgotten.

The flight home was uneventful, but the arrival back at their individual homes was joyful as tired parents and excited kids reunited. With the time change and the jet lag it was an early lights-out for everyone. By the first of the week everyone and everything would be back to normal, with just a good story to tell to the extended families and friends, and a folder of papers already starting to get buried under the more recently arrived magazines, bills, and sales pitches.

The kids had the last of their summer camps and activities to attend to, and the wives were getting organized for their fall tennis league. Dave was buried in a list of patients needing surgery, and Derek was meeting with the new owners of a piece of land on which they wanted him to build a 30,000-square-foot building to house a call center for upscale condos.

Brick had turned his attention to a new hot commodity coming out of the forests of Vietnam: wood shavings for newsprint. Even with the shift to paperless businesses, the presses were still rolling out printed material on paper and it seemed that Vietnam had an abundance of dead trees left lying on the ground from the carpet bombing of their forests forty-five years prior. On his first trade of the wood pulp, he cleared a cool thirty grand. *Who needs New York?*

He was at his desk at 1:00 a.m. that night awaiting the opening of the Hong Kong commodity markets desk when his phone rang.

"Is this Bricklyn Wahl?" asked the male voice on the other end of the line.

"Yes," he answered, slightly irritated by the unknown caller, and trying to keep his eyes on his monitor for the first signs of trading life in the Orient.

"Please hold for Mrs. Foster," the voice said. The next sound he heard was accompanied by a lot of static and background noise.

"Brick? This is Willow. I'm sorry to bother you so late at night, but I need your help."

"You might have to speak louder. There is a lot of static on the line."

"Brick, this is Willow, I'm in the foothills, outside Melbourne, Australia and can't get a very good connection. I need your help."

"What is the problem?" As he asked the question a cold chill went up his spine, and the hair on his arms stood on end.

"It's Edward. He has taken a turn for the worse. I'm 12,000 miles away and I'm buried in the last two days of setting up the TAG project here in Australia. I was wondering if you could fly to New York and spend a few days there at the town house. I just need someone there I can trust. He has a nurse, and of course the maid and butler, and the doctor comes by every day, but he needs someone to talk to and someone to go with him to his dialysis every other day. I should be home by next weekend. I can have a private jet ready to pick you up in Phoenix at ten in the morning."

"Wow ... Willow ... this is so unexpected," he said, leaning back into his chair and turning his vision from the monitor to a picture on his office wall. It was one of his wife and baby lying in the maternity unit bed—Debra grinning from ear to ear. "I'm in the middle of some critical trades and I have Debra and the baby here."

"Bring them with you if you like. You can stay in the guest suite at our place. The jet is like a flying tech center. You can work from there and I'll have the butler clear off Edward's desk so you can use it and his computers as soon as you arrive."

"I really don't see how I can ...."

"Please don't say no," she said, not really begging. Her tone was more like a warning.

"I need to talk it over with Debra," Brick said firmly.

"If I don't get these deals in Sydney approved and signed, there won't be any TAG project and your gift from Edward will be worthless by this Friday instead of worth a few million dollars by next month. You are the one person Edward says he trusts with his finances right now. I know that David can't do his doctoring work from New York and I think Derek's wife is skeptical about the whole project. Besides, they both have older children who probably wouldn't do well there in the mansion. Please do this for us. It's not just for Edward. I would consider it a personal favor to me. I'll make it worth your while. A car will be there to pick you up later this morning."

Before he could respond, the phone went dead and he was left staring at the screen of his computer wondering what in the world was happening. A flash on the screen notified him that his wheat contract was receiving a bid. By the time he executed all of his trades and put in his automatic sell orders, he had nearly forgotten about Willow and her bizarre request. Then his cell phone rang again. This time it was the pilot of the jet giving him an actual departure time and asking for an estimate of the weight of passengers and luggage he would be bringing on board.

"What in the world are you talking about?" screamed Debra. "I can't just throw the baby's things in a bag and fly off to New York again. What about your work?"

Brick talked in a soft voice of reason for nearly fifteen minutes before she started to show signs of caving in. As he did so he was putting his clothes into the suitcase and packing his shaving kit. He then laid her suitcase on the bed, put his arms around her and tipped her head up from the pillow with a finger under her chin. "You told me you didn't want to live the life of a boring suburban housewife—right?"

"That may be true, but I guess I forgot to tell you that I don't want to be a puppet dancing on the end of a string to some strange woman's eccentric tune," she said.

Two hundred twenty short minutes later, a stretch limo was parked in front of the Wahl house. Debra had things organized only because Melody had responded to her 7:00 a.m. call for help, bathing and dressing baby Lexy, while Debra packed and canceled a visit to the pediatrician and her hair and nail appointments.

"Don't worry about a thing," were the parting words from Melody as the limo pulled away from the curb.

If Debra didn't know better she would have noted a hint of jealousy in Melody's voice. Off to New York in a limo again! But this time in a private jet and to stay in a $20 million townhome—the whole trip planned and executed in less than two hours—what an insane, but intriguing life. She leaned her head back into the seat and patted Lexy's hand. Her mind was spinning, but she couldn't help thinking about her life as a teen when leaving home in the early morning or even the middle of the night wasn't all that unusual. Her dad had been a free spirit, a product of the sixties, when the idea of a stable lifelong career with the same employer and a lifelong faithful marriage to the same woman was never a real consideration for many of that era. Holding a real job just wasn't "his style." By the time Debra was in high school her dad was long gone. Today she couldn't even form a mental image of what he looked like.

The hard-working, stick-to-it nature of Brick Wahl's personality was one of the predominant things that had attracted her to him. Now, he was starting to act just like her dad. His split-second decisions with erratic swings in their bank balance and eccentric new friends were worrying Debra. Now, this TAG thing. She always heard the cliché, "If it's too good to be true then it probably isn't." How could she not believe that to be the case right now?

"T-A-G? Just what does that stand for?" asked Brian.

The four men were standing on the tee box of the par three, sixth hole at Troon North in Scottsdale waiting for the slow, foreign players ahead of them to putt.

Dave and Derek had invited Brian Smithson, a lawyer friend, and Mike Galley, a trusted accountant, to join them for a Saturday round of golf. The green fees in Arizona in the summer were a bargain, but only if one started early enough in the morning to avoid the medical costs of treating heatstroke. Dave and Derek had long discussions earlier in the week, and decided they needed some sound financial advice about their newly-acquired wealth position, and how it would affect their taxes. In addition, they were beginning to question the whole setup of TAG, especially after Brick and Debra had taken off on the spur of the moment to fly to New York to house sit for Foster.

"No one ever really told us what it stood for," Derek said, trying to explain the company Foster had—without their permission—involved them in. "Probably something like 'Total Asset Growth.'"

"Or 'Total Asinine Gullibility,'" said Mike. He was not the typical bean counter who just knew everything could be solved with green numbers. Mike's optimism in life ended with the assumption that the sun would come up each morning. Every other good thing that happened during life he attributed to either hard work or divine intervention.

Derek teed his ball low and cranked the perfect seven-iron shot 180 yards, sticking the ball fifteen feet from the waving blue-and-white checkered flag.

"Nice shot," the others said in unison.

Brian went through his pre-shot routine, then stopped and turned toward Dave. "If you're worried about the guy giving you this freebie, I'll take it off your hands; if you buy lunch. I could use another million or two, especially with the potential upside your friend purposes." To emphasize his statement he hit his tee shot inside of Derek's.

The joke negated the accountant's derogatory statement, but still didn't answer the question about the legitimacy of TAG.

Later, as they sat in the clubhouse, trying to rehydrate and cool down, Brian turned to Derek and Dave. "I've been thinking about your guy's situation for the last nine holes. Other than it screwing up my putting, I honestly can't think of any reason that you shouldn't embrace the gift for what the guy apparently intended—a gift of gratitude. Sure there might be some tiny glitches down the road ... there usually are with any big-dollar deals ... but, when in your entire life will you ever get a tax-free million bucks without working for it?"

Mike wiped the sweat from his brow then held his frosty glass on his forehead. "The more I think about it, I have to agree with Brian. Matter-of-fact, I want to look over the prospectus and do a little research. If it looks legitimate, I might just pull a hundred grand out of my 401K and put it in with you guys."

Derek and Dave looked at one another, shrugged, then clicked their glasses in an informal toast.

Brian, the older and self-appointed sage of the group, was quiet for a minute or two, ostensibly watching the baseball game playing on the clubhouse's big screen TV. Finally, he turned to the three. "Explain this one thing again. If I were to invest with one of you, then I'm allowed to get my own group of investors, who in essence belong under my name, thus as profits start coming in from the real estate sales, I'll make money not just on my hundred thousand, but on theirs as well? Is there a limit on the amount a single investor can throw in the pot?"

"That's the way it was explained to us at the meeting in New York. Commercial real estate nationwide and even worldwide is overbuilt right now, just like residential housing was three years ago. Prices per square foot are at a twenty-year low so buying now is a bargain. As the inventory shrinks and the prices go up—which they have to do—the profits, with the leverage of financing, will be as high as 200 or 300 percent. To answer your second question, I think the answer is that any amount over $100 thousand will be welcomed," Derek concluded, taking a long pull on his drink.

"None of my doctor friends have made a profit on their pension plans for the last two or three years. I've mentioned this deal to a few and they are all chomping at the bit. If you two think it's a valid deal, I'm going to push them to jump in as well," Dave said. "Each of us is allowed to bring in a maximum of ten investors. We don't want you to feel any pressure, but if you are interested you need to let us know in the next week or so."

Brian turned to the accountant and asked, "Are you sure that I can use 401K or IRA funds without any problem?"

"As long as you don't incur any additional obligation to the plan ... you know like annual or monthly payments."

On the TV screen, a grand slam was punched into the left field stands, giving the Yankees a three-run lead and the win. Dave gave a cheer and told the others how cool it had been to actually be in the Yankee's ball park. Conversations drifted to a hotly contested primary race for the Arizona senate, but lasted less than a minute because they all favored the same guy.

The limo ride into Manhattan was like déjà vu. The black, Lincoln limo was identical to the one from their first visit, the route was identical, and even the driver—a man with a strong Caribbean accent—looked and spoke the same, but didn't acknowledge remembering Debra or Brick. The atmosphere however, was quite different.

"I feel like a fish in a leather and glass bowl," Debra said, leaning close to her husband as the car rounded a tight curve. "I think I prefer riding around in the Tahoe to this boat. I can't imagine doing this every time you wanted to go somewhere."

"I'll bet you would get used to it," said Brick, pouring himself a glass of mineral water from the chilled minibar. "You sure you don't want something to drink?"

She shook her head and stared out of the tinted window at the skyline in the distance. Only the fussing of

Lexy regained her attention. She put a pacifier back in its place and patted the baby's tiny leg.

"Honestly Brick, I think this is a mistake."

"What are you talking about? We discussed this over and over. It's not like we are missing work or a family reunion. It's stinking hot at home and I can do the same amount of work in Foster's study as I would there. You saw the guest bedrooms. Lexy will have her own room and we'll have the cook and butler to wait on us. I'll bet that a week from now, you won't want to ever leave."

She shrugged and replaced the pacifier in Lexy's pouting mouth.

When the limousine arrived in front of the mansion, the driver hustled out and around to open the door. Before they could get out of the car, to their surprise, Willow appeared at the top of the stone steps. She stood there with her arms folded and the sun reflecting off of a very large diamond ring that Debra didn't remember seeing before. The woman was offering a polite smile. Only when Lexy appeared in Debra's arms did the lady venture slowly down the steps toward the car.

"You are the most precious little thing I have ever seen," Willow said, extending her hand to cup the chin of the baby. Lexy smiled and even stretched her arms out asking to be held by the strange woman. Willow made no attempt to accept the child.

Brick and Debra stared at the woman in disbelief, and Brick finally said, "I thought you were in Australia finishing up some mega-dollar deal?"

"It was Austria, and you'll never believe how lucky I was. The attorney for the investor took one look and signed off on the whole thing. I turned the plane around and just got back an hour ago. But I'm just picking up some clothes and papers from the office then I'm off to Vermont. More eager investors!"

The couple followed the driver and Benjamin the butler, who carried their luggage up the spiral staircase, to the main living area. They then headed down a long hallway past the master bedroom and past the two large guest suites that Debra and her friends had used to freshen up the night of the dinner. They climbed a narrow staircase to the third floor and finally stopped at the end of the hallway. Willow was already in front of the bedroom doorway.

"I hope you don't mind staying this far down the hall and up another floor? Edward isn't used to the cry of a baby," Willow explained.

"No problem," Brick said before he even had a chance to look at the room. When the door was opened and he glanced around, he immediately had a sick visceral feeling. It was nowhere close to the size and quality of room Debra had described.

"The bath is just across the hall and I had Margo find a crib for your little one," Willow said.

The room was dark and sparsely furnished with a single lamp on a small bedside table to light the room. A small dormer window over the head of the standard double bed was the only ventilation and it was high enough that Brick doubted he could reach it to open it. With barely enough room to move between the bed and the crib, the butler leaned the suitcases against the grey and brown floral wallpapered wall. That was when Brick looked at the floor and saw the carpet. It must have been the original when the house was constructed. What little wool was left after decades of vacuuming, didn't hide the hemp backing of the floor covering.

When Brick looked up, Debra was still standing in the hallway with Lexy—her mouth agape. Only when the maid appeared and opened the door to the bathroom across the hallway revealing the five-by-ten water closet with its small-footed tub, chain-pull toilet, and wall-hung sink with no counters or shelves, did Debra utter a word.

"My goodness, Willow, this bathroom must be nearly a hundred years old," she said.

"It truly is a museum-quality room. We seldom allow guests to use it so as not to destroy any of its original qualities. Note that even the vanity mirror is leaded as you can tell by the slight peeling from the back."

"Exactly how old is the house?" Brick asked, more out of anxiety than curiosity.

"I think Edward said it was his great-grandfather's. I know that the coal furnace and gas lighting pipes are still in the cellar. I had the front of the house remodeled three years ago when I joined the family. Well, I'll let you three get settled. Perhaps you could catch up with me in the parlor in half an hour and we can look in on Edward."

Brick nodded in agreement. Debra was still standing in the hallway, alternately staring into the bathroom and back into the bedroom. She didn't say a word until Willow had walked down the long hallway, past several other doorways, and disappeared down the front stairwell.

"There is no way you are going to force me and Lexy to live in this hole!" she said in a low but emphatic voice, facing Brick as tears appeared on her cheeks. "I don't care how badly we insult these people or how sick your friend is, we are either moving to a good hotel or the baby and I are catching the next plane home."

"Debra honey, it's not that bad. Everything looks clean. Look at the towels and the bedding, they are brand-new. I'm sure that after a couple of days we'll get used to it."

"You can barely stand to listen to Lexy in the next room with her moaning and fussing. How will either of us survive with her crib smashed up against our bed? And look at that bed. We have not slept in a bed that small since the first month we were married, and even then you pushed me out every night so I ended up on the floor."

"But we need to be here for—"

"Don't try to argue with me!" she said, raising her voice loud enough that he was sure those down the hall could hear. "I am not staying in this creepy, little, claustrophobic room! There are good hotels less than a block away and I will not be imprisoned here for another moment. Either you walk down there and tell her what the situation is, or the baby and I are getting a cab and going to the airport."

The Wahls wouldn't know what was behind the doors of the other rooms—possibly more bedrooms like the one they were offered—since Willow stuck her head out of the master bedroom door to investigate the ruckus and then came up the stairs to find out the news. In spite of the obvious availability of the larger suites and promises to keep Lexy quiet, Willow was adamant that Edward was not to be disturbed by the crying of a child.

An hour later, having spoken briefly to Foster, Brick had moved the girls and their bags to the Ritz-Carlton Hotel a few blocks away. There he settled them into a large suite overlooking Central Park. Willow, after hearing Debra's concerns, had insisted on making the hotel arrangement and covering the $800-a-night charges. The difference was night and day in Debra's mind. She hadn't quite understood that Willow had agreed to the move only with the understanding that Brick would remain at the mansion to look after Foster anytime Willow needed to travel. Since the baby wouldn't be staying at the mansion, Brick's things were belatedly moved into one of the mansion's luxurious guest rooms, complete with a bathroom larger than the upstairs bedroom.

"It just doesn't make sense," Debra said to Brick as he kissed her good-bye, "if Ned is so sick, why an occasional fuss from the baby would even be noticed? For what they are paying to have us here they could have easily afforded a full-time nurse."

"I don't know the answer to the question, but we'll only be here for a few days. You might as well enjoy the experience and see as much of the city as you can. I'm sure that I'll be able to join you most of the time. You know that I couldn't do any of my trading at the hotel. Ned's computer setup in his office is ideal for what I need. The bottom line is that he needs someone that he feels he can rely on ... not just a stranger."

"He does look pretty ill," she said, feeling jet-lagged and tired of disagreeing. She was ready to have some peace and quiet. Lexy was sound-asleep in the hotel's crib, and the huge bed was beckoning Debra.

"You have your phone, so please call me every time before you leave the hotel. I want to know where you are going and when you get back," he insisted, then kissed her one last time.

He walked back to the mansion, taking in the sights of the city as he went, ambivalent about what lay ahead. He was feeling guilty for leaving Debra and Lexy alone, but he was also dying with curiosity. Just what did the mysterious woman want him there for? He didn't have to wait long to find out.

As he approached the Foster's home, the limo was once again parked in front with its trunk and rear passenger door open. Approaching the front door, he was almost run over by the driver carrying two large, leather suitcases, closely followed by Willow carrying a black alligator laptop case and a matching purse. She was dressed in a black business suit, which emphasized her figure and height. The black patent leather heels looked unmanageably high. The only color she wore was a red-and-black checkered scarf around her neck, and of course, her diamonds.

"Did you get her settled to her satisfaction?" she asked, not waiting for an answer. "Sorry it didn't work out for her to stay here. I'm sure she'll be just fine at the hotel. I've instructed the concierge to check on her and act on her every request. As for you, I have left a list on Edward's desk of names I need you to call—"

"You mean for emergencies?" he interrupted.

"No, no. The house staff has the doctor's and hospital's numbers. I need you to call each of our investors in TAG and make sure they have sent in their checks for the initial investment. I will be in Frankfurt tonight. In the morning I will be closing on our first major purchase. My iPhone number is on the desk. If you meet any resistance or hesitation, call me. Also, check in with Edward every hour and make sure he isn't on the phone with anyone.

He is having some moments of confusion, and I don't want him screwing up any of the deals. One last thing, try to think of someone willing to donate a kidney to the poor man. His blood type is O negative. Tell them we'll pay all of their expenses and give them $500,000."

Before he could close his gaping mouth to formulate a question, she was down the steps and into the car. He could see her face through the tinted window, and was certain that she didn't even glance back at him.

Brick walked into the house and closed the door. The sound of the twelve-foot, carved wooden door echoed down the hall. The smell of sickness struck him for the first time as he ascended the curved staircase. The closer to the master bedroom he came the stronger the smell. Knocking on the door brought no response, so he slowly twisted the ornate brass knob and peeked in. Ned was asleep and snoring loudly. Brick tiptoed in, and though the heavy curtains were pulled, he could still make his way. He looked at the furnishings and at the silver tray holding a myriad of fat prescription bottles. In the adjacent bathroom were more bottles on Ned's half of the expansive marble-lined room, and on Willow's side were at least a dozen perfume bottles of different sizes, shapes, and colors. The enormous bathtub's edge was lined with candles and bottles of various lotions and oils. Curiosity rising, Brick looked into the first closet off the bathroom. As he stepped in to get a closer view the lights came on automatically, startling him. The closet held row after row of men's suits, sport coats, tuxedos, shirts, and ties. On the opposite wall there were at least fifty pairs of shiny dress shoes and some outdoor footwear. On the third wall were floor-to-ceiling shelves and drawers.

The lady's closet was twice the size of Ned's. Every rack, shelf, and floor space was stuffed with expensive-appearing clothing. The shoe rack alone took up an entire wall from floor to ceiling, and then there was the built-in bank of drawers. Brick heard Ned cough, sending a chill up his spine. Turning to leave he noticed an open drawer in the built-in dresser. He ventured a peek inside and found the drawer divided with suede-lined cubicles full of jewelry. He started to reach into the drawer to examine one of the necklaces when he heard a second rattling cough. That's when he saw the gun, lying flat next to a row of glittering rings. He was no handgun expert, but was pretty sure it was a 9-millimeter Glock.

"Benjamin? Is that you?"

Brick froze in place listening, but heard only his own breathing. He thought about turning out the light, but didn't know if the antique-looking switch would make a loud click or not. He opted to wait, breathing in and out as silently as possible. The next sound he heard was a door opening, then closing and the sound of running water. He flipped off the light switch and pushed the door open a crack. Ned's bedroom was empty. Brick made a quick step toward the door only to be met by the hallway door abruptly opening—nearly smashing into his face.

"Pardon me sir. Are you all right?" Benjamin asked.

"I'm fine. I'm waiting for Mr. Foster to finish in the bathroom. I think he was calling for you. Do you like to be called Benjamin or can I call you Ben?"

"Sir, please address me as Benjamin if you would be so kind," the butler said in his stiff, New England accent.

When the man turned to knock on the bathroom door, Brick escaped into the hallway and into his guest bedroom. He walked to the narrow window and looked out on the street below. "What in the world have I gotten myself into?" he asked of the silent audience beyond the rippled pane of antique glass. He turned to his suitcase lying on a low side table and began unpacking the few of his clothes and toiletries. He wanted to share his experience so far with Debra, or maybe one of the guys back home, but decided they would all be at work and he knew Debra had gone to the park with Lexy. A knock on the door broke his concentration.

"Sir, it is Benjamin. Mr. Foster would like to meet with you in the parlor in ten minutes if you would be available."

"I'll be right there," Brick said.

"But sir, I believe I said ten minutes."

"Exactly. That you did. I'll be there in ten minutes," Brick corrected himself, wondering what the old man wanted and if he could stand to remain in the mansion another ten minutes.

Edward Foster III sat on a massive, tufted-leather office chair. The oxblood color of the leather, and the rays of late afternoon sunlight shining through the partially opened velvet curtains, gave a healthy color to his face and hands. A sweating glass of ice water rested on a crystal coaster which lay on the hand-carved, teak desk. A twist of lemon adorned the drink. He smiled at Brick when their eyes met, then took a swallow of water before attempting to speak.

"I'll bet we both wish we were up on that Trapper's Lake mountain bike trail right now," he began in a raspy voice. "You can never imagine how much it means to me to have you drop your activities at home and come to my aid. And your sweet wife ... she is a great example of motherhood and what a loyal wife should be. I understand she is staying at the hotel. Trust me, it wasn't my idea that your daughter should be placed at the other end of the house. Willow has a mind of her own, and often life is easier for me if I let her have her way rather than putting up a debate. If you would prefer, have her move back in here—in the guest suite."

"I'm sure she and little Lexy will be fine at the hotel. It has a nice view of the park and plenty of floor space for the baby to roam without getting into trouble," Brick said, still standing in front of the desk like a buck private reporting to his staff sergeant.

Foster motioned toward a chair and Brick took a seat. His eyes glanced around the room, studying the art work and photos he had seen on their previous visit. The one he hadn't showed off to Brick was one of Foster standing arm-in-arm with a man—Brick was certain— that had to be Jimmy Hoffa.

"He was one of my first big investors," Foster said, hacking and then taking a drink to suppress the cough. "That was in seventy-three. He had been out of jail and trying to get back in the good graces of the Teamsters Union, but that crook Nixon blocked his way. Jimmy had a couple million in a Cayman bank account and wanted me to look after it for him. I had a brother-in-law in Detroit who gave him my name. Why he picked me I have no idea. Maybe he didn't trust anyone in the motor city, or perhaps he just liked bicycle racers."

Brick hesitated to pursue the matter, but his curiosity prevailed. "Didn't he just up and disappear?"

"That's right. Even the news dogs couldn't find him."

"So what happened to the money?" Brick asked, getting braver by the minute.

"It's still there ... in the Cayman Bank on Grand Cayman. Now that you mention it, I guess I haven't thought about it for years. Matter-of-fact, I don't think I have ever mentioned it to Willow." He looked Brick in the eyes and raised his bushy, grey brows. "Promise me that you won't mention it to her either."

Brick squirmed in the hard, wooden chair and nodded in agreement. The conversation was getting more intriguing, but also more uncomfortable by the minute. Unable to sit still he got up and examined some of the other pictures of presidents and celebrities. There was one with Arnold Palmer and another one with a very young Lance Armstrong. Then he saw Foster's Tour de France picture. It was in a simple stand-up frame, sitting on the book shelf in a darker part of the room.

Ned was standing between two gorgeous, brunette women holding bouquets of flowers. He was wearing the bright-yellow jersey—awarded to the winner of each day's "stage" of the race—skintight biking pants on his skinny legs, and a grin from ear to ear. There was no indication of the date.

"That was 1972," Ned said, with a soft laugh. "It was an unimportant stage of the race that the team let me have for being a solid team contributor. I had been riding for six years, and it was the nearest I came to getting my name in the papers. That little bit of glory however, was enough to help me raise the few bucks I needed to start Foster Ltd. The rest, as they say, is history."

"No wonder we couldn't keep up with you on the mountain," said Brick. "When did you retire from racing?"

"That was it. My business took off and I didn't have the time to train anymore. I still rode on weekends and for an occasional fundraiser. Within a couple of years, even the major riders didn't know my name. Fame is a fleeting thing," Ned mumbled, coughed, and took a drink.

"But that's not why I requested for you to come here," he said. "I need your help, and not just because I'm under the weather. I need some fresh people outside the mainstream loop of the cement jungle of Wall Street.

How would you like to come to work for me on a full-time basis?"

This gave Brick a bizarre feeling; almost like he was an actor in a movie instead of real life. He even went so far as to reach under the desk and pinch his own leg to be sure he wasn't dreaming—it had been a long day. He looked at Ned to see if there was any nonverbal message, but the old man was just staring back at him.

"What exactly is it you want me to do?" he asked.

"All of my current executive-level employees are busy in their own divisions, and as you can imagine, recovering from this recession has stretched every one of them to the breaking point. This new program that we call TAG needs a couple of men to work with Willow and get the jump-start it needs. Since you already have a financial stake in it, I thought you might be motivated to make it work. A part of it I didn't mention was our other potential investors. We have substantial contacts in the Middle East. The Arab businessmen don't necessarily like to deal with women. My Asian investors love women but don't like to do business with them. Then there are the contacts I have in Bahrain, and the United Arab Emirates already have asked that I send a man to pitch the program. Trust me when I say that these fellows are loaded.

"The Feds are watching all of the banks like buzzards circling over a desert road kill, so the biggest cash pools available for buying real estate right now are the Arabs and the Asians. You and your friends might be able to round up a few million in growth funds from your buddies in Arizona and California, but the Arab players can dump a billion dollars into a pot and not even notice that it's gone."

"But I've never even been to that part of the world," said Brick, his mind still trying to make the conversation seem real.

"That isn't a problem. I have a facilitator in the company who can smooth out those types of experiences so that after a couple of trips there you'll start wanting to buy a camel."

"What's a facilitator?" asked Brick trying to suppress his laugh.

"Did you ever see the movie or the TV show *MASH*?"

"Sure. That was a long time ago."

"Remember the sergeant they called Radar? The little squeaky guy who could get everything done or found or fixed or forged? That, my friend, is a facilitator. I have a guy named Boycie who is just like Radar. He has the answers before you think to ask the questions."

Brick noticed that Ned was starting to sit a little lower in his chair and that the color in his face was getting chalky. He had a thousand questions, but sensed that he better put most of them on hold. There was one more thing he had to find out.

"Mr. Foster, maybe we could talk more a little later, I'm feeling a little jet lag. I have just one question that I need to know. How close are you to finding a match for your kidney?"

"I'm glad you mentioned that. I was getting so excited about TAG that I forgot to mention it. That's also a thing I might need your help with. As you know the computer and modern science have given us the ability to do a lot of things. Some of them might seem a bit intrusive, but they can also be life-saving. And please continue to call me Ned."

Brick nodded in agreement, having no idea where this bizarre conversation was headed.

"Please don't take this wrong, but when you and your friends ... my friends now ... when the six of you were here at dinner that night, I took the liberty of running some basic tests from the drinking glasses. You've got to understand that Willow and I were getting a little desperate. Anyway, we did a little bit of DNA testing and with that the brainy guys over at NYU could do some cell typing. As it turned out, one of you is a near perfect match with me."

Brick was speechless. A wave of nausea swept over him when his first thought was that the matching person was Debra, then, a hot flash and beads of sweat followed.

"Who is it?" he was finally able to ask, barely suppressing his anger.

"It's your good doctor friend, David, the man who already saved my life once. Now he has the opportunity to do it again. If he is willing to do it. If you can persuade him, I'm willing to make all of you wealthy men. I would propose that you and our friend Derek and Doctor Dave all come to work for me. The details can be worked out later, but I can promise each of you a king's ransom if you can save my life and get TAG funded." Ned sank back in the chair as he finished the sentence, apparently relieved to get the offer off of his mind.

Brick couldn't sit still a second longer. He arose from the chair and paced the room. The aura of master-servant was gone. Brick's emotions were jumbled. The man at the desk had suddenly taken on a new role, but what it was or what it would become was far from clear.

"You'll have to excuse me sir, maybe we can talk

later. I'm not feeling well," Brick said, bolting for the door.

He grabbed his wallet and sunglasses from the bedroom and headed for the front door. He had to walk and think. He cut through Central Park and started to head toward Debra and the hotel, but then turned down a path toward the main lake. After an hour of brisk walking and thinking he headed toward the hotel. He knew it wasn't safe in the park after dark.

"I can't believe he would do such an underhanded thing to us," Debra said.

Lexy was playing on the floor with a luggage tag while the parents paced the room. Brick had tried to soften the explanation a little, but his wife immediately saw right through Foster's (or was it Willow's?), apparent plan.

"He is desperate to get a kidney," Brick said. "He probably does tests on everyone he can entice into touching things in his place. He's probably tested every one of his employees too."

"That's no excuse and you know it. Are you going to call Dave?"

"I'm not sure just what to do," he said, sinking into a club chair next to Lexy. He picked her up and tried to get a smile out of her, but instead she started fussing, and then crying when he took the luggage tag's shreds from her mouth.

"Well, I think we should pack up and go home. He has lots of money and can get along just fine without you and they certainly didn't want me around in the first place," she said.

"I can't just leave the man."

"Tell me why not," she said, snatching the sobbing

baby from Brick. "He has a butler. He has a maid. He has a trophy wife. He probably has a whole list of doctors on his speed dial, and now he has you—but better than on a speed dial—he has you on a leash."

Brick made no response. There was nothing he could say that she would accept at the moment, so he got up and tried to give her an embrace, but she turned away. He was trying to think the situation through, but was getting nowhere when the phone rang.

By the time Brick made it back to the town house, paramedics were in the process of carrying Edward Foster III out of the building and down the curved steps. A crowd had gathered, requiring Brick to push his way to the front. Foster was still alive, but with his face covered by an oxygen mask it was impossible to assess his condition. The ambulance doors slammed shut, and the light and siren filled the evening air.

Benjamin was at the top of the stairs where less than twelve hours before Willow had stood—arms folded— giving a less than warm greeting.

"What happened?" Brick asked, trying to catch his breath.

"Mr. Foster was eating his dinner when he began choking. I performed a Heimlich maneuver on him which helped. Margo was in the kitchen and responded to my call for assistance. She called the ambulance. By the time the rescue gentlemen arrived, Mr. Foster was breathing on his own and was communicating with me. They are taking him to the hospital where his doctor will meet him. He did ask if you would stay here at the home and await his call."

Margo was nowhere to be found, and Benjamin announced that he was retiring to his room for the evening and disappeared. Brick went into the mansion and wandered the living areas. Every place he looked and everything he saw was of the highest quality, and most expensive, from the kitchen appliances to the furniture and floor coverings. He supposed that the newness of everything except the building itself, reflected the arrival just a few years ago of Willow and her expensive taste.

He settled into the massive chair in Foster's study and dialed Debra at the hotel. She answered in a whisper, saying the baby was asleep on the bed next to her so they kept the conversation short. He gave her a brief update on Foster.

"You better call your friends and tell them what the heck is going on. I wouldn't leave it up to Foster to tell Dave that his kidney is on the sacrificial altar," she admonished sarcastically.

After saying goodnight to her and apologizing for the crazy situation he had gotten them into, he sat and stared at the pictures on the shelves and walls, and tried to suppose how it would be to transfer his life to New York City or wherever else Foster might send him. He tried to imagine what Dave Felshaw was going to say when he heard the news about being a match as a kidney donor. His next thought was wondering if anyone had called Willow. Knowing that he couldn't just sit there, he scribbled a note to Benjamin and Margo with his cell number and headed out the door.

Six thousand miles away, Willow was standing in the window of the Savoy Hotel in London, looking at the faint hint of dawn through a mist of late-summer, morning rain. She never handled the jet lag well. She was used to working out every day with her personal trainer, and even missing one day made her muscles ache. She had slept intermittently on the airplane due to the ever-present ache at the site of her kidney surgery. She was drawing a bath when her cell phone rang. At first she just glanced at the number and ignored it but then she recognized the 602 area code.

"Are you sure he's OK?" she demanded.

Brick was standing in the waiting room of Columbia Presbyterian Hospital's emergency room surrounded by strange patients and their families. He had tried, but there was no way the staff was going to give him any information about Foster, so he had managed to slip down the hall toward the treatment rooms and had a lucky glance into the correct room. Foster was sitting upright, and though he had on oxygen he appeared alert. He returned Brick's glance and motioned vigorously for him to come into the room.

Foster removed the mask and introduced Brick to the doctor, calling Brick his nephew and giving permission for Brick to have access to medical information. The doctor gave Brick a thirty-second rundown of the situation and the management plan for the next day.

"I'm sure he will be all right. We'll probably let him go home tomorrow afternoon," the doctor advised.

Someone came in and slipped a plastic bracelet onto Brick's wrist and invited him to leave and return in the morning. They gave Brick the admitting room number and the direct phone number to the room, then shooed him out the door. Foster hollered a "Thanks for coming!" farewell and was then whisked down the hall to an elevator by an orderly.

"I've told you all that I know." Brick was walking along a rain-slicked sidewalk talking to Willow. "Actually, he looks good, better in fact than he did this afternoon after you left."

"What do you think, Brick? Should I catch a flight home?"

"He's going to be asleep for the next eight hours and then he'll be getting imaging tests all day tomorrow. I'll come by and see him in the morning and give you a call. Where are you, by the way?"

"London. I have a ten o'clock meeting with a group of investors from Saudi Arabia. The last time we met they treated me like a servant, but I still need to do a follow up. Then I'm flying to Moscow, or at least that is what I had planned."

"Why don't you just hang tight with your plans for now, and I'll give you an update in the morning," he said.

"Thank you for being there, Brick. I'm so grateful that Edward took my advice and called you. By the way, did he mention anything about Dave?"

The question sent a slight chill up Brick's spine. At first he thought of denying knowing what she was talking about, but then said, "Yes."

"Well, don't worry about that tonight," she said. "Call me as soon as you know anything. Promise?"

"I promise," he said, ending the conversation and coming back to the reality of his surroundings.

It took twenty minutes to find a cab, and then a ten-minute ride through the emptying streets of upper Manhattan before he was back at the Foster town house, or The Mansion, as he, Debra and the rest of his friends referred to it. Approaching the door it occurred to him that he didn't have a key. At first he panicked then thought, "What the heck?" He would just go to the hotel and sleep with his wife and baby. As he turned to leave, for some unknown reason he put his hand on the door knob and it turned freely then swung slowly open.

Feeling certain that he had locked the door on the way out, he began having second thoughts about the entire day. The ground floor of the mansion was empty and it felt damp inside. He could hear his footsteps echo as he walked down the hallway and up the wooden stairs, leaving lights on as he made his way to the large guest room.

To his surprise, a nightstand light was turned on in the room. He had left it in a jumble, but instead his clothes were all pressed and on hangers in the closet. His suitcase was placed neatly in the corner, even his hairbrush, his shaving gear, and toothpaste were lined up on the marble bathroom counter like little soldiers standing at attention. The bed was neatly turned back for him. The only thing missing was a Godiva chocolate truffle on his pillow. Margo had to be there, but where?

He showered, and failing to own, let alone bring along a pair of pajamas, he slipped between the sheets, feeling the cool smoothness of the fabric and within moments falling into deep, dream-filled sleep.

In what seemed like mere seconds, he was awakened by bright sunlight as the room's heavy curtains were drawn back.

"Good morning, Mr. Wahl. I took the liberty of fixing you breakfast," said the maid, Margo. She was dressed in a crisply-ironed, white apron over a light-blue, cotton top and a dark-blue skirt that barely reached her knees. She said nothing about the time, or having taken the liberty of waking him up, nor did she leave, but stood in the doorway as though waiting for him to immediately follow her to wherever his breakfast was waiting.

Slowly awakening and remembering his state of undress, thanked her and asked her to close the door. After another quick shower and shave he was ready to find his breakfast. He couldn't remember having eaten dinner, but knew for sure that he had missed his usual bedtime snack.

The dining room was alight with the morning sun and at the head of the table was a place setting complete with multiple forks, knives, and spoons. Margo removed a heavy-handed, tooled, silver cover as he approached the table, revealing a steaming plate of scrambled eggs, sausage, and hash-browns. More interesting than the food was a note placed on a china tray beside his plate.

"Mrs. Foster faxed that for your attention," said Margo, presenting him with the note.

Dear Brick,

I knew that you would be sleeping so I sent this note as I may be in flight when you awaken. My meeting here went well. TAG is now funded with a promise of millions of Arab oil dollars. More importantly right now is the need to help Edward. I am flying to Phoenix directly from London and wish to meet with your friends, David and Derek, and of course their wives. I thought it best if you could give them a call and arrange the meeting for me. The specifics of my arrival are below. I will be staying at the Phoenician resort and could host a dinner for them there. I trust that you will stay in NY to care for Edward. Thank you for your assistance.

Yours Truly,

Willow

"What! Are you nuts?" Dave asked. He stood at the operating room's scrub sink, his hands covered in antiseptic soap. The circulating nurse was holding his cell phone up to his ear for him so he didn't have to break scrub as he spoke. She nearly dropped it when he shouted.

"You have got to at least talk to the woman. I've already spoken to Derek. He agreed to pick you up at seven so you could have an early dinner with your kids. Willow's plane lands at five, so she will be at the Phoenician main dining room at seven thirty. If nothing else you can have a good lobster tail," Brick said, regretting that he had stated the reason for the meeting.

"Tell Doctor Bent I'll be a couple of minutes," he told the nurse, rinsing his hands and taking the phone from her. He walked down the corridor to an empty operating room and leaned against a gurney.

"What makes her think that one of us is a match for Foster?" he asked Brick.

"It's not just one of us, it's you. She took our drinking glasses from the table the night we had dinner and ran DNA. She also admitted that she paid someone to hack the Arizona Red Cross computer to check our blood donation records. She doesn't know for sure that you are a perfect match, but you are for sure close," said Brick leaning back in the heavy, leather chair, bracing for a tongue lashing from his friend.

"Melody is going to go ballistic when she hears this nonsense."

"Why don't you wait until you hear the entire proposal before you tell her everything? Willow is a very good persuader and will present the proposal in such a way that the reality of the thing will be softened."

"It will have to be softer than a baby's bottom for me to give up a kidney," Dave said. "Listen, my patient is asleep on the operating table. I'll call you back in a couple of hours. Plan on us going to the dinner, but that's all I can promise."

Brick looked at the phone in his hand and finally hung it up. He didn't know exactly how he should feel—like a humanitarian or a pimp—but was now committed to helping Edward Foster III receive a donor kidney from his best friend. The dilemma was taking more financial perks for doing it.

It was already ten thirty and he hadn't called Debra. Maybe she was still asleep. No sooner had the thought passed his mind than the phone rang. He didn't know the protocol of answering it and didn't want to hunt down the maid or butler so he let it ring. After six or seven irritating rings he picked it up anyway and started to say hello when he heard Benjamin's voice. He started to hang up when he heard the voice of someone he was sure was Foster's doctor. He listened and then slowly hung up the phone. Seconds later there was a soft tap on the study door.

Brick opened the door and Margo just stood there, with tears running down her cheeks.

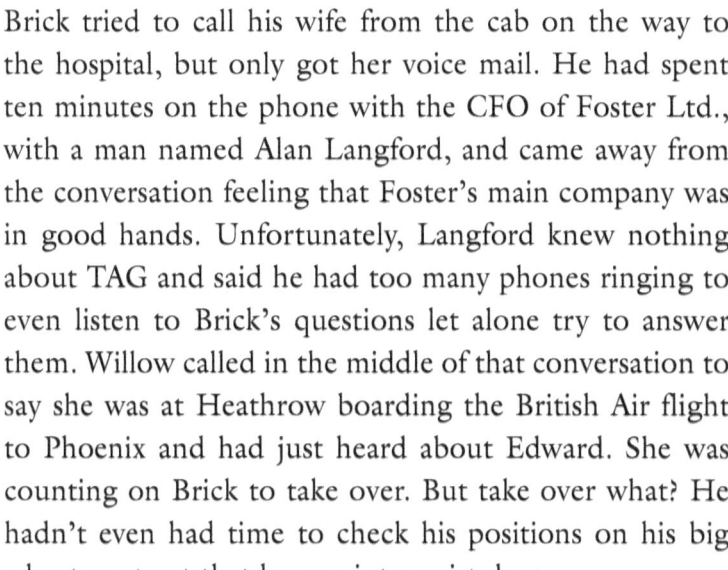

Brick tried to call his wife from the cab on the way to the hospital, but only got her voice mail. He had spent ten minutes on the phone with the CFO of Foster Ltd., with a man named Alan Langford, and came away from the conversation feeling that Foster's main company was in good hands. Unfortunately, Langford knew nothing about TAG and said he had too many phones ringing to even listen to Brick's questions let alone try to answer them. Willow called in the middle of that conversation to say she was at Heathrow boarding the British Air flight to Phoenix and had just heard about Edward. She was counting on Brick to take over. But take over what? He hadn't even had time to check his positions on his big wheat contract that he was into waist deep.

The doors to the ICU were open so he didn't have to call through the security phone. There was a flurry of activity around one of the rooms so he snuck by and found a team standing around Foster's bed. The room was alive with electrical sounds, reassuring Brick that he wasn't too late yet. He watched as medications were injected into the IV lines and as someone in scrubs, a hat, and a mask taped an endotracheal tube in place.

"He is alive. That's about all we can say for now," the teenage-looking doctor told Brick. "He was doing great this morning, reading the paper and joking with a nurse when he started seizing and then had a respiratory arrest. We got him breathing and moved him here to the ICU and then he did it all over again. His lab work last night looked pretty good. We're still waiting on the report from an hour ago."

"So, is he going to be all right?" Brick asked in a naïve, but hopeful tone.

"Unless he gets a kidney in the next few days, he is going to die," said the doctor in a matter-of-fact tone. "He might not make it through the week. Who knows? Humans are not machines that can be repaired with screwdrivers and pliers, as nice as that would be. Everybody responds differently to similar conditions. The best we can hope for is that he recovers from this morning's trauma and can hold on for a few more days. We'll run him through dialysis again, but that's losing its effect, and some of the kidney's functions can't be replaced by the machine. The bottom line is that he needs a new kidney."

As Brick walked out of the hospital entrance, Debra called him back. They agreed on lunch together. There was little he could do until he spoke with Willow again; so he went back to the mansion and brought up his trading accounts on Ned's desktop computer. Maybe he could still salvage some wheat or sugar money before the market closed.

Derek Morris was sitting at a breakfast meeting in the country club's restaurant, 19th Hole, when he received the call from Dave. He had just finished a sunrise tee time round of golf with a new client, and they were discussing the final plans for a new medical office building. It would be Derek's biggest construction project ever at 220,000 square feet and with a price tag of $20 million. The profit margin was mind boggling.

He listened for sixty seconds to his doctor friend's

message regarding dinner that night and quickly decided to go. Dave hadn't mentioned the real reason for the dinner at the Phoenician with Willow, but he sounded uncharacteristically worried.

Derek and Natasha had felt like the third wheel in the trio of friends ever since the chance encounter with the Fosters and the trip to New York. Derek had done as much as anyone to save Ned's life when they were up on the mountain bike trail, and even at the hospital in Meeker he had pitched in, but Dave had been given most of the kudos. Brick, on the other hand, had hated the hospital and yet had created some kind of unseen bond with Willow that neither Derek nor Natasha could figure out.

When the call came that morning from Willow—waking Natasha from a deep sleep—she at first rejected the invitation to go to the dinner. Only the uncharacteristic pleading from the woman had changed her mind. She knew better than to call Derek in the middle of his round of golf so she waited. In the meantime, Melody called her and asked if the husbands knew about the get-together. Eventually, everyone got the word about the dinner, just not about the need for Dave's kidney. Each of them made their plans and found babysitters for the evening.

When Derek picked up the Felshaws in his fancy new pickup, the tension dissolved for the time being. The ladies looked fabulous in spite of the short notice. The guys were dressed much more casually in cotton slacks and Aloha shirts. The girls always had lots to talk about, and Derek's new project was full of interesting conversation pieces, including a statue in the middle of the plaza with a life-size horse sculpture by Derek's artist

uncle, Carl Dahl. The office would be like an advertising
billboard for any of Derek's future projects.

The Phoenician resort is a massive complex of
buildings scattered among natural desert vegetation and
jungle-green golf course fairways. The main building
sits on the side of Camelback Mountain overlooking the
Phoenix valley. No sooner had the parking attendant
opened their doors and directed them into the cool
lobby, did they see Willow rushing toward them. She
was dressed in a glittering, emerald-green dress, with
a short hemline and low-cut neck. Diamonds sparkled
from every reasonable body part.

She greeted each of the four friends with an exuberant
hug and a peck on each cheek. Approaching Dave last, she
maintained her clutch on his arms, ignoring the chatter
of the others until he had looked her straight in the eyes.

"I'm so glad you could come tonight," she said to
him, still not releasing his arms. "I only wish Edward
could be here."

The table in the main dining room was awaiting them.
Willow was seated at the end of a rectangular table next to
the two men, allowing Natasha and Melody to visit across
the table and to observe the woman's obvious flirtation
with their husbands. She chattered on about Brick and
Debra coming to New York and her trip to London and
the cute little Lexy, but sidestepped questions about
Edward's condition or the progress of TAG. When the
main course was being cleared away she waved off the
waiters and pushed her chair back.

"It's been lovely visiting with the four of you. I would
invite you up to the room for a nightcap, but I know you
have children at home and babysitters. Ladies, could I be

so rude as to ask for a moment alone with your husbands? I promise it won't take long," Willow said.

Natasha and Melody didn't act surprised and left the table for the powder room. Natasha took the car's claim check insisting they would be waiting in the car. "Don't be long," she admonished Dave.

"We have a problem," she said, reaching out, taking each of their hands in hers. "TAG is just what we told you it is and it is growing quickly. Our main problem is that everything revolves around Edward. We have over $300 million in assets today and could have $1 billion by October, but only if Edward remains alive. His other company is, for all intents and purposes, in the public domain. The board of directors has everything ready to take it public, and with all the Securities and Exchange Commission rules, it might as well be so right now. Edward's and my stock will be a small portion of the proceeds, but more than enough to suffice our wants and needs.

"The question then is TAG," she continued. "Edward is very close to dying. The best doctors in New York and Boston agree that he can't live more than a couple of weeks without a kidney transplant. I don't know if you are aware, but I gave him my right kidney to save his life and the life of the Foster Company several years ago. The kidney would still been working if it had not been for the damn rattlesnake bite and the reaction to the antivenom."

"So cut through the fluff and tell us why we are here," Dave said.

"I need you two and Brick to take on TAG full time. Those working in the Foster Ltd. group don't have the time and are not invested or interested. Edward wanted

TAG to be his legacy and for me and him to run it by ourselves. Yes, he gave you a pittance of an interest in it as a reward, but the potential is much greater," said Willow.

"And?" Derek asked glancing toward the hotel lobby as the girls walked by on their way to the car.

"I will make it very simple. If the three of you are willing to come to work, full time, with me for the next year, we will give each of you 10 percent of the company stock and pay each of you a salary of $4 million for the first year. I have the first quarter checks in my purse for each of you if you agree. There is one big catch," she said, gripping their hands even tighter.

The men were looking at one another nearly holding their collective breaths.

"And that would be?" Dave finally asked.

"Dave, you must donate him one of your kidneys. We know that you are a close enough match, and it must happen within the week."

The forewarning the two men received had not softened the reality of the demand. Derek pulled his hand away from hers and started to stand. "This is bull," he said.

"Wait!" Dave said. "Is he really that bad?"

"You are the doctor. You know the disease and the outcome. I gave him my kidney for three reasons. One I admired him ... not loved him ... at that time, but I have grown to love him. Two, he in essence paid me for my kidney just like I'm offering to pay you. Three, it saved his company for me and him and all of his hundreds of employees and investors. Believe me. I know what I am asking you to do. I would do it again in a heartbeat if it were possible."

"I can't just take off and move to New York and neither can Dave," Derek said. "I'm about to start the biggest construction project of my life, and he has patients to care for and our kids are about to start the new school year." The list could have gone on, but Dave reached across the table and put his hand on Derek's arm.

"Maybe we can work it all out. Is there a reason we can't run it from here in Phoenix?" he asked.

She shrugged. "I suppose it could be worked out, after the surgery is completed."

"I don't want you or Ned to think I would do it just for the money," Dave said, "but we have obligations to be met each month and stopping my practice would essentially require me to start over again when TAG is up and running and I return to medicine."

"In addition to the salary for TAG, I have a cashier's check in my purse for each of you for a million dollars and one sitting in my dresser drawer in Manhattan for Brick, if you agree to the transplant. Obviously, David, we will pay for all the expenses of the surgery and I'm willing to set up a college fund for each of your kids for … let's say $100,000 for each. You have three children right?"

Dave and Derek just stared at her, and then Dave slowly nodded yes to the question about his kids.

"The annual salaries will be paid after the surgery is completed—successful or not. As far as I'm concerned, it is a take all or leave it all proposition. In either event, I need to know by noon tomorrow, before I leave for New York. It's all for one—one for all. Derek, I need your and Brick's business and management expertise, and Edward needs David's kidney. Everyone contributes and everyone benefits."

She held out her hand to shake on the deal. Both men looked, but waited. Derek said he needed to talk it over with his wife and sleep on the radical idea. Dave repeated essentially the same statement, and they left the side of the table with her still standing there, her hand unshaken.

The discussion in the car on the way home was heated. The wives were crying and the men were confused. What were they to do about work? What about the kids and school? What would they do with their homes in the negative housing market? What about the extended family who relied on them and the grandparents and their church jobs? The questions went on and on as though there was no answer, but then the money spoke. It spoke loud and clear.

It was 2:00 a.m. in New York when they woke Brick up from a sound sleep. The three of the men talked on the phone for over an hour with Natasha and Melody sitting by listening and asking questions. Brick didn't wake Debra, knowing the final decision would be up to him to make. By the time they had discussed all of the ramifications of the offer, fatigue finally set in. Melody insisted that they all sleep on it before they made a final decision.

Saying yes to drugs—sleeping pills—was the only way to make Dave and Melody's brains finally stop ruminating through the scenarios and all that money. Even if TAG failed, they would be multimillionaires. No student loans to pay off, no mortgage or car payments and their kids' educations funded. All of that for just one eight-ounce piece of Dave's body.

Dave was making rounds at the private orthopedic hospital where he did most of his hip and knee surgeries when a lab technician he had never seen before approached him.

"Doctor Felshaw, can I borrow your arm for a minute?" She showed him a requisition from Massachusetts General Hospital for several vials of his blood. Highly irregular, and yet reasonable under the circumstances, he agreed. He followed the cute blonde's ponytail as it bounced toward a nearby chair. She cleansed his arm, gently inserted a long needle, and removed six glass vials of his dark, red blood. He was surprised that when he stood he felt so dizzy. Perhaps the dizziness was because he hadn't gone to sleep until after 1:00 a.m. when his wife finally stopped talking and started a muffled snore in mid-sentence. He had left the house with the TV tuned to cartoons and a bowl of Cocoa Puffs in front of each of the kids. Melody was still dead to the world.

He went by the doctor's lounge and ate a doughnut and had two glasses of orange juice to quell his dizziness. While he stood eating, the TV news was telling the story of a medical malpractice case in Las Vegas where the jury had awarded $15 million to a woman who hadn't liked the results of her face-lift and breast reconstruction surgery.

In the before and after pictures the news channel showed, the woman was homely before and still homely afterward. It reminded him of his dad's saying, "You can paint a manure pile pink, but it's still a pile of crap." It was right then and there that he made his decision to abandon—at least for the time being—the practice of medicine.

"You are a near perfect match! Of course we knew you would be," Willow said, calling late in the afternoon. "The Phoenix blood lab was very efficient. All the tests were good. The surgery is scheduled at Mass General for 9:00 a.m. a week from today. You just have to be in Boston one day before. We'll fly Edward up in three days so the doctors can get him ready."

The next five days flew by in a blur. All three of the men's $1 million checks cleared the bank—there was a note from Foster's tax lawyer for the IRS that the money was a gift, and that Foster already had paid the taxes on the money. Dave broke the news to his medical partners that he was taking an extended emergency leave from his practice. The plan was for Melody and the kids to stay in Phoenix until he had recuperated from surgery, then they would find an apartment in Manhattan close to Derek and Brick. Natasha had started thinking of the experience as a big adventure, and already was looking at apartments online. Derek had hired a project manager to head up his medical office construction project, figuring that even with his absentee management he could keep the project alive and successful.

Brick put Debra to work—feet on the ground—helping Natasha search for suitable housing for all three families. He had resolved that he could easily drop out of trading for a few months, and then if necessary, he could get right back into it when the chaos of TAG settled down and was running smoothly.

"You won't believe the prices here!" Debra said, talking to Melody and Natasha on a conference call. "Six thousand a month will get you a three bedroom, one bath with a kitchen the size of my broom closet and view of subway tracks. I'm expanding my search to Connecticut and New Jersey tomorrow. The boys can ride the train into town every day and do some of their work while they commute."

After what seemed like a ream of legal paperwork was signed, arrangements for the surgery were finalized. Dave would fly to New York to catch up on things with Brick, and then the two partners would drive up to Boston. Saying good-bye to his kids and to Melody was bittersweet. Each of the kids had colored a get well card for their daddy, and Melody had made a fresh batch of chocolate chip cookies and packed them in a child's shoe box, with a photo of her and the kids under the ribbon's bow. Once in New York, he was met at the airport by Brick, Deb, and Lexy. He had no face-to-face time with Ned, who already had been carted off in an ambulance to fly to Boston.

Brick took Dave to dinner at a four-star restaurant and they stayed up talking until midnight. The next day was a day too full of anxiety for Dave to even remember. Brick rented a new Mercedes and drove them to Boston for Dave's afternoon check-in.

Cut time was Monday morning at nine o'clock sharp. Mass General was everything they had heard it would be and more—more confusing that is. The buildings seemed piled on top of one another and once inside, it was a maze of hallways with turns and elevators confounding one's sense of direction. More labs and x-rays filled the evening, and when Dave's dinner tray came, a tiny cup of green Jell-O was all it held. Brick said good night and left for his hotel. He had promised to be there in the morning.

As they wheeled Dave into the pre-op area the following morning, he was finally able to have a conversation with Ned. With their gurneys side by side they talked about Dave's family and the sacrifice they were making. They talked about Willow and how she had done a great job getting everything organized for the transplant, and they talked about TAG, about which Ned seemed to be a little unclear regarding any details from the previous several weeks.

As their pre-anesthesia medications began taking effect, they talked about another bicycle ride and about "that damn snake."

"Springtime in Switzerland is fabulous," Ned explained with a groggy voice. "I'll get a tour guide for the four of us and rent us the best bikes money can buy. We can ride every day for a week. I want you to take a trail with me up the side of the Jungfrau. It is truly a sight to die for, and best of all there are no poisonous snakes."

Willow and Brick walked into the pre-operative area together. After hellos and good-byes, she gave both men kisses and turned away toward the waiting area. Brick shook their hands wishing them both good luck and reassuring them that he would be there when they awakened. Within moments, the orderlies wheeled the patients toward the swinging double doors of the operating room. The ordeal really was going to happen.

The undersized waiting room already was full, except for a double settee that would put Brick and Willow hip to hip. At first he told her he would stand, but then gave in and slid into place.

She was not in a mood to talk so he pulled out his iPad and went to work. There was a good opportunity with wheat futures since the Russian drought was letting up. He made a call committing on four short-sale contracts. When she asked what he was doing he was surprised. She had never heard of a *put* or a *call.*

When he tried to visit with her about Foster's old and very successful business, she was elusive. Then he brought up TAG, which turned on a virtual faucet of positive pitch lines and promises, all sounding like she was trying to pitch their business plan to a new investor. When he asked about real specifics, she changed the subject to coffee and headed off to the hospital cafeteria.

Brick thought about calling Derek, but at the last second remembered that it was still 7:00 a.m. in Arizona. He went back to his iPad and began organizing his spreadsheet, and his mind left the hospital and the drama in the nearby operating room.

Lost in concentration on his work, he felt the pressure and then the warmth of her hip against his before he saw or heard her. He continued on his project for a few more minutes, and looked up to see huge tears slowly rolling down Willow's cheeks.

"Are you all right?" he asked, not knowing how to manage her unusual emotion.

"It just brings back all the memories of the last time. Everything that seems like déjà vu is, in fact, a real memory. Even the smell of this place is the same. This may sound stupid, but sitting here earlier even made my incision start hurting," she said, now starting to sob.

The little muffled sounds were attracting the attention of others in the room, some of them looking at him in questioning ways. Finally, he lifted his arm and put it around her shoulders which she immediately responded to, snuggling against him, leaning her wet cheek against his chest. And there she remained.

His iPad had long since shut itself off, and his arm had gone to sleep, when a young female walked out of the operating room, tearing a paper mask from her face.

"Are you with Mr. Foster and Doctor Felshaw?" she asked.

"I'm Mrs. Foster," Willow said, leaning forward so Brick could remove his nearly-numb arm.

"I'm Doctor Jaden Allen, Doctor Rose's transplant fellow. The kidney was safely removed from Doctor Felshaw and he is headed to the recovery room."

"What about my husband?" Willow asked.

"He is stable. I understand they had some problem with the anesthesia at first, but he is now stable and they are beginning to place the donor kidney. There is always a lot of scar tissue when there has been previous surgery. It may take a while."

"How long is a while?" Brick asked, still wiggling his sleeping hand.

"If all goes well, they should be done in about an hour," the pretty brunette said, pulling off her pink, paisley scrub hat and shaking out her long hair. She glanced at the clock on the wall saying, "They should be out of the operating room shortly after two."

Brick excused himself and left to get some fresh air

and a Coke. He walked around a small park for what he thought was half an hour, then returned. At first he thought he was in the wrong place, however there was a half-empty coffee cup with Willow's lipstick smear and the copy of Road and Track he had glanced at earlier. Before he left, there had been eight or ten people in the room. Now, it was empty. He tried to find a nurse or a secretary, but no one was around. Then he heard the sobbing again.

He walked down a hall to a door with a small, stained-glass window that he hadn't noticed before. There was a small plaque indicating that the room was a non-denominational chapel. The source of the sobbing coming from inside was unmistakable. Willow sat on an upholstered chair with two of the women he recognized from the waiting room on each side of her. When Brick entered the room the strangers rose and walked out. Brick's stomach immediately cramped and sweat broke out on his forehead. Now, anticipating the worst he put his hand on her shoulder and asked, "What's happened?"

Slowly Willow raised her head and looked up at him, giving a tiny smile. "He made it," she whispered. "The doctor said everything went perfectly well and he is going to be fine."

"That's terrific!" Brick said, kneeling in front of her, taking her into his arms and holding her close. "That's just terrific! So why all of the tears?" he whispered.

"What tears?" she asked, leaning back away from him, tossing her head to straighten her hair, and then standing and brushing the wrinkles out of her skirt, as if she had just concluded a business meeting.

"When will he get out of the recovery room?" asked Brick.

"Dave is already supposed to be in his room, and they might release him tonight or first thing in the morning. Edward will go to the ICU for the night and then remain here for about a week. As soon as Dave can leave in the morning, I would like you to take him back to Manhattan. You can all continue to stay at the town house. I need you to get to work on TAG. I'll e-mail you instructions on what I need you to do next," she said.

"That's such great news ... about Ned, I mean."

He stepped toward her to give her another embrace, but before he could touch her, she turned and bent down to retrieve her purse, leaving him in an awkward position. She then turned and left the room.

He ate lunch, then found Dave's private room and was allowed to sit by the bedside waiting for his friend to come out of the effects of the anesthesia. It was nearly dark when Dave was able to speak to him and even then it was gibberish. Brick was pacing the room when the nurse came in.

"Doctor Rose usually makes rounds at eight in the morning, so your friend can probably be discharged about ten. He should rest until then," the head nurse said. "You look like you could use some rest as well."

He thought about trying to find Foster's room, but was sick of the hospital's atmosphere and decided instead to take a cab to Fenway Park and watch the Red Sox clobber some poor visiting team. He was just in time to watch the last five innings, eat a bratwurst, and make it to his hotel in time to call Melody and give her an update on Dave.

The drive back to New York was uneventful. Dave was awake and ready to leave the hospital by noon. He had a bottle of pain pills and a large sterile dressing on his flank. He had been given the name of a doctor in Manhattan to visit for follow up in a week and was wheeled out the door. The conversation with Dave was fine for the first twenty minutes, then he reclined the seat as far back as it would go and was instantly snoring. Brick tried to access his e-mail while he drove the turnpike, but couldn't get a good signal, so he gave up.

He tried to call Debra, but only got her voice mail. He checked his voice mail, and when he heard her voice, he nearly ran the car off of the road. His wife was alternately crying and yelling at him. She had spent the whole previous day looking for places to live and couldn't find any place in the area that she felt safe, and knew that Natasha and Melody would hate it too.

"It's no place to raise a family and I won't spend another day in that museum with a maid and butler standing over my shoulder. I'm on the way to the airport with Lexy. If you want to see us, you'll have to fly home to Phoenix," she said as the message ended.

He had no idea what had triggered that reaction, then suddenly remembered that he had forgotten to call her the night before. He had called Melody, but not his wife. He tried again to call but she wouldn't answer.

Benjamin and Brick helped Dave walk up the stairs and into his assigned bedroom on the third floor. Margo had the room made up fresh, and even had a bowl of fruit and a plate of homemade cookies on the bedside table. Dave thanked them and went right back to sleep.

Brick wandered down to Ned's office and settled into the massive chair. He checked his futures account and sold a corn contract, then bought a contract on January sugar. When he opened his e-mail and deleted the spam, he found a message from Willow. True to her word, she left him some instructions: eight pages of them. *The woman is a cold-hearted slave driver.*

The first item was to arrange an appointment at J.P. Morgan Bank to sign in as a co-signer on the TAG bank account. He caught a cab to the bank, making it just as they were closing. A pleasant female officer escorted him to a room where he was given the necessary paperwork. Reading the first page, he discovered that he was listed as Vice President of Investments. He sat back and chuckled at the title. *Me, a vice president?* He felt like he had one foot in his family home in Arizona, and the other one in a bucket of cement in New York that was slowly starting to set up.

It was after eating the dinner Margo had prepared for him and Dave that he finally got ahold of Debra. She had chickened out about flying home, and was just six blocks away—back at the hotel. He checked on Dave and gave Benjamin instructions to keep an eye on him. Then he shaved, showered, and caught a cab to see his wife.

Derek was in a free fall. He had been up half the night with his sick three-year-old who had thrown up on herself, her bed, and her dad. When he finally was able to drag himself out of bed at seven, Natasha told him he had a dozen new e-mails and a FedEx package sitting by the door. Three of the e-mails were from Brick: the first outlining why he needed Derek in New York as soon as possible, the second insisting that the whole family come as soon as possible—to keep Debra and Lexy company—and finally insisting that he come up with the names of some people in the real estate development business that they could call about investing in TAG.

His head was pounding and his daughter was still sick and was screaming like a wounded cat when he opened the FedEx package and found a cease and desist order from the county attorney, demanding that his construction team not break ground on his new office building project until it could be proven that the land contained no ancient, native burial remains. The project was already into the bank for $600,000 in building permits, architectural charges, and engineering fees. The daily interest alone was more than the monthly lease payment on his BMW.

Just as he was ready to dive into the swimming pool

to work off some of his fatigue and frustration, the phone rang.

"Derek? It's Willow."

"Hi, how are you Willow? How is Ned doing?" he said, trying not to show his morning's frustrations. "Brick already e-mailed me, telling me to get back to New York as soon as possible."

"There is an urgent change in plans," she said. "Edward has taken a turn for the worse. I thought he would be home in another couple of days, but he is running a high fever, so they have put him back in the ICU. I have a meeting in Dubai in three days. It's a meeting that could make or break our TAG project. Anyway, I don't feel that I can leave Edward right now and someone of our group must be there. Dave obviously can't go. Brick is dealing with his angry wife and has already assumed responsibilities for us in New York. Derek dear, I need you to go in my place."

"To Dubai? In the Middle East? You have got to be joking! I don't speak any of those languages," he said (it was the first thing that popped into his mind), when suddenly a feeling of light-headedness nearly made him drop the phone.

"The people you will meet with speak better English that either of us. They are probably Harvard or Princeton graduates."

"But Willow, I can't just drop everything here and fly off halfway around the world."

He walked to the edge of the swimming pool and slowly descended the steps into the lukewarm water until he was up to his chest. The cocoon of the water seemed to settle him.

"Are you in the bathtub?" she asked, beginning to laugh. "Even I don't expect you to take my calls from the bathtub."

"I'm sitting waist-deep in my swimming pool. The water is warmer than a bathtub. It's supposed to get up to one hundred and fifteen degrees today."

"There you go! Dubai will be a pleasant relief for you. I read that it's only forty-two there. That's forty-two Celsius," she said with a laugh. It was the first laugh he had heard from her in a long time.

He didn't respond for a few moments, thinking how he could make the trip work. He obviously couldn't do anything for a couple of weeks on the office building—his attorneys would have to run with that ancient burial ground ball.

He finally laughed with her and said. "I guess I will be fine making the trip. Natasha and the kids are leaving in two days for Newport Beach with her parents and won't even know that I'm gone. I'll just have to drive them over to California a day early and fly out from L.A. How long will I need to be there?"

"They will want a day or two to entertain and impress you, and then they'll play word games for a day or two. Finally, they'll get down to business. I've made your reservations at the hotel for a week, but you can always leave sooner. I'll get you a flight from Los Angeles. I need to FedEx you a ream of paperwork to look over."

"Are you sure I'm the right person to do this?"

"You are not only the right person, you are the only person I can trust," she said.

"What about the guys who work for Ned in the Wall Street office?"

"Like I told the three of you already, that is an entirely separate company. It is controlled by a board of directors with a bullheaded chairman and a CEO and a CFO. Those people are completely separate from TAG. Edward is emphatic that they have nothing to do with TAG. TAG is Edward's new baby and now it's our new baby. We can all nourish it, and watch it grow or throw it out with the bath water along with all the millions it will earn for us." The impatience and frustration in her voice was increasing.

"All right! I get it! I'll make it work out," Derek said, feeling pushed into a corner with no way out. "You'll just have to stay close to a phone and do some coaching as we go along."

"Watch for the FedEx package," she said and then hung up.

He took a deep breath and laid his phone on the pool edge. Diving down toward the drain, he held his breath as long as he possibly could, then emerged and swam a dozen fast laps until he was completely winded. He took a quick rinse in the outdoor shower then went dripping into the house.

"Honey, there's been a little change in plans."

Natasha was standing at the stove, barefoot, cooking pancakes and sausage. She was a wise woman and had rolled with lots of unpredicted waves during their ten-year marriage. "Surf's not up," she thought.

Thirty hours and 400 miles later, the couple leaned against a small retaining wall and watched their three kids play in the sand with Natasha's parents sitting nearby. They already had unpacked the week's-worth of beachwear and food inside the rented condo. Derek was dressed in a tan, summer-weight suit and a blue-and-red striped tie, while Natasha wore just her bikini with her blond hair pulled into a ponytail. She smelled of coconut oil and shampoo. They both heard the honking of the cab, so they kissed, looking into one another's eyes. Any necessary words had already been spoken.

"Bye kids," he said, trying in vain to get their attention.

"Hey you guys, come give your dad a kiss," Natasha said, getting immediate results.

"I love you guys. Take good care of your mom. Promise?"

He pecked Natasha on the lips, waved good-bye to his in-laws and picked up his bags, feeling the sand on his hands from hugging the children. Tasha followed him as far as the garage by the street, then stood waving as the cab turned the corner.

His flight was late departing, giving him plenty of time to visit on the phone with Brick and Dave to catch up on what was going on with their lives. He caught Dave as he was dressed and heading out for a short noon walk in Central Park. Melody and their kids were due in town and later they planned on driving out to Long Island, to the Foster's ocean cottage where Dave planned to continue his recovery. If all went well with Ned, he also planned to complete his surgical recovery on Long Island. At this point, Foster's recovery was still more of a hope than a plan.

Brick was barricaded in the mahogany-paneled study, already feeling that he had become the hub of the TAG enterprise. Debra and Lexy had moved back into the mansion, taking an extra room for the baby. Willow hadn't been seen at the mansion except to pick up some extra clothes and pay the household help. She spoke to Brick several times a day and yet refused his offer to come sit at Ned's hospital bedside to give her a break. His condition was stable, but not necessarily improving. He still was not able to even take a phone call.

Benjamin and Margo had accepted the reality that Brick and Debra, as well as the recovering Doctor Felshaw, were more than temporary houseguests and had fallen into their silent and efficient modes. There was no need for Brick or Debra to shop for food, cook, clean the house, or do the laundry. Debra had used the time to get caught up on her Facebook and had even invited her parents to fly to New York—staying at a hotel of course—to visit with her and the baby while Brick worked, which he was doing now from dawn until dusk.

"Have a good flight, partner," Brick said to Derek over the phone, looking out of the small window to the park across the street and wishing that it was he who was flying off to the Middle East to be wined and dined by the oil rich Arabs.

"Anything I can bring you?" Derek asked. "I hear their camel cheese is to die for."

"You mean die from … right?"

"Something like that. By the way, how many of those London investors sent their final checks?"

"You think she would tell me? I'm working all day writing a new prospectus and preparing investor kits and making phone calls from a fifty-page list of potential clients, but the actual checks—assuming there are any—go straight to the Barclays' Bank account in the Caymans.

So far she hasn't given me the access numbers. Foster pays an accountant in Grand Cayman to keep the books. How many sets there really are, we'll probably never know. I told her that I need to meet with him and she agreed, but won't say when."

"That sounds pretty fishy to me," Derek said. "I thought this was supposed to be a transparent deal for all of us."

"Oh it's transparent all right. She can see right through each one of us," Brick said, looking over his shoulder to be sure no one was lingering in the hall outside the office door.

"You sound like you need a night off. Maybe the big city life is too much for you. Maybe you should stick to trading pork bellies and corn. Perhaps an office in Sioux Falls or Fargo would be more your style," Derek kidded. The problem was that he didn't hear Brick laugh at the joke.

"You'll find out in a couple of weeks—when you get back, just what a drag the city can be. Debra was all starry-eyed the first couple of days she was at the hotel, but soon learned that you can only go up in the Empire State Building or browse through Macy's so many times and the thrill of the city starts to wear off."

"So, how is the old man? I mean really? Willow makes it sound like he's got both legs on the crematorium table," Derek asked, just as he heard the last call for his flight.

"Let's just say that he may have experienced his last rattlesnake bite—at least from the Colorado variety."

Derek hadn't realized just how really "first class" Virgin Atlantic's treatment could be. By the time he arrived in Dubai, he didn't want to get off of the plane. He was used to Arizona's hot summers, but when he walked out of the Dubai air terminal into the desert air he thought he had entered the mouth of a blast furnace. He followed a grey-haired man holding a printed sign with his name on it. They walked straight out of the main door to a white Rolls Royce, where he was invited to wait inside while his luggage was retrieved. Ten minutes later they were cruising down a wide boulevard, lined with new modern buildings taller than anything in Phoenix. Each had the look of an entrant in an architectural contest.

The Burj Al Arab hotel was the most fantastic building Derek had ever cast his eyes upon. It looked like the sail of a giant racing sloop, soaring a thousand feet into the sapphire-blue, desert sky. The hotel's foundation sat on a man-made peninsula a half mile from the shore. He was led to a glass elevator, and then whisked directly to his room, where a huge bouquet of flowers and a bowl of exotic fruits awaited him. When he looked out of the window of his suite, he had to grasp a nearby table to keep his balance. His room was so high up that helicopters were flying by halfway between him and the water below.

The next seventy-two hours seemed as though he was playing a role in a movie. He had meetings with strangers who acted like his long-lost, best friends, ate meals of broiled lobster tails and Kobe filets, and slept in silk sheets so slippery he couldn't keep the numerous pillows from sliding off of the bed. When he showered, it was in a marble vault large enough to accommodate his whole family at once.

He had hoped to see some of the countryside, but quickly learned that this wasn't a sight-seeing trip. His schedule was e-mailed to him each evening by Willow and was filled with appointments and meals. By the end of the third day he was exhausted and ready to come home, but received a text message that she had an extra day of meetings planned for him. These would be the more difficult ones since they all were repeat visits. Thus far, his job had been merely to present the idea of TAG to the prospective investors. It was now his responsibility to close the deals.

Derek's jet lag, combined with too much to eat and drink, and no time to use the enormous fitness center or swimming pool the hotel provided, was taking its toll. His face muscles hurt from smiling at strangers and potential clients, and in spite of the quality of the food, it was all starting to taste the same. The list of names of the men he needed to meet with all started to look and sound the same. By the end of his second-to-last meeting in Dubai, he had insulted two of the men by mixing up their names. Then came the meeting with Prince Abraham Assad.

The billionaire prince was waiting in the hotel's reserved business room. He was wearing flowing white robes, and was surrounded by a cluster of attractive, but serious-appearing women, all dressed in business suits. The first time they had met, Assad had worn a plain, but elegant business suit with the traditional black-and-white, plaid head scarf, and they had met alone in the dining room. Derek offered the thirty-five-year-old prince some refreshments, but they were declined. This, he thought was not a good sign.

"Thank you so much for returning this morning," said Derek, not positive how to address the man or the four women sitting around the small conference table.

"It is our pleasure," the prince said in a friendly, but formal tone. "I have brought my legal team with me to listen and ask you a few questions. When and if the ladies are satisfied, we will decide whether to join with you and your company."

Derek passed out glossy information booklets to the five women. The ladies picked them up, but the prince left his on the table. Derek began to repeat a rote sales pitch—just like the other three days, but was interrupted, not with a voice, but a hand resting on his arm.

"Dear Mister Morris, I recall everything you told me the first time and have shared that with my staff," he said, smiling and nodding toward the brown-eyed beauties seated across from Derek. "What we would like to know is how my investment would be guaranteed?"

In all of his years of study in business and finance, and even in the construction business, he had never heard the word "guaranteed" used in any real sense. The nature of the business held risks, and no one he ever worked with spoke about guarantees except maybe the title companies. He swallowed hard, took a large gulp of water and looked across the table at the women. All four of the women were looking at him as though he was a strange, foreign animal in an exhibitor's glass cage.

He turned toward Assad and looking straight into his eyes said, "Only a hopeless dreamer would think there are any guarantees with high-yield investments. You know that, as well as I do. Rest assured that my team will do everything to make your money grow as quickly as possible. After all Abraham, I have my own money invested in TAG, and I plan on making a killing."

The stern face of the man deepened and then morphed into a sly grin. The women's eyes were directed toward Derek, but he could sense that their peripheral vision picked up their boss's change of mood and they all began to smile.

Later that day, riding in the cool comfort of the hotel's Rolls, he questioned his choice of the word "killing." He had read enough Daniel Silva novels to believe that the value of life in the Middle East was thought of in different terms than in the West.

He used the airplane's phone to place a call to Willow. He couldn't wait to relay the good news, but got only her voice mail. He still hated text messaging, so elected to wait. He called Dave's cell phone and again got voice mail. He was about to dial Tasha when he finally remembered that it was the middle of the night in California. He settled into his fine, Cordovan leather seat and fell soundly asleep. Next stop—Hong Kong.

Dave Morris had been through ten days of living hell. From the moment he heard about Foster needing his kidney, he felt like something was crushing his adrenal glands. Every time he had thought of actually going ahead with the transplant donation, his heart started racing, his breathing came in short gasps, and his bowels cramped and churned. He was in the middle of consulting with a patient and his mind wandered, losing track of the present conversation. Even at home he couldn't concentrate on the simplest tasks. He went to church on Sunday with a brown penny-loafer on one foot and a black one on the other. He put sugar on his eggs and Neosporin ointment on his toothbrush. He was used to excellent health, and worried that he would now become sickly or worse. No matter how hard he tried, he couldn't get the thoughts out of his mind, nor could he make himself back out of the commitment.

Once the basic plan for the transplant was agreed upon, he felt like he was on a slippery slide into an abyss. All of the stress and anxiety, however, was balanced by the millions of dollars involved and the guilt-trip Willow had given him. The other aspect of the conundrum was that he really liked Ned Foster, and didn't want him to die for lack of an available kidney. All of the alternatives had been carefully considered, including continuous dialysis, artificial kidneys, heterologous kidneys, and travel to Bangkok or New Dehli to buy a kidney on the black market. None had the potential for success for the billionaire like the donation of Dave's kidney.

Saying good-bye to his wife and kids in Phoenix had been hard for everyone but it was especially hard on Melody. The kids sensed something different this time about Daddy's business trip. They hadn't mentioned the money to the kids—not that it would have meant anything anyway—but they still sensed that Daddy was leaving for what seemed to them to be a long time. His last night at home with Melody had been bittersweet. No matter how hard they tried to ignore the inevitable, the potential of lasting negative effects or even worse, an unpredicted inter-operative or post-operative death, still hung in the air.

The flight to New York and the drive to Boston with

Brick were quickly forgotten, replaced immediately after the surgery by the pain in his flank, where the incision had been made and his kidney gently ripped from inside his previously normal, healthy body. Dave had encountered numerous Percocet and Oxycontin addicts over his short career who had developed their innocent habit following their orthopedic surgeries. There was no way he was going to let himself step into that trap. He decided that after the first post-op day he would just let himself suffer the pain. That had sounded good in theory, but his bravery rapidly faded the second day when he couldn't even sit up to drink water without unseen daggers stabbing his right flank.

It was Benjamin who saved him from the abyss of drug dependency. On the morning Dave returned to the Manhattan mansion, the stoic butler removed the pill bottle from Dave's bedside table and would only hand them out one at a time and only after a full discussion regarding the levels of Dave's pain. The man would never smile at Dave, but did give Brick a big grin on post-op day five when he ceremoniously poured the remaining pills into the toilet and announced, "The doctor won't be needing these now." He then removed a bottle of Advil from one pocket and a small crystal candy dish from the other and emptied the pills into the dish and set it on Dave's bedside table. "Enjoy," he said.

Melody and the children arrived in a black stretch limo on post-op day seven. Willow, although not ever actually visiting with Dave—she had remained in Boston with Foster—had given Mel daily e-mail updates as well as encouragement to remain in Arizona until her husband was "up and around."

"You look fantastic," Melody told her husband. "The kids are thrilled to see you." Though he wouldn't have known it, since after a thirty-second hug and kiss they were off to explore the four stories of the mansion, giving Benjamin a near-ulcer. They returned to Dave's room twenty minutes later insisting that their mom take them to the zoo in Central Park. "That old man told us it was lots of fun and we could spend all day looking at the lions and tigers and eating cotton candy."

"I've found a beautifully-furnished, three-bedroom apartment for you just six blocks from here," Debra told Melody later that day. Dave, Brick, and the girls had just finished a light meal and were watching the kids play in the mansion's great room on a real tiger rug complete with a real tiger's head with giant teeth. "It's only two buildings away from the one I found for Derek and Tasha. He's supposed to be back the first of the week and Tasha will bring the kids then. It will be just like living back home in our old neighborhood."

"What about you and Brick?" Melody asked.

"Willow insists that we stay here at the mansion, at least until Edward comes home from the hospital and everything gets back to normal … we'll just wait and see. I told you how lonely the hotel room got after a few days."

The words "back to normal" seemed to hang in the air like black smoke from a burning house fire. They all wondered when and if that would ever happen.

Edward Foster III would return to the mansion, but not in the style one would expect from a mogul of Wall Street. It happened without warning to the temporary residents of the mansion and its employees. No one had heard a word from Willow for two days—something Brick was getting used to. He had talked to Ned daily, but seldom spoke with him long enough to talk about anything except TAG, before the man would complain of fatigue and hang up.

Just before noon on the first Friday after Melody and the kids had temporarily moved into the mansion, the black stretch limo showed up. Melody had found a couple of small bedrooms on the mansion's third floor and had settled in until they could decide on an apartment. The Morris kids and Lexy were playing in the garden, being watched by Dave—still in his pajamas. Debra and Margo had gone to the grocery store to try to find food the kids would eat—brie and lox just weren't footing the bill. Brick was off to the Foster headquarters downtown to find more investors' names. Melody was in the shower, softly singing to herself, confident for the first time in months that Dave was going to recover and get back to normal. She heard a car horn honking through the bathroom window and then recognized Willow's raised voice as well.

"Benjamin, get down here immediately! Mister Foster is in the car and we need your help to get him into the house," she hollered through the open front door.

Within minutes the entire place was a beehive of confusion. Dave and the kids came in from the garden. They were carrying tree branches they had been using as swords, and Dave was struggling to hang on to the toddler.

Willow led the parade from the car, carrying three shopping bags from Saks and bossing everyone out of the way as Benjamin and the driver half-walked and half-carried Edward Foster III up the steps of the town house and into the entryway. They paused as the driver struggled up the steps with a collapsible wheelchair and finally got it opened and secured behind the peaked Foster. He was gently lowered into the chair and his feet lifted onto the foot rests.

"Welcome home Ned," said Dave, standing barefoot in striped pajamas and struggling to contain the wiggling Lexy. The Morris kids were hiding behind him, peeking out at the old, pale man sitting in the wheelchair frowning back at them.

Foster looked up at his kidney donor with barely a sense of recognition. Just as Dave was bending down to shake Ned's hand, Willow popped back out of the master bedroom and barked the order to keep the children at a distance from her husband.

"Don't shake his hand you idiot. You haven't washed your hands and are holding that filthy child."

Melody had come down the stairs into the hallway— her head wrapped in a towel and wearing a robe, with wet, bare feet dripping on the Persian rug. She started to speak out in protest at the insult to the baby, but took a deep breath instead and approached Foster.

"Welcome home, Ned," she said, bending down and giving him a kiss on the cheek. "What a wonderful surprise! None of us were expecting to see you back home so soon, but we are so glad you are here." As she released her arms from his slumped shoulders she glanced up—more like glared up—at Willow.

Dave already had fled to the upper floor with the kids leaving the two women facing off. Benjamin pushed the wheelchair toward the crackling fireplace. The driver had gone back to the car for more of the luggage.

"Where are Brick and Derek?" Willow demanded.

Melody looked at the overdressed woman and crossed her arms across her gaping robe, trying to control her voice. "Brick has gone downtown to work. I don't expect him back for a couple of hours. I'm not sure where you have sent Derek today. I don't keep his agenda."

"Why isn't he here? And where are the other wives? You should have all been here to greet Edward when we arrived." Her voice was not just angry, but condescending as well.

"Just hold on a minute. No one advised us that Mr. Foster was returning home today. The last I was told he was too ill to even have visitors. As a matter-of-fact, I haven't seen or spoken to you for days. Benjamin and Margo didn't mention his homecoming, but then I doubt that they were aware."

"You were all sent an e-mail memo this morning," Willow insisted. "It seems like the least you could do as houseguests is to stay abreast of the goings on."

"I'm very sorry that we didn't know. I'll call Brick and the 'other wives,' as you prefer to call Debra and Tasha. Debra and Margo should be here any minute. They are grocery shopping. Tasha and her kids are arriving in town today. Perhaps we can prepare a nice welcome home dinner for your husband," she said, trying to tame the conversation.

Willow didn't respond, but turned toward the study then paused in its doorway. "See that the children stay upstairs and don't make any excessive noise to disturb Edward and tell your husband when he gets home to remove his computer and papers from my desk. I need to work in here. They can use the dining room table."

Melody had tears in her eyes as she quickly ran up the two flights of stairs to find her kids and the baby. Dave was laying on the bed holding a toy in front of Lexy in one hand and his flank with the other.

"There you are sweetie," she said, picking up the baby. "Thanks for watching her, Dave. Are you hurting?"

"I just took the stairs a little too fast."

"Maybe it was all the weight from the filth from this child," she said sarcastically.

"Don't take anything she says personally," Dave said. "She lives in a different world than the rest of us. There's been a lot of pressure on her with the markets in the tank and trying to get TAG off the ground, let alone deal with Ned's illness."

"You sound like you like the woman," Melody said, sitting down on the edge of the double bed.

"I like Ned, and if he likes her, she must have some redeeming quality."

"Well I can't wait to get out of here now that Willow

is back. I was getting used to the place, but I know that this mansion is too small for the two of us, let alone the five of us. That rude display of her personality was enough for me. We need to find an apartment near Deb and Brick."

"My, but you two do look cozy," Willow said, standing in the bedroom doorway looking at Dave lying on the bed in his pajamas and his half-dressed wife sitting on the bed with Lexy close beside them. Before they could move or respond, she wheeled around and was gone.

Derek quickly was getting used to the luxurious lifestyle of the ultra-rich. The jet landing in Hong Kong was bumpy, but that was quickly forgotten when he was waved through customs and immigration, and found his luggage already on the cart of a driver wearing a navy-blue suit and a little, squatty drivers hat. The man smiled at Derek and held up a small card with his name neatly printed on it.

Five minutes later he was in the backseat of a pearl-white Bentley, speeding along the new airport's highway toward the most densely populated city in the world. Observing out the car window, he noted that the stark contrast between wealth and poverty was blatant. The doorman at the Peninsula Hotel led him past the desk straight to the hotel lounge, assuring him that after his refreshment, everything would be ready in his room—no checking in at this motel six.

In the lounge, he enjoyed a late lunch of lobster salad and blueberry gelato, and then he took the elevator to the twenty-eighth floor and found his suite. His clothes already had been ironed and put away and a steam bath was started. Next came a shave and haircut by the room service barber, then the steam bath was followed by a cool shower. As he dried off in the stadium-size bathroom he saw the message light flashing. Hopefully it was Tasha saying she and the kids had arrived in New York.

"You can't believe the day we had here," his wife explained when he returned her call. "Edward came home from the hospital in the morning and within two hours Willow had made everyone so mad that we all moved into a hotel. When Brick picked me and the kids up at the airport he was in panic mode. 'She's gone psycho on us,' was all he would tell me at first. Apparently, during the lunch that Margo had fixed for everyone on the patio, Willow marched out and started yelling at Dave's four year old, Emi, for having picked some of the flowers. This set Melody off and by two o'clock the whole place was in a cat fight. At one point Willow accused all three families of being a big commune and not even knowing whose kids were whose."

Derek stared into the phone, then back out through the window at the teaming city across the harbor. "So where are all of you now?" he asked, "the Waldorf?"

"Heck no! We're all crammed into three rooms at the Weston with a view of the side of the city bus building. Every hotel Brick tried was full because of some stupid bowling alley owner's convention. Brick tried to get Dave to stay at the mansion with him, but he was the angriest. I guess she made some insinuation about him and Melody being together with Lexy when they weren't fully dressed. Brick is ready to kill the woman, and here I thought she adored him and that he respected her."

"Why are you still up? It's got to be the middle of the night there," he said.

"It's a long story—the long flight then getting moved and settled in and feeding all of these kids was a challenge. I'm fine now. We'll all sleep in, and then go apartment hunting. How's the money harvest going?"

"It's like picking up pine cones in the forest. You just have to go to the base of the trees and the money is lying around like some unnecessary refuse. The people I met in Dubai make more money in a day than we could ever make in a lifetime. I have a check in the briefcase for €25 million—not dollars, and that Arab guy has three cousins who also want to throw their money into TAG, but they just need to sell some wives or oil wells or camels first. I can't remember which."

This brought a loud laugh from his wife who made one of the kids stir and ask for a drink of water.

"So what are you doing in China?" she asked, while getting water in a plastic cup from the bathroom sink.

"I'm meeting some casino mogul here this evening who is taking me to Macau in his helicopter. He is the friend of a man in Dubai and already has been involved with Foster in some type of construction fundraising project. These people all love Ned. None of them are too fond of Willow. According to the prince, they all call her 'the snake.' They say she crawled into Ned's life and wrapped herself around his little finger or some part of his body. A lot of the time I don't quite get what they are saying. They think they are speaking English, but it is half a planet away from our accent."

Tasha laughed again, and then gave her husband a warning to be careful and to call her when it was daytime in New York.

"I love you sweetheart," he said, feeling a sudden sense of loneliness in the big luxurious room. "I sure wish you were here with me right now."

The next twelve hours were some of the most interesting and frightening Derek had ever experienced. A shiny, black helicopter landed on the roof of the Peninsula just before sunset. A bellman had escorted Derek up to the helicopter pad. He was dressed in a rented tux and felt like a fool on his way to a Halloween party. When his host wasn't in the chopper, Derek almost turned around to go back to the room.

"Put on these headphones and tighten your harness, the winds can be a little harsh over the water," said the pilot of the MD helicopter. He wasn't exaggerating about the bumpy ride, and flying mere hundreds of feet above the ocean added to the thrill. By the time Derek saw the light of the massive casino hotels he was feeling nauseated, and his temples were throbbing right along with the helicopter's blades.

From the air the skyline of Macau looked like a bigger and brighter Las Vegas. The helipad at the Venetian Macau Hotel was attended to not by normal-looking porters, but by tall, beautiful women in silk, split-leg dresses and spike heels. Derek was led by one of the ladies to a glass elevator that descended two floors to a private roof garden. There he was shown into a red velvet-lined room where he found six men playing baccarat. They stood and politely introduced themselves. The only name Derek remembered was a Mr. Stanley

Ho, who he later learned was one of the richest men in Hong Kong.

Derek was served a drink and asked to join the gambling, but declined. He sat at a side table watching them play hands where $10,000 chips were tossed about like children's toys. He marveled at the total lack of emotion of the losers. The winners often smiled or shouted an exclamation of joy, but the losers just shrugged or sat quietly, sliding out more of the square plastic chips to stay in the game. Within a short time, millions had passed back and forth across the table.

Two of the men, Ho and a Mr. Chee, finally excused themselves from the game and motioned for Derek to follow them into a private dining room where he was introduced to a Mr. Chen, who apparently was waiting for the three men. He was stout, bald, and apparently half blind with wrinkled, weathered skin and narrow, dark eyes distorted by very thick, wireless-rim glasses. He was at least twenty years older that Ho and Chee. Unlike the tuxedo-clad men at the gaming table, he was dressed in a conservative dark suit and no tie. His diamond-studded cufflinks were the only hint of wealth. He invited Derek to sit at the table. Immediately, a hidden door opened and a parade of waiters began loading the round table with platters of food, the identity of which Derek couldn't recognize. Being a good sport, he tried most of the dishes, finding that even the fish, with its head still on and eyes gazing up at him, was quite tasty. The four of them ate in relative silence, and Derek was doing fine until Mr. Ho insisted that Derek have more of one of the dishes he already had tried and nearly gagged on.

"This is very delicious and interesting," he said. "What exactly is this?"

"Sweet and sour duck tongues," Ho said with a grin. "Take many ducks to make."

That was when Derek lost it. His long ignored stomach did a reflex reversal, barely giving him time to stand and rush from the room. Fortunately, one of the waiters read his mind and opened the door to the adjacent restroom. Ten minutes later he was back at the table with an empty stomach and what would probably be a life-long aversion to Asian food.

At about midnight, the men adjourned into a small conference room and the business meeting began. Derek was given the floor to explain TAG and the potential its inceptor held for its future.

"And how is our friend Edward Foster?" one of the men asked. "We were told that he has been ill."

"He's doing great!" Derek exaggerated. "As a matter of fact, he's back home and ready to go back to work. His first task will be to sign the papers on the properties he intends to buy for the investment group." He was hoping no one would ask details about the London property Willow supposedly had made a deposit on.

He went on to explain the structure of the investment and how additional money could be made by the investors by bringing their friends into the partnership. He never mentioned the word pyramid, but wondered if these savvy businessmen weren't reading his mind. By 2:00 a.m., he had a verbal commitment from one of the men—Mr. Chen—for $30 million. They promised to invite other friends into the partnership and from the appearance of their dress and the bling they wore, Derek had no doubt that he had just made a huge score.

"Enough work for one night," said Chen and arose from the table motioning Derek to follow. They entered another elevator and within seconds were on the main casino where Chen was met by four beautiful, young, silk-and-jewel-clad women, who immediately latched onto the two men's arms. Fearing what might come next when one of the women began stroking his fingertips, Derek leaned close to Chen's ear.

"I must apologize, but I have meetings tomorrow and need to get back to my hotel. Would it be possible to have the pilot fly me back now?"

Chen looked at him like he had gone crazy. "What? You don't like Asian hospitality. Surely you can spend a few hours with your new friends. The night is still young."

"Actually, I'm feeling ill and must insist on going back to the Peninsula."

Chen barked an order to the beauty clinging to Derek's right arm and she left. Two minutes later two burly-looking security men made their way through the crowd, and after whispering with Chen, motioned for Derek to follow.

"Would it be possible to see you tomorrow?" Derek asked, but Chen already was casting dice onto a roulette table and ignored the question. When he asked a second time, Chen turned to him and smiled.

"I will be off to Bali tomorrow Mr. Morris," Chen said. "But, my secretary will bring my check to your hotel tomorrow and you can be on your way back to your family. I apologize for the rudeness of my lady friends. They were just doing their job."

He was led through another maze of hallways and elevators and moments later he was standing on a windy rooftop watching the helicopter approach the building. By the time he could see the skyline of Hong Kong, dawn was lighting up the eastern sky.

Motion sick and beyond exhausted, he peeled off his clothes and collapsed onto the turned-back bed. He felt something hard against his face but was too tired to reach his arm up to discover what it was. He was in bed less than three hours when the phone rang.

Derek strained to sit up on the edge of the bed and was finally able to reach the phone. Natasha's voice sounded like it was at the end of a long tunnel. She reiterated how she had arrived in New York in the middle of turmoil and confusion with everyone mad— mostly at Willow. The three wives moving into the hotel with the kids had been a circus, initiating at least three calls from the front desk requesting a reduction in noise.

Still in a stupor, Derek had reached up to scratch his cheek and found a sticky liquid stuck to it. *I'm bleeding*, he immediately thought. He rushed to the bathroom stumbling over his shoes on the way. Once in-front of the mirror with the lights turned on, he saw the foil wrapping of a Godiva chocolate melted and smeared on his cheek and ear.

All this time his wife was telling her story of the plane trip from Phoenix and the kids' activities and then she dropped the bomb. "Did I tell you that Michael Pierson's daughter and husband who were going to stay in our house are being transferred to Chicago?"

"So who will watch the house and pool and feed

Winston?" he asked, trying to wipe the dark chocolate from his face.

"That's just it. There's no one, and they are leaving next Monday. They didn't even move in," she said.

"Well, I'm sure we can find somebody …."

"We won't need to. I'm taking the kids back to Phoenix. This is no place to raise a family. I don't know why I let you talk us into it in the first place."

"But sweetheart, we're committed to work for TAG and that means—"

"You're committed to work for TAG. There is no way that I'm going to live in the same town with Willow and play nursemaid to your friend Ned," she said, cutting him off in mid-sentence for the second time.

"I thought you had made plans with Debra and Mel to see the East Coast and visit all the historical sites?" he asked, finally getting his eyes open and realizing that this conversation was pivotal to his business plans. "I need to be back there where the money is to help grow the TAG business."

"There is lots of money in California and Arizona. You can let Brick handle the East Coast and that woman. The kids and I are going home to Arizona. We'd like you to join us. We love you and miss you, but there is more to life than the money."

After she hung up, her words kept playing over and over in his pounding head. "We'd like you to join us." He filled the tub and sank into the scalding water, trying to erase the headache and stiff joints. It had been over a week since he had ridden his bike or even swam his usual twenty laps in his pool. Half an hour of soaking and a cool shower and he began to feel normal.

When he found himself going through the mini-bar he remembered why he was so hungry—he had tossed his dinner. Twenty minutes later he was shaved, dressed, and at the breakfast buffet in the elaborate dining room. He made a circle around the room looking at a variety of strange foods. *How could these people eat this stuff?* The smell alone of the boiled fish and steamed meat dumplings nearly turned him away. He finally settled on some generic brand of Frosted Flakes and a banana and ordered an omelet. At least they had good fruit.

He was making good progress on his meal when a woman, holding a filled plate in each hand, stopped at his table. "Do you mind if I join you?"

He glanced around the dining room and though there were a few other open places, the room was getting filled up and his table was set for four.

"Absolutely," he said, making a gesture to stand—just like his mother had taught him. He pulled out her chair and helped her be seated.

She didn't make any effort to converse at first, but as he was finishing his cereal she asked where he was from.

"Arizona—in the United States," he said.

"You wouldn't happen to be with the Foster Group, would you?"

Derek studied the woman for the first time. She was in her mid-forties, with dark, auburn hair; smooth, tanned skin; and turned out like a role model for a middle-age super mom. Her watch and jewelry were elegant, but not extravagant. Her clothes were tailored, and he now noticed that her hair had just a hint of blond highlighting. As she spoke she didn't look him in the eye at first, letting her eyes dart around the room as though on the lookout for something.

"My name is Trent—Ashlyn Trent," she said, extending her manicured hand.

"Derek Morris," he said, reciprocating and at the same time feeling that he was being set up. There was no way that this was a coincidence. Her bony hand was ice cold and now, when she looked at him, her eyes were equally frigid. "How did you guess that I'm connected with Mr. Foster?"

"I'm nosy," she said, giving him a smile that was more of a smirk. "I'm acquainted with Edward and also with his wife—at the least I could pick her out of a lineup."

"And why would she be in a lineup?" he asked without thinking about the implication of the question or her possible answer.

"Just a figure of speech—nothing intended. I was told that he wasn't doing well. Is he dead yet?"

The question made Derek choke on his orange juice. He managed not to spray any of it, but needed a minute to recover. When he finally caught his breath and was able to take a sip of water, he looked directly at the woman and asked, "Why would you think he is dying?"

"It's quite simple, my dear man, the wife—Willow—is killing him, so she can have it all. Why else would she marry the rich, old fool?"

Foster's medical history flashed through Derek's mind, the first kidney transplant with Willow being the donor, and the physical specimen of a man who had given him and the others a run for their money on the mountain bike trail—he was hardly an old fool.

"The rumor mill must be overactive," he replied. "Edward is home, nearly back to his normal vigorous health, and Mrs. Foster is hard at work on a new project."

"Well, it must be nice to be young and full of naive confidence. I suppose he has you out sniffing out new investors. I hope you'll be smart enough to only accept money from the weak and stupid. The last young hustler Willow sent out on the quest for investors got mixed up with the wrong crowd and disappeared."

Derek needed to hear more of the woman's story, but she took a long, last drink of her coffee then stood without warning. Before he could slide his heavy chair out to stand, she had waved farewell and headed for the exit.

He settled back into the chair and pondered the experience. *Willow trying to kill Ned for his money? A previous salesman disappeared? She's smoking something illegal.* He finished his breakfast feeling a knot growing in his stomach.

His flight back to New York wasn't until early evening. He had been told about tailors who could make a wonderful new suit for a person in just a few hours at a bargain price, so he walked out to the busy street and set out to find one. A tip from one of the bellmen headed him toward the Hyatt and the arcade of businesses in its basement.

The shop was the size of his kid's bedroom at home, but smelled of new fabric and was filled with the staccato chatter of men fitting and trying on clothes. Within half an hour he had picked out a wonderful navy wool pinstripe for a suit and a lightweight mohair material for a black blazer. The salesman, who had to stand on a worn chair to measure Derek, promised that both the suit and the blazer would be ready by five o'clock. As he left the shop and found his way to the street, he saw Ms. Trent. She was getting into a black Mercedes limo. The man holding the door was the same stocky guy who had met Derek at the hotel the night before to lead him to the rooftop heliport.

Without thinking he ran toward the car arriving in time to knock on the rear passenger window. The car started to pull forward then stopped and the window went down.

"Hi, it's me, Derek, from the restaurant. Sorry to intrude, but I was wondering if you had any suggestions of what to see here in Hong Kong? I've got several hours to kill before my flight."

"Why don't you get in," she said, this time giving him a smile, which he thought was sincere.

Ashlyn gave instructions to the driver, and then pressed a button which raised the smoked-glass partition behind the man's head. The car pulled into the dense traffic and turned toward a road sign indicating a tunnel. Derek was getting used to the soft leather and rich smell of the world's most expensive cars, but wasn't used to the idea of being in the backseat alone with a mysterious woman. When the car descended into the tunnel under Hong Kong Harbor and the light grew dim, he began to question his impulsive dash toward her car.

When the car dropped him off in front of the Hyatt, six hours later, he was a much wiser man. He felt he knew the island and the city like a tourist guide, and he felt like he had just received a crash course in the world of international finance. Ashlyn was a shrewd and cunning businesswoman, who happened to have an MBA from Wharton's School of Finance and fifteen years of running international hedge funds. Her identical twin, Haley, whom they had met at an exclusive British club for a late lunch, was a vice president for Scudders and ran its Pacific Rim mutual funds. The women had homes in the Hamptons, Tokyo, Paris, and a permanent suite at the Peninsula.

When they said farewell, the woman first offered her hand, then leaned across the seat and gave Derek a kiss on the cheek. "It's a European thing," she said, but still left him feeling guilty, not because he didn't like it, but because he was storing up all of the stories of the trip to share with Tasha, and wasn't so sure he could share this one without hurting her feelings.

The light on the bed stand telephone was flashing when he returned to the room. He hung his new suit and blazer on the silent butler and punched the message button.

"Derek, I've been trying your cell phone for hours. You must keep it charged and on audible at all times," Willow's voice commanded. "Something has come up and I need you to change you flight plans. I need you to meet with a new investor in Bucharest. I tried to get the man to come here to New York, but he has some kind of visa problem. Call me as soon as you get this message."

Derek wasn't sure whether she had said "Bucharest" or "Budapest." *Where is Bucharest?* He dialed her cell number and she answered immediately. He started to protest having to take another diversion in his travels, but was cut off before he could utter a word.

"The man's name is Nikoli Constantini. He owns real estate all over Romania. He was a former assistant chief of something or other in the old communist government. When it fell apart, he ended up with a lot of office buildings and farmland. He and his brother have cash and lots of it, but have trouble getting it out of the country. He heard about TAG from an investor here named Armon Dupree. Apparently, Mr. Constantini wants us to trade some of our assets for some of his. It could be a sweet deal for us—maybe buying quality real estate for twenty cents on the dollar."

"That sounds like a ridiculous idea to me. I have been telling the investors that we deal strictly in cash," Derek said. "I've heard about the grab-fest that went on in all of the communist countries right after the Berlin Wall was torn down. Romania was one of the worst. The man sounds like another of the Russian mafia moguls. I don't think we want to get mixed up with them, and I can't imagine getting any New York investors excited about owning real estate in Romania."

"Well, we need a real estate presence in Europe— just like we have told our investors that we already have. A couple of office buildings with nice pictures of international signs on their buildings would go a long way in convincing our friends that we are for real," she said. "Constantini claims that he has a twelve-story building in the north part of town near the airport with a big Coca-Cola sign on the top."

"I think I'm too tired to meet with anyone again on this trip and my wife needs me to help with the kids for a few days," he protested. As she was speaking he was peeling off his clothes and filling the tub.

Acting like she hadn't even heard him she started giving instructions. "I've had your flight changed to a direct flight to Athens. There is a connection there to Bucharest. You can be there by noon. The travel agent has you booked into a hotel and your meeting is at ten tomorrow morning. Check your e-mail for your itinerary, and call me when you finish the meeting."

"How's Ned?" he was able to interject before she hung up.

"Edward is fine. He is at home, as I'm sure you know, and your families are fat and happy. Now, forget about what is going on here and make a deal with Constantini. Your e-mail will contain the bargaining guidelines you need to follow. Remember your old real estate catch phrase: location, location, location."

Before he could mention again that the actual country might make a difference, she had hung up. Four hours later in the dead of night he was chasing a full moon westward. He tried to sleep on the flight but his body's biorhythm was so totally confused that all he could do was worry.

Dave Felshaw awoke from another nightmare. At first he didn't know where he was, and when he did recognize the surroundings of the mansion's bedroom, he felt a sense of panic at the situation he had gotten himself into. It was over a week since his right kidney had been removed, and he was still feeling like crap. His incision had healed well enough thus far, needing only a light dressing to protect the tender, red scar, but the muscles beneath the skin felt like they were being seared with a branding iron. The after effects of the pain medication were still tormenting his sleep with strange and frightful dreams. He had never been able to remember his dreams until this past week. As though the nightmares weren't bad enough, now he had to spend the nights alone in the mansion with relative strangers.

"Maybe if you would clean up, put on some clothes, and give Brick a hand with the calls you'd feel better," Willow suggested to Dave at breakfast, after listening to his complaints. It was a rare appearance for her. Benjamin had helped Ned get dressed and into a wheelchair. Ned cleaned up really well, and yet he was barely able to feed himself without pain meds on board.

"He's not sleeping well," Brick said, coming to his

best friend's defense. "His pitching in with the work can wait until he feels up to it. I've got an extensive list of our neighbors and friends in Arizona, and have been real successful getting their attention. Dave can start back on his medical school classmates in a few days when he's feeling better."

Melody and Debra had moved to a new hotel with the kids; Natasha had repacked her bags and was flying home to Phoenix that morning. Usually, at this time of day, Brick was sequestered in the office burning up the phone lines cold-calling his never-ending list of contacts.

"I just think if he gets his mind on something else, he'll feel better," Willow said, backing off little. "Look at Edward. He's up and around. He's doing better every day. Aren't you, darling?"

Foster gave her a glassy-eyed look and started to speak, but took a shaky sip of coffee instead, spilling part of it as he replaced his cup in the saucer.

"So Willow," Brick said, "by my calculations and the e-mails I received from Derek, TAG has a gross balance of over $100 million. I need you to get the list of purchased properties to me so I can start some investment versus return charts. Most of my contacts want something visual to help them make their decisions. The story I tell them sounds great, but a nice, color pie chart showing some profitable sales would go a long way to quelling their fears."

"We've been working on some new purchases this week," she said, diverting the question.

Brick didn't like her answer, or the way she had been riding Dave. "The quarterly return payments for our first group of investors are just around the corner. We need the records on the purchases and the sales. Didn't you say one of the guys at the Foster Building was in charge of re-sales? You've never given me the guy's name."

She looked first at Brick and Dave, then finally at her husband and back to Brick. "You just do your fundraising job and let me worry about the sales and quarterly payments, and get your friend here well enough to pitch in. The money is already in the bank to make the quarterly payments. Profits from real estate are not like your pork belly trades. Inspections, court recordings, appraisals, and closings all take time. But the profits are huge. You'll be very surprised a year from now, when your buddies back in the Arizona desert will think you're some kind of King Midas with a golden touch," she said, laughing at her lame analogy.

Her rare touch of levity brought a polite smile to everyone's face. Even Ned seemed to clear his brain from the drugs in his system long enough to smile and make a comment. "You boys need to trust in this woman. She has made hundreds of millions for our clients the last ten years. Just because she's beautiful doesn't mean she can't be ruthless when it comes to money."

Dave gave Brick a glance and then pushed his chair away from the table. *"Ruthless" pegs her personality to the wall.*

The rest of the day went by without much drama. Brick kept working and Dave slept a couple of hours, and then tried to climb the stairs a few times to build up his strength. The two wives came to dinner at the mansion that night. The entire spread was prepared and delivered by a gourmet, home delivery service. It was served by Margo and Benjamin. The meal had been pleasant and the two empty places for Ned and Willow were offered to Margo and Benjamin. Of course they refused the invitation to join the group.

"Mr. Foster is taking dinner in his bedroom and the Mrs. won't be joining you," was the only explanation given.

The children had been relatively well-behaved and the food was scrumptious. Little of the day's earlier discussion had been shared with the wives until Dave and Melody were alone.

"Well, at least he got the ruthless part right," Melody said to her husband as she tucked him in bed and he told her about the breakfast discussion. Dave was still staying in the mansion, surrounded by all of his medical trappings. "I've got to go sweetheart. Debra was waiting downstairs for the cab to take us to the hotel."

"I'm going to try and get dressed in the morning so I can go to the Foster building with Brick. We're going to meet two of the managers of Foster Ltd. to pick their brains. Willow wants me to take over the public relations for TAG," Dave said. "That should be fodder for a good laugh. She says it won't be any different than trying to sell a hip replacement to someone's grandmother."

"Well, see if you can get by without taking so many Advil tonight, and maybe you'll feel more energetic tomorrow. By the way, don't call the hotel until after one. Deb and I are taking the kids over to the new apartments first thing in the morning to try to decide what furniture we want to ship from home and what we should buy. Willow told Deb to just buy whatever we thought we needed and send her the bill, but I want some of my own things here from home and the kids need their playthings."

"So Natasha is staying in Arizona for sure?" Dave asked for the third or fourth time.

"That's what she claims. Her kids are older and are more attached to their friends, and she says she can't stand the city noise, let alone Willow and all the confusion. I think part of it is the way the woman bosses Derek and Brick around. Tasha thinks it's demeaning to them and doesn't want to be here to listen to it."

"Everything will be better when we get moved in the apartment and I'm back to full health," he reassured his wife. "Now how about a little kiss?"

"Don't you surgeons ever say 'please?'" she asked in a playful tone, giving him a little more than he asked for.

Derek had his face plastered against the airplane window as the Boeing 767 made its approach to the Bucharest airport. He would never understand why someone would want the aisle seat with people crawling over you, and the flight attendants brushing by every few minutes. He was expecting to see horse carts on dirt roads and oxen pulling plows in the fields, but instead saw clusters of industrial buildings and new highways under construction. Once on the ground he was met by a driver in a shiny, black Audi sedan and taken to a fancy new Ramada Inn just a few miles from the airport. There he was shown to a large, well-appointed room to refresh before his afternoon meeting. He was astonished at the relative level of prosperity in the north end of the city, with the only visible stigma of the previously oppressive communist regime being the numerous stark-looking, "block" apartments lining the main roads and the ornate government buildings. Later, riding in the car, they got closer to the downtown area where statues of past heroes and war monuments filled nearly every intersection.

"Who owns all of the apartments and office buildings?" he asked his two hosts that afternoon. The three men were sitting on the patio of an exclusive, private club on the edge of one of the city's parks. The two Romanians could have been brothers. Both were in their early forties, tall, dark, and quite handsome. Both were dressed in tailored suits with crisp, black shirts and solid-colored ties. Neither asked if he minded their smoking, nor did they ever stop—lighting each rancid-smelling cigarette off of the previous one. Luckily for Derek, a gentle breeze blew away most of the smoke, allowing him to breathe.

"None of the buildings or land we represent ever belonged to the old communist party. It was all private. The buildings all have been built since our democracy began. Individuals and some companies like yours make up the major ownership," the taller of the men told him. He did remember that neither of them was named Constantini like Willow had said.

Derek had missed the correct pronunciation of their names, and though they had given him business cards when they picked him up at the hotel, he had been shy about staring at them until now. He laid the cards on the tablecloth and read them carefully.

"So Alexi," Derek asked the quieter of the two, "what do you think is the best investment here in Bucharest at the moment, land or commercial buildings?"

"That would depend on how much money you want to invest. For a few million we can show you some nice pieces of commercial land in the growing north part of the city. For several millions, we have available a fantastic new office building which is 60 percent leased out and will double in value when it is completed," Leonardo answered.

Derek looked at the man and tried to read his intention, but found only a cold stare masked by a cloud of smoke. He turned his attention toward his soup and salad and pondered the situation. These two men had to be some of the winners in the land grab of the early nineties when the Communist Party collapsed, leaving ownership to the first or fittest to claim it. Neither of them struck him as being overly bright, but definitely they were rich, greedy, and wanted to expand their wealth.

"Well, let's see what you've got."

Sitting on the edge of the hotel bed eight hours later, waiting for Willow to answer his call, he couldn't help but wonder if he was in a trap. The properties he had seen were a far cry from the type of investment he thought TAG should be making. The so-called "new" buildings were at least ten or fifteen years old, still not completely finished, and were in locations no respectable international company would touch. The nice, really new buildings they had passed near his hotel—the ones with Sony or Intel or Marriott signs on their fronts—were dismissed as too expensive or not for sale. As for the raw land, the parcels he was shown were distant from any active development, and needed complete infrastructure brought to them before any type of development could occur.

When Derek didn't act all that interested, his Romanian hosts became somewhat abusive; claiming he was wasting their time. To placate them he had them return to one of the buildings, a twelve-story office building with an insurance company as its primary tenant. The only Coca-Cola sign he spotted was painted on a vintage vending machine in the lobby. As they walked through the building, floor by floor, he couldn't help but notice stained restroom doors with broken hinges and rat droppings swept into the corners. Also, there were obvious vacancies on every floor.

"I'll have to put in a call to my partner, and let you know in the morning," he had told the men when they dropped him back at the hotel. They had named a starting price of $25 million, and wanted cash and a quick closing to make the deal go down at that price.

"You need to act quickly," Alexi said, blowing smoke out the open car window. "These kind of bargains don't come up every day."

"This is not where we want to leave our investor's money," Derek explained to Willow, hoping the room hadn't been bugged. "I know used car salesmen in Phoenix that I'd rather invest our millions in than these guys. There is no way for an outsider to know whether the leases or even the titles to these properties are valid. I wouldn't put it past these two to take the money and skip the country. The whole place gives me the creeps. The common people look like hard-working, honest folk, and the women are beautiful, but these business guys are downright scary."

"I didn't send you to them to become golfing buddies," she said. "They were recommended by some of my best clients who already have made major investments in the country. Ask them to show you one of their remodeled apartment buildings tomorrow, and tell them we won't go over $20 million for the insurance building."

Derek was astonished. He couldn't believe that she was actually going to insist that he leave TAG's money—some of it supposedly his money—in this city with no more guarantee than the word of one of her unnamed clients. He tried to go to sleep without drugs, but resorted to an Ambien at 2:00 a.m.

When he came down to breakfast, Alexi and Leonardo already were there, sitting in a cloud of smoke and smiling.

"Good morning my friend," Alexi said, giving Derek's hand a vigorous shake. "We have a busy day planned for you. You get some breakfast and we'll be off to see the best places in our city. We have saved the best for today."

By noon he had a splitting headache and was sure he was in the process of perforating an ulcer. The "best" properties turned out to be more aging dogs, just like the day before and try as he might to like them, all he could see were piles of concrete with peeling paint and chipped floors. The elevator in one of the apartment buildings—an eight-story one at that—didn't even work. After climbing to the sixth floor, he stopped the procession and feigned knee pain.

When they took him back to the hotel in mid-afternoon, Derek was resolved to buy nothing. He didn't care what pressure Willow or anyone else put on him, he was not going to commit his investors' and friends' money in Romania. He agreed to a meeting with Alexi and Leonardo for the next day, and then went to his room where he quickly went online and booked a flight out of Romania for that night.

He didn't bother checking out of the hotel for fear someone at the desk would call the locals, but took his rolling bag out a back door and caught a cab on the side street. At the airport he checked in and immediately went through security, then found a corner out of sight of the main waiting room. He was the first in line to board the plane to Vienna—the only flight he could get on that night. Not until the plane was in the air and had pulled up its landing gear did he take a deep breath.

Three hours later he was checked into the Vienna Hilton Hotel. He ordered room service then filled the tub with scalding water and sank into its comforting cocoon just as his cell phone rang. He hoped it would be Natasha, but when he saw Willow's name pop up on the phone's screen he ignored it. He had redirected his whole life's work because of the woman's insistence, but he was firm in his resolve not to redirect his integrity.

Brick and Dave took a yellow cab downtown to the Foster Building. Dave was moving slowly, but felt the acceleration of his spirit to be dressed and involved in the hustle and bustle of New York's financial district. Once in the building, they were escorted to a suite of offices on the mezzanine floor where a room was set up for them. A cute blond "temp" secretary was at the desk outside the door, anxiously twirling a pencil and waiting for instructions to do something for her new bosses—anything but sit and twirl.

"Liz, this is my partner Doctor Felshaw," Brick said, "Dave, this is Liz. Mrs. Foster has assigned her to help us with anything we need here in the main office. She has worked on the other floors in other departments so knows her way around the building. Right, Liz?"

"Exactly, Mr. Wahl. I have all of the duplicate files you e-mailed me on the TAG investors. They are in the rolling file holder by your conference table. I set up the laptop that the guy in finance sent down but it doesn't seem to be working very well. The spreadsheets are already copied to the documents folder. I hope they are still there."

She turned to Dave. "Is there anything else I can get for you? Coffee? Sodas? Anything?"

"Nothing for now, thanks, Liz. It's nice to meet you," he said to the young woman. He wandered around the nearly-empty room, and placed his briefcase on the table. He was anxious for her to leave so he could start the stream of questions for Brick that were filling his head.

Once she was gone, the two TAG owners took seats at the desk and Dave opened his briefcase and took out his laptop. There was little else inside. "Well, where do we start?"

"That's the problem," Brick said. "We start from the beginning. So far all I have been able to learn about the Foster Company is that this whole building is full of people who work for Foster's corporation, which is now owned by the public. Ned and Willow are supposedly major stockholders, but the board and the CEO really run everything. They are not about to allow us access to anything except this room and the water cooler. As far as they are concerned we are arm's-length renters here. I've tried to ask around but have found only a couple of the senior guys who have even heard of TAG."

"I guess that makes sense," Dave said. "Ned told us from the beginning that this was something new and separate. I guess we just didn't know how separate. So what's in the files that you have?"

Brick opened the metal top of the long, rolling, file drawer, revealing about fifty red, yellow, and blue manila folders. "You know all the calls we made and all the time I have spent since your surgery?"

Dave nodded, although he didn't really remember too much about the last couple of weeks. Even the last few days had some blank spaces in his memory. He guessed it was from all the medication he had been taking.

"Well, everything we have done is right here and on a spreadsheet on the laptop. I have duplicates of the hard copies back at the mansion. All of the records of the money we collected from your doctor friends, the records of the shares that Ned gave us the night of the first dinner, and all of the money Willow supposedly has collected is right here. Also, there is a list of supposed former clients of Foster's company who I've been trying to cold call. So, in three weeks we only have collected money for ten or twelve shares at a hundred grand each. Ned told me the investors were lining up to buy, but since he got sick, they all seem to have backed off. Willow assures me she has collected lots more, but the files don't bear that out. I don't know whether she exaggerates or lies or just can't remember."

"So where is the money? The millions that Willow said she already collected and the million and a half that my partners and the other docs put in?" Dave asked, starting to get a little red in the face.

"Oh, it's in the bank. She uses a bank in the Caymans. I've seen the statement. There is nearly $20 million there, but it's mostly committed on new property. Derek claims he picked up over $30 million in Dubai and another $30 million in Hong Kong. The problem is that I can't get Willow to send me copies of the investor's checks or the deeds, or even the closing reports on the properties that she has supposedly purchased before we came on the scene."

"I thought that the profit from the sale of property was the guarantee for the cash investors put in, and was to pay their six-month profit payment. If nothing sells then where will the money come from to pay the new investors their profit?"

"Now you are seeing the problem. Derek has been racing all over the world, while you have been sick as a dog. Ned is still sick, and if you ask me, isn't going to get much better, and Willow is like a shadow. One minute she is there and the next minute a cloud rolls overhead and she has disappeared. I'm starting to get calls from curious investors—did you know that I'm the CEO of TAG and that you are now the Secretary Treasurer? Foster's and Willow's names don't even appear on the new letterhead she had made up and had hand-delivered yesterday."

Dave was starting to get a headache. He waved through the glass partition at Liz and when she came in they sent her for a couple Cokes and some Advil. Brick went on to explain the mechanics of how they processed the investor's money and how the spreadsheet worked. His cell phone rang a few times with routine questions, and then Derek called.

"It's about time you guys woke up and went to work," he chided. He was on his way to diner in Vienna. "How are things going in the Big Apple?"

"Can you believe that our malingerer is finally dressed and sitting beside me at the Foster Building? He says he wants to go to work, but I think it's just so he can check out the girls here at the office."

"Put your phone on speaker, I need to bring you two up to date on my Romanian adventure."

Brick and Dave stared at the phone as Derek detailed his last couple of days. By the time he told of sneaking out of Bucharest like a criminal on the lam, they were both biting their fingernails.

"She really told you to buy a building for $20 million?" Brick asked in an incredulous tone. "I don't think we have $20 million liquid until you get your new investor's money deposited … unless of course, she has raised money without telling me."

"I still have the checks from Dubai and Hong Kong that are a lot more than $20 million, but spending this money on anything less than a sure thing would be out of the question. I must say that I found it odd that neither of the new investors would agree to bank transfers and insisted on checks."

As the conversation went on, more questions were raised. When Derek described the characters he had met in the Middle East and in China, neither Brick nor Dave could sit still any longer. Both were up pacing the room, firing questions at the phone on the table and getting answers that just raised more questions.

"So where is she right now?" Derek asked.

"We haven't seen her for several days. The only people who know anything about her are Margo and Benjamin. All they'll reveal is that she won't be to dinner or that she ordered this or that for Ned's breakfast. I guess she's in town, but it's hard to see a ghost," said Brick.

"I have a flight to JFK tomorrow midday so I'll see you at the mansion when I arrive. I'll call when I'm on the ground. I'm only going to stay part of the day, and then I'm flying to Phoenix to see my family."

Brick and Dave could feel the silence in the room when the phone went dead. After a couple of minutes, Brick gathered up some of the papers they had been studying and started to re-file them. Dave was rubbing his flank and staring out the window when the door opened.

Dave could smell her perfume first, before he slowly turned toward the woman.

"Hello boys," Willow said. "I'm glad I caught you here. I have a whole list of things I want you to do."

"Not until you answer a few questions," Dave said, motioning her toward a chair.

Two hours later the trio left the glass-walled office space and exited the building. Willow's driver pulled up to the curb and the three got into the car. Dave's headache and surgery site pain were temporarily gone, and the circles under Brick's eyes seemed to have disappeared. She dropped them off at their wives' hotel, with the promise that the car would be back for them and their families at six. She refused to tell them what else she had in mind for them but made a big deal about a surprise she had in-store for the trio.

"After the party," she teased.

The long, black limo arrived as promised, whisking them to the front door of the Foster's mansion. The entrance was decorated with pink balloons and large, white bows. Inside the place was similarly decorated and music was playing. The dining room table was set with the finest china, and fresh flowers were in vases everywhere. It didn't take long to figure out that it was Willow's birthday and she was throwing herself a party.

The meal was served promptly upon their arrival and was eaten amid laughter and joking. Ned was wheeled to the table and was the most alert and affable the Arizona guests had seen him since weeks before the surgery. The children behaved like angels, and even Lexy had honored the birthday girl by giggling and smiling throughout dinner.

After the main meal, the table was cleared by a staff of caterers and reset with an extensive buffet of finger food, and a cocktail bar in the corner was prepared to serve the next wave of guests.

At eight, the front door was opened wide and more guests began to arrive. It was soon apparent that the Wahl and the Morris families were underdressed for the rest of the evening, so they made an exit for the hotel. At the last minute Dave grabbed his shaving kit, whispering to Benjamin that he was spending the night at the hotel. He was exhausted and his flank pain had returned.

"Why didn't you tell me it was her birthday?" Melody asked as the limo pulled away from the mansion. The kids had the sun roof open and were standing on the seats, hollering at the passersby.

"She didn't tell us," Dave said. "We were too busy getting the business straightened out regarding TAG. She didn't even mention dinner until the last minute when she dropped us off at the hotel."

"Well it was a fabulous dinner and she was so sweet to the kids."

"She must have been on something. Trust me. Her personality couldn't change that much in four hours."

"Well, whatever it was, she made me feel at home and happy to be a part of their business family," Melody said, leaning her head on Dave's shoulder.

"That's a good thing, because we are in the family now, whether we want to be or not. Let's just hope it's not like the New York families in the gangster movies."

"What is that supposed to mean?" asked Debbie.

"Just that we are committed to make the business work," he said.

The hotel room was more crowded than he had imagined, but the kids were good sports and slept on a rollaway and the floor, giving up a part of the bed for Dad, and falling sound asleep as soon as the lights were out. For the first time in weeks he was with his wife with his kids nearby. The place was a far cry from their luxurious home in Arizona, and he was missing a kidney, but after his afternoon talk with Brick and Willow he was assured that he was in fact a multimillionaire. Time would tell if he would ever actually be able to spend any of it.

"She did what?" Derek asked. He, Brick, and Dave were in the back of the limo with the driver's partition raised. The two friends had picked Derek up at the airport in order to have more time with him.

"She signed her entire interest in TAG over to the three of us. Ned still holds 52 percent, which is the majority of the stock, but she said she wants us to run the whole thing for him. She wants to spend more time with him at their country home," Dave said.

"I didn't even know they had a country home," Derek said, still astonished at the revelation that he had just been given a 16 percent ownership in TAG. What that actually meant in terms of money, he had no idea.

"It's somewhere on a lake in Vermont. She offered to let any of us use it whenever they aren't there. She and Ned plan to use their place in the Caribbean as their winter retreat."

Again Derek was taken aback by the new information.

Maybe it was jet lag, but things seemed to be moving at him a bit too quickly for him to assimilate. He had just gotten off the phone with his Natasha while he was waiting to clear immigration and she hadn't said a thing about Willow or TAG. He guessed she knew less than he did.

"When did this all happen?" he asked his partners.

"We had an unplanned meeting yesterday, right after you called and gave us your Romanian mobster report," Brick said. "There were lots of questions and she had all the right answers including the surprise announcement. I think she was going to save it for when you got back, but we pushed her with some hard questions so she broke the news."

"Well that's a real one-eighty," Derek said. "Forty-eight hours ago she tried to force me to buy a $20 million pile of concrete garbage in Romania. Now she wants out completely? I don't get it. Something smells like fish, and it's not your aftershave."

"All we know is that Ned's personal accountant came by the mansion this morning and showed us a fresh set of books on TAG. Brick and I studied them. The way it looks at the moment, her 30 percent ownership is worth around $15 million if we were to sell the business. Who knows for sure what the real market is without putting it out there? Anyway, that's what she told us. We're each now worth $5 million more than we were yesterday morning," Dave said, with a huge grin on his face. "That's ten or twelve years' worth of very difficult joint surgeries."

Derek looked at his two buddies' smiles. Dave with his sickly pallor and Brick with bags under his eyes from too many nights up with Lexy, and too many hours sitting at Edward Foster III's desk trying to run this phantom business.

"Tell me one thing. We have raised all of this money and I guess it's all accounted for, but what actual property does TAG own? Just because there is money in the bank doesn't mean any of it is ours," Derek said.

"She has bought properties all over the country and in Europe and in Hawaii," Brick explained. "Nearly everything TAG is buying, owns, or is selling right now, is in escrow with set closing dates. Her accountant's books show that not a single piece of property is selling for less than a 20 percent profit."

Derek turned his face toward the passing buildings. He couldn't believe it. Not any of it. From what he had seen, the woman was a reckless investor and the real assets of the company were a few computers and desks, if that. They owed investors millions and had promised millions more in profits. He reached in his travel bag and retrieved four Advil and took a bottle of water from the limo's minibar, drinking the whole thing in four swallows.

His final conclusion—until he could examine the books himself—was that Willow Foster had just freed herself of all of the legal and possible criminal responsibility of dealing with TAG and its investors. The original investors, including his friends and family in Arizona, not to mention the shady people in the Middle and Far East, were expecting a huge return on their money and the only money to meet that obligation was that of the newest investors. Until he could see some title reports and deeds Derek continued to question whether or not Willow had bought and sold a single two-by-four or roof shingle. Without any real assets there was only one honest name for the business plan, and it started with a "P."

"I thought you were just going to catch up with the guys and then catch the next flight home," Natasha said in frustration. "It's Mom's birthday dinner tonight at Fleming's and you're buying. All of the family is going to be there. We planned the time based on your flight schedule."

"I'm sorry sweetheart, but I need to spend more time with Brick and with the accountants, not to mention that Willow has made some changes ... I can't wait to tell you the best part of the news." Derek was sitting at the desk in Ned's home with Brick standing over him looking at account ledgers. Dave had fallen asleep on the leather couch in the corner, and was snoring to the point of distraction.

"Please, Derek! Just come home and see us for one day, then you can go back to New York. One day can't make that much of a difference," Natasha pleaded.

"It's two o'clock here. If I get on the five o'clock flight and you pick me up at seven Arizona time, can we make it to the dinner at Fleming's?" he asked, knowing that he was in for a mental battle with her if he didn't agree.

"That will be perfect," Natasha said. "I love you. Got to run and pick up the kids. On second thought, why don't you just take a cab to the restaurant?"

He pressed the off button on the phone then looked

212 Steven I. Dahl, M.D.

at Brick and shrugged his shoulders. "What could I say that was going to make a difference? I'll be back tomorrow night and we can go over the properties and ledgers then."

There were in fact lots of properties listed on the information Willow sent—one even in Paris—but, there were no deeds of trust or closing papers included in the file boxes stacked beside the desks. They had spent over an hour searching when the first hopeful document was found. It was a title report on an office building in Chicago which listed a purchase price of $12 million with the previous selling price being $7 million.

"Look there," said Brick enthusiastically. "There is a cool $5 million profit in that one property alone."

"But where are the others? I thought that all this time you had been sitting at this desk, you and Willow had been buying and selling high-end properties for TAG," Derek said. "What have you actually been doing?"

"I've been meeting and talking to investors just like you, and Ned asked me to take over the day-to-day management of their personal stuff. They have a lot of bills to pay and things to sort out," Brick explained.

Derek got up from the desk and pushed the heavy window drapes to the side. He couldn't believe what he was hearing. His commodities-trading friend Brick had been made into a personal secretary; his orthopedic friend had abandoned his lucrative practice, donated his kidney, ignored his family, and now looked like a war refugee; and he personally had talked an Arab sheik and a Chinese underworld kingpin into giving him millions to invest with the personal promise of huge returns. Now, he was finding out that his earliest suspicions about the new company were probably correct. "If it sounded too good to be true," rang in his ears like the lingering ring of a high-caliber pistol shot. He was starting to think that there probably wasn't any real property to back up the sales hype that he had been spewing into anyone's ears who would listen.

"So Brick, with the exception of the one piece of property in Chicago, where is all of the money right now? Is there any other actual real estate? And if not— where is the money?"

"Like I've already told you, it's tied up in deposits on forthcoming deals and in options on properties that haven't been put on the market yet. She wouldn't just hide it or run off with it. She and Ned have plenty of their own," Brick said in Willow's defense.

"Just how much money are we talking about?" Derek asked. "You just told me that Willow gave us her $15 million in equity. Was that her own investment, or is that including the money everyone else has put in?"

Brick was standing, facing his friends, and their voices were getting a bit louder. Dave had awakened and was sitting on the couch, rubbing his side and trying to catch up with the conversation.

"I don't have all the answers," Brick said in his defense. "I just know that Ned is an honest man and that he trusts Willow."

"I know that when you trade commodities you seldom see the actual property," Derek said, trying to control his emotions. "But real estate is quite different. One has to actually own the property and hold a title or deed of trust before it can be sold."

"I'm not stupid, Derek."

Dave could tell that the conversation was getting out of hand, but when he stood to try to cool the situation he became light-headed and had to sit back down.

"No one is saying that you are stupid," Derek insisted. "I just get the feeling that she has been stringing us along, and that there might be fewer big real estate deals in the works than she has implied. I see lots of proposals and appraisals, and offers on land and buildings, but where are the deeds?"

"I don't know!" Brick confessed. "She is gone so much of the time and there always are lots of other things to do around here to keep me busy, including my family and Dave. Asking Ned for any information is forbidden by the woman."

"Well," Derek said. "Somebody better find out where either the deeds or the money is. We've taken in millions from our friends and family and I have checks for another $60 million for deposit into the account today. Trust me. The guys I have been dealing with are not the kind you want to make angry. Right now, I've got to leave or my wife is going to kill me before the others have a chance. Can you call Willow and get the lowdown on where the money and the deeds are, and what sales are in progress? I thought she had you in the loop."

Brick glared at his partner, resenting the accusatory tone in Derek's voice.

"You fly on home to Natasha and we'll stick around here and sort things out," said Dave, trying to be the peacemaker. "I'm sure that there is a logical explanation to everything. She couldn't have just pocketed the money, and besides, I know that Ned has plenty to make things right if there is a problem."

"Well, you just keep believing that, but in the meantime let's get some documentation before somebody asks for their money back and all we can give them is a hollow promise and a pat on the back. If my new Arab friend in Dubai doesn't see a return on his investment, he'll have all of our hands cut off, but it won't matter because my new casino-owner friend in Macau, Mr. Chen, already will have us diced into fish chum."

With that happy thought, Derek picked up his carry-on and computer case and headed out the door. He had barely enough time to make his flight. He could not miss the birthday party. Of all his potential enemies, the last person in the world he wanted mad at him was his mother-in-law.

CHAPTER

Edward Foster III died on Halloween afternoon, amid
the falling leaves, orange crepe paper bunting, and
the enormous jack-o'-lantern Brick had carved for the
mansion's doorway during an afternoon of boredom. For
the previous three months Ned had been making slow but
steady progress with his health. A personal trainer came
to the mansion every day to take him through a gentle
workout, and Margo and Benjamin had been spending
hours every day walking slowly with him up and down
the sidewalks of New York City. Willow and the staff had
spent time with him at the mountain retreat where he
actually had ridden his favorite mountain bike around the
bridal path. In mid-October they had taken a long cruise
on the Silver Chalice Cruise Ship up the coast of New
England and around into the waters of Newfoundland,
into the Saint Lawrence Seaway, all the way to Quebec,
to see the fall leaves. He hadn't strayed from the ship,
but had been well enough to enjoy the brisk air and the
change of cuisine.

Home from the cruise just three days, he had insisted
on a walk to get a fresh bagel and a cup of hot coffee
at his favorite local coffee shop. As he came down the
steps to the sidewalk in front of the house he let out a

small gasp and his knees buckled. He reached out for something to hang onto, and went to his death grasping only the stem of the giant carved pumpkin. By the time Benjamin could dial 911, Foster already was losing his facial color. Benjamin tried to perform CPR, but by the time the paramedics arrived there was no possibility of a successful resuscitation. The broken-hearted butler sat on the steps of the Foster mansion and wept as the ambulance slowly drove away.

The sad news made the front page of *The Wall Street Journal* and *The New York Times*. Brick was in Chicago at the time evaluating an apartment building that had just come on the market. He and Debra had left Lexy with the Felshaws to have a weekend alone. When he received the phone call from Dave, he became lightheaded. Dave had been at his apartment working over the figures for the purchase of a shopping mall in Las Vegas.

"How could that happen? I was just with him yesterday and he was fine," Brick said.

"He just collapsed. We won't know until they do an autopsy—if Willow will consent to one," Dave said. He had been on the scene moments after Ned's death and thus had to make the important phone calls, including the one to the new widow.

"Where is she?" Brick asked.

"Your guess is as good as mine. Just like always, she answered her phone and sounded next door, but wouldn't commit on when she would be here. She gave me the name of a funeral parlor, which was weird. It was like she had it on her phone's address book."

"Well, I can't do anything there today so I might as well finish my appointments, then fly home in the morning. If that's all right with you, or should we come back now?" Brick asked.

"Like you said, there isn't anything you have to do today. Take Deb out to dinner and we'll see you tomorrow night. I'll track Derek down and hopefully get him here by the day after tomorrow."

For the previous few months TAG had finally been operating in the way the three young owners had expected: a cash-rich investment firm. Money was coming in from the investors Derek found, properties were being discovered and purchased by Dave, who had developed a nose for the smoking "fire-sale" real estate, and Brick then followed through with the actual purchase and later the resale of the properties. They relied on Willow's contacts for the marketing. The big stink over missing deeds and titles during the late summer had softened, although there was still a hiatus between what had been taken in from investors and the money spent on properties.

The Morris and Wahl families had settled into life in their apartments in New York. Both had kept their houses in Arizona, relying on Derek to check on their homes and pay the yard and pool maintenance men—it was Arizona, where cash was expected for manual labor. Debra and Melody had learned their way around the Big Apple and were enjoying the change into the fall season with the colorful leaves falling from trees—unlike the desert with its brown fall and winter landscape. Shopping for winter clothes was an additional novelty and was proving to be lots of fun.

The Morris kids were involved in their usual Arizona life of school, sports, dance, and music lessons, but with dad now a real millionaire, times were really good. Derek was still on the road a good deal, but lately it was to meet and entice investors whom he, Brick, and Dave had found, not the shady people Willow had lined up those first couple of months.

Ned's death came as a huge surprise to each of the families. They might have expected it three months earlier, but now everything had settled into a false state of normalcy. Ned had started spending time with Brick and Dave, mentoring them, in the mansion office, or even in the office space they used in the Foster building. He ate most of his meals at the dining room table and often had the boys join him for lunch. One of the things that had allowed TAG to function better was the advice Edward Foster III had begun to hand out.

"Teaching moments should never be passed up because of outside pressures and interruptions," he was fond of saying. Once he started into an explanation he would ignore the phone and any other confusion until he completed his point.

One of the things he insisted on was keeping a daily log of the business activity, including the people contacted, the acceptances, the rejections, the purchases and the sales. The only exceptions were Willow's activities. When she would join them and tell about her meetings she never produced records. Although she had, in theory, relinquished her ownership in TAG—with Ned's apparent blessing—she still liked to eat out and travel under the guise of TAG company business and continued to solicit investors. None of the young partners dared to complain, but some of the missing property deeds still had not been produced.

"What can I possibly wear to the funeral?" Natasha bemoaned. "I have no black winter clothes. Debra just called and said the mayor and possibly one of the Clintons are going to be there and probably at the wake at the mansion as well. Who knows who Willow will invite?"

"Can't you call Mel and have her pick out something for you?" Derek asked, trying to sound concerned.

"Are you kidding me? She doesn't have time, and her tastes in clothes are completely different. I need you to get home and get packed. I can probably get us an earlier flight, and then I can go to that dress shop Debbie told me about. We need to make a good impression with all of the Foster people."

"Don't count on anyone even noticing us. We will probably be sitting at the back of the church and won't meet a soul."

Instead of sitting in the back of the church, Derek found his name in the program, along with Dave, Brick, and five unknowns. They were to be the pallbearers. The men's wives didn't get to hide in the shadows either. Margo called the night before the funeral with a request from Willow that Debra, Melody, and Natasha help serve the food at the wake.

After the funeral and the long caravan to a very old, exclusive cemetery, the wake began. The mansion was packed shoulder-to-shoulder with strangers. The guys recognized a few familiar faces from the main office and one or two investors.

"It looks like everyone who walks by the front door with a white shirt and tie on has stopped in for a free meal," Brick commented.

Gratefully, the caterers had anticipated the crowd.

The Arizona wives really didn't have to lift a finger, and reasoned quite quickly that the plea for assistance was a ruse to be sure that they attended. All three of the ladies looked fabulous, as did their husbands in their jet-black, matching suits worn at the insistence of the new widow.

The funeral had been very formal and quite brief. The sermon and eulogies were outclassed by the organ music, played by a master on a two-hundred-year-old organ, with bass pipes that rattled one's tooth fillings. Flowers were omnipresent and tears of sadness flowed from the eyes of Edward Foster III's friends and business associates. It was evident to all present that he had been a truly good man.

As for his widow, the woman could not have been colder if she had been the one lying in the open casket. At the funeral home, she stood her ground behind the coffin as mourners passed by, seldom glancing upward. At the funeral, she was the last to come into the church and the first to leave. She remained in the limo at the cemetery telling Brick, whom she had assigned to escort her, that she had a splitting headache and to go ahead without her.

Back at the mansion, Willow made a short appearance to greet the mayor of New York and also a former senator, then excused herself and retired to her room, leaving the hosting to the new owners of TAG. Foster's former employees all seemed appropriately saddened by Foster's death, and clearly enjoyed the food and drink at the wake, but not a one mentioned anything about TAG. Brick and Dave had spent considerable time at the corporate headquarters the last three months, and yet not one of the main officers or board members gave more than polite nods to the three men.

When all of the guests had left, the caterers cleaned up the place and were gone. The three couples collapsed in the mansion's living room, kicking off shoes and peeling off neck ties. Benjamin and Margo had excused themselves and retired to their quarters on the fourth floor, leaving a cold stillness in the massive old house.

Their silence was broken by the sound of the floor creaking, a door closing and water running on the second floor, causing all six of them to look up at the hand-carved beams of the vaulted ceiling, like a choir of school children singing the last note of a hymn.

"At least she's not dead," Melody said in a flat voice.

"She might as well have been for all the help she was today. The least she could have done was introduce us to some of his family and friends," Tasha said. "I couldn't believe that she didn't even act like she knew his younger sister ... what was her name?"

"Kristen," Debra answered. "She's from Virginia, but also has a home here. She is as sweet as can be. She wrote her number on a notepad for me. She said that Willow was probably still in shock and to let her know if the woman wanted any help when she starts sorting through Ned's things. She called him Ned too, just like he always wanted us to call him."

"Willow won't let her touch a thing," Brick said. "Ned wasn't dead two hours when she went through his office locking and taking the keys to every cupboard and drawer that has a lock. I'll be surprised if she doesn't ask us to return our front door keys."

"I'll bet she has his clothes and toiletries boxed up and out of here by the end of the week," said Natasha.

"Maybe you guys are being too harsh on her. She

has been through a lot the last six months and certainly hadn't expected him to die. Now is when she is going to need us more than ever," Dave said, leaning his head on his wife's shoulder.

The whole time Derek sat quietly, as though lost in his own world of thoughts. When Brick asked him what he was thinking about, he looked up at the ceiling again and just shook his head.

Willow didn't ask for their keys to the mansion. They had gone back to their apartments—Derek and Tasha were crashing at Brick's—late that night. The next morning they slept in, then got the kids fed and dressed, and all took cabs to the mansion with the kids to pay a cordial visit to the widow.

"She left this morning at nine thirty," Benjamin said, standing at the front door. Brick had started to open the door with his key, but the door was pulled open from inside before he could turn it.

"What does that mean … she left?" Brick asked as Lexy tugged at his sunglasses.

"At seven she rang for Margo and asked her to bring breakfast to the room, then asked if I would bring the four largest suitcases in the attic. Margo and I assisted her for over an hour, and then the driver and I moved the luggage to the car. She had her normal travel bags as well. I believe there were three of them."

"Did she say where she was going?" Dave asked.

"No, sir. We just loaded up the suitcases and she left."

"Do you mind if we come in? I need to make some calls," Brick said.

"Unless you have an extra key to the study, you'll have to use the phone in the kitchen." Benjamin said.

"Well, there must be a misunderstanding or some-body's made a big mistake," Brick said, beginning to lose his patience with the atypical condescending tone Benjamin was using. "I have all of the company's business paperwork in there. I have calls I need to make and appointments to confirm for tomorrow."

"Actually, Mrs. Foster told Margo that she wouldn't be back for quite some time and that we should take our accumulated vacations starting Friday. She said for Margo to clean out the pantry and refrigerator, as she wouldn't be returning for a while. She gave strict instructions that no one was to be allowed in the house."

"But you just said that we could use the phone," Natasha said, leaning closer to get the gist of the conversation.

With the three families standing on the sidewalk with the kids, the conversation at the door became impossible. Dave finally stepped forward and insisted that they be allowed in the house. He still had personal items in the bedroom.

"I'm sorry, Doctor, but the lady of the house implicitly forbade me to allow anyone in the house until she returns," Benjamin said, apparently having changed his mind. He was standing up straighter and filling the doorway with his large frame.

"This is ridiculous," Derek said, handing his youngest child to Tasha. "Step out of the way, Ben. We all three have business files and paperwork that needs our attention. You know as well as we do that we run part of the new business from Mr. Foster's study."

"Sir, if you don't settle down and leave, I will have to call the police."

The cold, robotic voice wasn't that of the Benjamin they all knew and had grown to think of as a friend, nor was the wide-eyed anger on his face that of the gracious servant who had waited on Ned and on Dave in sickness and health.

Derek stepped back, afraid that the stranger was about to attack him. He started to speak again to reason with the butler, but before another word could be said, the huge door was closed with a solid clank and the sound of the dead bolt was heard over the noise of the traffic behind them.

Natasha stepped forward to bang the large brass knocker, but Derek grasped her arm and shook his head. "It won't do any good," he said. "The man is just doing what he has been ordered to do. He obviously doesn't like it any better than we do."

Like a large family of refugees being turned away from a border crossing, the three families with their children turned toward the street and began walking away.

The six adults and their several children huddled around small tables at a breakfast deli near the Foster mansion, trying to make sense of the conversation that had just occurred at the town house door. Debra and Melody had been standing back far enough that the conversation had to be repeated before they would believe it.

"I left my beaded purse and lipstick in the living room last night. I'm going back and getting in there," Natasha said, getting up and walking away from the group. She went back up the street and approached the door then rang the bell. When there was no answer she repeatedly slammed the brass horseshoe-shaped clapper against its iron plate, again with no response.

Derek, thinking the kids were with the Felshaws and the Morris clan at the deli, ran after her as his children trailed behind him. "Derek, try your key!" she insisted, banging the clapper again.

Just then a black-and-white, NYC police car pulled up to the curb. An officer in the passenger seat rolled down the window and leaned out toward her. "Lady, you need to hold on to those children when you are standing by the street." Tasha looked back to see her seven- and five-year-old standing behind their father.

Afraid that Benjamin had phoned the police, Derek insisted that they all leave and that the men could come back later and straighten things out. They returned to the deli, and after picking up their orders, one by one the families flagged down cabs and headed back to their apartments.

"We have to go back," Brick said. He was pacing back and forth in the small living room of his and Debra's place. Melody was getting ready to take the older kids to her apartment so that they could play and the men could talk. Natasha insisted on staying with the men. She wasn't about to let them lose control of the situation.

"We need to talk to an attorney at the corporate office and see if anyone there knows what's going on," Dave said. "I've been on the phone with the guy several times in the past month. He is Ned's biking friend, his name is Dennis Toleman. Maybe he can check around and find out something about what's happening."

"That's fine," Derek said, "but the account information for the TAG bank accounts and the safe with most of the deeds of trust and purchase documents are in the mansion office. I wrote down the bank account and routing numbers and have them at home in Phoenix and on my smart phone. At least that's something."

"How hard can it be to go back there tonight and simply walk into the place like you've been doing for the last three months?" said Natasha. "I don't know why we bothered knocking anyway." She was sitting cross-legged on the floor trying to entertain Lexy while Debra made sandwiches in the kitchen. "What is the worst thing that could happen? Margo hits one of you guys with a frying pan?"

This brought on a laugh—the first in a couple of hours.

"Why don't you just do the obvious and call Willow?" Dave suggested to Brick. "She has always had her eye on you, ever since you ate dinner with her at the hotel in Meeker."

"That's just not true," he said, blushing and looking toward the kitchen and his wife.

"It is true," Derek confirmed. "Why do you think they had you living at the mansion for so long?"

"That's bullcrap and you know it," Brick said, turning to face the others. "If she has the hots for anyone it's Dave. The woman is trouble. She has been since the first day we met her, and now that she has us all dragged into her little snake pit, she is going to play with our minds and lives until she gets bored; and then she will bite and kill us just like the snake that she is. In fairness to her, she did her rattling in the beginning to warn us, but we didn't heed the sound."

Everyone stared at Brick as though he was nuts, then Natasha jumped up, handing Lexy to her mother. "You can all sit around and hypothesize about some snake in the grass, but in the meantime we can't all give up our new lives and TAG. I'm not going to let some stuffed-shirt butler with an attitude keep us from getting what is ours. And Brick, if you won't call Willow, then I will. And Dave, if you won't go back to the mansion and get your clothes and all of the account information we need, then Derek and I will."

She headed toward the door shouting for Derek to

bring the luggage; she was going to get the kids to the hotel.

"Let's everybody cool down," Dave suggested, delaying her exit. "We all still have some of our $1 million and our share of the company. We'll just have to use the downtown Foster Building office to run the business."

"That's the worst idea I've heard all day," Brick said. "The minute the word is out that we are not working with Willow, any potential new clients will evaporate and the old ones will be serving notice to get their money back. She is still part of the company—like it or not, she probably just inherited all of Ned's money, shares of stock, and his power. We need to let her finish her grieving; then I'm sure we can get her to be reasonable."

Debra came in the small family room carrying a tray of sandwiches and a pitcher of lemonade. The mood changed for a few minutes, until Natasha, now back in the room, reopened the subject. "If you aren't going to have to work at the mansion, then why don't we all just go back home and run the business from Arizona? You guy's leases are month to month," she said turning to Debra and Brick. "You can fly back and forth when you need to and we can get back into the happy lives we were living before this waking nightmare began."

"So that's how you think of it? Getting a million bucks for saving a guy's life is a nightmare?" It was Brick who had stood up and assumed a stance like he was going to attack his best friend's wife.

Debra immediately grabbed his arm and jerked him away.

"Have you all lost your minds?" Brick said. "We're all multi-millionaires and will be even richer if we just chill out for a few days. Willow isn't stupid. She stands to lose as much as we do if this thing tanks. Everyone just needs to give her a few days."

"That's fine with me," Dave said. "Everyone is in an agitated state of mind. A close family member's death is the worst stress a person can have."

"Well, it's not fine with me," his wife said. "My kids and I are missing our house and friends back home and Dave is out a kidney. As far as I can tell, TAG was just thrown out on the street with the three of you men. Any hope of keeping any of it viable, is reliant on a psychotic woman who seems to be playing some sick game with all of us. I'm packing up and moving back home!"

Everyone looked at Dave for some sort of confirmation or negation. Slowly he stood up from the table and took a place behind his wife's chair. He leaned down and kissed her on the top of her head then looked at the others. He was going to honor his wedding vows—*for better or worse.*

Natasha and Derek remained still, comfortable with the thought that there was no pressing decision for them, having long since made the call to stay in their home in Arizona. Derek had even been keeping up with the real estate market, and had just sent in the annual renewal for his license and the building permits on his big construction project with the city. He pushed his chair away from the table and stood. He put his arm around Brick's shoulder and gave a little squeeze. Everyone took a deep breath, letting the tension escape from the room.

"Your impression to give things a few days is the right one, Brick. Things have changed however, and I don't see any reason why we can't run this company from Arizona.

Willow will be happy to have us and the kids out from underfoot. If you and Debra don't mind staying here in New York for a while, that will be great. Thank goodness for e-mail and iPhones."

Everyone gave a little chuckle at Derek's comic relief. Brick turned to Melody and apologized for his burst of anger and the group scattered to check on their kids. Conversations were kept at a minimum until the coats were buttoned up and the door was opened, then it was Natasha who put her hand on Brick's shoulder and whispered in his ear. "Before we leave for home, I'm getting inside the mansion. You need to let me know what it is you have there that is most important. As for Willow, you need to stay far away from her. She has your number. She will try to use you against the rest of us. Don't call her or talk to her. Just let me take care of her and the mansion."

Brick couldn't believe his ears. The mild-mannered and yet crafty Natasha was ordering him to back off so that she could take care of things? He looked for Derek in order to dispel this insanity, but he was already standing outside on the curb holding his three kids while a cab pulled to a stop.

"We'll be at the Marriott. The kids need to practice their swimming," she said to Brick. "Derek will come back for the luggage. I'll call you later or just text me a list of everything you need from Ned's study. I'll get a list of the things Dave left behind. And Brick, don't worry, I won't forget my purse and lipstick either."

Natasha left the hotel just after dark. The kids had enjoyed a swim and the adjoining rooms with their large windows overlooking Broadway and 42nd street proved to be better than a Disney movie. They were in their pajamas and lined up at the windows watching the lights of the famous intersection, the police cars, and the nutty-looking people on the sidewalks. McDonald's wrappers were on the coffee table behind them and the lights were mostly turned off.

Derek had handed over his mansion key to his wife with reservation, and yet had known her long enough to realize the futility in arguing with her. She had been on the phone with Dave and then with Brick, making a list. He sent her off with a kiss, a charged cell phone, and the code for the Foster's alarm system written in ink on the palm of her hand.

She had the cab drop her off a block away from the town house. It wasn't completely dark yet and the street lights were just starting to flicker on. With two fabric shopping bags slung on her shoulder, she looked like any upper Manhattan lady on her way to buy groceries.

She walked casually past the entrance twice, looking at the upper floors from different angles. No lights were visible in the mansion's windows. On the third pass, she walked up to the door and inserted the key. The heavy double bolt resisted, and then gave way with a grinding sound as the lock released. She turned the ornate knob and the door was free. Brick had explained that the alarm made no warning chirp or buzz, but that she would only have a sixty second delay before the sky would begin to fall.

She stepped into the foyer, closing the door behind her then immediately groped for the alarm key pad. A dim yellow LED light was the only assistance. She tapped in the six numbers and held her breath waiting until a green light popped on. It was ten seconds that seemed like an hour before she saw the green; only then was she able to take a deep breath. Why Derek had brought his xenon bicycling head lamp to New York was a mystery—heaven knew there were plenty of lights on the streets, but now it would come in very handy. She slipped it onto her forehead and clicked the switch to the dim position.

The light suddenly threw shadows in the room that took on a life of their own. She thought she knew the rooms of the mansion pretty well, but now realized that she had missed a lot of things—big things—like the stuffed ring-tailed cat on a shelf near the stairs; its glass eyes picked up the light and glared back at her. From the kitchen came a grinding sound that at first sounded like a door opening, but then she remembered the commercial ice maker that they had often used. Working her way toward the study, she noticed that the living room had several packing boxes stacked in one corner. She knew for a fact that they hadn't been there twenty-four hours before.

Her heart rate jumped another ten beats per minute as she put her hand on the study's door handle, not knowing if the room would be locked. Her cotton gloves were slippery on the heavy brass knob, giving her the sinking feeling that the door was in fact locked, but then it turned. Closing the door behind her a solid thud couldn't be avoided.

Natasha advanced the switch on her headlamp to full brightness and surveyed the room. She only had been in Ned's office twice. Once was on their first visit to the mansion four months prior when Ned had given the three couples a personal tour of his home, and again one day when they were considering living in the city and one of her kids had disappeared. Looking for Cali, she had entered the closed room and had searched under the massive desk behind the chairs and the couch where she found her little sweetheart sound asleep in a padded window nook.

It took her less than sixty seconds to find the drawer with the TAG files and the Sure Save backup hard drive that Brick and Dave used for their laptops. Missing was Brick's actual computer. Frantic, she searched through all of the drawers and then the shelves and in the storage closet. She had filled her bags with the items she already had found when she heard a different sound.

Tiptoeing to the door, she turned off her headlamp and opened it to listen. Voices echoed from the front of the house, but the longer she listened the more sure she was that they were outside.

She made a dash for the stairs and with her headlamp back on low, silently climbed the two flights to the third floor. Dave's convalescent room was more familiar to her, having visited him several times right after the surgery. Why he had left anything behind was a mystery to her, but then so were lots of things about this whole last four months.

On a built-in shelf next to the bed were the objects of her assigned task for Dave. There were a stack of DVDs, most of which were old movies, and a few soundtracks, but then she saw the answer to her question. Written in Dave's crimped hand was a CD labeled: *TAG dates and promises*. Apparently, he had taken the time to record and copy the early affairs of the business. She stuffed it into the shopping bag with the other things on her list, leaving most of the DVDs behind. As she was heading toward the stairs, the lights on the landing of the fourth floor came on.

"How could you let me sleep so long?"

It was the voice of Benjamin. *Who was he talking to?*

"You know you loved it. You were exhausted and so was I. Can you believe we actually had a long nap during the day? That had to be a first. I love it when the cat is away."

It was the voice of Margo. *A much friendlier and less formal voice. So they are a couple.*

In Dave's bedroom with the door pulled nearly closed, she waited. Her heart sounded loud enough to her to be causing an echo down the hallway. She listened as the two servants walked down the stairs, talking and laughing. Willow's name was mentioned in a derogatory way and the leftover food from the wake was discussed with chuckles, saying that they had hidden some of the lobster salad from the guests and planned on eating it now. As the voices disappeared into the kitchen on the main floor, Tasha's panic grew. She had to get out of the house, but first she had to find Brick's laptop.

Her shoes were a problem. The hard heels clicked on the wooden floor as she walked. She slipped them off and tried to find room in the bags for them, but had room for just one, so she tucked her blouse into her pants and stuffed the other one down the front of her blouse. It felt uncomfortable but secure. The laptop had to be in Willow's room.

Tiptoeing down the curving staircase, with each step creaking and groaning, she made her way to the second floor. She could hear the two servants talking and rattling dishes, which gave her some sense of security. To

Natasha's surprise, Willow's bedroom door was ajar and a light was on in the bathroom. She was positive that the woman wasn't there so she slipped into the room and silently closed the heavy door. The room was a mess. Drawers in the nightstands were open and the bed hadn't been made. Clothes were in piles on the floor as though sorted and discarded.

The widow's closet was in worse shape. Nearly every drawer was open and clothes were everywhere. A white ermine, full-length coat worth thousands lay in a heap. Row after row of shoes were picked over, leaving behind some that Natasha would have gladly exchanged for her own. Even the velvet-lined jewelry drawer was open exposing row after row of rings, bracelets, and necklaces, glittering in the overhead light.

Just as she was reaching for the light switch to leave, she saw an alligator briefcase. Natasha pushed a pile of skirts aside with her foot and bent down to snap open the case. Staring up at her was a manila folder bearing a neatly printed label that read, *TAG SUCKER LIST.*

Laughter on the stairs brought her out of her momentary concentration. She edged the closet door closed then lifted the briefcase strap to put on her shoulder. Sitting beneath it was a small HP laptop with an Arizona State Sun Devil sticker on the well-worn case. She lifted it out of the briefcase, revealing three red flash drives lying in the bottom. Again the voices resonated through the door. She quickly turned off the light and searched the room for cover should they enter.

"What a pigsty," she heard Margo say. "I hope she doesn't expect me to pick up this mess. And look at the bathroom. The idiot didn't even flush the toilet."

"Just forget it," Benjamin said. "Just turn off the lights and let's go to bed. I'll call the Merry Maids tomorrow. Well pay them with the grocery money you've been skimming. You can probably find some of her older clothes in the closet that we can unload at that second time-around store. It's not like she will ever miss them. I already talked to the owner about buying some of the old man's stuff."

There was a flushing sound, then the light under the door went out and the bedroom door clicked shut. Natasha took a deep breath and turned the closet light on again. Her tote bags were too full to add the laptop so she put the folder and laptop back in the briefcase. If Willow missed the case so be it.

Again on the stairs, slowly taking one creaking step at a time, she made her way toward the front door. That's when she remembered the motion detector. Not ten seconds later the warning flash of the red light began. Brick had warned her that the warning allowed just sixty seconds before the full alarm came on, along with the inside and outside lights as well as a signal to the local police precinct. "The bedrooms must be on zones of their own," she thought as she scanned the wall panel for the keypad.

She was barely able to hang onto the two bags and the briefcase and now she had to enter the six digit code that was written on her hand. If only she could remember it. Then the unimaginable happened. The brass clapper on the outside of the door, not five feet from her face, began to thump, sending an echo throughout the foyer and down the hallways. Someone was knocking on the door.

Salvation came through the wonders of electronics.

Just as she was about to slip into the guest closet on the other side of the foyer a voice sounded from the outside intercom.

"Is that you Angelo?" It was the distinctive voice of Benjamin speaking through the intercom outside the door.

"Yo, Ben, it is me, and I have the case of wine you ordered."

"Would you be so kind as to bring it around to the side of the house? I'll buzz the gate open. Just leave in on the back stoop."

With that, the red flashing light went off and the back porch light came on, casting a pillar of light from the kitchen. Steps could be heard on the sidewalk. Tucking the briefcase under her arm, she reached for the door knob and gave it a turn. That's when the lower button on her blouse came apart and her shoe thudded to the floor.

Truly in a panic now, she set the briefcase on the floor by the half-opened front door and swept the shoe up and into the top of the bag. Briefcase and bags in hand and still barefoot she slipped through the doorway and tugged the door closed. The night air was freezing cold so she set down the briefcase and pulled her navy blue scarf up around her neck and the back of her head. She looked up and down the sidewalk for the wine delivery man, but saw only a woman walking in her direction leading a large black manicured poodle.

"Good evening Mrs. Foster," the woman said. "I'm very sorry to hear about your husband."

Natasha had no choice but to acknowledge the condolence, which she did with an immediate small smile and the nod of her head.

"My Egbert was such an admirer of your husband's skill. He made us a small fortune you know?"

Natasha didn't speak, but smiled and nodded again, turning the opposite direction from the woman, praying that an available cab would come by.

"Have a pleasant evening," the lady said, her voice growing distant. "And be careful where you step with those bare feet. These sidewalks can be filthy."

The rain was cold and coming down as hard as the desert dwellers had ever seen it pour. The limo driver tried to keep an umbrella over them as they threw the last of their suitcases into the auto's trunk. Derek motioned for the kids and a bellman held an umbrella for them as they dashed to the open door. The windshield wipers slapped at the rivulets—fighting a losing battle.

"Do you mind if we wait here a couple minutes until this cloudburst lets up?" the driver asked, leaning through the privacy window.

"Do what you need to do to get them to the airport safely," Derek said. "I'll just wait here inside with them until you're ready to leave."

The three sleepy kids all had given their dad hugs and kisses and were snuggled together on the back-facing seat. Derek held Natasha's hand, giving her reminders about the house keys and the mail and everything else that came to his mind.

"Why don't you just come with us instead of later in the week?" she asked for the dozenth time.

"I'm worried about Brick and Dave. You know that. Dave said he's been running a fever the last couple of nights and Brick is still too emotional—especially after having been locked out of the mansion. We've talked this subject to death," he said.

"Fine, but don't call on Friday and tell me you're staying over the weekend. Your ticket is on the dresser in the hotel room. Get everything straightened out here then come home. I'll get a sitter and pick you up at the airport. You can take me to Tia Rosa's on the way home for a shrimp taco." She gave him a kiss and pushed him toward the door.

He stood in the hotel entrance watching the car pull onto the street and disappear around the corner. "She and the kids will be fine," he told himself. It was the rest of them he was worried about. The night before, Natasha had only been back to the hotel from her secret mission for thirty minutes when his cell phone rang. It was Brick, telling him that Willow had just called and wanted to know who had stolen her briefcase.

"I didn't have to play dumb—she didn't even give me time to say hello, but immediately started screaming that she was calling the police to have us all arrested," Brick told him. Twenty minutes later, Natasha and the kids were booked on an early morning flight to Phoenix. Derek feared that Willow had recently become just nutty enough to follow through with her threat.

The three men met at the Marriott coffee shop and looked out of the window onto the madness of Times Square. It was a fitting continuum to the confusion and anger each one of them was feeling. Their lives had been turned upside down twice in the last four months, having walked away from the success most young men long for, and now having their dreams of untold wealth shattered by a beautiful but crazy woman—a widow—who they could only hope was being temporarily unreasonable due to the sudden loss of her husband and business partner.

The conversation thus far had been trivial, but as the plates were cleared away and the pancake syrup wiped from the table, Dave took a notepad from his briefcase, ready to take notes. He wrote the date and time then clearly wrote out the name of the three men. Across the face of the page in capital letters he wrote *MINUTES OF THE REORGANIZATION OF TAG—A FINANCIAL CORPORATION.*

The three men voted with raised hands to make Brick the president, Dave the secretary, and Derek the treasurer. They also voted to remove Willow Foster from the board of directors and to file a lawsuit against her for obstruction of the business affairs of the corporation. With those probably vain efforts completed, they turned to the real problem: The hard drive on Brick's laptop had been wiped clean. Not even the pictures of Lexy remained. The paper files Tasha had found contained a few notes and a list of present and potential investors, but no bank account numbers and no signed agreements with the property sellers or buyers. The flash drives had spotty information—mostly old e-mail notes sent to Willow by apparent clients.

"I still have copies of my investor trips to Dubai, Hong Kong, and Bucharest and copies of the checks I received, but the deposit receipts were sent to you by UPS," Derek reminded Brick.

"I have them in the file cabinet in Ned's office, unless she has taken them too."

"I just had a positive thought," Dave said. "The few days before Foster died, he rode with me to the bank and to his downtown office. We met a woman there who had been his personal secretary before Willow showed up on the scene. They obviously still had some chemistry between them, but I didn't think about her because I didn't see her at the funeral or the wake. MaryAnn … I'm sure her name was MaryAnn. I'll go down there this afternoon and see if she'll talk to me. She was wearing a charm bracelet that had a bicycle on it and I remember Ned commenting something about her still wearing 'that old thing.'"

"Good idea. Go for it," Derek mumbled, happily relinquishing the president title to Brick, who was still conducting the meeting. "I made a couple of contacts at J.P. Morgan. I'll go by there and see if they can look up some numbers for me—since my records were eaten by the family dog."

"So I guess I'm stuck with meeting with the attorneys?" concluded Brick. "Let's hope she hasn't already banned us from meeting with them or worse still, followed through with her threat to call the police."

"Don't worry about the police, Brick. If she called anybody it will be either the FBI, since our company does business across state borders, or maybe her friends in Bucharest who make the Gambino family look like the Muppets," Derek said with a smirk.

"Wonderful," said Brick.

"The reality is that she won't call anyone," Dave said. "She has too many skeletons in her closet and we have stretched too many rules and regulations to want anyone to look into them."

As the three stood to leave, and Brick went to the cashier to pay the check, Derek noticed Dave take a little extra time getting up and then rubbing his incision side.

"Are you okay?" Brick asked him.

"Yeah. It's just a sore back. I need to get back to my good mattress at home. The lumpy thing at the apartment is killing me. Thanks for asking. Listen, Derek. Melody thinks she and the kids need to get back to Arizona as soon as possible. You think Brick can manage here if we take off?"

"I think all three of us need to get out of town as soon as we get an idea about what is really going on with TAG. You tell Mel to call the movers and make the flight reservations. As soon as Tasha gets unpacked I'll have her send our cleaning ladies over to your place and get it spruced up for you. Your folks will be thrilled that you are moving back home in time for Christmas," Derek said.

"I'm afraid if you two leave here my wife won't want to stay here either," said Brick, rejoining the men. "We leased out our place in Scottsdale for a year and still have eight months to go. The problem is what am I going to do here for an office? I can't have investors coming to meet with me at my tiny apartment."

"I think you really need to hang around here. Just use the office at the Foster building ... you know the one on the mezzanine? It is always empty. Matter of fact, we ought to go by there and put our name on the door before someone else takes it over. Ned told me he was going to make it the main office for TAG anyway, but just hadn't gotten around to it."

They shared a cab, and twenty minutes later were standing in the shadow of the Foster Building. There were several familiar faces they recognized from the funeral and wake coming and going as they made their way to the sweeping marble staircase. The large office suite was on the mezzanine level. The four connected rooms hadn't changed since the previous month when Derek and Willow had met there to review the list of potential investors. Although there wasn't a secretary at the entrance, and the main office had just a minimum of furniture, it looked to be available, and even had a computer-generated reserved sign taped to the door as though expecting them.

They pulled up chairs around a small conference table and started making notes and reviewing the business plan as best they could remember it. Derek asked a secretary in the next suite of offices to borrow some materials and within an hour they had a working outline drawn on the chalkboard and yellow legal notes scattered on the table. The mood had elevated since the earlier, dreary meeting at the hotel. Then someone knocked on the door.

Derek opened it to find a young, very serious-looking guy with a grimace on his face. "What are you people doing in here?" the man inquired.

Brick stood and offered his hand and a business card to the man explaining that he was the president of TAG, Edward Foster's spin-off company, and that this was their assigned office. He said that they would be moving in and using it on a permanent basis. The bluff sounded believable, and the guy excused himself for interrupting their meeting. Ten minutes later he was back. Standing beside him was a security guard.

"I don't know what you fellows are up to," the man said. "But we have checked with the Foster Building superintendent and no one is assigned this office except Mr. Foster's widow and she sent an e-mail just yesterday that it was to remain empty."

"That's because she has reserved it for our company. It is called TAG. She is on the board and Mr. Foster was the major shareholder. She is out of the country right now. I'm sure when she returns she can take care of the necessary paperwork." It was Derek this time, trying to convince the two men. "We now are managing the company and Mrs. Foster's shares."

"Until we have a use agreement in the office file, you will have to vacate the building. Mr. Murphy here will show you out," the preppy guy said, pointing to the security man.

"Let's just go," Dave said, standing and gathering up his papers.

Derek and Brick looked at each other, both feeling another avalanche of defeat crashing down on their attempt to keep TAG viable.

"Could you just give us ten minutes to put away our paperwork?" Brick requested.

"You need to go now," the security guard said in a rough Bronx accent. The guy was itching for an excuse to back up his authority with the Taser gun he had strapped in his holster.

"What's going on here?" All five men turned at the sound of the authoritative voice.

"I repeat, what is going on here—oh Dave, it's you. What a nice surprise," the stately older woman said, moving between the bully guard and the doorway. She gave Dave a peck on the cheek and turned to the other two. "These must be your partners."

She extended her hand to Brick and then to Derek. "I'm MaryAnn Carpet. I was Mr. Foster's executive secretary."

"These guys are trying to use this room and it's supposed to be reserved for Mrs. Foster," the preppy guy explained.

"Mrs. Foster doesn't work here anymore, Billy. Now be a good boy and go to the lounge and bring a tray of assorted drinks and some snacks for these men. They have a lot of work to do."

"But this morning we got an e-mail from Mrs. Foster ...."

"There are no butts allowed around here, Billy, it's a non-smoking building. Now run along and do as I asked you. And Mr. Murphy," she said, turning to the security guard, "please see that the Cuban man in the management office makes up one of those shiny brass signs for the door here. It is simply to say, 'T A G.' Would you do that right away?"

As the two frustrated men turned away, Ms. Carpet took Dave's arm and led them back into the suite of rooms. She insisted that they all sit down, and then she walked to the window and began talking.

"Long before the present Mrs. Foster showed up in this building, I had the privilege of working for Ned Foster. We started out in a small office up the street that had more broken bicycle parts scattered around than business files, but his energy and magnetic personality couldn't be contained in such a small space. Over a period of ten or so years, he became a legend here on the street and yet always maintained a humble and approachable personality. When he became ill the first time we had just moved into this building and had more employees than I could count. By then Willow had caught his eye and was planting her fangs in the poor man. After the transplant, Willow began wedging her way into the management, so it became necessary for Ned to divest himself from some of the original company and to lease out space here in the building.

"Just days before the first transplant and their wedding, Ned ... Mr. Foster ... signed a document giving me a small partnership in this building and giving me a lifetime job here as the executive secretary of Foster Inc. Now that the company has gone public, the real managers, the CEOs, CFOs and every other big-headed snob that works here have all tried to get rid of me. But they can't. I have a very nice office and my own secretary, and I am the dorm mother ... so to speak."

Brick, Derek, and Dave were listening intently to the story.

"When Ned invented TAG and you gentlemen came on the scene, I noted a change in his attitude—a marked improvement—but also a change in Willow in a different way. He became much happier with a positive outlook on the future, while she became more secretive. It was Willow who insisted that all of the TAG work, or at least most of it, be done at the Foster house. I suspected that she didn't want me to know what was going on. When Ned had his relapse, she must have seen her opportunity to take her money—and everyone else's—and run. Did you know that she has a new home on Grand Cayman? I seriously doubt that we'll ever see her again."

"But what about TAG? Why would she try to stop it after she signed over all of her stock to us? Did you know that she has locked us out of the mansion?" Brick asked.

"It's simple. She wants you to fail. She wants you to take the responsibility for TAG's soon-to-be-lost millions and she wants the investors to be angry at you—and they will be. Everything she can do to bring TAG to a quick death is good for her. By the way, who controls the bank accounts?"

The question was never answered. Dave let out a strange sigh then abruptly stood up with his hand on his flank. His face turned white, then his knees buckled and he collapsed onto the floor, pulling his chair and a table lamp with him.

It was like old times, sitting in the waiting room of a hospital. Derek and Brick were staring at each other, but not speaking, both lost in their thoughts and remorse over how they should have stuck with their lives in Arizona and left the glitter of the big city and big money alone.

A tall, skinny, East Indian doctor wearing a white lab coat and a white turban walked out through the automatic doors and called out, "Mr. Brick Wahl?" When the two men arose and approached him, the doctor introduced himself and led them to a vacant corner of the room.

"Your friend is quite ill. He has developed an infection in his blood which is now affecting his remaining kidney. It is very possible that the kidney will quit working and he will have to have it removed."

"How could he have gotten something like that?" Derek demanded.

"There is no way to know for sure, but probably

some contamination at the time of his first surgery ... he donated a kidney if I am correct?"

"But he's going to be all right isn't he?" Derek asked.

"He is stable right now, but he has received a great deal of antibiotics over the last few months. It is possible that he has developed a resistant strain of bacteria. We must wait until all of our cultures are completed then we will know more," the doctor said in his peculiar, staccato accent.

"We need to let his wife know what is happening. Is he going to be okay?" Brick demanded, grasping the stunned doctor's coat sleeve.

"Sir, would you please let my sleeve go loose, or I will be required to notify the security guard. Now you must leave. In the future I will only speak with Doctor Morris's wife." With that said, the doctor turned away, leaving the two friends to deal with their frustration without his help.

"I'll go back to the Foster office and gather up the paperwork. You go pick up Melody. See if Debra will watch their kids. I'll meet you back here around six," Derek said.

The men had left the building's office in a shambles. Four paramedics had arrived just minutes after Dave had collapsed. By the time they left with him on a gurney, their medical trash was strewn around the room and tromped onto the floor along with the some TAG business papers, which just minutes before had seemed so vital. Tangled, plastic IV tubing was lying on top of Brick's laptop, dripping a sugary electrolyte solution onto the keypad. MaryAnn Carpet was nowhere to be found.

It was past seven in the evening when Derek arrived to pick up the papers and the computer. It had started snowing, making taxis almost impossible to obtain. The office complex was nearly abandoned, the last of the workers heading out to catch their commuter trains and subways. He was choking with thirst and after assessing the clutter he headed for the lounge and vending machines. His coins made a loud clatter and the Coke fell to the bottom of the slot with a clunk. Reaching for the can he caught the movement out of the corner of his eye. At first he thought he was imagining her when Willow stepped out of the doorway's shadow.

"You are a sorry sight," she said. "Did you just run the marathon or is a sweaty, stained suit the new image of TAG?"

Derek was startled and dropped the soda on the floor. Ignoring the fizzing and pinpoint spray from the punctured edge he stepped forward to confront her, their faces just inches apart.

"Why did you lock us out of the mansion? You arrogant shrew!" Derek demanded, getting straight to the point.

"Why should I allow a bunch of strangers to wander around my house with your children running wild, taking and breaking as they go? A better question is why did you break into my home and rifle through my bedroom? I had Benjamin call the police, but then out of the kindness of my heart he called them back to say there had been a misunderstanding. You see, I'm not as coldhearted as you would like to think."

"Do you know about Dave?" Derek asked, taking a

step away and fishing for more coins for the machine—his throat was still burning with thirst and now bile.

"I just this minute got back in town. There was a text message that I should come here. What happened to Dave?" The tone of her voice had softened and she pulled out a chair to sit.

The conversation lasted nearly half an hour. Derek sharing the recent catastrophe while they split a Coke using water cooler paper cups. She actually got tears in her eyes when he told her about Dave having to be admitted to the hospital and Natasha abruptly flying home. A janitor finally showed up with a mop and bucket to clean up the spilled soda, thus breaking the mood.

She claimed that she had left the mansion shortly after the wake. With her old college friend, she had gone to a resort in Vermont. Too upset to sit around in the forest, she had come back to the city. The call from her servants regarding the break-in had spurred anger that surprisingly, she apologized to Derek about.

They walked to the conference room and found that the janitor had straightened the room and cleaned away the trash.

"I see you've taken good care of my briefcase," she said, reaching for it.

He put his hand on the handle and slid it in his direction. "I need to borrow it for a few days."

"What else did your cat burglar take from my house—my jewelry and furs?"

"I thought it was our house too. Remember *mi casa es su casa*? Trust me, nothing was taken that wasn't ours. You knew that the computer was the only complete record of the TAG business dealings, including the money I accepted from your friends in Dubai and Hong Kong. Did you plan on just throwing us out on the street with the leftover food from the wake?"

Willow was silent for a long moment. Her hands had a slight tremor and tears glassed over her corneas, then beaded on her made-up eyelashes, until finally two symmetrical tears fell as though in slow motion, splashing onto the conference table. She made no attempt to brush them away, but instead looked Derek in the eyes.

"I don't know what I was thinking. Matter of fact, I still don't know what I'm thinking about the business. Edward's death has obviously changed my life. I see no reason why it shouldn't affect yours as well. We will just have to work it out. How, I have no clue."

Willow turned toward the door then turned back. "This is a cold, lifeless place to conduct business. Clients will not be impressed. I'll inform Benjamin to leave the door to the mansion open tomorrow and to give you the new alarm code. You can use Edward's office for the TAG main office. I'll have his personal things moved out. But Derek, don't you or your partners ever invade my bedroom again."

He bit his lip to not make a comment about the way she had treated all of them, especially Dave, but decided to let her have the last word. He watched her walk down the corridor, narrow hips swaying and spiked heels clicking on the tile floor on her way out to a waiting limo. He had to admit to himself that she was quite the beautiful and regal woman. What she would do next would be anyone's guess.

Alone, with each motion echoing in the empty building, he took the time to make sure the files were straight then replaced them into the briefcase. He placed the laptop in its carrying case and snapped the lid shut.

If only I had made a recording of that weird conversation for the others to hear. He felt strongly that someday he would need proof that he hadn't dreamed up the whole encounter. The last two days had been strange enough that he wasn't sure himself that she hadn't been an apparition.

It was three long and very anxious days before Doctor David Felshaw was released from the hospital to his apartment in Midtown Manhattan. Debra had stayed at the Felshaw's place to tend the kids while Melody attended to her sick husband who now looked and felt 90 percent better. They were anxious to move forward with their plan to give up the apartment in New York and return to their luxurious home in Arizona.

With new keys and alarm code in hand, Brick and Derek had spent the last few days transforming the mansion office into a real business office. They ordered new file cabinets and bought a bigger, faster desktop computer to manage the business. Brick was often in communication with the bigger investors. When he felt confident they had control of the overall view of TAG's holdings and obligations, he gave Derek the okay to fly back to Phoenix.

When the two men first showed up on the mansion's doorstep the day after Derek's heart-to-heart conversation with Willow, Benjamin and Margo had fallen all over themselves making apologies for their earlier behavior. The TAG plaque Ms. Carpet had prepared for the downtown office was fixed to the gate of the mansion, although the men still planned to use the downtown office for additional staff as the need grew.

"You've got to go ahead with your plans to move back to Arizona, the weather here is only going to get worse," Brick told Melody. His best friend Dave was lying on the couch in a warm-up suit. Debra had fixed dinner for the Felshaw clan and had come by to drop it off.

"Are you sure you will be all right here by yourselves?" Melody asked, Debra holding her hand.

"It will be a relief to have you and your kids out of our hair," Brick joked. "As a matter of fact, maybe we'll send Lexy with you so we can really be alone for a few days."

"Not in a million years," Debra said giving him a slug in the shoulder.

"I'll set up my Skype account as soon as I get home," Dave said. "Then we can confer on a moment's notice."

"By the way, did you get the final word on the type of infection you picked up?" Brick asked Dave.

"Nothing ever grew out of the cultures. That Indian doctor you guys confronted insisted on a toxicology screen and they did pick up some sort of strange chemical in my blood, but they think it must be a contaminant. By the second day in the hospital, my kidney function was almost back to normal and my fever completely gone."

"I think she poisoned him," Melody said. "Willow had gone bonkers that week and hated everyone. It wouldn't be surprising if she wanted us all dead and out of her life, not just her house."

"No way," Dave protested. "She may be strange, but I don't believe that she is evil. Besides, there is no way she could have done something like that."

The conversation was interrupted by a crying child and the subject dropped. A week later the moving van picked up the Morris family's household goods and they were on their way back to Arizona. Brick had surprised them with a limo to take them to the airport. Dave was back to 90 percent of his strength. He had even contacted his old medical practice partners about the possibility of returning to work part-time. The farewells were brief, knowing that they would all see each other frequently.

Back at their own apartment Brick and Debra ate a lunch of leftovers, played with Lexy, and talked about how their life could finally settle down to a routine. At least that's what they thought.

It snowed again that morning in Manhattan. Brick had decided to walk the six blocks to the mansion from their apartment. He didn't even own a winter dress coat, so he looked a bit out of place in his North Face ski jacket on top of his white shirt and tie. His penny loafers, which always looked stylish in Arizona, picked up slush as he walked. The passing pedestrians had on some sort of strange rubber covers for their shoes which he was beginning to covet. By the time he turned the corner to the mansion his socks were soaked and his toes were numb. If he was going to make this place his home he would need to commit to additional clothing.

As he approached the mansion he noticed a man standing at the gate, staring at the brass TAG nameplate. He was a stocky man in his mid-thirties, wearing a wool overcoat and a felt hat. He had a three or four day growth of whiskers, and was wearing dark sunglasses, which in the heavily overcast sky, seemed out of place.

"Can I help you?" Brick asked.

The man looked Brick up and down before he spoke and then said, "I'm looking to find a Mr. Derek."

The accent was hard for Brick to place, but the next sentence made the guy's background clear. "I come from Bucharest," the word Bucharest coming in a guttural groan from deep in the guy's chest, more like a belch than a location, "to get money Mr. Derek promised to me. Where does he living," he said, in an even stronger accent.

Brick was stymied, not knowing what to say or do. He had heard the tale of Derek's Romanian encounter with some angry gangsters, but was sure that Derek had skipped the country without accepting any investment money or purchasing any property. He could play dumb, but the TAG nameplate was most likely all that the guy needed to make a connection.

Brick wished he hadn't spoken to the man; thinking in retrospect that he could have just walked on by the mansion had he known who this stranger was and what he wanted.

"Mr. Derek used to work here, but quit and moved away. He doesn't even live in New York anymore," Brick said, proud of himself for being able to fabricate a half-truth.

"You have telephone number? I want it. And I want address. I come to America to check up on money. I don't go home without knowing that it in safe place ... maybe in my pocket." The pauses between his short sentences, Brick quickly decided, were more for effect than a lack of language skill.

Again Brick was trying to remember if Derek had taken any investment money from the Romanians.

He was positive that no transactions had taken place. Looking through the man's dark shades into his snake-like eyes elicited a feeling of darkness and evil—the same feeling that Derek must have experienced.

"It is cold out here. Why don't you invite me into your building and you can call your friend and we can make arrangements to meet."

"Actually, I'm on my way to a meeting and won't be going inside. Besides, I don't know how to get in touch with the person ... you said his name is Derek?" Brick said. In spite of the cold, he was feeling sweat beading on his forehead.

"You find him for me and I come back at sixteen hours. You be here and take me inside and I talk to Mr. Derek. I don't want trouble from you, but you are a very bad liar."

He watched the man turn and walk to the curb where the first car to come up the street was a black, monochromic Maserati four-door with blacked-out windows. It stopped at the curb where the back door opened and moments later the Romanian was gone. Brick looked up and down the sidewalk before he turned to the mansion's front door and inserted his key into the lock.

"I swear, I didn't take a penny of those hoodlums' money," Derek insisted. "And I for sure didn't promise to buy any of their pathetic real estate. I ate lunch with them and they insisted on paying since it was their private club. Other than that they didn't give me a nickel. I can't believe they have come to New York thinking we owe them anything. If I was to think someone would be after us, I'd think it would be the people in Macau. Those people were really scary."

"So what should I do when he comes back? I can't just avoid them by not coming to work. I have the closing agreement on the apartment building in Denver that I've got to finish by tomorrow," Brick said.

"I'll call Willow and see if she knows anything about what's going on with them. She's the one who hooked me up with the Romanians in the first place," Derek said. "For all we know, she may have taken their money after I left there."

"When was the last time you talked to her? I've tried to call her all week and I just get her voice mail."

"She sent me a text yesterday, saying she is on a yacht in the harbor at Monte Carlo. She wants me to look into putting some TAG money into an old hotel there that's on some kind of a plaza nearby an old casino. I guess the big Grand Prix race actually passes the hotel. She thinks the place is in a prime location. She wants me to fly over and check it out."

"We don't have enough money to do a deal like that," Brick said, "unless she's still getting investors from sources like the Romanians."

"Well, the money keeps coming in and we have to put it someplace. I'm all for being diversified in both types and location of our real estate. I'll try to reach her and see what the Romanian deal is all about."

Derek called Willow numerous times over the next three days without success. He was back in Phoenix with his family, but still kept trying. He gave up at 2:00 p.m. on the third day, knowing it was already bedtime in Europe. At three in the morning his cell phone rang, startling him and Natasha awake. Middle-of-the-night calls were never good news.

"Derek, I noticed that you left me a text? Something about Rome? I didn't quite understand it," Willow said. Although the connection was good, there was loud music playing in the background and her words sounded a bit slurred.

Derek struggled to get his eyes open and staggered into the hall, closing the master bedroom door behind him. Once in his office his brain had cleared enough to answer the widow.

"I called because the mobsters you sent me to Bucharest to meet with showed up in New York this week. They claim we have some of their money. I didn't take a nickel from them. You want to tell me what's going on?"

"Calm down Derek. I'm sorry to call you in the middle of the night, but I just got your message."

"Did the Romanians send you any money to invest?" he demanded.

"It's not a big deal. They called the day after you so rudely stood them up for their appointment and I told them one of your children had become ill. You did such a good sales job on them that instead of wanting to sell us property, they insisted on sending $20 million to invest. It arrived just when my world was falling apart with Edward, so I must have forgotten all about it. It's in one of the Cayman accounts. I'll have to track it down, but I have just the place to invest it. We can use it to buy and renovate a cute little boutique hotel here in Monaco that I told you about. You'll love the place. It has a view of the harbor and the Royal Casino is just a stone's throw away. It even has a row of balconies looking right out on the formula one race course."

Derek was at a loss for words. TAG had over $200 million in investors' monies with expectations of rapid turnover and profits. That was what Foster had promised and what was realistic when he was alive. Now those returns seemed impossible, especially since this woman couldn't keep track of $20 million chunks of investors' change, and she wanted to spend it on renovations and hotels to impress her friends.

"Could you please send me the details of the money's location so I can get it sent back to the Romanian gangsters? I told you then that they were dangerous and that we shouldn't do business with them."

"But Derek, love, this little hotel will be the perfect place for their money. Those people love to gamble and with the casino and the car race and the film festival at Cannes, the property here is like gold. With $20 million we can tie up the deal and make the building a showplace. Then you can put the place on the market and triple our money," she said with a conviction that was beginning to impress him. "Think of how fun it would be for all of us to get together here on the Riviera. I'll bet your wife looks great in a bikini."

"Brick said these guys want some kind of accounting now. Not some dream hotel in a couple of years. Incidentally, there are two of the original investors who are due their semiannual profit payments this month. That's going to take $4 million. We need to close some fast deals. Ned never intended for us to make any long-term investments. You know that?"

Derek was now fully awake and pacing the small study. He had never liked the business plan Edward Foster III had established, where each investor was promised

5 percent of his initial capital, plus 8 percent interest returned to him every six months. It was a sweet dream investment that normally would have been too good to be believed, but with Foster's contacts and his own personal wealth to back it, Derek, Brick, and Dave had bought into the idea—especially since their positions were free and guaranteed them a healthy cash flow along with the other investors. The first few deals Derek handled already had turned over and were getting ready to close for huge profits. Things were looking good with the Arab and even the Chinese investor's money, but everything about the Romanians tied his stomach in knots.

"Willow, you need to just return their money. We don't have the time to oversee rebuilding a hotel in Monte Carlo or anywhere else. It's just Brick and me to do all the work. Dave is going back to his medical practice when he gets stronger. His health can't handle the stress of this business. Unless you want to take care of the hotel thing yourself and make it a separate deal, you need to return the money."

"They will probably want their 50 percent return right now if we give them the money back," she said in a matter-of-fact tone.

"I didn't promise them any 50 percent return!"

"But Derek darling, that's what we promised everyone. Remember? You have been telling them that they would get 5 percent every six months and a 100 percent balloon of their principle at the end of the five-year investment or when we return their principle. That's 50 percent where this girl went to school. You've forgotten about the interest … but they certainly won't."

"That was based on you and Ned continuing to bring

in investors. How can we keep up that pace with him gone and you off to who-knows-where, on yachts and tropical islands? Brick can barely keep up with the paperwork and I'm doing my best to find and make real estate deals. The investors will just have to settle for a little less until the economy turns around."

Derek didn't know if he was feeling anger at Willow, or a sense of sinking into an abyss of panic as the reality of the situation became clear. His previous vision of grand wealth for himself and his partners was evaporating into the reality that TAG's obligations were growing out of control.

There was a flurry of static on the phone. "Willow, are you still there?"

"I am, but just for a minute more. Derek, my friend, you have got to work a little harder. You can't just lie around your swimming pool and expect the bank drafts to float down from heaven. Edward worked seven days a week for forty years to build his organization. You boys have been at it for what? Six months now? You can't expect success to happen without lots of work and a few tears. Tell that sweet friend of yours, Dave, to forget medicine. He made the decision to quit his medical practice back in July when Edward brought you all into the company. He needs to stick with his decision and help you out. He is a very convincing salesman. After all, he talks people into letting him cut on them and even remove their knee joints and replace them with titanium contraptions. Surely, extracting money from rich folks can't be that much harder for him."

"I'll talk to him, but before you hang up I've got to know what to do about the Romanians."

"Forget about the Romanians! They are a bunch of spoiled bullies. Wave a couple of real estate contracts at them and they will be happy. Did they really tell you they invested $20 million in TAG? The idiots were so wasted on whisky and cocaine when they gave me the check, that they probably forgot that it was really $30 million," she said with a wicked laugh.

"Where exactly is the money now? I need the name of the investment bank. We need the name of the bank and the account numbers," Derek asked in a near frantic voice. "I haven't seen any deposit slips for that amount and I'm sure if Brick had he would have told me."

"It must be in my purse somewhere. I'll look for it and e-fax you a copy, but only if you promise to at least take a look at this hotel. It's a bargain that won't last long. You boys and your wives will love it here. You need to hop on the plane and have a look-see. Bring Natasha if you like. They also have some favorable tax laws in Monaco. We might even want to move the company here."

Derek heard another clatter of static, then loud music and then the phone went silent. He immediately started to redial her number, but then stopped. He had too much to think about already. He needed to talk to Brick and Dave. First, he needed another four hours of sleep.

Two weeks later, Doctor Dave Felshaw was wearing his best suit and a new, light-blue shirt with a red-and-blue striped tie. He hated to dress up, but glanced at himself in the floor-to-ceiling glass wall of the hospital corridor and pulled his shoulders back. He looked good, but a bit older than he did five months previously, when he had last walked down this hallway. Perhaps there were even a couple of grey hairs mixed in his sideburns. He was on his way to the medical staff office to tell them he was finished taking his leave of absence. Now he had to make a quick appearance before the executive committee to have his operating room and admitting privileges reinstated. Within ten minutes of explaining to his friends about his time in New York, he could be on the way to the OR to assist one of his partners on a total hip replacement. He had spent the last twenty minutes of the drive to the hospital going over the steps of the procedure in his mind.

He had been feeling pretty good lately, but not perfect. He had considered taking another month of lying around the house and working on his golf swing, until Melody brought up Christmas. She had grandiose plans for the kids and the extended family. The problem was that the bonus money they had received from Mr. Edward Foster III seemed to be blowing away in the desert wind. After the income tax pre-payment, the church donation, payments on their home in Arizona and the apartment in New York, the new wardrobe Melody had picked up in the city, not to mention the hospital bills that Willow had promised to cover but hadn't yet addressed, they were going to need an infusion of cash before the fifteenth of April next year. The idea of going back to work was growing on him. His older brother had once told him, "A big mortgage payment can make the simplest bone fracture and casting seem exciting."

Ever since the third month of working in private practice, Dave never had taken home less than $20,000 a month. The last year, before the rattlesnake bite, he had made nearly half a million dollars as a partner in his group practice. Now unfortunately, he had to get back into the hospital operating room to fire up the money machine.

He was greeted with warm smiles by the eight men and women who surrounded the conference table. He knew them well. He even knew their spouse's names. They were his friends, his golfing buddies, and one of them was his previous business partner.

"It's great to see you back, Dave," the chairman of the committee said with a smile. "You have had quite an adventure according to your statement and the articles I read in *Business Weekly* about your new company and the unfortunate death of it's founder. I must say I admire you for trying to save his life. I suppose you know that *Forbes* magazine is even doing a story on his life and you three heroes bringing him down that mountain on your backs. You guys were fantastic. I know that I couldn't have done that."

"Twice he saved that Foster guy's life. Twice," said Mary Platt, the attractive internist, and Melody's close friend, who was sitting immediately to his right.

"We discussed the situation of your kidney donation and subsequent infection here with the group before you arrived. We are all looking forward to having you and your expertise back in the hospital; however, the boys at legal and our infectious disease committee have laid down some pretty strict rules regarding possible carriers of MRSA. We received the lab data from your hospitalization in New York and they were 99 percent sure that it was the methicillin-resistant strain of staph that you had."

"They were never really sure because I had started on Cipro the day before I got deathly ill," Dave said.

"And Dave, that's the second reason we have some concern. We understand that you self-administered that medication. We all know how the Board of Medicine frowns on that practice."

Dave felt like he had been kicked in the gut. A wave of nausea nearly brought up his breakfast. He started to say something about how everyone there had probably self-treated themselves and their families, but Mary put a restraining hand on his knee, giving him the signal to remain quiet for his own good.

"Before we can approve your reinstatement, we will need two blood cultures thirty days apart and a letter from your personal physician that you are infection-free. I'm sure that you recognize that this is for your protection and the safety of the hospital," the chairman concluded.

"How can they do that?" Brick asked Dave, staring incredulously into his phone. "You still have your license don't you?"

"Sure, but without operating room privileges I can't really practice. I have to get in the hospital to operate. That's why I'm calling. I need to get back into the loop with TAG. We've been spending money like drunken sailors."

"I can relate to that," Brick said. "A million bucks sounded like a fortune in August, but living here in the city is at least four times as expensive as at home in Arizona and we only have three mouths to feed."

"Didn't Foster say something about a year-end bonus?" Dave asked.

"Year end, month's end, what does it matter? There isn't any extra money to pay anyone. Derek just got back in town from Frankfurt where he signed a contract on a parking garage and Willow tried to get him to dump money into restoring some old, firetrap of a hotel she found. He told you about that didn't he?"

"He said he was going to Europe, but I was busy or sick when he called and didn't quite get it."

"Well, it doesn't really matter in the short run. He had to act interested in it to keep Willow from pulling the plug on the whole company. Luckily he put her off for a couple of months. We owe investors almost $10 million on January first. It's their semi-annual profit money. If we can't raise it these next two weeks we are going to be in a big hurt."

"Well, I can't do any procedures in the hospital for about two months. What can I do to help? There are still our parent's friends that have some money."

"Willow just faxed me a new list of names. Everyone's looking for an end-of-year tax break. Maybe we can get lucky. Catch the next plane back here to New York and you can go to work on raising money. And Dave, it's freezing cold, bring your best warm clothes."

"There is no way that I can miss Christmas with the family, and you and Derek shouldn't either. I'll come for a week then come home and be back there in New York for New Year's Eve. I always wanted to see the New Year come in at Times Square."

On New Year's morning the three Arizona men sat huddled in a coffee shop on Madison and 68th Street. The wind was howling and the temperature was pressing the mercury lower by the hour. None of the men had ever felt more chilled. They had just mailed out twenty-seven checks, all of which they printed off of the small HP printer at the mansion using a Quicken program they had borrowed from Dave's old office secretary. The holidays had come and gone almost without notice. It had taken every ounce of their energy and every minute of their time for the men to contact and convince the people on Willow's list to invest in TAG.

Brick's brainstorm and Derek's fast action had saved the day. Brick had been reading *Forbes'* year-end tax saving hints when he found the website for a wind machine company. Dave did some late-night tax law study, and in twelve hours Derek had partnered with a Colorado clean energy company that builds electricity producing wind machines. It was old technology used in California clear back from the seventies, but was now in the public's focus again with bigger, more powerful fans and generators, and new government incentives. Their project wasn't even out of the ground yet, but the funds they raised before the

year-end would probably qualify the American investors—
"for sure qualify," was their sales pitch—for big income tax
credits and deductions. The three men had spent an all-
nighter at Kinko's printing the documents on December
29th in order to have them delivered and signed by the
31st. By New Year's Day, they had raised the essential $10
million, plus enough to each take a small salary bonus.

Having now met the old investor's profit requirements
had bought them some time. TAG had another three
months of life. Christmas had consisted of a two day-
visit to Arizona to be with the kids and wives—Debra
had locked up their New York apartment to spend the
holidays with her parents in Arizona. The men had taken
over the mansion, giving Benjamin and Margo the rest of
the month off. Willow spoke with them on rare occasion,
but stayed out of their business and away from the
mansion. Each of the partners' Christmas present to their
wives was a promised trip in the late spring to Monte
Carlo for the grand re-opening of the Hotel Saule, which
they would later learn was the French word for "willow
tree." The men had taken to calling it "The Snake Pit."

None of the women were pleased about the abbreviated
Christmas together, but the kids were happy with their
toys and didn't even mention their dads' absences. The
men bought their own Christmas presents, new iPhones,
and a faster laptop for the office at the mansion.

By New Year's night, the crisis was averted and all
three men were on their way back to Phoenix to warm
up. They promised each other that they wouldn't let a
cash pinch like that one ever happen again. They planned
to take a week off and then be back on the job with a
renewed physical energy and enthusiasm.

The winter break was awesome. The men spent time playing with their kids and extended family. They played golf, did household repairs, yard work, and romanced their wives, without any significant business distractions. Brick even managed to complete a couple of very profitable pork belly trades—once a gambler, always a gambler. But the seven days went by rapidly.

For Brick and Debra, the trip back to New York was painful. It had been shirtsleeve weather in Phoenix. When the town car pulled up in front of their Manhattan apartment, the snow was blowing, and a four-foot-deep snow tunnel led the way to the front door. Later that day, Brick made his way through the blizzard to the mansion. Benjamin had scooped a path to the front door and had a roaring fire in the office fireplace. Brick was greeted inside by the two TAG staff members who looked tan, rested, and happy to have him back. On the corner of the entry table was a tall stack of unopened mail addressed to TAG. In addition, Brick had a visitor.

Sitting on a straight-back chair next to the dining table, was a small middle-age man of apparent Asian heritage. He had a nearly bald head, full, broad shoulders, and small, black eyes that looked like they had been painted on his round, amber face.

"Allow me to introduce myself," the man said in an obvious second-language English. He stood and made a slight but formal bow. "My name is Yong Lee. I am employed by a gentleman named Chen. My employer is an acquaintance of one of your partners, a Mister Derek Morris. I also had the pleasure of meeting Mr. Derek on his recent trip to Hong Kong."

A very sick feeling struck Brick as he heard the words

"Hong Kong." He knew that Derek had solicited money from the billionaire Chen, but couldn't remember seeing the written record of the amount invested or its paper trail in the information that Willow had given him. In reality, there had been so many things going on at the time of Derek's return that Brick had nearly forgotten about the China connection.

"It is a pleasure to meet you," Brick said, extending his hand. "Could I offer you something to drink? Perhaps you would like a cup of tea or hot cider?"

"Tea would be fine," the man said with a smile.

Brick had not played host to anyone in the mansion before, and was at a loss when he went into the kitchen. To his relief, Margo already had prepared a tray with a pot of hot water, a selection of herbal teas, and a glass of Diet Pepsi for Brick.

When she delivered them and the men were settled in the parlor, the stranger removed an envelope from his breast pocket and began speaking. "We have heard very little from your office the past three months. Mr. Chen gave a Mr. Derek a check for $30 million to be paid to the account of his old friend Edward Foster III, with the prearranged agreement that it would be invested in an entity called TAG. I have no idea what those letters mean, but the promise was to invest the money in American real estate. A suggested return amount on Mr. Chen's investment was discussed and a timeline was set up for that return. Since I was to be here on other business I was asked to stop by, as you Americans like to say, and obtain an update on the investment."

The skin on Brick's neck and face—still cold from his walk to the mansion—suddenly burned. Thinking it better to say nothing rather than to lie, he held up his index finger indicating that the man should wait for a moment. He walked into Ned's massive study and searched until he uncovered a stack of brochures explaining the wind machines. On the cover was a picture of twelve of the massive, three-bladed generators lined up along a beautiful Colorado mountain peak.

"Here is where the money is temporarily invested," Brick said, handing the glossy sales information to the man. "The United States real estate market is still depreciating, so for the time being, we have made a decision to put our investor's into a bit of a longer-term, but much more profitable, venture. Once the market hits its bottom, we'll be buying commercial property again, in a fast and furious manner. Then the profit margins will be enormous. Your Mr. Chen may want to invest even more with us in a few months. We'll keep you advised."

The visitor looked at Brick for an uncomfortable length of time before he spoke. "Mr. Chen is not interested in electricity machines or old houses. He is only interested in making a substantial profit on his investment; a profit that your partner guaranteed. I believe the first return on that money will be due in April. Please see that Mr. Chen is notified a few days before you transfer the funds in order that he might have another location arranged to invest those profits."

The Chinese gentleman then set down his full cup, stood and walked toward the door. Brick tried to convince him to stay, to let him explain the wind farm or some of the other potential future investments, but the man was silently insistent on leaving. When they got to the curb, a stretch Bentley was waiting for the silent Yong Lee.

Brick hadn't even waited until the Chinese man's limo pulled away before he was dialing Derek's number.

"I didn't promise the man anything except that the funds would be invested in American real estate," Derek said into the phone. "The profits and the payout were Willow's part of the deal before I ever arrived in Hong Kong. She probably promised the Arabs the same thing. Whatever she told those investors, I'm sure they would like the wind farm idea if they would just give us a chance to explain it. The numbers are looking better every week. Congress is considering even better tax incentives to add to those already in place," Derek continued.

"Derek, listen to me. This Chinese guy is downright scary. I don't think tax incentives are part of their vocabulary. He emphasized that his Mr. Chen isn't interested in electricity or wind or anything else—just the money—every nickel of what is now and will be owed him. And he made it pretty clear that he expects every dollar of his money is to be in American real estate. Not wind or air or water or Monte Carlo hotels."

Derek had been sitting out on his patio watching one of the kids fly a balsa wood airplane and keeping track of the others while Natasha went to the store. He didn't have any figures in front of him to back up his next statement, but said it anyway. "I could transfer the accounts around so that it looks like Chen's money is in the big Chicago office building. Why don't I go ahead and do that, then we won't have to worry about it."

"If you can do that then I agree, but we also need to start planning now for the March 30th when we'll owe the semi-annual profit payout."

"I already have it in my planner. That's the same time

the Arab's payout on their money is also due," Derek said.

"How's Dave holding up?"

"He is still weak but improving. One of his friends from med school, John Glenn, is part of the original U-Haul money family and has hinted that they would like to put some cash into TAG. Maybe we can use part of it to cover the interest on the Asian man's money."

"Great! If it comes through, we'll use some of it to cover the March payments," Brick said. "I've got to go; the phone in the study is ringing."

"He can't be serious!" Natasha said. "Cover the Arab and Chinese interest payouts with the new investment money from American investors? Is that how this scheme is supposed to work?"

She looked across the table at her husband and then at Dave. They were in the middle of an emergency meeting when she returned home. Dave looked up at her with a worried expression and Derek—always the optimist— smiled and shrugged. "It will all work out," he said.

"This whole TAG business sounded too good to be true from the first," she continued, giving the men a disgusted look. "Now it's sounding more and more like a Ponzi scheme than a business opportunity—rob Peter to pay Paul? Or is it rob Chang to pay Ahab? Is that the plan? What happens if the real estate market doesn't come back and you don't reap those huge profits you're promising everyone?"

"Do you think for a minute that we haven't thought of that and worried ourselves sick about it?" Dave asked, in a tone he seldom used with anyone, let alone a friend's wife.

"But maybe it would have been good to have thought it through a bit before the three of you gave up you life's work and dragged us all to New York like a flock of rockstar groupies chasing an idol. You were all so enamored with Mr. Edward Foster III, you couldn't think straight. Or was it Willow who seduced you into believing you could all be the new Ned Fosters or Rockefellers or whatever?"

"What we did, we did with common consent and each of you wives. The three of you were just as enamored and seduced—if you like that word—as we were," Derek said, keeping his voice low and objective. "Think about it, sweetheart. It's only been six months since we started into this thing. Think of all the things we've seen, the places we've been, and all the new interesting people we've met, not to mention the money. Dave might have seen a million dollars all together at one time, but you and I certainly haven't and probably wouldn't. Even after taxes we have more money in the bank than we have ever dreamed of. That's opposed to the huge debt we had six months ago. Brick was on the verge of going completely under six months ago. Dave is the only one who is worse off financially, and we're going to keep working until we can get him and TAG on their feet and making everyone money."

"That's my Derek," Natasha said looking at Dave. "He is the most optimistic person on the planet. However, he forgot to mention just now that he is the only one who has been seeing the world and meeting the new interesting people, while you have been cut on and infected and I've made more moves with the kids than the United Van Lines drivers."

Dave laughed at her sarcasm, not refuting it, but not entirely agreeing either. When he stood up to leave, he had to pull himself up from the table. This awkwardness drew their attention to the thinness of his formerly muscular arms. They had been told by Melody that he had lost over thirty pounds since the original kidney donation, and the subsequent infection was still taking its toll.

"I'll leave the debate to the two of you," Dave said. "But, Natasha, you need to look around at this nice house and at the cars in the driveway and at your cute kids. All of this came before Foster and TAG and it was your husband's hard work that got you here, not Foster or Willow or your imagined Ponzi scheme. If anybody is to blame for the problems we face right now, it is that damn rattlesnake." He put his hand reassuringly on her shoulder. "Don't discount the possibility that five years from now we'll all be wealthy beyond any of our dreams."

"Or we'll all be working on some chain gang and our kids will be in foster care," she quickly quipped back at Dave as she snuggled up to him and gave him a peck on the cheek.

Everyone faked a chuckle as they walked Dave out to his car. Each trying to believe that the problems they were facing, although they seemed quite insurmountable, were not life threatening. At least not yet.

Brick worked in the mansion's office every day. Once or twice a week he would venture downtown to the Wall Street district to work in the Foster Building. He liked the first floor suite of rooms where, just as MaryAnn Carpet said would happen, a second brass plate had been installed on the door. *TAG World Headquarters* read the sign. Inside the office was a secretary's desk complete with desktop computer, fax, printer, letter baskets, and other necessary equipment. There was however, no secretary, and the rest of the rooms sat empty as well, but all were kept clean awaiting the arrival of whoever might need to meet or work there. There were even small nameplates on three of the desks naming Brick, Dave, and Derek with their formal titles.

On a rare sunny day in late January, Brick entered the office building. The main desk information secretary had called him insisting that he come to the office to meet with a client of Mr. Foster's who refused to meet with Brick at the mansion, and likewise refused to leave a name. He felt like getting out into the fresh air anyway so had agreed to meet the person.

He could smell a hint of perfume as he opened the

unlocked TAG door. Sitting in a straight-backed chair was an attractive, older woman. She was wearing a soft, beige wool suit, alligator pumps, and had a full-length, sable coat draped across her lap. The woman stood and offered her hand, which was adorned with two fabulous rings. Her fingers were thin and her skin was cold and parchment-like. Though her hair was a silky, dark brown and her figure trim, the leathered skin under her blue cashmere collar hinted of years far beyond her wrinkle-less face. The woman had a warm smile, which jogged Brick's memory enough that he knew he had seen it before. He had met this woman, but couldn't recall where.

"It is kind of you to travel all the way downtown to speak with me Mr. Wahl," the woman said. "We met at Edward's funeral. I'm Edward's sister, Kristen Bent."

She waited for the light to go on in Brick's head, but he was becoming good at faking and didn't flinch. Instead he came back with a cordial, "Of course I remember you, Mrs. Bent. Ned—he wanted all of us to call him Ned—had spoken often of you. I must admit that in the confusion of the funeral that I have forgotten where you live."

"I spend my winters in Palm Beach, but live here in New York most of the time ... in Westchester County. I flew into town to meet with the attorneys—Edward's attorneys. They have finally decided to read the will. It is going to take place on Wednesday at ten o'clock. Since I have no communication with any of his three widows, I thought that you might be available to accompany me to the reading. I believe that it is in both of our interests that we are there."

Trying his best not to act surprised he said, "Did I hear you say widows?"

"That is correct. There are three, you know. Or perhaps you didn't know that," she said, nodding at the chairs. They both sat down on a couch in Brick's office before she went on. "First there was Wendy—his high school sweetheart. She loved the country and sports life. She followed him everywhere when he was riding his bike in Europe. That was a hard life for her. Living alone in dumpy French apartments by herself all day while he trained with the other teammates, and then putting up with his moods when he didn't ride well. They still were very happy, until the money started to roll in and he was forced to move here to New York to build on his name and to satisfy the sponsors. She just couldn't handle the city's crowds and soon moved back to her hometown. Fortunately there were no children.

"Then there is Wanda. Edward picked her up on the rebound. She was a knockout runway model. She was a sweet girl, but had her eye on having her pictures in fashion magazines, not celebrity charity photos. Her looks and sensuality knocked him off his feet and his bike. They were only together for a few weeks when he first got sick, and she asked for an annulment. She packed up and left without even saying good-bye. It broke his heart. He became reclusive for a time and thought only about making money. And then of course you know Willow. She worked for him for a long time before he even noticed her, but once he did get to know her, she manipulated her way all the way into his home."

"He liked the W names didn't he?"

"He liked all of the women in his life, but most of all he liked riding his touring bicycle and making money for himself and for his friends. He often tried to include his extended family in the excitement of the big city, but there always seemed to be some last minute reason to cancel the birthday dinners or holidays at his beach houses. Our other siblings and our parents—of course—have long since passed. Now there is just me and my daughters. I don't need or want any of his money. I married a good man who left me comfortable and my children are fine, but I would like to see just how he handled the wives. Call it curiosity."

"What time is the reading?" Brick asked, then remembered that she had already told him when she repeated the ten o'clock time.

"Actually, the attorney suggested that we meet at a neutral place here in the city and this location was mentioned. I suppose that unless you don't allow it, we might meet here? There is a larger conference room on the second floor I'm told, but there will just be a few of us. Do we have your permission?"

Brick nodded his agreement, but was very confused about the reasoning behind this woman requesting to use the TAG offices, and even more curious as to why Willow wasn't calling the shots.

"I'll have the secretary reserve the larger room and have it ready with some refreshments," he said, knowing that he could call on MaryAnn to help. She was always pleasant and seemed more than willing to be of service.

"I hope you will be here for the reading. Also, your two partners should be present. I wouldn't be surprised at anything Ned might do with his property. He always liked an unpredictable outcome, especially if it made people smile."

Mrs. Bent stood and held her coat out for him to

assist her. She slipped on long, brown leather gloves, and then turned in order for him to slide the luxurious fur onto her slender shoulders. She then faced him, extending her hand to him along with a warm smile. He walked her to the building's main exit and down the steps, where a frosty-white Mercedes sedan waited at the curb with a chauffeur holding the car's door. As she settled into the rear passenger seat she looked at him and waved.

"You both have got to be on the plane tomorrow morning," Brick explained to Derek, who was not being easily convinced.

"That would be a total waste of time. I'll be surprised if Willow will even allow you in the room, let alone all three of us. It's the reading of his will. Not a stockholder's business meeting!"

"But you haven't met the woman I just spent an hour with. This sister is without a doubt the classiest lady I've ever met. She looks and acts like she is important in the overall picture. When she said we should all be there, I believed her. She knows something that we don't."

"I'm already scheduled to be in Seattle to look at a warehouse. It's just a mile from the Microsoft campus and is a sure bet to appreciate quickly when they expand their new cell phone line. I can't reschedule with this guy or he will dump us and sell it to someone else. We need the buy more than he needs the sale. Besides, Dave can't come to New York. He is still not feeling well enough for an unplanned trip. You go and represent TAG for us.

And Brick, take good notes! In the meantime, I'll make us some big bucks."

"Do you think we need to hire our own attorney?" Brick asked.

"You know more about TAG than any attorney we can hire," Derek assured him.

The idea of having their personal lawyer had been discussed before, but the cost of a Manhattan lawyer was ridiculous. Dave's brother-in-law, Trevor Allen, had done some work for them on a few of their smaller real estate deals. Other than that they had always used Foster's old legal firm and had never seen a bill—guessing that those hours were blended into the large corporate account.

"Okay, I'll go to the meeting, but you promise to stay by the phone just in case we have to do some quick negotiating."

The following morning, the sky was colorless. The wind was gusty and freezing cold. Brick left his apartment early and luckily caught one of the cabs that normally were scarce on stormy days. No one was walking the city's traffic-jammed streets, and by the time he arrived he thought he would be late for the meeting. MaryAnn had arranged for a large conference room, and had several dozen chairs set up in a double semicircle facing a table to be used by Foster's attorney. There was a side table of light refreshments and a video camera set up on a tripod fifteen feet in front of the attorney's table. When Brick arrived, most of the chairs already were occupied by people that he didn't know.

Brick looked around the room and saw that MaryAnn was busy serving coffee to the attendees. She acknowledged his arrival and his glance at the camera and just gave a little shrug, nodding toward the back of the room. There was Willow, huddled in conference with two strangers, both wearing very expensive suits. Brick took a seat next to a woman he had seen at the funeral. He introduced himself and smiled, but she didn't reciprocate.

At 10:20 a.m., the final chairs were filled and the attorney called the meeting to order. Willow never greeted Brick or even looked in his direction. Her chair was at the far end of the row of chairs.

"She is too weird for words," he thought.

Just as the attorney was introducing himself and his partner, the conference room doors opened and in walked Kristen Bent, the deceased's sister, followed by a tall, thirtyish woman with long, blond hair, a tight, grey skirt, and a suit jacket that only an attorney would wear. She was pulling a small, rectangular, leather briefcase with wheels that clattered on the tile floor as it rolled across the room. A slight commotion ensued as seating was adjusted and the two women were settled.

Foster's attorney again began speaking. "Thank you for being here. My name is Mitchel Platt, and I have been asked by Mr. Edward Foster III to prepare and maintain custody of his last will and testament." He held up the leather-bound document as though he were offering it at auction. The attendees all stared as he began to open it.

"It is now my responsibility to open and read the document. Please rest assured that this is the only will in existence. I have represented Edward Foster for twenty-five years. Every two years, like clockwork, he has reread and adjusted his will to comply with the changing laws of the State of New York and with the changes in his personal life."

There was a quiet shuffling of chairs and a few murmurs as Platt laid the leather case on the desk and withdrew a single sheet of paper. This was followed by absolute silence from the audience. Platt coughed twice and then began to read.

"I, Edward Foster III, resident of the State of New York, being of sound mind and body and under no duress, leave this last will and testament. To those who mourn my passing, please accept my gratitude but also my request to get on with the rest of your lives and choose to be happy. Rest assured that I have lived a full and generally happy life. I was never blessed with children, but have felt the joy of close friendships. I have never achieved greatness in the world of academics or politics, but have reaped the reward of hard work in competitive sports and in the world of business—those were my children. I have enjoyed the companionship of many lovely women, three of whom I married. For their patience and indulgence of my numerous idiosyncrasies, I wish to reward them with the following:

To Wendy Foster, my first wife, I leave the sum of $5 million and my ski lodge in Vail, Colorado.

To Wanda Foster, my second wife, I leave the sum of $5 million and my beach house in Grand Caymans.

To Willow Foster, my present wife, I leave the town house in Manhattan, and the remaining cash in my J.P. Morgan IRA.

To my loyal secretary, MaryAnn Carpet, I leave $3 million dollars and my condo in Palm Beach, Florida.

To my sister Kristen Foster Bent, I leave the remainder

of my estate, including my outstanding shares in TAG, LLC. Said shares are to be split equally with her daughter, Valencia."

Mr. Platt cleared his throat and then replaced the single sheet of paper in its leather case. The room was silent as he slid back his chair and stood. He was nearly to the door when her voice shattered the silence of the room.

"That is all a damn lie. You were supposed to leave everything to me!" Willow's voice had a hollow tone to it, as though she was speaking to Edward Foster's ghost standing in front of her. "No one else deserves a penny. I gave you my life. I gave you my kidney. How could you do this?"

The question went unanswered as the witnesses to the reading stood and filed out of the room, anxious to be away from the woman before the situation worsened. The two men who had surrounded her at the beginning sheltered her now, keeping others at arm's length.

Wives Wendy and Wanda apparently were not present, but Brick looked for MaryAnn Carpet who stood near the door conferring with Mr. Platt. The deceased mogul's sister remained seated, visiting with the young blonde at her side.

Having no real idea of the extent of Foster's estate, Brick couldn't calculate the value of her distribution. The one question in his mind at the moment was the amount of TAG stock not owned by himself, Dave, and Derek. Did it really now belong to Ned's sister and how would she manage it?

He was watching Willow, and then turned to speak with Ned's sister, but she was gone. He had to nearly run in order to catch up with her in the corridor of the Foster building. She wasn't leaving the building, but heading toward the elevators with the blond woman at her side.

"Mrs. Bent, may I speak to you for a moment?"

"Oh, Mr. Wahl, I'm glad you could be at the reading. I didn't see your partners though." He started to make an excuse for their absence, but she waved off his reply.

"I'm sure we will have plenty of time to meet with them and get to know them. Allow me to introduce my daughter, Valencia. She is also my attorney. You can call her Val." Brick nodded at the young woman who gave him a cold stare, not extending her hand or opening her mouth.

"I would like to meet with you tomorrow," she said. "It would be best if our partners could be here as well. Is there some reason Mr. Morris and Mr. Felshaw can't get here?"

The cordial personality she had exhibited previously was momentarily gone. Brick tried to explain that Dave was still ill and that Derek was in Seattle on TAG business. She considered his answer and then suggested they meet in three days in Phoenix.

"I'll book us a conference room at the Phoenician," she said. "Please make sure you are all there and bring your computer with all of the information regarding TAG. As a matter-of-fact, why don't you e-mail Valencia the files so she can have a preparatory look. Let's say ten o'clock?"

Brick didn't have to ask Debbie twice. She literally jumped into his arms when he said that they were taking an unexpected trip to Phoenix. Any excuse to get out of the cold and stormy New York weather was good, but a chance to go home to see her family and friends was even better. Dave had no problem clearing his schedule, motivated by the need to be close to his wife and kids. Derek already had a ticket to fly home the day before the planned meeting.

The flights occurred without any delays and their family reunions were sweet. Three days later the men arrived at the Phoenician hotel together, leaving the car with the valet. The lobby was busy with well-to-do winter visitors from all over the world. The hotel was a favorite of travelers from the Arab world ever since King Feisal had stayed there during a prolonged illness. He had required extensive neck and facial surgery that was performed by Richard Pavese, a world-famous plastic surgeon and close friend of Dave's father. Dave had spent his honeymoon at the palatial hotel, so he knew the property well.

One of the bellmen had been on the lookout for the three men and handed Dave a note that they were to meet in suite 607. A six-seated golf cart drove the men past the shimmering pool, already surrounded with sun bathers, past the golf pro shop, and finally to a building separate from the main hotel. They were shown to the suite. The door was already wide open.

The room was spectacular, with floor-to-ceiling windows looking out onto the golf course and the valley beyond. A large dining table in the suite was prepared for the meeting with bottles of chilled water and dainty pastries.

"Gentlemen, thank you for coming," Kristen Bent said as she flowed into the room from an adjoining bedroom. Moments later, Valencia entered from a separate doorway. Both were dressed in casual, but elegant, silk pants and tops, spiked heels, and flashy, day-time jewelry. To Brick's surprise, both women were smiling. Introductions were made and the five partners settled around the large table.

"Let me just start off by saying how happy I am to be associated with you handsome young men," Kristen said. "Prior to Edward's passing, he shared some of his stories with me regarding your life-saving efforts and especially the selfless sacrifice of your kidney, Doctor Felshaw. On his behalf, Val and I want to thank you."

Smiles were exchanged and a moment of spontaneous silence ensued.

"Let's get down to business," Valencia said, opening her iPad and looking at the men over her gem-encrusted reading glasses. "To the best of my calculations, each of you own 16 percent of TAG. You have no other financial connections with my late uncle's estate. Is that correct?"

"It was our understanding that we each owned a third of Willow's stock. At least that is what Willow told us when she signed over her shares. The exact number of outstanding shares was never revealed," Brick said.

"Edward was no fool. He would never have given away a controlling position to Willow or to you or anyone else for that matter," Valencia said. "The estate settlement is very clear that Mother and I own 52 percent, and the three of you together own 48 percent. By giving you her shares, Willow absolved herself of any legal or criminal responsibility with TAG. I guess she feels that her other $100-plus million will see her through. I think that for her, TAG was just a game. Now she is tired of it and is on to the Monte Carlo social scene and her new toy, the hotel she has bought with quasi-TAG funds. Trust me when I say that what she did at the time was not ethical, but technically will most likely hold up in court since it was before the will was read. I believe the funds for it came from investors in Romania … if I understand the rather vague accounting notes."

"But she led us to believe that she and Ned loved the company and that she only gave us the majority because she didn't have time; and of course, he was not well," Brick said.

"Nonetheless, that is the way it is. My mother would like to continue to employ the three of you to manage TAG and hopefully get it back up and running in the black," Valencia said. "Another alternative is to liquidate it, but that would take time and probably reduce the value substantially. From my quick look at the books that might be the best option."

"I had the impression that things were going okay for right now," Dave said.

"Going okay? Only if you consider owing our investors $300 million in principle, with 5 percent of that due payable to them every six months, is doing okay. And, that we have no possible way to reduce the initial principle on their investment without profitable sales. Where I went to school, that means we have to generate at least $15 million in profit every month. That's just to keep our heads above water. In order to make a profit for all of the stockholders, and eventually repay the principle investors, we need to do a lot better than that—probably a miracle or a winning lottery ticket. It would appear that Willow, unbeknownst to my dear Uncle Ned, left us with a daunting task."

Derek slid his chair back from the table and began pacing the room. All eyes were on him as he began to talk. "When we were invited to join TAG, we were told that there were large real estate parcels that were on the market and nearly in escrow. The three of us have raised nearly $200 million in investments and have more lined up, but the profitable parcels of land and buildings aren't what they were outlined to be. We have searched the books that Willow originally hid from us and as far as we can tell, much of the later investment money has been returned to the earliest investors as profit and not invested in tangible property."

Brick took the floor and explained. "Last fall, there were in fact several pending sales, and it appeared that those profits could be there, but the economic conditions worldwide are having a negative impact on everyone, thus the properties' values are relative to which buyers we can find."

"What you are telling us," Valencia said, "is that in order to meet our obligations to our present investors, we have to have new money from new investors? It appears to me that the profit on your present properties won't ever meet the obligations?"

"That about sums it up," Brick said.

"So what you are saying," Kristen summarized, "is that Willow, unknown to my brother, had been running a Ponzi scheme, and was smart enough to give you three, and now us, all of the obligations with no chance of paying off the debt in the foreseeable future? And that in order to keep the business alive, and us out of jail, we have to find new money and profitable investments?"

There was a silence in the room that lasted far longer

than anyone's comfort level. The whine of a lawnmower outside on the putting green was the only sound to cover their sighs and breathing.

"Perhaps you could tell me about our investors. How willing would they be to restructure the debt?" Valencia asked Derek.

"Several of the ones we know are reasonable businessmen and thought they were getting a super deal. They will probably understand the problem. However, we barely know the names of most of the early investors. The biggest problem is that Willow recruited some money the last couple of months from people that we are definitely not real comfortable with," Derek explained.

"Like Arab princes, Chinese gamblers, and casino owners, and worst of all are the Romanian mafia guys," Dave said—apparently the only one brave enough to call the investors what they really were.

There was another long silence and then the calm was broken. "This is ridiculous. How stupid can all of you be?" Valencia screamed, slamming her iPad on the table. "All of you should go to jail, including Willow."

Her mother tried to calm her down, but she would not be placated. She ranted for the next five minutes that they were in over their heads and that the whole thing should be turned over to federal investigators. She maintained that since her mother and she had nothing to do with TAG, prior to the reading of the will, they should just walk out and deny any knowledge of the whole thing.

"It's as though Willow created this whole business to play games with people's lives, and when Uncle Ned appeared to be dying, she placed Mother and the three of you in front of the firing squad while she conveniently left the country. It's like she got off the elevator and threw a cobra in with the rest of you as the door closed."

"It was a rattlesnake," Dave said in a soft voice. "A big, diamondback rattlesnake."

There was another silent pause as the truthfulness of the analogy was pondered.

"Well, we have got to do something," said Kristen. "We need to talk to these people—these investors. I'm sure they'll understand."

"Mother, you sound like a naive idiot! What we need to do is find out what Willow did with the early money, the money that was supposed to show up as property holdings in the TAG inventory. The numbers just don't add up. Somehow she managed to skim off lots of money, or buy property that is not on the books."

Derek's cell phone rang, and at the same time a maid knocked on the door, asking to make up the bedrooms, both thankfully interrupting the hopeless scene. Brick made a hollow promise to try to contact Willow. Derek nodded in agreement to call the investors in Macau and Dubai. Valencia suggested contacting a professor of banking and lawyer that she knew at the University of Virginia. They set a date for a future meeting and the men left, electing to walk back to the lobby. The day was sunny and beautiful. They followed the cart path past the golf pro shop and were nearly to the swimming pool when Derek finished his phone call. He glanced back behind them for some reason. That's when he thought he saw one of Willow's Romanian investors.

With their husbands sequestered in the TAG business meeting at the Phoenician hotel, Natasha organized a ladies luncheon for the visiting Debbie. Babysitters were found for the kids and the three ladies met some of Deb's best friends at the Quilted Bear—their favorite lunch spot in Scottsdale. The girls decided to eat outside on the veranda near the back of the restaurant. Surrounded by a scattering of propane heaters with the bright sunshine beating down, Deb hadn't felt so warm and happy in months. The soups, salads, and sandwiches just had been placed on the two round tables they had scooted together, when the waiter reappeared with a folded note which he handed to Debbie's sister. Written on it was the name, "Mrs. Morris."

The note was passed to Natasha who read it, and then with a confused look on her face, excused herself from the table and walked into the small main building. The chatting ladies barely noticed her absence. Melody had nearly finished her sandwich when she heard Natasha's phone ringing beside her plate and untouched salad. She leaned across to Deb.

"Do you think she is okay? She didn't say anything about being sick, did she?"

"The waiter brought her a note and she left. I'm finished eating. I'll go check on her."

Debbie looked around the front of the restaurant and then checked the ladies room. She asked the waiter that brought the note if he had seen her, but received only a shrug. She went out onto the sidewalk and walked up and down along the boutique shops in each direction, then returned to the ladies' table fully expecting that Tasha would be sitting there eating her greens and have a logical explanation for her absence, but her place was still empty.

"Melody," Debbie said. Would you please call your husband and see if he is still with Derek? Maybe they came by for her."

The next three hours were spent on a flurry of phone calls back and forth between the eight or ten cell phones owned by the wives and husbands. No one had seen or heard from Natasha. Her car was at home and the kids hadn't been picked up from the babysitter. Debbie had Tasha's phone and answered it a few times before she had to remind Derek that it wasn't helping for him to keep calling that number. His anxiety turned to anger and fear at four o'clock when a call came from one of the men with whom he had eaten lunch at the private club in Bucharest.

"Mr. Morris?"

"Yeah, this is Derek."

"I have a message for you from your wife. She would like to see you and your children again someday. She knows that it will never happen unless you return the money and the interest payment you owe to your proud Romanian investors."

"Who is this? You better not hurt her or I'll—"

"Mr. Derek, do not threaten me or my colloquies. You do not know how to take action against us and will only get yourself and your wife hurt by trying to do so. Trust me when I tell you this. You are from a country of peace and prosperity with soft hands and narrow minds. We are from a country that can't exist without threats and occasionally an act of violence. For you, the threat should be enough. You do not want to experience the violence."

"But I didn't take any of your money," Derek screamed into the phone, and then putting it back to his ear for a response, heard the buzz of a dead line. He turned to the cluster of friends beside him; all who were staring at him with shocked looks on their faces.

"What did he mean by 'the proud Romanian investors'?" Melody asked sarcastically. "And how much money is he talking about?" She had always been the one person who didn't want to know the details of TAG, and tried to avoid conversations about it, especially in front of her kids. Now, she wanted to be brought up to speed.

"I didn't take a dime from the thieves. Apparently, after I flew home, they cut a deal with Willow and gave her $30 million. She didn't mention that it was a result of my visit. She said that she wanted to use it as a short-term loan for the purchase of her new hotel in Monte Carlo," Derek explained. "I thought it was her private deal with them. I told her not to do it at the time because I thought they were just laundering drug money."

"Great," Melody said, "now we're not just running a Ponzi scheme, but a money laundering business as well. And if we don't call the police or the FBI, we'll all be charged with obstructing justice."

The others in the room looked at her with a questioning appraisal about her summation of the situation's legality, not quite sure whether she was making it up as she spoke.

"So what are we going to do?" Dave asked, his question aimed at Derek and Brick. He was lying on the couch in his family room. His face was flushed and his voice weaker than it had been for weeks. The stress of the day had gotten to him.

"Call your new friend Kristen Bent," Debbie said. "She's got lots of money. Maybe she'll loan it to you until you can track down Willow and make her pay them back. You can't just sit here while your wife is kidnapped."

Five miles away, tucked in the back bedroom of a suite at Camelback Mountain Inn, Natasha was sound asleep. She had been more mad than afraid when the two Mediterranean-looking men told her to get into their car. She had told them to go to hell and had turned to walk away when one of them grabbed the handle of her purse, which was looped through her arm. One of the men had opened the side of his jacket revealing a pistol in his belt. They then simply explained that they knew where her children and husband were, and that it would be easier for her to come with them than to bother the kids and her husband, who had serious work to do. They promised her that they wouldn't so much as touch her if she would cooperate.

"Get your hands off of me … let go of my purse," she hissed.

"Let me say it again. We know where your kids are.

Just behave yourself and in a couple of hours everything will be back to normal," the one with the gun said, raising his black bushy eyebrows.

Looking around for any sign of help and seeing no one, she slapped the hand away from her purse and got into the car. Surprising her, they had stayed true to their word. The hotel suite they led her to was stocked with food and her bedroom and bath were separate from the rest of the suite. The door locked from her side. They had even let her call her kids during the drive to the inn, but no one had answered. She had a splitting headache, so she took four Advil, ate half a bagel and went to sleep. She had full confidence that her husband would resolve the situation—whatever it was.

Brick and Derek were staring at the laptop, looking at TAG's numbers. Trying to telephone Willow had been a waste of time. They studied the current cash assets of TAG and were so short of the $30 million the Romanians wanted that they gave up on the idea of raiding TAG for the money. Derek dialed a number and handed Brick the phone.

"Mrs. Bent? This is Brick Wahl ... thank you for hosting the meeting this morning. Yes, we enjoyed meeting her also. She is every bit as attractive as her mother .... I'm sorry to disturb your afternoon .... Oh, it is warm out by the pool! Great! Listen to me please, we have a new problem."

"She is the majority stockholder, she has to do something!" Melody insisted.

"Her daughter said to call the police, and she is probably right. They have no intention of giving in to any kind of demand for money. Maybe they don't have that kind of money anyway," said Brick, still holding the phone in his hand.

"That's easy for you to say," said Derek. "Your wife is safe and your baby has her mother holding her. What am I going to tell my kids? That their mother has been kidnapped and that the police might be able to return her safely, but then again maybe the mean guys will just kill their mom and dump her out in the desert?" The hopeless reality of the situation had finally sunk in.

"You can't blame Ned's sister for not handing over money that she doesn't have, and the daughter, Valencia, is probably thinking more clearly than any of us. Handling this thing yourselves is just plain foolish," Debbie said.

"I need to find Willow. She has the money and she has the responsibility to pay up," Derek said, driving his fist into the closet door. There was an audible crunch. The others didn't know if it was the wood of the door or the bones in his hand, but he seemed oblivious to any physical pain at the moment. "She took money from those mobsters and made the promises."

Debbie took baby Lexy to her parents' house, and Derek called his sister and asked her to pick up his kids. Dave had gone in his bedroom to sleep. He was looking feeble and complained of pain in his side. In spite of nagging from Melody, he refused to call any of his doctor friends to come have a look at him. Melody had her own brood to worry about and asked Derek and Brick to move their negotiations into Dave's study, but they packed up and went to Derek's house instead. The two of them would have to resolve the problem by themselves. They had just pulled into the driveway when luck turned in their favor.

Parked in the circle drive was a small Cadillac sedan with a Hertz company sticker on the rear bumper. Leaning against the front fender was a tall, slender woman, dressed in jeans and a snug, black cotton top. Her hair was pulled back on her head and she wore large, round sunglasses against the glare of the setting sun. Instead of looking at the men when they got out of the car, she looked in the direction of the sunset. Only when they approached the car did Willow turn toward the two men.

Brick and Derek were too astonished to speak. They stood facing her, waiting for her to acknowledge their presence, just a little bit in awe of the powerful image she portrayed.

"I understand that you fellows have had a tough day," she said, finally looking at them.

Brick gave a disgusted sigh then took a step to the side when Derek moved in front of her, putting his face mere inches from the sullen woman. He deftly plucked the sunglasses off of her face. He took a deep breath, and was ready to begin screaming at her, when he saw the tear tracts and the smudged mascara. Her nose was red and running. He noticed the scuff on her cheek as though she had fallen. Her voice shuddered as she drew a breath and started to speak.

"I heard about Natasha," she said softly, in a hoarse voice, which they would never have recognized as hers without actually seeing her lips move as the words came forth. "Please believe me. I had nothing to do with those animals taking her."

"If you were a man, I would beat you into the ground," Derek said, trying with all of his might to restrain himself from doing just that. "Where is she?" he demanded.

"How would I know? They lured me here—to Phoenix—promising to help me with an investment purchase and then attacked me at my hotel. They said that they wanted their money back and a year's interest on it. They told me they had taken your wife as insurance and that if we would pay up this week, that they wouldn't hurt her."

Brick was at her side now listening intently. He was prepared to physically stop Derek should it be necessary. "Why do they suddenly insist on their money being returned? Did they do that to your face?" Brick asked.

"It was just a slap," she said sarcastically, touching her reddened cheek. "I've had a lot worse."

"Why did you get us mixed up with them?" Derek said, anxious to move back to the beginning and to find out about Natasha.

"It's a long boring story, but it goes back years, long before I ever met Edward or had even set foot on Wall Street. What is important now is helping your wife. I tried to call my sister-in-law, but she won't return my calls."

"What a surprise," Derek said, spreading his hands to mock her. "Imagine being needed and not returning calls. We have been calling you for days, and don't tell me you didn't notice."

"Forget all of that. That has nothing to do with the present situation. My sister-in-law Kristen can help us if we can find her. She now owns part of TAG. She is very nice and just needs to understand the situation."

The innocent inflection of her voice was astonishing to the two men. Did she actually not know that they were at the reading of the will and that they had been in contact with Ned's sister and daughter? They looked at one another and waited for her next revelation.

"She is loaded with cash. If we can contact her, she can get you off the hook. Officially, I now have nothing to do with TAG, but those brutes don't seem to care. They want their money plain and simple. They want their money and don't care how they get it or who they have to hurt."

Derek's phone rang and he turned away to answer it. Willow brushed a hair out of her eyes and stared at Brick. He felt his anger building. Did this woman think for a minute that they were going to buy this pack of lies?

"Tell me something, Willow. What did you do with the money that the Romanians want back? I've studied the books nearly every day since we started into this catastrophe that Ned presented to us as the greatest business plan on earth, and for the life of me I can't find anything about millions of dollars coming to TAG from anyone in Romania. Could you have forgotten to turn the check into the bank? Maybe you put it in the wrong account by mistake? Or did you use it to order furniture for the hotel in Monte Carlo?"

She continued her cold stare at Brick and then abruptly turned and reached for the car door. Brick reached out and grasped her wrist and held it firm.

"You aren't going anywhere. You need to stay right here. You are way too accomplished at disappearing for us to let out of our sight. I think the best thing we can do right now is trade you for Natasha."

Willow jerked her hand away from Brick and slapped him across the face. "How stupid are you?"

she screamed. "There never was any $30 million. They are playing us against one another. They told me that they gave the money to Derek. They even showed me a canceled cashier's check to prove it, but I'm not so stupid that I can't spot a counterfeit check—they misspelled 'certified.' I don't have their money because there never was any. And as for their demand, I couldn't raise $30 million today if it were to save my own life. Edward's estate was in shambles. All the palatial houses he left to his favorite wives are mortgaged to the rafters and the millions in cash that came with them isn't liquid. It's all in solar energy stocks. Each of the wives will be lucky to get enough from the shambles to pay this year's property taxes. Why do you think he started TAG? He was going broke. We went to Colorado last summer to get a break from the bill collectors. TAG was a last-ditch grasp at the golden goose. None of his buddies and protégés on Wall Street would touch it, so when he met you boys, he thought he had found new financial life—and maybe he had, until he got sick again."

By now Derek had finished his call and was listening—mouth agape as this exotic and oh so baffling woman told her story. He shook his head in disbelief.

"I think you are a damn liar," Derek said. "You stole the $30 million and probably another $100 million as well and have it stashed away somewhere. We need $22 million right now and then the rest of the money I've raised. We need the money from Macau and the money from Dubai and every other investor's money that you have hidden in your bogus real estate deals."

"Maybe you have the money and are hiding it from your friends, because I don't know what you are talking about. Every penny I collected from investors went into the J.P. Morgan account. And every cent I took out for property purchases, you, Mr. Brick Wahl, wrote the checks for. If there is money missing then it's on you boys' side of the ledger."

Derek's phone rang again, and again he turned away. Willow took the opportunity to grab her purse and try to get in her car again. This time Brick couldn't restrain himself any longer. He grasped Willow's shoulder and began to squeeze. She dropped the purse in her right hand and swung at him, but he caught it and slid his hand onto her neck, pushing her head upward against the car window.

"Stop it!" Derek screamed at Brick. "Get control of yourselves. Both of you! I just got a call from Natasha. She is in a taxi on her way home. She has a note from the Romanians."

Willow twisted away from Brick and scurried around to the front of the car. "Give me my bag and get out of my way. I'm calling the police and having you arrested for choking me."

"You are not going anywhere until we have this settled," Brick said, scooping Willow's purse off of the ground and walking toward the entrance to Derek's house.

"If what you are saying is true, not that I believe a word of it, we've got to work together to resolve the issues," Derek said. "Come inside until Natasha gets here. I promise you Brick won't hurt you."

She looked at him for a moment, then picked her sunglasses off of the hood of the car and began walking toward the house. Before they could close the front door a yellow cab was stopping at the curb. The trio stopped to look at the unexpected car and then saw Natasha get out and run toward them calling Derek's name. She had a big smile on her face and was carrying a bouquet of white roses, but tears were streaming down her cheeks.

Derek nearly crushed his wife in his arms. Tears were streaming down both men's cheeks as Natasha told them of the polite, but firm control exhibited by her afternoon captors. Unlike Willow's story of brutality and threats, she had been frightened, but not harmed or even threatened with anything violent.

"After the first hour, they were actually quite nice to me," she said. "They ordered lunch for me and let me watch TV. I even had a short nap. Then they said everything was arranged and they would send me home in a taxi. They paid the driver $200. My gosh! We were only five miles from the restaurant where they abducted me. Before I left, they gave me these flowers and this gold bracelet." She held up a bouquet of white roses and a heavy gold chain bracelet which sparkled in the fading sun.

"You said, 'except the first hour.' What happened the first hour?"

"Those two guys are pretty scary at first, but the younger one was cute, and after a few minutes was nice to me. They had to listen to me yell at them for interrupting my lunch. And I didn't quite know what they were going to do to me so I just pouted about missing lunch with my friends."

"That's got to be the fastest case of Stockholm syndrome on record," Willow said in a sarcastic tone. "They didn't treat me quite so nice. Neither did your husband and his friend here."

Tasha turned toward the source of the last four months of business troubles, and matching Willow's tone of voice asked, "What rock did you crawl out from under, Willow? The last I heard you had flown off to the Caribbean with all of the company's money. Or was it Monte Carlo?" She got no response.

At Derek's insistence, the foursome moved the conversation into the house and sat down in the Morris's living room. Willow tried to justify her absence and explain some of the shuffling of the TAG's funds. Finally, with all of the known facts available, at least as much as they could believe from Foster's widow, they arrived at a plan. Willow had a source—an old school mate at J.P. Morgan whom she would ask to search the bank records, and she remembered one of Ned's old investors, Armon Dupree, whom the men had met, and who had unimaginable wealth and connections.

Neither she nor Derek would admit receiving a check from the Romanians, and yet Willow insisted that she had seen the phantom canceled certified check. Brick and Derek were still hoping that Kristen Bent could be their ace in spite of her daughter's dismissal, but were not mentioning it to Willow. Derek had his wife safely home, so for him, everything else was secondary. Now, he could become the aggressor. He had a plan to deal with the Romanian hoods, but wasn't about to share it with anyone.

After a long debate, Willow was allowed to leave and

drove away saying that she was headed for the airport. She didn't want to spend another hour in the same city as the Romanian brothers. She promised to call Brick by noon the next day with more information. Natasha's sister brought the kids home and Brick went to meet Debbie. By the time the sun was down, life appeared to be somewhat back to normal. Pizza was ordered and baths were started.

Lying on the Morris's kitchen counter was the wrapping paper from the roses Natasha had brought home. She had no idea at which hotel they had held her, since they had forced her head down on the back seat during the drive, and once at the hotel they had kept her distracted. She had seen the stationary in the room but didn't recall the name. Fortunately for Derek, written on the wrapping paper was the name "Camelback Mountain Inn." It only took Derek a minute on his iPad to find the place and to make a plan of his own. The Romanian men wanted money, but would get more than they had counted on.

Natasha and the kids were sound asleep when Derek left the house. Natasha had reminded him to put his car in the garage, but he had left it out for a reason. He cruised the unfamiliar part of Scottsdale where a dozen new boutique hotels and time-share condo projects had gone up in the last ten years. He found the inn tucked on a side street behind a megaplex theater. The hotel was deceiving. It looked like a run-of-the-mill, winter visitor hangout, but the cars in the parking slots and the landscaping reeked of big money. His wife had said the place where they had held her was extremely nice.

Derek was wearing a ball cap and a long-sleeve turtleneck pulled down over the bulges in his loose fitting cargo jeans. He had considered carrying the 38 cal. Sig Sauer pistol his father had given him for college graduation. Arizona's new "wild west" law didn't require him to have the pistol registered, let alone have a concealed weapon permit. He had remembered the advice, "No gun—no gunfight," his policeman friend Burk had given him. By the time he walked in his room to retrieve it from the dresser drawer, he already had lost his courage to take a gun to the meeting.

He found a darkened spot in the hotel's parking lot for his car and walked past the tiny lobby and into the pool area. The gun laws in Arizona might be liberal, but the smoking laws weren't, and he figured that the Romanians couldn't go long without their sour-smelling, Turkish tobacco. He was right. Sitting at a poolside table were the two men who had tormented his life once too often the last couple of months. Their rooms appeared to be on the ground floor with adjacent, open French doors. Derek ducked down into a chair near the far fence and watched as the men smoked, drank, and laughed at their inside jokes.

The longer he watched them, the angrier he became. He couldn't just walk up and accuse them of kidnapping or extortion. He had to have more than that to make their lives miserable. He went to the lobby and found a house phone opposite the front desk. He knew that the clerk wouldn't give him their room number or ring it that late at night so he left a message and watched from across the lobby as the young woman put a note into the Romanian's pigeon hole. Each slot had a number. Minutes later he was at the door of the older brother's room. The golf ball-size magnet he had brought from home worked like a charm. Once he applied it to the box for the electronic key slot, the light above the door handle turned green and the door handle twisted open easily.

Once inside the hotel room, he started looking for the laptop Natasha had mentioned. It took him less than a minute to open the HP notebook and find the file—fortunately named TAG. The idiot didn't even use a password to lock the document file. Derek put an 8-gigabyte flash drive into the USB port and started downloading. When he finished he took the magnet and gave the back of the computer a brisk massage with the magnet. Next, he took another item out of his pocket. It was a 5-inch-diameter, plastic case that he normally used for fishing bait. Inside the case was a collection his son, Soren, had been acquiring in his terrarium. It was a family of twelve, small, tan-colored bark scorpions.

The two oversized beds were waiting for the goons, their bedspreads already turned back, and a foil-wrapped Godiva chocolate resting on the pillows. Derek hated the tiny insects and cringed at even opening the jar's lid but did so anyway. He could hear the men still talking, but suddenly the voices were getting closer. He opened the container and dropped two of the angry scorpions under one of the pillows and the other six under the second pillow. He then repeated the deposit of the remaining scorpions in the second bed. The French door onto the patio opened just as Derek closed the door behind him, sneaking into the hallway.

He heard a sound in the hallway and froze momentarily. Faking dropping his room key card, he bent over and faced the door across the hall from where he had just exited. He heard the clatter of a vending machine giving up a bottle of soda, and then footsteps and glanced in that direction. Walking straight toward him was the youngest of the Romanians. The man was concentrating on opening a plastic beverage bottle and didn't look at Derek's face, at least not yet.

Not having time to consider what would happen if the room he was entering was occupied, Derek stabbed the door locking mechanism with his magnet and turned the handle. The Romanian walked down the narrow hallway toward him and was just yards away when Derek finally slipped silently into the room, acting as one would if a wife or child was asleep inside.

Derek heard the door across the hall click shut just as he heard the loud snoring coming from inside the stranger's room. He counted slowly to ten and then silently he was back out the door and slinking down the hall toward the exit.

The only possible witness to his being on the hotel property was the clerk at the front desk. She had been busy when he called on the house phone, thus he doubted she would remember him. He walked out through the empty lobby and made his way to his car. He put the key in the ignition, but didn't start the engine. He lowered the driver's window to let the cooler night air into the car and catch his breath. As he settled into the car seat, he heard a piercing scream coming from the hotel's pool area. He hoped it was one of the Romanians.

As he drove home he was a confused bag of emotion. He was excited that the nasty little scorpions might have stung one of the Romanian idiots—or maybe even two of them, but he was not a violent person and was already feeling slightly guilty. What if one of them died? It was very unlikely that they would get anything other than a bad headache and an annoying electric shock feeling in the afflicted body part, but with a heart condition one could actually die. "At least I didn't take my gun and shoot one or both of them like they probably deserve," he rationalized. He was on the main road headed home when he saw blue-and-red flashing lights in the mirror and then heard the siren. A wave of nausea and adrenalin shot through his body. "The last thing in the world I want to do is resist arrest," he thought as he put on his blinker and pulled to the curb.

The police car slowed and then passed Derek's car, not giving him as much as a glance. Derek resumed his speed and in two minutes was sitting in the darkness of his own driveway, listening to the engine block making its cooling down, ticking sounds. He could hear his heart pounding and feel the blood throbbing in his temples. His clothes were soaked through and through with sweat. *What have I done? How has it helped with TAG?* The self-directed questions would go unanswered for days.

The phone rang at six in the morning. Since it was on Derek's side of the bed and he was nearly comatose—having tossed and fretted most of the night—Natasha had to crawl over him to answer it. The scene was comical: her leaning across his non-responsive bulk, trying to carry on a conversation.

"What do you mean he can't answer the phone?" the arrogant woman demanded.

"It's six in the morning and he got to bed late. He isn't a morning person. As a matter of fact, neither am I. Would you mind calling back later?"

"This is Willow. I have got to talk to Derek right now."

By this time, Natasha had crawled completely over Derek and was standing on the side of the bed, he finally started to stir. She covered the mouth piece with her hand and relayed Willow's demand.

"This is Derek," he said as he sat upright and then toppled back onto the pillow.

"Good! You finally woke up. I just received a call from a friend of mine in Bucharest. She told me that our Romanian friends spent some time in Scottsdale hospital last night. Apparently, their room was a hatching ground for scorpions. She said they left the hospital and went straight to their jet at the airport. They are in the air on their way back to Bucharest as we speak."

Derek was too exhausted to feel any sort of emotion regarding the news. He knew that—at least temporarily—he should feel good.

"Thanks for letting me know," he said and handed the phone back to Natasha.

"Willow? This is Natasha. Whatever it is you just told Derek, you better repeat to me. I think he fell back to sleep before you finished speaking." She paused with the phone at her ear and nodded as the widow repeated the message, and also asked to have the three partners meet her in New York in four days.

"I'll be out of touch most of this week, so have them at the Manhattan town house next Friday no later than ten in the morning. It will be essential that all three of them are there. Tell Derek that I will be there and Kristen will be there also. We are finally going to get this mess organized and make it profitable for everyone."

Three hours later, when Derek finally was awake enough to think, his wife repeated the message to him. His first inclination was to call and explain everything about the Romanians to his police friend Burk. He had probably committed a felony and Burk probably would have to report it to his boss. If he were to be arrested it would affect everyone, including his kids. He called Brick and set up a meeting after lunch at Dave's house.

Dave fortunately was feeling better. Once he was brought up to date on all of the bizarre events of the preceding day, he agreed to fly to New York with his partners. Derek had not mentioned his visit to the Romanian's hotel to either of them. He was still having palpitations every time he even thought about the scorpions and how close he had come to getting caught.

Dave, Brick, and Derek got out of the Yellow Cab looking like Wall Street moguls in their expensive suits, white shirts, and silk ties. It was the first time Dave had really dressed up in weeks. They paused on the sidewalk in front of the Foster mansion, each having flashbacks of happier and more solemn times. There had been a couple of warm days in the city and most of the previous month's snow was gone, leaving behind piles of dirty, frozen residue in the shady spots and slush on the walkways. The normally lush vegetation around the small yard in front of the town house was brown and dead. A light was on in the entryway, but otherwise the place had little warmth or charm.

Brick tried his key and the big brass lock turned effortlessly. The three men stomped the moisture off their shiny, black oxfords and entered, immediately feeling the cold emptiness of the massive old structure.

"Benjamin? Margo?" Brick hollered, getting back just an echo in the cavernous house. The heat was apparently not on. A fire had been set in the fireplace, but hadn't been lit. The men spread out and searched the first three floors, but found no one.

"Her bedroom is empty. It looks like no one has been

here since we were here last," Brick shouted down from the second floor stairwell.

"No one's been in the study either," Derek confirmed.

Dave lit a match to the kindling in the fireplace and the three partners took up places in the leather chairs closest to the fireplace. They waited less than ten minutes when voices were heard and the front door opened. Willow, Kristen Bent, and to the men's surprise, Valencia Bent, came into the mansion. All had polite smiles on their faces and were chatting about some sale at one of the department stores the men had never heard of. Greetings were exchanged as though it was the starting of a family luncheon or bridge get-together—all smiles and cheerful questions about their trip and families.

Brick suggested they sit at the dining table, but the ladies liked the warmth of the fire so they pulled more heavy chairs into a semicircle and settled down to business. Willow fussed with the thermostat, but couldn't get it to work so she gave up and found a wool lap robe. She then sat down next to Brick on the couch.

"Well, Willow, what is the purpose of our meeting?" asked Kristen in a voice so sweet it could have melted dry ice.

"We need to talk about TAG," Willow said, smiling at her sister-in-law and the perky, but cautious, Valencia.

The men could sense a tension, but didn't know the history of the two older women to begin to guess what was about to happen. Dave broke the momentary silence by finishing a conversation he was having earlier with Valencia about his kids' Christmas presents. Everyone listened politely and then all eyes turned back to Willow.

"It seems that in my exuberance to help Edward and

these men get TAG off of the ground, I may have made a few mistakes. I had turned to a couple of financial sources I had used in the past—before I married Edward—and probably should not have considered them. The worst of the mistakes involved the Romanian brothers," she said, looking straight at Derek. "That problem is resolved and their money is being paid back as we speak—without interest. They are lucky to get the money instead of a prison sentence. It seems that they have lost the desire to make any profit on the investment and are quite happy to be getting their principle back and getting back to their hometown. They mentioned something about having to go to the hospital in Arizona and not wanting to deal with my partners there anymore. I must say, you three underestimate your ability to intimidate."

"That's great news," said Brick without smiling. He had no idea what she was referring to regarding hospitals and wanting to avoid partners, but he could sense, as could the others, that the rest of the story might not be so great.

"Anyway, since I paid back their money for you, I expect that it makes me a part owner again—at least in principle. Since I gave you three my shares of the company, I presume that you will at least consider me a valued investor," Willow said, raising an eyebrow.

"Not quite so fast. As I understand the history of the transactions with the Romanians, you must have had their money all this time. Am I wrong?" To the surprise of everyone in the room, the question came from Valencia, not her mother or one of the men. Willow started to pull her head back in denial, but stopped short and with a twist of her neck toward Derek said, "I'm sorry for the misunderstanding with the deposited check. My accountant must have made a mistake as to which account to put it in and with the confusion of the funeral, I didn't follow up as I should have."

"So, my dear, exactly how does that make you a partner in this business?" Kristen glared at Willow as she spoke. "You own no stock in TAG and are very likely in violation of several federal laws on international money transactions. We all appreciate having your Romanian Mafia friends out of the way, but perhaps it is best now for you to leave the scene, just as we notice your household help has done."

"Oh they haven't fled," Willow said, raising her chin as she addressed the others. "Margo and Benjamin are at my beach house in Grand Cayman getting it ready for the arrival of the new owner. They don't have the time or the inclination to sit around this dreary place waiting for you men to come and go. Later in the spring, they will be with me in Monte Carlo. My hotel renovation is proceeding well and we need to be ready for the late spring and summer crowds. Benjamin and Margo will be there to help as I'll be living there in one of the suites. From now on, I will honor my promise to allow you to use this mansion for your office, but you need to make your own arrangements for domestic help. I can give you a list of names," said Willow.

Derek stood and began pacing. "Let me change the subject for a minute. What are we to expect from your other investors, especially Mr. Chen in Macau, and the consortium in Dubai that I accepted money from?"

"Well, sugar," she said in a voice they hadn't heard since the first day in Colorado. "You sweet talked them into investing their money and made them promises of rich returns. You need to keep those promises. My obligation to them stopped the minute you took their checks to the bank."

The questions went on for another hour with practical and logistic things discussed in detail. By the end of the meeting a more cordial and trusting mood was present, and more importantly, the three men felt for the first time that Willow wasn't trying to play some kind of game with them. Kristen and Valencia had asked good questions as well and had received straightforward answers. Willow announced that she was flying out that afternoon and already had texted her driver to pick her up at the house. She had cleared out her bedroom with the items she would need for the next few months. When they walked Willow to the door everyone was smiling. No faux plans were made to get together in the future, and she made no offers of future help. TAG would have the use of the house for the present—they agreed on a year—but, Willow would be unavailable to help TAG in any other way. Her departure was like closing the door on a cold draft of wind.

"I'm exhausted," Kristen said. "That woman has always drained my energy. It's as though she absorbs hers from others. Let's meet again tomorrow, but not in this dreary place. Come to my place tomorrow evening for dinner and we can talk about the coming year. Dress casually and bring your appetites, I love to show off my culinary skills. And for goodness' sake, find out how to turn the heat up in this place. Can you be there, Valencia?"

"Of course, Mother. Your new CFO wouldn't miss

it for the world, but I do have a date so don't set a place for me."

"What is that CFO comment supposed to mean?" Brick asked, acting startled and turning first to Valencia and then toward her mother.

"You're a smart man, Mr. Wahl," Valencia said. "TAG has just been reorganized."

It wasn't twenty minutes after the women had left that a FedEx delivery van stopped in front of the mansion, and the door clapper shattered the quietness. The envelope Brick signed for was addressed to him and sent from an address in London. The men had been in the kitchen trying to find something fresh to eat, and discussing how they were being nudged out of the management picture by the two aggressive women. "We probably would have been better off if we still had Willow trying to boss us around," Dave said.

They huddled around Brick and the FedEx envelope, standing at the counter as he withdrew the stapled stack of legal-size paper and read to them out loud. The Arabs— the ones Derek had met with in Dubai—now wanted their money back and their London-based attorney was making the request in legal terms. There wouldn't be any physical threats or kidnapping this time. Their attorneys would simply tie up the business in court and freeze all of TAG's bank accounts, if they didn't comply. They were being given thirty days to return the full amount plus the accumulated interest, which they were generously lowering to one percent per month, beginning on the date the initial check was written.

"Great!" Derek said, slamming the empty FedEx carton against the granite countertop over and over again. "I'm so sick of this mess. Why don't we just pack up and walk away like Willow is doing?"

"The last time I checked, I didn't have $100 million in the bank to walk away to. It seems that I recall each of us leaving profitable occupations because we wanted the adventure and thrill of Wall Street and the wealth that Ned promised if we would join him." It was Dave reminding the other two of their joint decision. He was now sitting at the breakfast nook with his head in his hands, looking pale and fragile. The hulk of a man that he was six months prior looked twenty years older and thirty pounds lighter. His voice, once a lusty source of mirth and reassurance to his friends, was now a whisper with words trailing off at the end.

"My million-dollar bonus, which seemed like so much money, is about gone. Between the April fifteenth tax man, the attorney, the accountants, my wife giving our tithe to the church, and the accumulated medical bills, we'll be down to less than a hundred thousand dollars. That's what I used to bill in a slow month. I gave up my practice and my kidney for Edward Foster III and TAG for the two of you. I don't think I can go backward in time. You two, can possibly pick up the pieces of your prior life and return to the trading floor and the real estate game, but what will I do?"

Brick and Derek looked at their friend with tears in their eyes. He definitely had sacrificed the most in order to make the business work. They joined him at the table and for the next hour, reminisced about their lives B.N.— "before Ned." Derek had been making lots of money doing land deals, but each one required capital from the last one and the market was beginning to weaken.

Brick reminded them of the mistakes he had made on the trading floor by over-leveraging wheat or pork belly contracts and not guessing the weather or market whims close enough to make a big killing. He had been in major financial trouble at the time of the snakebite.

They moped about their situation for a while, eventually dragging some cheese and stale bread out of the fridge and making sandwiches. Brick retrieved his laptop and as they ate, one by one they started reviewing the individual holdings of TAG and their individual investors—many of them relatively small sums of only a few thousand dollars, made by friends and relatives. Derek had even let his grandmother, May, put $20,000 into the venture when he knew in his heart that it represented a significant percentage of her remaining life savings. The others had accepted similar investments.

Looking at the asset column, it was not all bleak. Most of the money had been well placed with real profit potential. There were shopping centers, office buildings, and raw land in developing communities, all paid for in cash with TAG money. All of it was listed for resale and there was lots of interest in the properties. The problem was the time element. Big money sales didn't happen overnight like commodity trades or stock sales on NASDAQ. Every transaction took time. Now, the push by the Sheik and the Asian man to have their money returned was creating havoc. It was possibly being accelerated by rumors spread by the damn Romanian Mafia thugs.

It was getting dark and freezing cold outside. Inside the mansion it was taking forever to warm back up, thus the men decided to spend the night at the Marriott Marquis on Times Square. Within the hour they had checked into two rooms—giving Dave his own to get some rest. Derek and Brick went down to the coffee shop for cheesecake. That's when they ran into Lady Luck.

MaryAnn Carpet walked into the busy coffee shop, obviously in a hurry and obviously with a mission. When she saw the two men she grinned and headed their way.

"What a nice surprise," Derek said, pulling out a chair for the lady and helping her remove her coat. She made no pretense of being there for any other reason than finding and talking to the Arizona boys. She was dressed in a wool skirt and a purple, cashmere sweater that accentuated her figure and despite her age, drew glances from other men in the room.

"What can I order for you?" Brick asked.

"Whatever you're having will be fine as long as it's warm," she said.

They made small talk until the desserts and coffee arrived, then she admitted getting their hotel location from Tasha. They caught up on the apparent changes in the management of TAG and the men apologized for not using the downtown office that MaryAnn had arranged for them. Then she explained why she was there.

"I resigned my position at Foster Inc. after the generous gift from Mr. Foster's estate. I have however, still been going into the office in order to help make the transition for the building's new management. While I was at the office yesterday, a man came in whom I had never seen before, but have heard legends about. He is from South Africa and I could barely understand his accent. He was looking for Edward Foster. He said that they had been acquainted in the past and that he had the need to invest a large amount of money right away.

I explained that poor Edward had passed away. As the saddened man began to leave I suddenly thought of you and TAG. I gave him your name, but he didn't seem that interested. This afternoon however, he came by again requesting that I find you and set up a meeting. He wants to meet with the three of you tomorrow if possible. He has a flight back to Cape Town tomorrow evening. His name is James Rhodes."

Brick and Derek had been listening intently, both wondering how and why this freak event was happening just at this critical time.

"Do you have any idea how much he wants to invest?" Derek asked.

"He said that he is willing to buy all of the properties that Mr. Foster's new company owns. I asked around the office if anyone else has dealt with the man, but they all knew him only by name and rumor. I did Google him, but that was of little help."

Bad news is seldom as bad as it first sounds. Likewise good news, though in fact good, is rarely as good in the long run, as it first sounds. James Rhodes, a great-grandson of one of Africa's pioneers, was a huge hulk of a man, well into his seventies. He towered over Brick and Derek when they arose to greet him the next morning. His handshake was like a snapping bear trap that stopped just short of crushing bones. He had dark, green eyes which moved around, searching the lobby and lounge area in a continuous motion. On the middle finger of his left hand he wore a wide, gold band. Mounted on the band was an unpolished, clear rock that appeared to be covered with dust and grit. When Dave—who had excused himself from standing—was able to see the stone at eye level, he estimated the size to be that of a large black olive.

"Rhodes is my name," the stranger began. "I've been told that you boys are in the market for a new heart."

Dave, startled by the introduction, took the conversation's lead. "We have nothing to do with medicine sir. We are in—"

"I know, I know," the man said cutting off the clarification. "What I heard was that you don't have the heart for running this Ponzi scheme anymore. You know what I mean, the one that Ned Foster and his slithering lady friend sucked you into."

He didn't actually smile as he talked, but there was a subtle sense of mirth in his tone of voice. As he spoke his eyes continued glancing about the room, although he still seemed fully engaged with the conversation. His suit appeared expensive and though he wore no tie, the shirt's embroidered initials—"JBJ"—could be seen peeking out from under the cuffs of the coat. He wore western-style boots, which were glossy black, as though defying the sloppy, wet sidewalks outside.

"TAG is not a Ponzi scheme!" Brick said in protest. "It is a legitimate real estate investment company with stockholders, investors, and a long list of owned properties. There is nothing about it that is illegal. You need to question the source of your information, sir."

"Oh come on now, Mr. Brick Wahl. Don't be getting on any high horse. I had a little chat last night with a beautiful woman. Her former boss and I go back to our first bicycle race in Madrid—long before you were born. He was always the guy I drafted on, but could never quite catch at the finish. Now he has beaten me to the finish line again, but in this case that is not good news for him. I spent my working life searching for the right pit to dig—not the right pocket to pick like Ned—and now you boys. Oh, Ned was a genius in business, but when computers started making all the decisions on Wall Street, he began to lose his edge. He would call me once in a while and we'd chew the fat and reminisce, but for the last few years he would never let me trust him with any of my money."

Derek was getting restless with the story and couldn't help interrupting. "Excuse me, I appreciate your relationship with Mr. Foster, but we were told about you by a Ms. Carpet. She said that you might be interested to buy some of our properties."

"That's precisely my reason for being here. I received an anonymous call, though I think I know who it was, telling me that you boys were in trouble and were only two steps in front of some foreign investors' stilettos and only three steps in front of your Securities and Exchange police—rather like the Gestapo, I'm told. Ponzi schemes are illegal in South Africa as well as here in the USA, but the perpetrators there are simply thrown down deep mine shafts or fed to the famous white sharks of Cape Town Bay."

"We have no idea what you are talking about. We have always paid off our investors in a timely fashion and all of our holdings are legitimate," Brick said. "I worked side by side with Edward Foster for months and there was never a hint of illegality."

"Boys, I'm not here to accuse you or to insult you. I just want you to know that I'm not a blind pig looking for a truffle."

"So what exactly are you looking for, Mr. Rhodes?" Dave asked. He was sitting, working on a can of Coke he had retrieved from his overcoat's pocket. He still felt horrible, and it was all he could do to keep up with the conversation.

"I've been mining diamonds for forty years. I own a piece of land my ancestors left to me clear back when I was a kid. I tried to grow a green thumb and farm vegetables, but the land was useless for farm crops, so

I started digging holes in the ground. We've made a living—my brothers and me—but never anything big until now. Ten months ago we found a pocket of stones. It's not like with gold or silver where a vein runs at odd angles through the ground. It's more like a giant raisin cookie buried deep in the ground. Nothing for hundreds of feet in every direction and then in a twenty foot circle there could be a thousand raisins. All of our recent findings are very big, shiny raisins."

"These are diamonds you're talking about ... right?" Dave said, trying to follow the story and understand the stranger's heavy accent as well.

"Yeah, yeah, diamonds. Anyway, to get to the point, I now have a lot of money that I'm not comfortable having sit in some bank in Africa or Switzerland or in some hurricane-alley island. I always wanted to retire in the US and now I figure is my chance. So when De Beers wrote me and my brothers a big check, I thought of Ned. By the time I put all my affairs in order and tracked him down he was dead, and his wives are like finding shadows on a cloudy day. Luckily, I ran into the nice lady at the office building; I wish she would have found me twenty years ago."

Derek was finally getting a gist of what the man wanted and was becoming accustomed to the accent. "So if I may make a guess here, you want to invest some money here in the US and do it in real estate? Do I have that right?"

"Not exactly. I want to buy your whole company. I want to pay off all of your investors and buy your interests outright as well ... own all of the property myself. I don't have the time or knowledge to search out each deal and negotiate the thing. You see, there are hundreds of banks that have gone out of business and thousands of financial companies that have lost their investors' money, but to the best of my knowledge, with the exception of a rare volcano or torrential flood, no one has figured out a way to remove real estate from the earth. I want a foolproof place to put my money, and then I want to find a comfortable little mansion on a golf course in a sunny place and play golf every day for the rest of my life."

"But why TAG?" Derek asked.

"Because I want to be a part of the great American dream I've heard about all of my life. How much money are we talking about, by the way?"

This question hit the three men out of the blue. They each thought the other partner probably knew the answer, but when it came down to quoting an exact amount that the company was worth—subtracting the assets from the investments—Dave's wildest guess wouldn't have been even close. Brick, the one who had done all of the bookkeeping, was so totally lost because of the foreign money coming and going that he could only guess within $20 or $30 million. It was Derek who had a head for numbers. Sensing that this could be their only shot at unloading the company at a profit and not being arrested for failing to fulfill the promises Willow had made to the early investors, he picked up a pad of Marriott paper and a cheap pen.

"Just give me a few minutes. Why don't we order some breakfast for you?" In neat handwriting he created two columns of figures. He wrote down the assets on one side, including all of the known real estate's anticipated sale value, and the known debt on the other—the debt side being what he knew they owed the investors. The smaller ones he lumped into one group. Then there was the Chinese and the Dubai money. He took Willow's word that she had cleaned the slate with the Hungarian mobsters, but what else was there?

Ten minutes later, he leaned over to Brick and they looked over the pages together. Brick took the paper and carefully wrote a couple more names. Using his iPhone calculator, Derek added up the two columns, but wrote down only the asset total, giving the amounts that they projected the ideal sale price would be on the open market.

Suddenly, the last six months flashed through Derek's mind: the moving back and forth between Arizona and New York; the sacrifice Dave had made on the operating table; the threats and the abduction of his wife; the businesses they had each walked away from; and he remembered the night standing out in the cold, locked out of the mansion by the woman they had been forced to trust. Most of all he remembered his narrow escape from Bucharest. It all came flooding back like a nightmare, but he was wide awake.

"Derek, are you okay?"

He looked up realizing the other three men were staring at him. Waiting for him.

"Sorry. I'm just trying to be as accurate as possible," he said. Rereading the piece of paper, he added one last figure to the list of debts and then wrote down the total. He handed the list to Brick and nodded for him to give it to Dave when he was done. Finally, they handed the paper to Mr. Rhodes. The three men's eyes connected, Dave and Brick not fully understanding the last debt listed on Derek's accounting—$15 million in "commissions owed." This brought the debt to $460 million, but the predicted asset sales amount—using a "best case" scenario—was well over $500 million.

"Well," Rhodes said. "These amounts are, I'm sure, your estimates, and that is fine. I don't expect anyone to keep a whole set of books in their head. However, you haven't added the amount you are willing to sell it for. My question is, are you willing to sell it and for how much. I'll give you my offer, and usually I don't like to dicker back and forth. My next question is: Are you prepared to move forward now or are there others you need to consult?"

It would seem to a fly on the wall that they would have easily remembered Kristen and Valencia Bent, and that they were in fact the majority owners of TAG, but the three men had been stuck with the responsibility of the company so long that Mrs. Bent wasn't mentioned until now.

It was Dave who brought the woman's name up. "There is another owner in the business. A silent partner, if you will. Actually, its Ned's sister, Kristen Bent, and her daughter Valencia also is involved. Anyway, she will have to agree to the deal."

"Ned has mentioned her. If you think it will take a little extra to grease the skids on the deal, I could throw in a couple of rocks like the one on my ring."

Everyone's eyes looked at the stone on his ring. Seeing an uncut diamond for the first time can be pretty disappointing, and this stone was no exception.

"What is the carat weight of that diamond?" Dave

asked. He had recently priced a diamond pendant for Melody and his tenth anniversary.

"This stone is eight carats. If I were to have it cut, it would weigh about five."

"Isn't that over $1 million—a five-carat stone?" Dave asked.

"Depending on clarity and color, this stone would be about $1 million to $1.5 million. I only keep the clear, bright stones. I can't stand those yellow ones. They look like plastic to me."

The man spoke as though he was talking about a leg of lamb or a leather couch. Not knowing what to expect, they waited. The man had a sense of raw compulsion. He took a clean sheet of paper and within minutes had his own version of the list. When his totals were completed, he made a big circle around the bottom number then scratched his name beneath the figure. He laid it on the table beside Derek with a smile on his face. It was the first real smile he had shown all morning. "I believe in being up front with my business deals. I'll pay you cash for your company ... TAG, right?" The men all nodded in unison.

"Just to sweeten the deal, I'll throw in one of these rocks for each of your wives and one for Ned's sister," he said, slipping off his ring and passing it to the men for inspection. "Oh yeah, one for that sweet Valencia too."

It was the paper that Derek was stretching his neck to see. Not trying to be too anxious, he casually reached across the space and picked up the offer with Rhodes' signature scribbled on the bottom. Derek's calculation had shown a margin between debt and value of approximately $40 million, counting the padded commissions. Written in clear precise handwriting with a circle around it and a signature below was the amount of $550 million.

Derek was proud of his restraint as he calmly passed the sheet of paper to Dave who glanced at it for a moment and then passed it on to Brick.

"It will take me a few hours to contact Mrs. Bent and her daughter. Where can we reach you?" Derek asked Rhodes. They stood and shook hands, the three Arizona boys only too anxious to pass the buck to the African.

"I will stay in town until I have made a purchase. Let me remind you that you are not the only company in town selling real estate packages. My offer is good for forty-eight hours. I'll be at the Waldorf Astoria. If we agree to terms we can meet at J.P. Morgan Bank on Friday and exchange papers. My attorney can have everything ready in one day. Just let me know."

Rhodes walked out to the curb and caught a cab. The three friends watched him go, their minds racing, not quite sure whether they had seen a man or an apparition.

"I need pancakes," Brick said.

For the second time in twelve hours the men sat in the Marriott hotel coffee shop discussing the future of their lives. This time it was a little more cheerful, but there were still plenty of doubts.

"And just what would you do with your $20 or $30 million?" Derek asked, giving Brick a friendly punch in the shoulder, making him spill the syrup. "I'll bet you would leverage the whole thing on some pork belly or sugar future contract."

"Not a chance," Brick said. "I'm going to get it all in gold coins and bury it in the backyard."

"Not me," said Dave, "I'm going to find me a smart secretary to manage it, but is also a tissue match for me just in case I need a new kidney. What about you, Derek?"

"Me? I am going to give it to Natasha and let her hide it someplace that I not only don't know about, but that I couldn't get to even if I knew."

The rented town car pulled up the tree-lined lane in the plush, Connecticut neighborhood. The trees were bare except for the wind-driven snow slamming into the west side of their trunks. The streets leading into the lane had been piled up with dirty, brown snow from the passing cars and school buses. The house directly in front of them was an antebellum-style mansion, complete with white columns and a carved woodwork facade. The circular driveway passed beneath a covered portico where their driver stopped to allow them some protection from the wind and snow. An elaborate chandelier lit the expansive front porch. Twin, white oak rocking chairs stood beside the entrance door, adding an authentic touch to the colonial-style home.

Kristen Bent answered the door before they could knock, hurrying them out of the blowing snow. She looked like she had just walked off the set of an old *Dynasty* TV show. Her hair was perfectly coifed and her flowing, lavender silk dress hung on her shapely mature figure—more like a dressing gown than a dress. She wore matching silk slippers. Her makeup and jewelry were carefully balanced, prepared to dazzle or intimidate as the situation needed. Adding the air of

336

business to her casual dress was an iPad in a light-pink leather holder.

"Please come in gentlemen," she said, guiding them toward a brightly-lit living room full of furniture covered with carefully coordinated, floral prints. The carpet was deep enough to wade in and a white grand piano in the oval nook gave a degree of elegance, impressing all three men.

"May I offer you something to drink?" she asked.

"Just some water," Dave said. The others declined anything. "Your home is beautiful," he added. "Did you have it built?" he asked, but she didn't answer.

When they had settled into the chairs and couch and finished a round of small talk about the community, Derek cleared his throat and began. "Since we met with you last, there has been a surprising development. A gentleman was introduced to us, who claims to have a lot of money and who is offering to purchase TAG—all of it, including the debt and assets. He says he is an old bicycle racing friend of your brother's."

There was a pause as Kristen pondered the comment then she said, "Well, you three are free to do whatever you feel is best for you and your families. Any sale of the company would of course have to be approved by the majority of stock owners and the board of directors."

"I wasn't aware that we had an official board of directors," Brick said.

"That isn't official until we have a recorded stock-holder's meeting, but each of you are on the board and of course Valencia and I are the officers: the president and secretary/treasurer."

"It is what it is. Getting back to the man wanting to

buy TAG, he would like to buy the whole company, our shares and yours. He claims he has the cash to do so and is willing to pay a spectacular price," Derek explained. "He is a diamond miner from South Africa and has just sold out to De Beers. He would like to own real estate in the US."

Kristen arose from her chair and walked to an inlaid secretary desk on a far wall. Using the silk, rope-adorned brass key already in the lock, she lowered the lid and shuffled through a stack of photographs, removing one of the larger ones. She also picked up a leather bound notebook. She then closed the desk and carried the photo to Derek.

"Could this be the man who wants to purchase TAG?" she asked, handing him the photograph.

There, in living color, standing arm in arm with Kristen Bent, was James Rhodes. He was holding the reins of a docile-looking Shetland pony. Sitting on the saddle, looking like she was having the worst day of her life, was a six- or seven-year-old girl, wearing a yellow sunsuit and a straw hat with a blue flower in the brim. She had golden blond hair and the unmistakable facial features of the present day Valencia.

The photo was passed on to Dave and Brick, then Kristen took the picture and placed it face down on the coffee table. The room was silent as she sat and looked at the astonished men.

"Mr. Rhodes was a friend of my brother, as he might have mentioned. He was also my fiancé for a short time. That was a couple of years after Mr. Bent was killed during a hunting expedition to East Africa. Mr. Rhodes befriended us and tried to fill the gap Valencia's father left after his death. Then we found out that … unknown and quite hidden from us … that Mr. Rhodes was on the same hunting trip as my husband. It was quite a surprise, since he hadn't ever mentioned it during our months of courting and our rather extensive travel together.

"When we did find out the truth, my brother Edward confronted Mr. Rhodes with the rumor, and he admitted that he was in fact the person who had fired the wayward shot that killed my husband. I tried to be rational about the revelation, knowing full well that it had to have been an accident, but as you might well imagine, neither Valencia nor I felt forgiving enough to let the relationship continue. Valencia actually tried to reopen the investigation into her father's death when she started college at Vassar. Of course, the records were in a small province in Tanzania and were old and vague. By then many of the witnesses could not be found. I finally insisted that she stop. I doubt, however, that she will be willing to stay in the same city with the man once she finds out he is here, let alone agree to any sort of business arrangement with him."

"This is the chance of a lifetime for the three of us," Brick added. "We aren't cut out for the Wall Street world. The opportunity to sell our shares and be done with the past year's drama and stress would be welcome to me. He's our chance out. Otherwise, we could all be in enormous trouble with the investors and with the federal government. There is a possibility we could be charged with some kind of crime and all be sent to jail if we can't answer all the questions that have arisen from Willow's activities and replace the money we have accepted from investors."

"I merely inherited the company. I have had nothing to do with any of the earlier transactions," Kristen said. "You three and Willow are the responsible parties. If anyone goes to jail, it won't be Valencia or me. As for Mr. Rhodes, I seriously doubt that he has enough money to pay his hotel bill let alone buy TAG. His diamond mine, as he calls it, is a shabby plot of jungle that he inherited from his great-grandfather. It has no water, no electricity, and no improved road. The last I heard, he had lost his digging equipment in a gambling fiasco. That was a few years ago."

"But he says he found diamonds in a deep pit and sold the whole thing to De Beers for hundreds of millions. He is willing to pay us all in cash. He wants to buy TAG; all of it, including your share. We need to at least check out his story," Dave said with a pleading sense of emotion in his voice.

"You can do all the checking you would like gentlemen, but then come back here and explain to my daughter that the man who murdered her father wants to make us all richer. It will be an interesting encounter. In the meantime, we need to agree on how to satisfy the demand of your Chinese investor. Derek, as I understand it, you are the person who visited Macau and solicited the funds."

Reluctantly, Derek nodded.

"Then perhaps you could be so kind as to call the man ... I believe his name is Chen?"

"That's his name," said Derek. "I'll call him, but what do you want me to say?"

"Merely explain that the money is tied up and that he needs to remain agreeable to the initial contract. We didn't promise an immediate return of his principle, just the income on it. Let him know that he is not due any money until ... let me see," Kristen opened the leather binder and picked up a sheet of paper. She ran her long, manicured finger down a column. "Here it says that the first income payment isn't due until April. April 31st, to be exact."

"And what do I tell him if that's not agreeable?"

"Simply explain to the man that the information Mrs. Willow Foster has on file regarding his prior investments and business activity is damaging, and that he won't want it sent to the Chinese gambling commission."

"How do you know all of this stuff?" Dave asked with a puzzled look on his face.

"My dear boys, you don't think that my sister-in-law, Willow, would trust just you men with her files on the company? Do you?"

"But we don't even have some of that information," Derek said.

"Trust me. You really don't want to know everything that is in these files."

The conversation was interrupted by the front door opening and the entrance of Valencia. She threw her full-length, mink coat on the back of a chair and waved at the men. She was dressed for a night out on the town, in a low-cut, silky cocktail dress and spiked heels. She was dripping in jewelry and had on more makeup than any of the men's wives had ever worn.

"I told Frank to pick me up here, Mother. I need to impress him with your house. Hi guys. Please don't let me interrupt."

"No problem," said Dave.

The men already were on their feet as Valencia circled the room giving each man a cheek-to-cheek peck, which embarrassed all three of them, especially since they anticipated their relationship changing the moment she heard about Rhodes. Her perfume lingered long after she moved toward her mother.

"I've got a few minutes before my date arrives. Anything new with the business?" Valencia asked as if she was asking the score of a baseball game.

"I'll go over it with you tomorrow dear. These gentlemen are tired and still have to travel back into the city after dinner. We better eat now and worry about business later," Kristen said, turning toward the men. "Could we schedule a follow-up meeting for tomorrow afternoon? Let's say in The Palm Room at the Plaza at four. Then the two of you can catch the red-eye back to Arizona and Brick and I can finish tying up any loose ends. Oh, and we'll need you there also, Valencia. Will that work for all of you?"

Valencia's date arrived and the two immediately left. The three men and Kristen adjourned into the elegant dining room. There was no more discussion or business, just the remarkable cuisine.

The ride back toward the city was silent. All three of the men were lost in thought. Sitting in the front passenger seat, Derek's mind was deep in the memories of his trip to China and the stoic expression on the faces of Chen's bodyguards. He didn't know if he could muster the nerve to call Chen and refuse his request to immediately return the capital. Also weighing on his mind was the concern that paying out Chen could create the rumor on the street that TAG was in trouble, and thus precipitate a run of the company's assets by the other investors.

Brick was thinking about the potential windfall of cash that a buyout from Rhodes would produce. He always had far less in income and in discretionary cash than the other two men. Now would be his big chance to level the field. He was ignoring the roadblock that the relationship with Rhodes and the women presented, and dreaming about a new Lexus SUV for Debbie.

Dave was thinking about how his life would be, had they never gotten into this mess with Edward Foster III. He had nearly constant pain in his flank and his temperature never was less than ninety-nine. He hadn't felt well enough to be able to work out or even swim a few laps since the surgery. He had pretty well exhausted the $1 million bonus Ned had given him. The only bright spot was that for the first time since he started college, he was debt free. He had paid off his medical school loans, his cars, and even the mortgage on his moderate house. Fortunately, his wife and kids were in good health and his wife still loved him. He had faith in Derek's and Brick's business judgment, but had serious doubt that they would ever figure out something to resolve the present TAG conflicts. He was just beginning a little prayer of gratitude and hope when he heard the Town Car's driver scream. He looked up in time to see a huge red snowplow—its rotating yellow light clearly flashing and snowblade flat to the ground. It was speeding directly toward them. Unable to stop on the icy street, the truck ran straight through a stop sign, smashing into the side of the town car.

The first thing Derek saw was the snowplow blade as its gritty, grey mass covered the driver's side window. He felt the jolt of the sudden side impact and saw the window glass fragment into a thousand pieces. Next, he heard the driver's-side air bag deploy with the explosive sound of a .357 magnum fired inside of the car. The driver's head was buried into the airbag, and then the head came flying out toward him. Dave tried to turn his head to look away, but the momentum of the side force wouldn't let him. Then the passenger-side door smashed into a steel light pole, and Derek's side air bag exploded in his ear.

Brick had been staring out the car's right-side, backseat window. He didn't know what had hit them as he was thrown at first toward Dave and then against the passenger side glass. The older town car had no rear seat air bags, thus it was his head that shattered the window when they were stopped by the sturdy light pole.

Dave saw the truck's glaring lights coming toward them. His instantaneous calculation of its speed and angle of attack gave him time to save himself. For some reason he would never know, he bent his upper body flat onto his legs and clasped his hands over his head.

Just as he did so, the far right curved corner of the blade shot through the glass and steel of the upper rear door, stopping precisely where Dave's face had been less than a second prior. The second impact, the one stopping the car's lateral motion as its right side was crushed by the light pole, threw Dave toward Brick, compressing the seat belt into his flank—his surgically-tender flank.

The honking horn, the screeching tires, the shattering glass, the exploding air bags, and the creaking and grinding as metal was twisted, bent, and crushed, all came to a sudden halt. What followed was a seemingly endless silence as the heavy snowflakes continued to fall on the scene, drifting through the shattered glass onto the still bodies of the four men. The only light was the rotating yellow signal light from the snowplow truck, since the streetlamp had been shattered when its supporting pole was bent thirty degrees, causing it to lean over the wreckage like the neck of a curious giraffe.

Though his ears were ringing like church bells, Dave heard the truck driver's voice break the silence with a whispered profanity. He looked up to see the driver, a heavy-set, white man with a mustache and thick glasses.

"Can any of you hear me?" the truck's driver asked. "Can you hear me," he repeated. "I'm really sorry. My windshield wiper stuck and I didn't see the stop sign. I'll call for some help as soon as I can find my phone or get on the two-way radio."

"I can hear you," Dave said, trying to sit upright. But the man was gone. He heard the truck door open then there was the crackle of a communicating radio and distorted voices. He tried to unfasten the seat belt, but at first it seemed to be jammed and Brick was half lying on the arm rest covering the corner of the latch. Dave turned toward Brick and tried to examine him. He was unconscious, but had a strong carotid pulse. There was blood everywhere; however, Dave's first guess was that it was due to the shattered glass and that both of their face wounds were bleeding, as would be expected.

"Derek? Derek, are you all right?" Dave shouted toward the front seat, but got no response. With the snowplow blade still sitting above his head, he painfully freed himself from the seat belt, wondering if his flank incision had been torn open. That's how it felt. He knew he needed to get out of the car, but the snowplow blade was literally in his face to the left and he could see that a steel pole had the rear passenger door bent inward. Crawling over the front seat was an option but the body of the driver was pushed into the middle console and Derek's wide shoulders filled the rest of the space. He could feel the frigid air on his bloody, wet neck and turned toward the back window. It was shattered into little corn-size fragments, but still intact and bent outward. He turned, kneeling on the seat and holding on to the seat belt anchor for leverage, and pushed against the glass with his hand. To his surprise the entire sheet of glass popped out of its frame and slid off the side of the car onto the ground, leaving an open access and a blast of frigid air. Slowly and painfully, Dave crawled out of the back window frame, onto the snow covered trunk lid and slid off onto the ground. He needed the truck to back away from the town car in order for him to attend to the others. He staggered to the passenger side of the truck and pulled himself up to open the door handle. As he was trying to twist the handle, he heard the sirens. The next thing he knew, he was looking up into the face of a female paramedic who was covered in blood—his blood.

CHAPTER

The scene at the community hospital was chaos. Although it was just a short commute to the city, the facility was strictly hometown. There was just one emergency room doctor on call and he was a resident, moonlighting from his real job at Cornell Medical Center. Fortunately, three of the passengers from the car collision were stable and semi-conscious when the ambulances arrived. Of the four town car occupants, the paid driver was in the worst shape. Within minutes he was picked up at the hospital by a helicopter and transported to a Level III trauma center.

Through the sliding cotton curtain, Dave could hear Derek and Brick both moaning as the doctor and the nurses tried to communicate with them. Derek was complaining about his shoulder pain. Brick on the other hand was jabbering about jet skis and then went on about wanting sushi with ranch dressing—obviously suffering from a bad concussion. Except for the fifteen or twenty small lacerations on his arms, hands, and face, Dave felt pretty good. But then he tried to sit up for a chest x-ray and felt the fire in his flank. He reached back to his right and felt a wet, gaping cavity.

"Excuse me, nurse, I seem to have a hole in my back," he said as he sank back into the plastic mattress.

The young blonde rolled her eyes and stopped gathering dressing material, and came to his side. She lifted the thin pink hospital gown and bent down to have a closer look. Then she let out a gasp for help. There was a hole in Dave's side large enough to plug in a golf ball.

It was nearly nine the following morning when the three men saw one another in the surgical recovery room. Derek had a full upper arm cast extending from his shoulder to his wrist. His forehead looked like a botched Frankenstein face-lift with three separate lacerations and their train-track suture lines.

Brick was bruised from head to toe but had no broken bones. The CT of his head was at first questionable for an inter-cranial bleed, but a repeat two hours later was negative. The admitting doctor settled for "severe concussion" as a diagnosis. He had forgotten all about the sushi.

For Dave, the accident meant two hours in the operating room. Much of the time was spent picking glass shards out of his hands and then reclosing the wound on his flank, first made when he donated his kidney to Edward Foster III four months prior, and then reopened by the force of the seat belt. It never had healed properly after his first surgery. When the local general surgeon was called in to repair the reopened wound, he was flabbergasted to find that deep in Dave's retroperitoneal space, where Edward Foster's donated kidney had previously sat, was a small, round ball of clot, fibrin, and pus. When the foreign mass was untangled and spread out on the Mayo stand, close inspection revealed a Raytex four-by-four cotton pad—typically used in surgery to mop up blood. It was missing its tiny blue strip of opaque plastic, which would have made it show up on any one of the numerous x-rays Dave had been subjected to over the last few months. Pictures of it were taken, and the hospital legal staff was notified. At first the surgeon considered not telling the patient, but when it was mentioned that the patient was in fact a physician, and had had his kidney removed at Massachusetts General Hospital, he quickly changed his mind. It would later provide Dave with a small malpractice settlement—enough to buy him a new Range Rover.

The driver of the town car had miraculously survived—the driver's-side air bag took the brunt of the impact. The fortunate man was stable and would recover from his injuries.

Because the town car had last been dispatched to Kristen Bent's address, the police showed up at her door after midnight, awaking her. A burly police officer in a hooded winter coat looked cold and somewhat sad. "Sorry to bother you ma'am, but there has been an accident. We need your help identifying the victims. We were told they were at your house just prior to the incident." His demeanor sent a chill through her—colder than the frigid wind. Her first thought was that it was Valencia and her boyfriend, but the officer then told her there were four men in the car.

She dressed immediately and went to the nearby hospital emergency room. In their haste to get the four injured men to the hospital, the paramedics had tossed all of the wallets into a single plastic evidence bag. When Kristen arrived and assessed the situation, it was up to her to sort out the men's identities for the nurses and doctor. She was given very little information about their conditions, and she settled into a molded, plastic armchair to await the outcome of the imaging, tests, and surgeries. It would prove to be a very long night. Valencia joined her mother just before sunrise. Brick was the first person they were able to speak to. He was still somewhat confused, but thoughtful enough to ask the women to notify his wife and the other two families in Arizona.

It was still dark in Arizona when Natasha heard the phone ringing—dragging her out of a confusing kidnapping dream where she was the kidnapper. It took her a moment to recognize the voice on the other end of the phone. When she heard the words "car collision," her head began to spin, her body went limp, and she fell back into the pillows. With her heart pounding she listened, anticipating the worst.

"It was a miracle any of the four men are alive," Kristen said, trying to be as positive as possible. "The police said the snowplow was driving too fast and ran a stop sign. There is already a picture of the car in the local morning paper. It looks horribly destroyed. Derek is in the recovery room. His arm is in a cast and he has some cuts on his face, but otherwise he is awake and alert. The doctors say that he should be fine."

Kristen gave a rundown of the other husbands' injuries, but soon understood that Tasha wasn't listening well enough to reiterate the details to the other wives, so Kristen left her regrets and the hospital's phone number. "Listen dear, I'll let you go. I need to call Mrs. Wahl and Mrs. Felshaw."

Debbie and Melody knocked on Tasha's door an hour later. An hour after that, they had organized their lives and children and were ready to leave that evening on the eastbound red-eye for New York. For all three, it was one flight to New York too many.

For most patients in the hospital the days come and go quite quickly. For the families of hospitalized patients, those days can be the longest of their lives. Sitting in an uncomfortable chair watching a tiny TV and listening to the patient cough, breath, groan, and complain gets old in a hurry. After four agonizing days of it, all three wives were more than ready for the news that they could pick up their husbands and take them home.

"I'll need to see him back in a week," the surgeon told Melody.

"Won't it be all right if I have one of his surgeon friends in Phoenix see him?" Melody pleaded. She had had enough of the mansion's small bedroom with all of its negative memories and her kids needed her home. Natasha also had been staying at the town house. Debbie had been at their apartment, but had already given notice of leaving and had just four days left in the place.

"Sorry Mrs. Felshaw, but I don't think he is fit to travel just yet."

"It's fine," Dave said. "Besides, it will give us time to iron out some business problems before we leave town. Thanks, Doctor, for all of your help."

The caravan of three taxies left the hospital entrance and headed into Midtown—two to the Foster mansion and one to Brick and Debbie's apartment. A fourth car pulled into the line of traffic behind them, unnoticed by the men or their wives. Plans had been made to get together at the mansion for brunch the following day. Until then they were all on their own.

The next morning Natasha and Melody went out to pick up the needed groceries for another day's stay at the mansion. It was too early to call Arizona to check on the kids, but yesterday everyone had been doing fine. Melody was in the checkout line behind Natasha when she noticed a man staring at her. It wasn't a rarity for her to draw looks from men, being a beautiful woman with a great figure, but this guy looked different. In the first place, he was Asian and much older that she. More eye-catching was the fact that he didn't remove his sunglasses inside the store and followed her so that she was never out of his sight. Several times he stopped to jot something in a notebook.

When Melody pushed her cart to the side and began filling her cloth satchels, she asked Natasha if she had noticed the man. Natasha was in no mood for another abduction or anything else that would compromise her family's future. She acted as though she was leaving the store and then pivoted just as the man came through the electric doors. In a move that would have made her high school basketball coach proud, she dropped her shoulder and swung her elbow up as though trying to keep her balance. Her forearm struck the man's directly on his Adam's apple. He grasped his throat and stumbled into a snow shovel display, dragging a dozen clattering plastic shovels with him to the ground. Natasha made a quick apology and was out the door.

"What did he look like?" Derek demanded when he heard the story.

"Short, muscular, and well-dressed," answered Melody.

"Also, he held a cell phone in his hand like he was constantly communicating with someone. He was scary like that character in the James Bond movie. You know? The one that kept cutting people's heads off with his top hat—tossing it like a Frisbee."

"We better warn Brick and Debbie," Dave said. "Do you think it's the guy you took the money from in Macao?" he asked Derek.

Derek shook his head and leaned toward the phone on the table, trying to reach it with his good hand. "I don't know. Why can't everybody just leave us alone for a few days?"

Derek told Brick about the Asian-looking stalker and then, on the spur of the moment, put a call in to Willow. To his surprise she answered her phone.

"I'm fine, love. I'm stuck here in Monte Carlo watching paint dry—literally. I heard about the auto accident. Kristen called me. She said you were all recovering and that I could help you the best by staying out of the way," she laughed.

"Have you heard anything from your Chinese contact, Chen?" Derek asked.

"Well, not directly, but one of the people Edward used to do business with did sent me an e-mail, asking if TAG was in financial trouble. Rumors always fly around the business world. I wouldn't worry about it if I were you."

"That's easy for you to say, but then you weren't the person that was kidnapped. The girls were in a store here in New York this morning and were followed by a guy that sounded like one of Chen's buddies."

"Well Derek, maybe you should call Chen and see

why he's having you watched. Perhaps he just needs some reassurance that you three are well enough to manage his $30 million."

"Listen to me, dearest," said Willow. "You just need to make some more good purchases and some spectacular sales and then everything will be just fine. All of the investors were given an honest pitch, and all of them are smart enough to know that not every business deal goes just as planned. If things get a little tight for TAG just give the investors a call and reassure them that things are fine. Explain that Edward's death, and now the auto accident, has changed the timelines. I'm sure they'll understand."

Derek started to ask her another question, but was cut off in mid-sentence.

"Sorry, but I have to run to meet the decorator in Paris. The hotel is coming together nicely. You should bring the wives and all come to the grand re-opening on May Day. But Derek, don't worry about Mr. Chen. He is a lover, not a fighter. He is the one that got me my job with Edward's company years ago. Tell him I said hello."

Derek tried to explain the conversation to the others, but it hardly put their minds at ease. The fact that Willow and Chen were connected prior to her knowing Foster gave them lots of reasons to worry.

Brick had invited Kristen and Valencia to stop by the mansion. There were lots of loose ends to tie up before the Arizona couples left town, and they still hadn't heard back from Mr. Rhodes. He wasn't looking forward to giving the man the news that his money wasn't wanted. Valencia had made it very clear that she would bring any such deal to its early grave.

When the door knocker sounded, echoing through

the mansion, Dave looked at his watch and wondered why they were early. The wives were in the kitchen putting the final touches on brunch and Brick and Derek were in the study pouring over the ledger so Dave dragged himself out of a chair and went to the door. Assuming it was Kristen and her daughter he opened it without looking through the peephole. Standing in a cluster on the stoop were four serious-looking men in dark suits and short, cropped haircuts. The oldest of the men held out a leather wallet that he opened to reveal a heavy-looking, gold badge. Standing further out on the sidewalk were four more men, all appearing to have been cloned from the one standing at the door.

"My name is Preston Rosen. I'm with the Securities and Exchange Commission. These men are with the FBI," he said, motioning to the men behind him. "Is a Mr. Derek Morris, a Mr. Brick Wahl, or a Doctor David Felshaw here?"

"I'm Doctor Felshaw. What can I do for you?"

Rosen produced a tri-folded paper from his inside breast pocket and unfolded it. "This is a search warrant for the contents of this house and any material present that is related to the operation of a company called …" he paused to reread the name on the paper, "TAG. Would you please step aside and let us do our work?"

"Can you tell us what this is about?" Dave asked in a loud voice, but received no answer, as Rosen brushed by, waving for the others to follow him into the mansion.

"Ladies, gentlemen, please remain in this room and let us do our job," he said to the couples who were now all standing by the door with mouths agape.

"I have food on the stove," protested Melody.

"Attend to whatever you must, but please don't attempt to interfere with our search. Trust me. We shouldn't take more than a couple of hours."

Rosen was a gentleman as were the other men. They didn't trash the place as they searched, nor did they damage anything. They started in the upper floors and worked their way down to the main floor, curiously leaving Foster's—now Brick's—study for last. This gave Brick time to slip a flash drive into the computer on the desk and download the vital information regarding the TAG accounts. He then deleted the information leaving only the files of Edward Foster that Willow had neglected to delete. When the investigators came into the study they were thorough. Two of the men went out and returned with empty file boxes that they used to carry away all of the paperwork, the printer, and the desktop computer.

Natasha offered the federal agents something to eat or drink, but they politely refused, saying they were nearly finished. As Brick was thinking about his laptop lying on a desk back at his apartment, Rosen produced a second paper.

"Mr. Wahl? This is for you sir. We have already searched your apartment and removed your computer. The doorman let us in so we didn't have to damage the lock. We left everything in good order," he said with a friendly smile as though he had delivered furniture or cleaned the carpets. "Here is a receipt for you. We'll have it ready to return to you in two days."

Lexy broke the silence that had fallen over the room with a cry as the door was slammed shut by the wind. She had been fast asleep in her stroller seat throughout the search.

The brunch was getting cold in the kitchen, but no one had an appetite for it anyway.

"How can we go on living like this with insane situations arising every day?" Debbie asked, taking her baby in her arms, tears running down her cheeks.

That was the question on all of their minds.

Kristen and Valencia arrived in the middle of the post-search-and-seizure wake. They listened to the account of the surprise search. They didn't seem at all surprised at Willow's nonchalant attitude. What did seem to worry Kristen was hearing that a copy of Edward Foster III's will also was seized.

"But it has my name on it as an owner of TAG. Surely they wouldn't search my home as well?" She began to insist that she and Valencia return to her home to be in attendance if a search should take place. After a discussion with the others, she finally conceded that not only was it unlikely, it would make no difference anyway. Her housekeeper was there to oversee any search and Kristen said, "I have nothing there to hide anyway."

It was just a few minutes later when the phone rang and MaryAnn Carpet called to report to Brick that the federal agents were searching TAG's office in the Foster Building.

"They won't be here long," she said. "There is nothing in any of the file cabinets or desk drawers but paper clips and old pens."

"Do you have any idea what they are after?" Derek asked her.

"That's easy," said MaryAnn. "They want information about Willow."

"But, why just her?" Melody asked the others after Brick hung up the phone.

"Most likely it's because she is the only one with a suspicious background of probable illegal transactions. Before she showed up on Edward's doorstep, she had been investigated by a Canadian court for illegal solicitation of funds," Valencia reported. She loved telling the undocumented story. "Why do you think she gave the three of you her holdings in TAG without any compensation to herself? She must have known that the SEC had finally checked on her and were curious about what she was up to."

"Da! And here we just thought she was being generous and wanted to simplify her life," Brick answered.

"Oh, that she did. She wanted to keep from going to prison. As part of her getting a green card, she had been forbidden to ever hold stock or deal in transaction of international business. She never had so much as a credit card here in this country until she met Uncle Ned. He loved her business mind and her ability to make every financial idea that she came up with seem like a gift from God. The problem came after the snakebite, the transplant, and then the rejection when it began to look like he wouldn't make it. She needed an easy way out of the country with a big stash of money."

Valencia paced in front of the ornately-carved fireplace as she laid out the series of events that had occurred over the last several years.

"She and I first met on a trip I took to Quebec. I needed to get away from a jealous boyfriend. She had just been cleared after spending six months on probation for defrauding some British guy out of his hotel investment. She was working at a travel agency at the time and I went in to ask about a day trip. We struck up a friendship—two single, hot women out for a good time. It was months later that I learned about her criminal activity. By then, I had introduced her to Mother and to Uncle Ned. She also had an in with your friend from Macao, who had invested money in Canada and with Uncle Ned. He was lonely and he had a branch office in Toronto that needed a manager. Within a year she was here in New York and was becoming more and more a part of his business and his life. Then when his kidney failed and the business started to suffer, he handed off the foreign operations to associates and concentrated on his New York office. Money was never the problem for him, but it was painful to see his business and his body losing momentum at the same time. When he couldn't find a donor for his kidney, Willow made her offer. He had no one else to talk to so he used my mother and me as his sounding board. In spite of her questionable past, I still liked her and so did he. And so I suggested he take her offer and he did. Eventually, he learned to love her."

"So donating her kidney was a business arrangement, not a lover's sacrifice?" asked Tasha.

"Honey, one can learn to love someone, but loving great wealth requires a great deal less learning."

"But when we first met her she seemed genuinely in love with him," said Brick.

"No doubt she was! He had transformed her from a clever secretary sitting behind a desk wearing headphones to a spoiled wife and multinational business partner living the life and style of a New York socialite. The cost of the deal to her was a kidney, and a willingness to ignore the handsome young men she was surrounded by daily. Now that Edward is gone and she has her freedom I doubt you'll see her in any geriatric bars. That's probably another reason why she chose to live in Monte Carlo."

During the entire explanation, the couples sat mystified, and even Kristen was surprised at some of the revelations her daughter was airing. They sat quietly for a few minutes and then it was time for action.

Of the group Dave was thinking the clearest and stated, "There is nothing we can do about the Feds. The thing we can do is to be sure that the other investors are taken care of the best way possible, starting with the Chinese and the Arabs. If we can make them happy and remove any physical threats to ourselves, we can deal with the rest of the problems. Maybe we need to make them our partners."

"They don't want partners, they want a return on their money," Derek said.

"What about us going to the federal investigators and explaining everything and letting them take over from there?" Melody's idea was met with an equal lack of enthusiasm.

"I think we need to follow Willow's advice and go to work. We need to sell more and buy more and turn a profit," Brick said.

"But Brick, we have been doing that and it isn't getting the job done," Dave said.

"I have an idea," said Debbie. "What if we buy the Arabs and the Chinese their own individual properties and then sell them to one another? We'll present them as such good deals that they won't be able to resist, and we'll present them as being too good to keep in the TAG inventory. In the meantime we can stop taking any outside money—not that there is any to be had anyway—and sell all of the properties we now own. Then we pay back the smaller investors and announce that since Ned's death the legend of TAG has come to an end. Then we can just close the company down and go back to our boring but peaceful lives." She sat back with a smile on her face as though her plan was already signed, sealed, and delivered.

The first thought each of them had was that Debbie's idea was fanciful and unrealistic, but suddenly Kristen stood and began to pace, drawing the attention of the group.

"Do you think that you can find a property in Hong Kong or Macao that the Arabs would consider owning?" She had stopped in front of Derek, and looking straight at him went on, "What about the Chinese? Do you think that they would consider buying a hotel or office building in a country where there is no alcohol served and the women are all wearing burkas?"

There were chuckles from the group, but then Valencia spoke up. "Mother, Uncle Edward and that snake, Willow, got you into this mess. I think you should get out of it. I think we should all get out of it and if Debra's recommendation works, I'm all for it."

Derek had his iPad turned on and was scanning the properties under construction in Dubai. It wasn't going to be easy, but he could see merit in what Brick's wife had presented. Both Chen and Prince Assad prided themselves in their shrewdness making money. To the best of his knowledge, TAG owed them both around $32 million plus some upcoming interest. If he could find a property in each country that was worth enough to pad a commission for TAG into the price, he could possibly make it work and have something real to show for all of their effort and sacrifice. The one constant in the deal would be that both the Arab and the Chinese man were enormously greedy.

There were no upgraded seats available for the Emirates airline flight. Derek and Brick were in the back of the coach class seats with the UN soldiers from Canada and the US on their way to deployment in Yemen. Crowded together with the GIs and starving student crowd, they were trying to get some sleep. They knew that they would have to survive the inevitable jet lag and yet be mentally sharp. There was no Bentley to meet them at the airport and their meals would be in street-front cafes instead of $300-a-plate restaurants. Low-budget and under the radar was their plan.

They had done their homework and arrived in Dubai anxious to go to work. Finding the nearly constructed buildings lining the waterfront main highway was easy. Five of them bore Prince Abraham Assad's company logo—a Falcon clutching a snake. Each building was towered over by cranes, and each one looked bigger and more extravagant than the previous one.

Unannounced to Assad, the two men wandered about Dubai appearing to play the tourist role, taking pictures, and reading all they could on the construction billboards in front of the skyscrapers. They bought lunch for a couple of British-looking chaps who emerged from one of the construction trailers at noon and the Big Mac turned out to be worth a thousand times its ten-dollar price tag. It seemed that the economic slowdown had finally hit the Arab gulf, and buildings previously constructed on an open budget were now counting bolts, nuts, and nails. There was a twenty-story bank building of glass and steel that looked like a giant flower vase with a flared top. The men said that it was their biggest headache. It was over budget and under-funded, yet the prince was adamant on getting it completed. Brick and Derek were offered a tour through the nearly-finished building. They loaded up on photos and then headed back to the airport.

Eight hours later they were checking into the new Trump Palace in Macau. They ate a buffet breakfast—a mere thirty-nine Hong Kong dollars—and slept for seven hours. Then they went casino hopping and shopping. Their online sources said that Chen owned at least half of the casinos on the tiny island. They found them all and did a street front appraisal of each. The closest in value to the new flower-vase-appearing hotel in Dubai was a garish, inverted pyramid that looked like a blown-up version of the city hall in Tempe, Arizona. How the thing kept from toppling over was a defiance of logic and gravity. They wandered through the building's shops, restaurants, and casino. They even asked to see one of the suites with its glass-walled bay window, giving the sense that the building was falling toward the waterfront thirty stories below. It looked like it would fit the bill.

They called Arizona and woke up Dave and Melody to explain the plan, and with Dave's approval they called

Kristen. She laughed at their success thus far, "I give my verbal blessing and full support. Now it's up to you men."

It took a full day of work in the casino's business center before they had the proposals completed. On a sunny Friday morning they set off for the horse races. It was a thirty minute hydrofoil ride to the Hong Kong Island track. Mr. Chen had his own box at the luxurious racetrack and getting past security was an issue. Derek had visited the place before and remembered the route in from the water taxi station. They loitered at the entrance until they saw Chen's entourage leave the helipad and make their way toward the private entrance.

"Oh my goodness!" said Derek, stepping between Chen's lead body guard and the billionaire. "What a surprise!"

"Ah-so, Mr. Derek. My favorite cowboy. What brings you to Hong Kong? Perhaps you are lonesome to see or even ride the horses. I'm afraid you are far too heavy to get on the back of one of my speedsters." Chen laughed at his own joke. He was apparently in a good mood, and after meeting Brick, immediately invited the Westerners into the private club to join him for lunch and to watch the races. It was well into the second pre-race parade when Chen asked the true nature of their business.

"We have a client in the Middle East. He has a new building for sale, but doesn't want to just sell it for cash. He is building five massive office and apartment buildings and has decided to diversify. I remembered the beautiful buildings here, especially that unique building that looks like the Great Pyramid of Giza turned upside down. Do you happen to know who owns it and if it is for sale?" Derek had worded the statement and question in a polite, but somewhat disinterested way, looking most of the time at the horses approaching the starting gate.

"And they're off!" yelled the voice over the loudspeaker.

It was two races and a platter of delicately fried shrimp and calamari before the buildings came up again in conversation. It was Chen who raised the question. "How much does your Arab friend want for his sand castle?"

"I suspect that he wants to make a trade. We have run a few numbers and feel that the building in Dubai is worth about $1.7 billion, but that is a negotiable price depending on what he gets in trade. Who owns the pyramid?"

Chen laughed at Derek and Brick. "You two are far too smart to approach me not knowing everything about my holdings and interest. The 'pyramid' as you call it is my property. As it turns out it is a bit too non-conforming for the tastes of most Chinese. I could become interested in liquidating it from my inventory."

"Would you be interested in seeing photographs of the building in Dubai?"

"Do you remember where we met the last time you were here Mr. Derek?"

"I believe I can find it."

"On second thought, I will have my driver pick you up in front of your hotel at 2100," Chen said in a tone of finality as he raised his binoculars to his round, bald head. Neither Brick nor Derek had mentioned where they were staying.

The multilayered lacquer on the Rolls Royce was so shiny it looked like a pool of black water instead of paint. The driver didn't speak a word, merely nodding in the direction of the rear open doors and later nodding at the front door of Chen's mansion. Derek and Brick had rented white dinner jackets for the evening—Derek remembering how underdressed he had felt the last time he had met with Chen. The printed real estate information they planned to give Chen was in a new, leather Coach briefcase that Brick had spent way too much for, but the appearance of prosperity was essential.

Surprising both men, the car glided past casino row and headed to the opposite side of the island. It drove through a neighborhood of eight-story slum buildings and then rolled down a curving hill toward the ocean. A massive steel gate halted the car. The driver, who had yet to speak a word to the men, mumbled a series of numbers into a tiny speaker and after a moment the gate slowly opened. It was too dark to see much until the driveway curved toward a palatial building aglow in the exterior's blue lights.

Mr. Chen stood on the upper steps of the entryway and waved them into his home.

"What a pleasure to see you again, Mr. Derek," Chen said, vigorously shaking Derek's hand with both of his. "And Mr. Brick Wahl. What an interesting name. I once knew a woman named Glass Window. Or maybe it was Grass Willow." He laughed at his own stupid joke and shook Bricks hand with equal vigor.

"It's a pleasure to meet you, sir. Thank you for inviting us here," Brick said, trying to not dislike the man.

"Please come into my humble home," Chen said leading the way into a foyer the size of most hotel lobbies.

There was a footman waiting to take their coats, which of course they didn't have. There was a butler standing like a statue holding a tray of assorted drinks. Both men choose the bubbling water with fresh limes and cherries. They were then led through a series of columns to a courtyard that opened outward to a view of the ocean and starlit sky beyond. On the far horizon a cruise ship was departing the bay, casting a reflection on the still water. The running water from a chain of koi ponds was the only sound heard as they walked toward a poolside table set with white lace tablecloths and crystal goblets.

"Please, Mr. Derek and Mr. Brick, take a seat. I would like you to join me in a light dinner then we can discuss business. Later, if you are not too tired from your journey, we can visit one of my clubs for a game of cards or perhaps you would like to try your luck with the dice."

"Thank you for finding time in your busy schedule to meet with us," Brick said.

Chen lifted his chubby left hand, giving a small wave to a servant, and within seconds silver platters of steaming seafood and chilled fruits were being placed in front of the men. Their glasses were filled and they began to eat. The glazed scallops were the best Derek had ever tasted and the giant prawns with just a wisp of crusted batter melted in his mouth. Several unrecognizable entrees were also served, the men hesitating to try them until coached by Chen, who took obvious pleasure watching the men's hesitation at eating the eel and hot, pickled sea snake.

As the plates were cleared Chen motioned them to another part of the pool area where over-stuffed chairs surrounded a low-lying table holding trays of petit fours and chocolate-dipped strawberries. As the men loaded up another plate of food, Chen sipped from a wine glass and studied the men.

"Tell me what it is that I can do for you gentlemen?" Chen said, switching to a more business-like tone of voice.

"We have been looking at available properties all over the world and have found a very special building in the Arabian Gulf. It is a newly-built, multi-use structure that will contain a hotel, apartments, business offices, and a high-end shopping gallery. It is on the water and will have its own small private yacht club as well as several restaurants. The owner has several such buildings in Qatar and Dubai, all of which are fully occupied and earning huge profits. He would like to diversify his holdings and would be willing to trade his newest project for a casino here in Macau. Since I know and trust you Mr. Chen, your name came to mind. And as I said yesterday, I wondered if you might be interested in taking a look at the project." Derek opened the leather case and produced several glossy photos of the prince's new building, which he had printed at a self-serve printing shop in Hong Kong. Though taken by Derek, the photos had a professional appearance.

"These are very impressive. I must admit that I like the architecture. What amount of money would we be talking about?" Chen said, laying the photos on the table.

"He really doesn't want money, but as I mentioned would like to accomplish a trade—his property, for something of equivalent value here in the Hong Kong area. He has never owned a casino, but has spent lots of time and money in them in London, Monte Carlo, and of course, Las Vegas," Brick explained.

"As you know, I own a few casinos here and have recently built three more in other cities in China. They are becoming very popular. Why would I want to invest in a country where they have no respect for women and where they are hypocrites regarding the consumption of alcohol?"

"We are told that the ruling families are concerned that when the oil reserves of the region become depleted, they will have nothing else to fall back on except tourism. Therefore, the ruling families are considering allowing legalized gambling ... gambling out in the open in the form of casinos. That is why our client wants to obtain some experience with the gambling business. For you, Mr. Chen, it could be an inroad into the Arab world where you could be the king of gambling when they open the legal doors."

Chen bent down and picked up the photos again, studying them this time.

"Tell me this. Would your friend insist on having a new building or would one of my older casinos interest him? Casinos are like women to me. It is much harder to put aside a young pretty one than one who is aging and perhaps not as interested in making me happy as she used to be. I think one of my properties could be of interest to your Arab friend, but of course I don't know if we are in the same baseball park, as you Americans say. I couldn't possibly let the lucky lady I'm thinking about—somewhat aged though she may be—go for less than $800 million."

Brick glanced at Derek who was quickly doing the math on conversion. "I think we are in the area at that figure." He had hoped for an amount around $1 billion. Eight hundred million pounds was over $1,200 million. Maybe too far from the amount the prince could ask for his new building.

"If I may make a suggestion," Chen said. "Why don't the three of us and a couple of my advisors fly over in the morning and take a look at the Arab's building?"

This offer came as a shock. The TAG boys hadn't even seen the inside of either building let alone approached the prince about any trade or sale.

"We need a couple more days here. We want to look at your property, and also you must know that we are businessmen, and need to look at the other possibilities here in Macau," said Derek, stalling for time.

"Mr. Derek. I do not mean to sound rude, but trust me when I say that there will be no other properties here in Macau available for sale. We have a very closed society and will welcome new participants only on our terms," Chen said. "I will honor your wish, however. You may take two days to look here, and then please use my airplane to fly to meet with your Arab client. If he is interested in my property, feel free to bring him back here. If there is still the possibility of a deal we can all return to Dubai. Perhaps I too will want to ... kick at the wheels ... of the other properties available there as you are doing here."

The Rolls Royce left the compound as quietly as it had arrived. Chen had been mildly insulted that the men were not staying at one of his own hotels, and made them promise to do so when they returned with the Arabs. It was past midnight when they got back to their rooms. They agreed to get some needed sleep and crunch numbers in the morning. Their brains weren't sure when that was supposed to be.

Breakfast in high-end hotels around the world is quite consistent, but of course the regional favorites are ever present. Add the local flavors like pancakes in the US and miso soup in those places favored by the Japanese, to the cheeses, smoked meats, pickled vegetables, breads, and cereals and you've got breakfast. In Macau there were some strange-looking smoked insects and odd-looking fruits neither Brick nor Derek had previously seen or tasted. Thank goodness for corn flakes and croissants. Derek was feeling adventurous and was just slicing into what the waiter called "a wonderful fruit," which looked like a soggy, shrunken, white tennis ball, when his phone vibrated.

"This is Derek."

There was a stream of static then a voice, unfamiliar to him, began giving him a travel itinerary. It wasn't his.

"I'm sorry but you must have the wrong person," he said, making an annoyed face across the table at Brick. Suddenly his face lit up. "I'm so sorry; we must have a bad connection. Yes, we can be there in an hour. It's navy blue with a falcon on the tail. Got it! Thank you."

He put down his phone and wiped his mouth with

the linen napkin. "Finish your corn flakes. We have to leave for the airport in ten minutes. Prince Assad's jet is refueling and will be ready to take us to Dubai in an hour. I sent him a text message just before I turned out the lights last night. He sent his jet for us and wants us to have dinner with him and his father, the emir."

"Do you think it's a good idea to accept his hospitality? Shouldn't we be neutral in the deal? You know, like we are representing both parties equally?" Brick asked with a serious look that he couldn't maintain a second longer before he broke into a grin.

The Gulf Stream VI was the royal-blue color of the US Navy's Blue Angels precision tomcats. The Americans were met at the private terminal by a serious-looking young man wearing a white head scarf and a lightweight robe over an expensive Savile Row suit. He led them through the metal detectors where they showed their passports, then asked them to stand, one at a time, in a small side room where he subjected them to a very thorough frisking. "I apologize, but we have to be very careful about foreign visitors nowadays."

They were led out to the plane, where they were greeted by a beautiful woman in a uniform who showed them to soft, white leather seats near the front of the aircraft. She asked them to sit side-by-side at a table configuration. They fastened their seat belts as the engines revved up. They didn't see anyone else until they were in the air and leveling off, then the door to a rear compartment opened. To their surprise, Prince Assad and an elderly gentleman emerged and walked forward taking the seats across from them.

"It is nice to see you again, Mr. Morris, and I believe

you must be Mr. Wahl. Allow me to introduce my father, His Majesty the Emir of Dubai."

The two westerners were speechless. The whole situation was surreal. The whisper of the jet engine, the sensation of climbing into the heavens at near-Mach 1 speed, the smell of the new leather ... and now these two serious and yet accommodating men sitting face-to-face with them. There was no way they could stand to shake hands, thus it was accomplished somewhat awkwardly across the polished, walnut table.

"This is such a pleasant surprise," Derek said.

"We had a cancellation of the day's plans and Father had always wanted to see Hong Kong from the air. I was intrigued by your e-mail. I have been a little bit nervous about our investment in your company, TAG, correct? I was in Monte Carlo last weekend and happened to encounter Mrs. Edwards. She told me about the unfortunate demise of her husband and that she had withdrawn her management of the company."

Derek and Brick listened to Assad talk, wondering what in the world this weird roller coaster ride was going to bring next. Aside from the conversation, they had the feeling that the airplane was not going straight, but making a wide, circling pattern.

"Well sirs," Brick began, not being sure of the correct terms of address with the royal twosome. "An opportunity has come up that made us think of you and your investment."

Using a tag team approach, Derek and Brick described the opportunity of swapping the newest building in Assad's Dubai inventory for one of Mr. Chen's hotel-casinos in Macau. Derek had hinted at it in his text the night before, so the fact that the Arabs were there assured them that the man was definitely intrigued, if not interested. They talked about the end-destination resort atmosphere in Macau and how the numbers of visitors per year was skyrocketing. No dollar figure was mentioned. Instead they discussed square meter size of the buildings, the number of rooms and suites, and the number of gambling tables and slot machines, and finally the net income the casino produced.

"I get the sense," Derek finally had the courage to say, "that we are still in the area of Hong Kong. Would you like me to call my contact at the casino and arrange a tour for this afternoon?"

"That won't be necessary," said the prince. "Our local people spent most of the night making a short video presentation for us. We have examined the property in its entirety."

Assad pressed a button on the side consul and flat-screen monitors around the cabin lit up, and soft music began to play. Appearing as though it was a professional advertisement for the casino, the video showed the front entrance, then lobby area, then proceeded throughout the public areas of the hotel, and finally through some of the hotel rooms, including two large suites, all in Hollywood-quality, high-definition.

The prince pressed the button again and the screens went blank. He sat back, and for the first time the old man spoke in a heavy accent using his most basic English. "It is a very beautiful hotel. I have always wanted to have private place to visit away from my homeland. Often we go to London, but it is too cold for my old bones," he said with a rare smile, rubbing his hands in imitated warming.

Derek was flabbergasted. He had expected a long, hard sell, with a lot of concessions to be made by both parties. Right now the old adage of the grass being greener on the other side of the fence appeared to be a prevailing mood with the Arabs.

"Brick took a few pictures of your building in Dubai when we were there recently and we showed them to the present casino owner. We feel that any negotiations are best done through a third party, thus we are willing to help you and our other client come to an agreement," Derek said. "The appraisals of the two properties are very similar."

"We like to do what you Americans call 'barter,'" the prince said. "The Chinese, however, do likewise. Often it makes for a long and tiring negotiation. What we would propose—since we are very impressed with what we have seen—is a swap. We wish to trade straight across. We will take over your client's property below us here in Macau in exchange for our new office-hotel complex in Dubai. Thus, there is no need for cash changing hands. Would you please make him our offer?"

Derek and Brick were both sitting up straight in their seats. With this card on the table they took simultaneous deep breaths. The deal was almost half done.

"We will be happy to go to them with the offer," Brick said. "There is just one complicating factor."

"And what would that be?" asked the prince.

"Your investment in TAG, we need to make it a part of the property swap," said Brick.

"And just how does that complicate this arrangement?" Assad asked. His tone was one of patience—almost as if he had anticipated the problem.

Derek sat up straight to explain. "We would like to liquidate your position in TAG. It's not that you are not a treasured client but, since the death of Mr. Edwards, we feel the need to liquidate the company. Since the exchange of properties—your office complex for the casino-hotel—would under any circumstance incur a commission, we would like to propose—assuming that we round off the sale price to an even billion American dollars for each of the properties—a six percent commission is fair. This would include your forgiving the debt owed to you by TAG and a $20 million commission to be paid for organizing the trade. We of course would cover any business expenses incurred."

The prince and his father sat expressionless. The prince finally retrieved an iPhone from his jacket pocket, opened the computer application and tapped in some numbers. Derek and Brick could both feel the airplane continue to make its gentle banking turn, but now it seemed to be losing altitude.

Finally, the prince looked up and said, "The only missing figure is the five percent quarterly dividend on the TAG investment. As I recall, it is due in two weeks. If we can conclude the exchange agreement immediately, meaning in the next twenty-four hours, I will waive that interest payment and pay you the $20 million in cash and forgive the $42 million."

A nod of Brick and Derek's heads was all that was needed to seal that half of the deal.

To the men's surprise, the prince and his father went on to discuss staying in Macau, but their security chief, who had been hidden away in the back of the massive private jet, insisted that they return to Dubai where he could protect them more efficiently. The Yale-alumnus emir agreed and within minutes of touching down, the plane was back on the departure runway.

Brick leaned on the hood of the car trying to reduce the spinning in his head. The up and down and round and round flight combined with the inconceivable monetary numbers spinning through his brain were making it hard to not feel intoxicated.

Derek was pacing back and forth in the parking lot trying to get Chen's secretary or the man himself to answer. "No one will pick up," he said. "Let's just go back to his office at his hotel and try to track him down."

"I'm so sorry," the petite woman at the greeting desk of Chen's business office said. "Mr. Chen does not accept visitors until 1800 hours."

She offered no explanation for the odd hours of doing business, but in retrospect, Derek told Brick that the afternoon was probably the billionaire's nighttime, since the casino was a nocturnal business. They took a room for themselves, and went to the fitness center for a workout and a swim. Brick was having the hardest time with the jet lag. It took forty-five minutes on the elliptical, and ten laps in the Olympic-size pool before he was finally starting to feel human.

At 6:00 p.m. sharp they were scrubbed, rehydrated, dressed, and pressed. They reported to Chen's office and were offered comfortable chairs, ink-scented copies of the *International Herald Tribune* and scalding-hot cups of tea. At 7:00 p.m. sharp they were led by another petite woman, wearing a snug, silk dress embroidered with pink peacocks, back out through the hotel's casino area, past the baccarat tables and $10,000-minimum blackjack tables, to a darkened room with large, French doors. The woman tapped on the door in a rhythmic code and it was opened by a stocky man that fit the description perfectly of the man their wives had seen following them in New York. Across the room Chen was sitting at a round gaming table playing some sort of domino game with three other men. A cloud of grey cigar smoke hung over the table like a suspended false ceiling. The only light in the room was a mosaic-colored, Tiffany lamp hung low over the table.

"Come in gentlemen," Chen said without looking up from his white tiles. "If you will excuse me for a moment, I must finish here before we talk. You are both welcome to watch. We'll be done in just a moment, but first I need to relieve Mr. Wong and his two brothers of their money." He laughed and then again the room became silent, except for the clicking sound as all four men toyed with and rearranged the tiles they had been dealt.

Derek's feet and legs were aching and Brick was getting dizzy again, but finally one of the anonymous men threw his remaining tiles down, cursing in Mandarin and pushing his chair back—obviously out of the game. Moments later the others abandoned their places and left Chen alone at the table.

"Come with me gentlemen," he said. "I need something to eat."

They followed Chen out through the high-rolling end of the casino to a private elevator hidden in a nook. Onboard there were only two buttons. Chen pressed the up arrow. They could feel the acceleration remembering the thirty-some-odd stories in the main elevator. When the car stopped, the doors opened to a lush garden of manicured trees and shrubs covered with a glass roof. Off to one side there was a lounging area where a dining table already was set up for the three men.

Chen motioned them toward the table. The view was fantastic, including the lights of the city, the bay, and more radiant still, the lights of the surrounding dozen or so casino marquees. Derek and Brick both walked to the edge of the garden to take in the view.

Three waiters appeared and pulled out chairs for the men to be seated. Steaming platters of food immediately were placed on the round table and glasses were filled. Chen muttered a few commands and the three men were again alone.

The food was colorful and delicious. Some of the dishes were on the too-spicy side, but the Westerners ate it anyway. Chen made no hint of discussing business until he was finished. As he pushed away from the table, waiters again appeared as though from thin air and cleared the table. Business was about to begin.

With little fanfare Brick presented the exchange deal as he had outlined to Chen previously. Again the Americans knew that like the prince, Chen was interested. Otherwise, there would not have been a meeting. Derek carefully explained the beauty and profitability of the building in Dubai, again showing him a number of photographs and a summary of the lease income. He offered Chen the same commission pitch of forgiving $40 million of the real estate commission in exchange for Chen's $40 million TAG investment and $2 million in interest. When the additional $18 million in cash commission was presented, Chen seemed to stop his slow nodding of agreement. He looked into Derek's eyes and asked the question both young men feared: "Are you charging commission on both ends of deal?"

There was a silence in the air until he continued. "I am all right with that as long as I know that Arab boy is paying you same fee I'm paying."

Derek took a long silent breath. "Actually sir, we are charging you $2 million less than the prince is paying," he said, knowing that the final charge for the commission was $40 million, regardless of how the allocations were made.

This seemed to please Chen, who nodded his head in agreement and then to their surprise smiled a toothy grin and extended his hand giving each a hardy shake.

Chen waved his hand in some sort of sign and waiters appeared again. To Derek and Brick's surprise, the table was reset for four people and an additional chair was placed. Following Chen's lead, the men stood as a fourth person approached from the shadows.

"Hello, Brick. Hello, Derek. And hello, Fong."

The two men could not have been more surprised if Adolf Hitler himself had walked up to the table. Standing in front of them in a slinky, red silk embroidered dress, with a slit nearly to her waist, was Willow Foster. The jewels on her neck, wrists, and hands caught every ray of light on the rooftop garden. Smiling, she gave each a double cheek embrace, saving Chen for last and letting his embrace linger longer.

"I'm so glad to see you two again," she said as the attendant seated her. "Please be seated," she directed.

Brick started to speak, but no words came to his mind. Derek's brain was scrambling to make sense of her appearance and then suddenly the pieces started to fit together. He remembered that at their first meeting in Colorado her mentioning that she had been the Asian liaison for the Foster Group when she first came to work for Ned. Chen had to have been an early and long-time contact—perhaps even more. Now, what the heck was she doing here at this meeting? But then he recalled earlier conversations with Willow and her knowing Chen prior to going to work for Foster.

"Well, this is certainly a surprise," Brick was finally able to get out. "We thought you were tied up with work in Monte Carlo."

"My friend here, Fong Chen, invited me here months ago to learn as much as I can about renting hotel rooms to gamblers ... you know that my little hotel is less than a block from the casino in Monte Carlo?"

"And how convenient for us that you just happened to be here today," Derek said, trying unsuccessfully to hide his sarcasm. "It seems funny now that I realize that the first time I came here seeking Mr. Chen's investment, neither of you mentioned your friendship."

"But love, you need to remember that friendship is not necessarily business."

Both men were having the sinking feeling that all they had worked for the last several days was suddenly going to go up in an invisible cloud of $1,000-an-ounce perfume.

As dessert was served, Mr. Chen was smiling and taking in the whole scenario, but not saying a word. Willow made small talk asking how Debbie liked New York and about Lexy and her new front teeth and when she was going to take her first steps. Meantime all Derek could think of was the millions that were probably going down the drain—once she said whatever it was she came here to say.

Did she want in on the deal or was she warning Chen off?

Just when he thought he couldn't stand the suspense any longer, Willow abruptly stood and straightened her skin-tight skirt. She squeezed Chen's hand, bent over to give Brick a kiss on the cheek—inadvertently giving Chen an inches-away view of her bare thigh.

Derek stood as she turned to him. She leaned toward him and in the midst of a faux kiss whispered, "Make sure you get all the cash due to you, before you leave the island."

He was so surprised by her comment that he started to ask her what she meant, but it was too late. She was back at Chen's chair bending down again to thank him and say good-bye. Then she was gone.

Brick stood, noting Chen's body language and thinking that the meeting was over, but Chen insisted that the men retake their seats saying, "I still have a few questions about the transaction."

"Oh no," thought Derek, "here comes the second shoe."

"What can we clarify for you?" Brick asked.

"The money amounts are in line, but we need to agree on the transition of the management. We cannot merely swap properties without having a plan in place for my employees."

Brick looked at Derek, watching the worry lines on his face relax.

"We can have our partner, Dr. Felshaw, assist you with the management questions. He helped run a large orthopedic clinic in the United States and has a college degree in psychology as well as a medical degree," Derek said, not having the slightest idea where that thought came from.

As much as the Americans wanted the meeting to end, Chen called for another round of dessert and began talking about the history of Macau. A lucky call on Chen's cell interrupted his monologue and the men made a break for it.

Assuming that the prince would be agreeable, a closing meeting was set for the next afternoon at the office of Barclays bank in Hong Kong. It was meant to be a neutral location with both parties there, but not necessarily in the same room. The axiom, that buyers and sellers are natural enemies, was their thought.

The men still had to present the final plans to the prince, who probably needed the approval of his father. Their commissions also needed to be confirmed. Both American's stomachs were churning when Derek's cell phone began ringing. It was answered immediately. It was the Arab prince.

Derek explained Chen's proposal and the agreed price. Once again he mentioned that the forgiving of the TAG debt would be half of the sales commission. Next, he mentioned the extra $20 million in commission for arranging the transaction. The prince laughed. "What a fortunate day for both of us. I get a beautiful casino where I can entertain my friends and it just happens to be a day when my stocks in the DAC, the German stock market, performed especially well. Your commission will not be a problem. Please be sure to have your bank routing information with you when we meet tomorrow."

Derek assured him that they would have everything necessary and hung up. The exchange was set.

Attorneys the world over love to drag out contracts and the negotiations of business deals as long as anyone has any patience left. Call it job security through billing hours or the suppressed dislike of their clients, but it happens just the same. On Friday morning in Hong Kong, there occurred the exception that made the rule. There was no dragging out any of the transactions. Faxed documents, e-mailed instructions, witnessed signings, and transfer of funds were all carried out with expeditious precision.

At 4:00 p.m. Hong Kong time, Derek and Brick watched from the marbled mezzanine of the bank as first a pearl-black Rolls Royce and a white Mercedes Auerbach, with a Chinese crest on its door, pulled up to the bank's private drive. The crown prince and his attorney-aide, then Chen and his three "assistants," exited their respective automobiles. A bank officer was at the door to greet them and lead them to adjacent conference rooms. The manager then came out and waved for Brick and Derek to join him.

They entered Chen's conference room first. Greetings were exchanged and then they reviewed the paperwork. Everything was in good order. The papers

were promptly signed and the commission money—
$20 million—was electronically transferred to IMC Bank
in Grand Cayman. The Chinese billionaire was asked
to wait while Derek and Brick went into the room with
the prince. When they entered, the man was frowning.
There was a typo mistake on one of the final purchase
agreement pages. It would have to be redone and
re-signed by both parties.

"Take deep breaths and count to ten," Derek
whispered to Brick.

The bank officer appeared within minutes at the
door and waved a new sheet of paper that was read and
promptly signed. The bank officer disappeared into the
next room to get Assad's new signature. It should have
taken seconds, but instead, ten long minutes went by
before the banker appeared again.

"May I speak to you gentlemen?" he said to Brick
who was pacing at the door.

Outside in hushed tones he said, "Prince Assad just
noticed that he was to pay you $20 million commission
and yet Mr. Chen is paying you only $18 million. He
insists on being treated equal. I'm afraid he won't sign
this last document until the matter is resolved."

Derek and Brick stared at one another and then
realized that in the rush they hadn't mentioned the
$2 million quarterly payment on the TAG investment
that was due both Assad and Chen. In their panic they
thought the whole deal would be nullified. In a moment
of brilliance, Derek went into the room and apologized
to the prince. To his relief the man accepted the mistake
with a nod. Derek then signed a transfer permission
form, returning $2 million to the Arab's account. By

5:30 p.m., all of the men were led into a third conference room where the two principle buyers were introduced.

"Prince Assad, please allow me to introduce you to Mr. Chen," Derek said. "Mr. Chen, please meet Prince Assad of Dubai."

The men shook hands and within a short time were exchanging pleasantries and had invited one another to visit their respective countries and to be guests at one another's mansion and palace respectively.

Brick stepped outside the room and called Debbie, knowing he was awakening her, but doing so at her prior insistence.

"We did it!" he said. "The papers are signed and the TAG debt is gone, not to mention that there is $36 million sitting offshore waiting for us to visit sometime soon."

"Fantastic sweetheart!" she said with a sleepy voice. "I'll call the others and let them know. You call me back before you go to bed. I'm going back to sleep."

Derek opened the door to see where Brick was and saw the phone in his hand. "Did you tell her?"

"No, I was just checking to make sure she fed the dog," he joked.

Chen insisted on hosting an impromptu party to celebrate his new purchase. It was to be held that evening at the best of the six restaurants in Prince Assad's new hotel. The two men had already agreed not to let the employees know just yet that there had been a change in ownership, thus Chen made all of the arrangements for the party. It was in a lovely room with live music and the food was fantastic. Eventually, the host's drinking became excessive. Derek and Brick excused themselves from the party and went for a swim and then to bed. They had made plans to meet Prince Assad to ride back with him to Dubai. From there they would catch the Virgin Atlantic flight on to London and New York.

When they arrived at the airport the next morning, a sleek, black jet was waiting for them, all fueled and ready to take off. As they began to board, Derek was handed a note from the prince, stating that he was staying on in Macau for a few days, but that his jet would deliver Derek and Brick directly back to New York or Phoenix, whichever they preferred. They couldn't believe their luck.

Several hours later they were in the middle of a game of chess when the copilot joined them in the cabin and announced that they would be landing to refuel. Neither one of them had bothered to ask where they were landing. As the plane taxied to a stop at the international airport's general aviation terminal Brick and Derek stepped to the plane's door to get a breath of fresh air and to stretch their legs.

"Where exactly are we?" Brick asked the pilot.

"Bucharest, Romania. We're about halfway between Hong Kong and New York," the pilot said. "Incidentally, we really need to take a four-hour rest here to comply with FAA regulations. Perhaps the two of you would like to hire a car and see some of the local sights or have a late lunch at a nice restaurant?"

Derek looked at Brick and the men simultaneously said. "Thanks, but we'll stay right here in the airplane."

Epilogue

Five weeks later, the three Arizona buddies were sitting on the fantail deck of the Silver Spirit cruise ship, watching their wives sunbathe as the ship steamed toward George Town, Grand Cayman. Dave was still not back in biking condition, but 90 percent healthy. He was even feeling good enough to threaten Melody with a mandatory scuba dive when they reached the island—perhaps to keep her out of the George Town jewelry stores.

"You better hold off on the scuba diving until you're back in full condition and we've done some long bike rides," Brick warned Dave. "Don't forget that Prince Assad is expecting you to spend a week with him at his new casino in Hong Kong next month and I understand from the article in Forbes that he is a serious sand dune biker."

"And while you're halfway around the world you might as well stop in Dubai to spend time with Mr. Chen. He claims he needs to reorganize his staffing at the office complex. We told him you were the best staff manager in Arizona," Derek chided. "It's time you started picking up your share of the workload."

"Oh, there you boys are," came a cultured female voice from behind the pink-and-white pool canopy.

Everyone looked up to see Kristen and Valencia—dressed to the nines—approaching the pool. The men stood to greet the mother and daughter—their soon to be ex-partners.

"Is everything set at the bank?" Valencia asked.

"Just like you said you wanted it to be," Derek said. "The $36 million is waiting to be divided as soon as we arrive at the IMC Bank, giving you two your 52 percent of the commission from the Hong Kong/Dubai deal. The bank manager said he would have the checks cut. We have also faxed the paperwork to the FTC, officially transferring our ownership in TAG to the two of you in exchange for total relief of any responsibility. And don't forget, you will pay each of us $2 million for our stock in TAG. Did I miss anything?"

"I don't believe so," Kristen said. "You men have done a wonderful job of straightening out the whole mess. Edward's old friend Armon Dupree is taking care of whatever misunderstanding there might be with the FTC. Thus, you don't have to give that any further thought."

"By the way," added Valencia. "My mother just received an invitation to the grand opening of Willow's new hotel in Monte Carlo. Rumor has it that she spent nearly $80 million on the renovation. No one has any idea where or how she came up with the money. I've also been told that the lounge at her new hotel is decorated in a Western motif, with branding irons, longhorn steer heads, saddles, and ten-gallon hats adorning the walls. Apparently, right in the middle of the bar is a large glass case holding a live six-foot-long female rattlesnake. People are already calling the snake 'Little Willow.'"

The End.

An excerpt from Steven Dahl's latest adventure, "Onion Dome" ...

CHAPTER

1

"Brayden? Can you hear me?" hollered his wife, Paula Ballard. Her voice carried as if from a megaphone up the narrow spiraling stone staircase, which led to the balcony of an ancient, Orthodox church. "You've got to get down off of that ladder right now! It's starting to rain again and everyone else has already gone back to the bus."

She couldn't see her husband, but she knew he had climbed a rickety wooden ladder that led from the top of the spiral stairs into the building's onion dome. She knew because ten minutes earlier she had led the ascent to the centuries-old, copper-sheeted dome. She had returned quickly to ground level when low clouds had moved in, decreasing the ambient light, and the cannon-like boom of thunder had flushed out raven-size bats. One had flown straight down from the dome's darkness, momentarily tangling itself in her curly, auburn hair. That did it for her. She had scrunched her lithe body to the side of the passage and let Brayden squeeze by on his way upward.

"I'm not coming back up there to get you," she yelled again, this time from the stone floor of the ancient church.

"I hate bats!" Paula said to her best friend Julie standing at her side. She had returned to the church in search of Paula and Brayden.

"Why were you even up there in that spooky place anyway?" Julie asked.

"Brayden wants to see how the architects constructed the framing and trusses inside the onion dome. He's mentioned it a dozen times as we've driven by all these majestic churches. He must have taken a thousand pictures of them the last couple weeks. I was a hundred percent on board with my goofball husband—checking out the inside structure of the dome seemed like a fun idea—until I was attacked by that bat. You should have seen the thing. It was as big as a pigeon, with beady, red eyes! It gets really dark at the top of the spiral stone staircase, and then there's a ladder that goes straight up. I'm sure he can't see a thing up there."

"I'll go tell Dennis to make sure the bus waits; he's probably out in the cemetery studying some new kind of flowers that grow best above the dead," assured Julie. As she left, she smiled at the withered, little woman sitting beside a table near the heavy, wooden exit door, hoping to sell one last candle or postcard before the church closed for the night.

The bus was waiting in the driving rain, its door closed until the driver saw Julie running toward it. The nearly-full bus held an eclectic group of tourists who had spent the last twelve days touring the flatlands of western Russia, beginning the tour in Saint Petersburg and then driving south into the Ukraine and then circling northwest into Poland. The final destination was to be Prague. This particular tour was a favorite of people who had seen all the usual sights of the big cities of Europe and wanted to connect with the real people and history of the smaller villages of Eastern Europe. By now some of the group had grown restless—the quaintness of the country farms, tiny brick houses and communist-style apartment buildings were losing their savor. Tonight in particular, they were tired and hungry. Many resented having to wait for the curious couple and just wanted to get to the hotel for dinner and bed.

Eighty feet above the worn, stone floor of the three-hundred-year-old Russian Orthodox chapel, Brayden Ballard was on his hands and knees—his tiny, Magnalight flashlight stuck firmly in his mouth. Thank goodness he had worn his jeans instead of his usual cargo shorts. He was examining the space between the curved roof close above his head and the trusses, girders, and crosspieces supporting the ceiling of the church beneath his knees. The space was tight for his six-foot, three-inch frame—requiring both of his hands to maneuver. Fortunately he wasn't overweight and had been working out regularly.

In all of his architectural training he never remembered seeing drawings or photographs of the inner structure that supports the uniquely shaped onion domes adorning the thousands of eastern European churches. It was the end of a long day of mostly driving when their tour guide allowed the group an extra hour to wander around the quaint little Polish town of Chelm. Brayden took one look at the red-and-blue dome with the late afternoon sun glinting off of the gold cross on its apex and was immediately drawn to it. He hadn't even mentioned climbing into the dome when Paula grabbed his hand

and they headed for the chapel, leaving the rest of the group to wander the town to eat gelato and barter for trinkets.

Now saliva drooled from the corners of his lips surrounding the flashlight and ran down his chin. He wasn't about to touch his face and remove the light just to answer the plea echoing from Paula's voice below. His hands were covered with bat guano, rat droppings, and probably a lot of other unmentionables. Scanning the three-foot, narrow space ahead, he could make out what looked like old rags, scraps of wood chips, plaster, and broken dowels left over from the time the dome was erected. The builders hadn't had nails at the time of construction so they had attached all of the beams with hardwood dowels pounded into hand-drilled holes.

"I should have brought a note pad and pencil," he thought, doubting that he would remember some of the unique bracing techniques the ancients had employed.

"Get down here! The driver is insisting that the bus leave now and will leave both of us behind," Paula's voice echoed up the hollow space. "Are you still even alive?"

"Crap!" he muttered, pulling the wet, slippery light out of his mouth. "I'm coming!" he yelled back. "Tell him I'm saying a special prayer for each of the passengers to save us from his reckless driving."

Reluctantly, he started to back his way around the narrow curved space toward the ladder. He shined the light back toward the opening then wiped the slippery flashlight handle under his armpit and stuck it back into his mouth. "If only I had brought that headlight I use for night bike riding," he mumbled incoherently to himself.

"Ouch!" he yelled out, as deep burning pain shot

from just above his wrist, up his arm and into his brain. The flashlight fell from his mouth clattering into a space a couple of feet below. He could see blood pouring from just above his wrist as he grasped unsuccessfully for the flashlight. It rested momentarily on a ledge, then rolled and toppled three feet downward into a narrow crevasse. The pain from the laceration was intense, but the throbbing worried him much more. "It has to be an artery that's been severed," he thought. He looked to see what he had cut himself on and noticed a sharp, pointed, metal flashing sticking out from a corner of the beam—probably someone's modern attempt to patch a leaking roof.

The flashlight was still glowing but was definitely out of reach. Feeling his way with his feet and good hand Brayden backed toward the faint light at the top of the ladder's crawl space. He felt the irregular angles of the hand-hewn beams pressing into his already sore knees as he inched his way along. His left hand was slick with blood, but he had to use both hands to balance between the floor trusses. Then his hand slipped and both arms fell, straddling the wooden beam. Gravity jerked his head and chest forward banging his shoulder and face on the beam between them. In the scramble to right himself he felt something—something definitely out of place.

The crusty, soft object was quite firm inside. It wasn't wood or tile or bat guano. He would never know what compelled him to reach down into the darkness a second time, but he did it anyway. It felt like fabric, or maybe leather, but it was encrusted—probably with bat guano. His right hand worked its way around the object, giving it a slight tug to loosen it from the angled space. His chest and face lay on the crossbeam as he raised his arm toward his eyes to get a look, but it was too dark. The object felt like a sack or satchel, but was heavy. Something solid was inside.

"Hey, Brayden. You still up there? You need to come right now. The bus driver is honking the horn!" The firm, male voice was that of Julie's husband, Dennis.

"I'm almost down!" he screamed, wishing it were true.

He struggled to hold on to the object and get back up on all fours and finally managed to wiggle his body around to face the exit. Five minutes later he was able to make it to the top of the ladder where he finally had enough balance and headroom to sit up. With both hands on the ten-by-six inch object he figured out that it was in fact a leather bag of some sort secured at the top with a drawstring. It felt crusty on the outside as well as moist—probably from the blood that still ran freely from above his wrist. He unbuttoned one button above his belt line and tucked the object inside his shirt for safekeeping.

He now had a hand free to probe the burning spot on his arm and became dizzy when he did so. It was a long, deep laceration. At its deepest place he could feel the tendons between his elbow and wrist. He awkwardly reached around and dug a handkerchief out of his hip pocket. This he wrapped around his arm, and with his good hand and with his teeth snugged down a half-hitch knot creating a makeshift bandage. Wiping his bloody hands on his shirt and pant legs, he took a deep breath and began the struggle down the ladder to the spiral staircase, one rung at a time—the last thing he needed right now was to slip and fall the ten or twenty feet to the stone floor. When he finally made it to the ground floor of the building, his head was spinning and a wave of nausea was forcing his afternoon snack of granola bars and Coke up into his throat.

Dennis was waiting at the base of the stairs, patiently stirring the wax in a votive candle. Without a word he turned and led the way through the steady rain to the waiting bus. The dense clouds made the early evening seem like night. The tall tour bus had its engine running and widow wipers slapping back and forth; then the headlights came on as the two approached. The men were just inside the door when the booing and hissing started and continued until Brayden was settled into his seat next to Paula. There were no questions as to why he was late. No one seemed to care.

"I'm really sorry I made you all wait for me," Brayden said in a loud voice, addressing the bus full of fellow travelers, most of whom he now knew by name. He was answered again by hisses and boos—this time more subdued.

The driver turned on the interior lights, something he hadn't done to help the two men to navigate to the seats. Instead he stood and made the pretense of counting heads. That's when Stacey, a legal secretary from Tulsa, looked at Brayden and screamed.

"What's all over you? Oh my gosh! Brayden Ballard, you're covered with blood!"

About The Author

After thirty years of medical practice—delivering more than seven thousand babies—and raising five children with his wife, Paula, Doctor Dahl now splits his time between their homes in the Arizona desert and the mountain peaks of Utah.

Their most recent travels took them to central Europe, where for over a year they managed the medical care of the Latter-day Saints missionaries and researched the health care systems in such fascinating countries as Poland, Romania, Moldova, and Serbia. These European adventures added to Dr. Dahl's experiences of living on the tiny islands of the Pacific, his Vietnam experience on a navy hospital ship, and time spent in a struggling Liberian hospital.

His previous fascination with ranching, flying, scuba diving, sailing, and serving his country as a major in the US Army all add credence and a realistic twist to his stories.

The best days of his life are those spent with his wife and family, especially with their children and grandchildren. With his fifth novel penned, and another taking shape, he and Paula will stay put in the United States for a while to watch the grandkids grow.

RATTLESNAKE

Steven I. Dahl, M.D.

www.authorstevendahl.com

Publisher: SDP Publishing

Also available in ebook format

TO PURCHASE:

Amazon.com, BarnesAndNoble.com, SDPPublishing.com

Other books by Steven I. Dahl, M.D.

Chicken Fried Steak, Action-Adventure
HOA Gold, Action-Adventure
Picasso's Zipline, Adventure/Medical Mystery
Onion Dome, Murder-Mystery
Missing Mercy, Adventure/Medical Mystery

SDP Publishing

www.SDPPublishing.com

Contact us at: info@SDPPublishing.com